CIRCLE OF INNOCENCE

by

To Katie,

LYNDA DREWS

Lynda Drews

WHISKEY CREEK PRESS
www.whiskeycreekpress.com

Enjoy the read!

Published by
WHISKEY CREEK PRESS
Whiskey Creek Press
PO Box 51052
Casper, WY 82605-1052
www.whiskeycreekpress.com

Print ISBN: 978-1-61160-856-4
Ebook ISBN: 978-1-61160-689-8

Cover Artist: Angela Archer
Editor: Marsha Briscoe
Interior Design: Jim Brown
Printed in the United States of America

Dedication

To Jim and my Boys:
for their patience, encouragement, and love.

Acknowledgement:

My first book RUN AT DESTRUCTION: A True Fatal Love Triangle was very personal. It was a work of non-fiction, based on my memories, research, and interviews. CIRCLE OF INNOCENCE is a work of fiction that involved the help of many people: Bill Larson (retired Door County Sheriff's Department) provided insight into the local county environment, Mary Beth Ryan (friend) who gave me valuable critiques, Paul McComas (friend and author) who provided excellent editing support, Fun Run Friends for helping me select a title, and Jim (my husband of forty years) who put up with all my years of rewrites and submissions.

Chapter 1

The whisperers—oh God, they'd found her! It never failed. Their pity-filled eyes caught hideous glimpses and twitched away.

She hugged her body and wept: "Help me, Mama! Hug me, Daddy!" But across the void, her parents' arms could no longer reach her.

His, however, could...

Sydney Bernhardt jerked awake, amidst a duet of beeps and barks. Her thudding heart joined in to make it a trio. The nightstand clock read 7:15 a.m. Light filtered in through the shades. Rather than rested, she felt exhausted.

Her nightmare, her same damned nightmare, had to stop.

She slammed off the alarm and dipped her shaky hand over the bedside, slipping her fingers into her dog's silky fur. "Damn it, Lloyd..."

Upon hearing his name used, even in vain, he smacked his tail on the slanted plank floor.

"I know... It's up to me."

Lloyd's head snuck over the bed sheet, his wet nose touching hers.

She couldn't help but laugh, staring into his woeful eyes as they mirrored hers. "We make a pathetic pair, don't we, boy?"

He smacked louder.

For the past two years, Syd hated to admit her Golden Retriever had been the only male who'd crossed her bedroom threshold. And what was more, her bedroom was situated inside a former migrant cherry-pickers' cottage on her family's Wisconsin acreage. Syd knew that no self-respecting thirty-two-year-old single woman would resort to living an arm's length from her kinfolk—that was, if she had any sort of life.

Syd climbed out of bed and—avoiding the mirror—dressed in jogging shorts and a long-sleeved top.

It *had* to be long-sleeved.

From her cedar shake cottage, she and Lloyd started off on their Sunday run, following the quarter-mile path adjacent to the orchards. On this kind of September day, under swirling white clouds and blue-iris sky, Syd could still picture herself frolicking with her brother and Mama among the leafy greens of the trees, Mama's apron strings flapping in the wind, her auburn hair feathered around her freckled face, their laughter abounding as Mama pretended to be Al Capone; Bobby played Dillinger; and Syd, of course, was the law-abiding Sheriff...

Syd's eyes smarted as she jogged by her family's fieldstone home where Daddy and Grandmother Bitsy still lived. They all so missed Mama's laughter, her wit, and her good soul.

Syd and Lloyd wound down the drive to the Bernhardt Cherry Chalet and made a left onto the county road, their shoes and paws to the pavement. A number of vehicles passed. Many carried bicycles secured to carriers. About 2,000 recreational riders had taken to these back roads the previous day for the Door County Century, held annually, after the summer crowd's departure and before the fall color invasion began.

The population of Door County is about 30,000, but it can reach eight times that number by July. One-third of the full-timers live in Sturgeon Bay, the county seat, with the rest sprinkled throughout the small waterside communities and nearby islands. Surrounded by the waters of Green Bay to the west and Lake Michigan to the east, the Door County "thumb" has more coastline, lighthouses, and state parks than any other county in the United States.

It was nearing 8 a.m. when Syd and Lloyd reached one of them: Whitefish Dunes State Park. The two followed a tranquil forest path, bordered by birch and spruce. With each stride Syd took, her iPhone banged against her hip. It was irritating, but necessary, for even when she wasn't working, she was still on call.

Most young people from the Door County peninsula spent their growing-up years looking for ways to get out. Even though Syd had an opportunity to make her break after attending college in Milwaukee, the "Door" had beckoned her back. She'd realized it was simply impossible to leave the good people—her people— especially one. But rather than focusing on a more traditional profession in, say, tourism, or her family's orchard business, Syd had wanted to emulate her Uncle Barry, a Cook County Sheriff. Whenever he'd visited, she'd been glued to his side, begging him to share his yarns about dealing with bad guys. Much to her family's amazement, Syd had followed through. She'd earned a

3

degree in criminal science and landed a job with the Door County Sheriff's Department.

Now, at an easy pace, Syd and Lloyd emerged onto the beach. The wind off Lake Michigan was strong but sweet, and the water foamed with chalky waves. Screeching gulls dotted the shoreline, miles of goldenrod danced in the breeze, and fox tracks dimpled the sand. Because this beach had been Syd's favorite place to hang out in her teens, it habitually triggered nostalgic thoughts. So often, they included her two high school cohorts, Gina Kaufmann and Eli Gaudet.

Back then, the three had been inseparable—all independent and idealistic—yet so different in other ways. Gina was gregarious; Eli, introspective with a streak of carelessness; and Syd settled comfortably in between their extremes. On an old bedspread, she and Gina would lie slathered in sunscreen, due to their fair coloring, while Eli refused to use the stuff. Year round, his supple skin remained the color of caramel. He'd lounge at Syd's side, his tall frame spilling onto the sand. She loved his slim yet muscular body and his hairless chest, smooth as polished granite. Being fifty percent Potawatomi, Eli had honored his mother's Native-American ancestry by wearing his raven hair long and pulled back with twine. Syd remembered how Eli's violet eyes would meet hers and, without a word, she'd find his large hand and sneak her small one into it. Gina, pretending she wasn't jealous, would simply roll her eyes...

Now, as the beach path converged into a wooded trail, Syd's breathing was uneven for that god-awful ache of regret had settled into her gut. She slammed her feet onto the wood chips to push her memories aside and headed for the adjacent Cave Point County Park.

What sounded like muffled thunder permeated the

forest. It gradually grew louder until Syd and Lloyd reached the source: the wave-worn limestone ledge jutting out high above the lake. She could feel the rock shudder beneath her feet as waves pounded the shore below. Syd was always careful along this ledge. There was a substantial drop to the water…and no fence for protection.

Lloyd stopped suddenly—nearly tripping her. He then began to sniff frantically along the uneven rock bordering the escarpment. Syd yanked on his leash, but he wouldn't budge. Instead, he lay down, his body facing the lake, and began to whine.

Syd knew this was a favorite place for scuba divers and kayakers, seeking a bird's-eye view into the caves below; either could be what Lloyd sensed.

For stability, Syd grabbed onto to a leafy bush growing out from the ledge's perimeter, and she leaned forward, squinting down.

Fear gripped Syd: a pair of running shoes bobbed in the water—attached to bare legs. Around the ankles, jogging shorts billowed. The rest of the torso was hidden under the carved-out ledge.

Commanding Lloyd to "Stay!", Syd scrambled down to the lower plateau of rock for a better view, her heart racing.

"Oh, no…" Her voice cracked. It couldn't be worse.

A child-like body in a running t-shirt, floated face down—arms spread—dark hair haloing the head—the power of each wave rhythmically butting it against the deadly wall.

Chapter 2

Syd swallowed and tried to steady herself, suddenly glad she carried her iPhone.

With shaky fingers, she punched 911. "This is Detective Sydney Bernhardt." She attempted to control the quaver in her voice. "I want to report a suspected drowning at Cave Point. Please send help."

Syd assumed the victim was dead, but hoped she was wrong.

Worried about Lloyd, Syd yelled some reassuring words up to him as she removed her shoes and socks. She then crept down another five feet onto wet rock.

From there, Syd was able to ease herself into the chilly lake.

Waves pummeled her, and she gasped for air. Holding onto the edge with one hand, she reached for the nearer leg and propelled the body toward her.

She managed to pull herself back up onto the embankment while securing the victim. Lying on her stomach, Syd then inched the body up onto the slippery rock, thankful it weighed far less than her own 120-some pounds.

6

The running shorts, she noticed, were ripped at the waistband—and there was an ugly laceration on the back of the victim's head.

Syd turned the body over to reveal the face of a beautiful young woman. Her dark doe eyes stared up at Syd. She wasn't sure if the victim was even twenty, and, for some reason, she looked familiar.

Syd checked for vital signs. "Damn!" she said under her breath at finding none.

An object seemed to be inside the waistband pouch of the woman's running shorts, still gathered around her ankles. Syd decided to wait on that.

Gently, she closed the victim's eyes, grateful the young woman's t-shirt was long enough to provide some modesty.

Syd cringed, hoping this was not rape. Most any death was horrendous, but when someone this age died, it did crazy things to her mind.

Once again, Syd called 911 to update the situation. Using her iPhone, she then took a photo of the victim's face and sent it on to Gina, who now worked for the Brown County Sheriff's Department.

It helped having a best friend with an inside track into all the inner workings of the office.

Syd tugged her socks back on over her wet feet, then put on and retied her shoes as she considered different scenarios. Had the ill-fated woman tripped, like Syd nearly did, and fallen over the ledge, hitting her head and tearing her shorts on the way down? Or was she attacked before her body was tossed into the lake? Or was she out in some water craft when a mishap occurred, and she ended up drifting to shore?

Last year, the body of a young boy was recovered after his boat had overturned in rough weather. Syd knew

Whitefish Bay had claimed its share of shipwrecks, one of which Gina and she'd made plans to dive down and see. But on Syd's last call to dispatch, the operator had said there were no water crafts reported missing or in trouble.

The predominant crimes in the county were burglaries, auto thefts, a few bar assaults, and an infrequent rape—though Syd was currently working a child-enticement case. There'd been no homicides for two years.

Still, Syd had been trained to assume the worst until the evidence proved otherwise.

A muffled male voice reached her ears: "Hey, pooch, what are you doing here?"

"Sir, that's my dog," Syd shouted and crawled up toward the overhanging abutment. "It may not look like it..." she reached the top "...but I'm Detective Bernhardt from the Sheriff's Department."

Syd saw the shock in the hiker's eyes. She was sure he was getting an eyeful. She wasn't wearing any sort of bra.

Syd judiciously adjusted her wet shirt and shorts, then used her fingers to comb through her tangled mass of damp curls.

The middle-aged man before her was a hippie throwback in a tie-dyed Grateful Dead t-shirt. A pair of binoculars hung around his neck.

"There's been an accident here." Syd picked up Lloyd's leash. "I've already called it in."

On impulse, she made an unorthodox choice. "Sir, until assistance arrives, could I ask you to give me a hand?"

For all Syd knew, this guy could be her perp.

Through wire-rimmed glasses, he gave her a concerned-citizen look. "How can I help?"

"I'd like you to detain any hikers. But, tell me first— do you have a vehicle?"

He nodded. "My VW camper's in the Whitefish Dunes lot, about a quarter-mile back."

"Did you see anyone on the trail?"

"Nope—well, no humans." Then, with a note of pride: "But I did spot a red-breasted nuthatch, a downey woodpecker, and a great horned owl."

Rather confident her volunteer deputy wouldn't hurt a fly, Syd released him to do his job. Then, because this could well be the location from where the victim fell, she moved Lloyd from his "watch" and carefully began to walk the rock shelf. Eyes peeled, Syd looked left, right, up, and down, searching.

But she found nothing to explain the young woman's death.

Syd turned away, confused, but relieved as the sound of distant sirens filtered in through the trees.

Moments later, Detective Marv Robbins and Deputy Phil Larson materialized from a wooded path. Marv, unlike Syd, was actually on duty.

"Well, hello, Sydney!" he shouted, as if she'd been selected as a contestant on the *Price Is Right,* but with a twinge of nastiness.

Syd had expected as much—Marv treated everyone as if they were intruders in his space.

He shook his head, eagle eyes surveying her. "Even when you're not on duty, you manage to beat me to a scene."

"Looks that way." She tried not to grin. It never worked when she rubbed it in. Syd knew this was a tragic situation, but there was still this rivalry between them.

She'd known Marv her entire life. He and her brother Bobby were like blood brothers. She'd always been the pest, the turd, the cow pie—unless Mama had been around. At six foot five, Marv was a giant with a masterful swagger. His shaved head could blind you at high noon. And behind his "just try to take me down" attitude, he could be an absolute prince—if he so chose.

"We left Deputy Foster in the parking lot," Marv reported. "He's taping off the trail entrances and checking anyone who returns to the existing vehicles in the lot. The Deputy Coroner will be here shortly."

Syd pointed out the victim, then asked Larson to interview the detained hikers. As he proceeded toward them, she turned back to Marv. "It's been difficult to keep curiosity-seekers at bay."

"I'm sure your get-up didn't help!" he snorted, elbowing her arm.

She jerked back—upset she'd done so.

"Get over it, Syd."

Marv's words stung, yet she knew he was right.

"Well…" He frowned, back to business. "Were you able to i.d. the victim?"

She shook her head. "No—but there's something inside the waistband pouch of her running shorts. I waited for you."

Syd again told Lloyd to "Stay!" then led Marv down the abutment. She carried his black evidence kit, and he brought the camera.

Marv analyzed the victim's face. "Doesn't she look a little like Jenny Tyler, only older?"

Syd tilted her head. "Yeah… I guess she does." The two detectives had interviewed ten-year-old Jenny earlier in the week, after she'd been the target of a potential pedophile. Maybe that was why this recent victim looked familiar to Syd—though she still believed there was more.

She pointed out the location from which she'd recovered the body. Marv began to shoot photos of both the victim and the spot.

Syd put on latex gloves and slipped her hands into the woman's running shorts. Inside the small pouch, Syd found a key attached to a brown plastic tag. She extracted it, holding it by the edges, so as not to blot out any fingerprints.

The tag was stamped with a big number "3".

Marv opened an evidence bag, and Syd dropped in the key.

"Let's see if we can find its home," he said. "I'll call in a request for two deputies to canvas the surrounding hotels and rental cottages."

As Marv turned away to do so, Syd saw the hawk nose and silver head of Deputy Coroner Bradley Hutton pop over the ledge.

"Hey," he shouted, "anyone down there?" Then he saw her.

Before Hutton could make a snide comment, Syd nipped it in the bud. "Don't say a word!"

Instead, she got a smirk. Then, in his tailored suit and slippery leather shoes, he crawled down the rock to join them.

As Syd explained how she'd recovered the victim, Hutton squatted to begin his examination.

Syd's troubled eyes found his. "Does it look like a drowning?"

"Not necessarily. I don't see any foam exuding from this young woman's mouth or nose."

He turned the head. "This laceration to the back of the skull might have been the result of a fatal blow." He frowned. "How tragic."

"What about the time of death?"

11

"There's slight rigor evident in the jaw and neck, but none in her extremities."

He lifted the victim's flaccid wrist, which wore a thin silver watchband. "We may be in luck. This Seiko is not the waterproof kind, and the hands stopped at 8:07— see? If I took a calculated guess, she died this morning, close to that time."

A whoosh of adrenalin set Syd's heart into motion. That was just about when she'd entered the state park.

If this was indeed an attack—this body could've easily been hers.

Chapter 3

Syd took a deep breath. She needed to pull herself together.

About six months ago, she'd been promoted to detective. Even though Marv had five more years of experience, Syd had been first on the scene, as he'd so aptly pointed out. According to protocol, she should get this case.

Right now, her goal was to prove *she* was in charge. "For the moment," Syd's eyes caught Marv's, "let's assume the victim didn't come from a water craft." She pointed to the ledge. "I didn't find anything up there. So, let's continue the search beyond this immediate area."

Marv frowned. He didn't like taking orders, so he barked out his own: "I'll walk south, and you head north."

"Sounds good," Syd readily agreed and clambered to the top. Her route seemed more promising: it was territory she hadn't jogged through that morning.

She picked up Lloyd's leash and the two began to follow the northerly trail, which paralleled the lake. As the forest noises enveloped her, Syd began to have second thoughts. Her eyes kept bouncing in all directions. If there was a perp, she knew that he or she could be out there. And of course Syd wasn't carrying a firearm. Her Glock was locked away at home. But thankfully she had Lloyd. He was bound to alert her if any stranger approached…right?

Syd tried to refocus. She knew evidence had been found in this area of eight ancient occupations, beginning around 100 B.C. One of those was from the Potawatomi, who'd arrived in the mid-1600s. But two centuries later, to fend off starvation, they'd virtually been forced to cede their land to the U.S. in exchange for money—and not much of it.

Now, trekking along the path Eli's ancestors had walked, Syd was determined to find a new strain of occupation—or anything, really, that might shed light on this young woman's death.

Lloyd began to sniff the ground. Excitement radiated from his body.

It was the same for Syd, for on a protruding flat rock, about a yard from the cliff's edge, she saw a pool of drying blood.

This has to be the spot, she thought, as her palms started to sweat.

On close observation, Syd could see a few strands of short, dark hair mixed in. Several trampled footprints were also located in the soft dirt surrounding the area, possibly from a struggle. Although in September, Syd knew hundreds of people might have passed this point each day. Because there'd been no recent precipitation, she couldn't tell whether any of the prints were fresh.

Lloyd suddenly began to bark.

Heart pounding, Syd jerked her head up.

A branch snapped.

"My God!" She spun around and squinted into the dark foliage.

Two eyes peered out at her.

Lloyd barked and barked, pulling on his leash.

Syd let out a huge sigh of relief. It was a white-tailed deer—just as startled as Syd.

"Quiet, boy." She gave a nervous laugh.

As the deer bolted away, she took a calming breath and resumed her search. Syd looked down into the frothy lake below. This spot was known for frequent riptides. She wondered whether the unfortunate woman had somehow fallen and hit her head on the rock, then, in an attempt to regain her footing, stumbled over the cliff and drowned? The day's wave action could have propelled her body to its current location.

On the other hand, if she'd been dead before she hit the water, Syd realized someone else, most likely, was involved.

Syd checked the ground for any possible drag marks without success. Then again, given the victim's small size, Syd knew she could've been carried.

Syd was psyched. She really didn't want to screw this up.

She phoned Marv. "You'd better get over here." And she told him what she'd found and where she was.

Her eyes kept watch until Marv and Deputy Larson arrived. Syd felt much better knowing the two men were armed.

"What do you have?" Marv looked peeved.

Syd figured it was because she'd been the one to locate the evidence. As she pointed out the rock, Marv squatted down for a better look. Syd then turned to Larson. "How did your interviews go?"

"Disappointing. Nobody saw nothin'."

"Damn!" Syd frowned. "Okay, then, Deputy, could you please tape off this area? And Marv, could you take more photos? I'll gather both the blood evidence and the hair samples."

Marv stood up, his lips tight. "Certainly, Sydney." His voice was condescending.

She rolled her eyes.

Once those assignments were completed, all three began to scour for additional clues.

Within a bush along the water's edge, Syd found some broken branches. "Check this out." She pointed to the spot. "Maybe this is where the body entered Lake Michigan."

"That looks likely," Marv acquiesced.

Syd checked to see if there were any threads from the victim's running shorts—and she was rewarded.

"The shorts might've ripped during an earlier struggle," Marv said. "Or—"

"Or gotten caught and ripped as she fell into the water." Syd shrugged. "Without more evidence, there's no way to tell."

They resumed their search and found some weatherworn plastic soda bottles, a couple of aluminum beer cans, and a few candy wrappers—nothing suspicious.

The wind continued to whip through the heavy foliage. In this shaded area, clad in wet clothes, Syd started to shiver.

Marv's eyes caught hers. "Come on…" He sounded a tad too nice. "Larson can drive you and Lloyd home. I've got things under control."

Sure you do, she thought, and forced a smile, suspicious of Marv's sudden generosity.

But as a major shudder racked her body, she reluctantly said, "Okay."

Chapter 4

In Syd's bathroom, steam rose and moisture dripped from the bead-board wainscoting. Inside the claw-foot tub, hot water kept running from the tap, yet Syd couldn't quit shaking.

Submerged, she considered the car she'd just seen.

When Deputy Larson drove her home, he'd paused before turning left onto Clark Road, and a Honda Insight Hybrid had passed. It was silver—identical to the fuel-efficient one she'd insisted Eli buy three years ago. She caught just a glimpse of the driver.

But it was him.

Syd hadn't soaked in a tub since she'd shared the space in Eli's bath, right before that life-changing week. They were being silly and sexy. He'd washed her "perfect" arms and kissed their vulnerable undersides. On her chin, he'd made a pointed beard of bubbles and suggested she could now join the circus. She'd agreed—after their ensuing acrobatics left as much water on the floor as in the tub.

Her eyes welled with tears. *Everything*, she thought, *was so easy, then...*

Her iPhone rang. Syd searched inside the towel she'd

placed on the floor, and found the device.

It was Gina. Clearing her throat, Syd answered, "What's up?" She knew her tears were foolish. In comparison to the young woman's death at Cave Point, Syd's issues were trivial.

Gina's husky voice filled her right ear: "You know that photo you sent me?"

"Yeah." Syd grabbed the towel to perform a one-handed dry off.

"Well, Deputy Sam Jeffers radioed in. He believes he has a hit on the young woman's last whereabouts. He wanted me to contact Marv."

Syd's heart sank. Marv must have told Jeffers to get back to him rather than to her. "So, is Marv already following up?"

"Well…not yet." Gina's words had a conspiratorial ring. "Since it was you that found the victim, I told Sergeant Morrell I'd try to reach you first."

Syd grinned. "Thanks, Gina, for always having my back."

But, still, Syd worried.

Jeffers could've reached Marv on his cell as well.

* * * *

At 10:22 a.m., with Lloyd in her family's care, Syd put her Dodge Caravan into gear and sped out. Because of the peninsula's seventy-mile length, every detective was provided with his or her own take-home vehicle, which could also be driven for personal use.

Syd headed toward the Solstice Cottages on Clark Lake Drive, retracing her earlier running route. Her hair was still wet. Her face was au naturel. At least she was dressed in the more appropriate attire of a navy-blue pants suit, her Glock secured in a holster on her left hip.

Hopefully, she'd arrive before Marv.

Syd checked the odometer as she passed the entrance to Whitefish Dunes State Park, then made a left and continued to follow the road bordering the inland body of water known as Clark Lake. As the resort came into view, she checked the odometer again: 1.8 miles. At a ten-minute-mile pace, the victim could have jogged to the park in under twenty minutes.

Beside the Solstice Cottage sign, a Hobie Catamaran was loaded on a trailer with a "For Sale" sticker attached to one of its hulls. Syd made a mental note to tell her brother.

She turned down the drive and noticed four rental bungalows, just like the many others in the county built in the '50s and still family-owned and family-operated. A Door County Sheriff's vehicle was parked next to the building marked "Office."

Syd breathed a sigh of relief. Marv's van was not in sight.

Inside, an aviary of parakeets chirped from within white-lattice cages. Syd heard Deputy Sam Jeffers' folksy voice, then saw him talking to a woman whose frizzy hair encircled a matronly face. The woman was scrutinizing a registration card clasped in her quivering hand.

Sam's eyebrows lifted when he saw Syd. He was holding up his cell that displayed a photo of the key, taken into evidence. "Detective Bernhardt, this is Mrs. Overlund."

The woman slid a matching key across the counter. "This nice young man said a key like this was found on the unfortunate woman."

A smile twitched across Sam's pockmarked, fortyish face. "Mrs. Overlund confirmed a young lady by the name of Carli Lacount rented Cottage Number Three for the weekend. I've already knocked on the door, but I got no response."

Syd turned to Mrs. Overlund. "Was the young lady alone?"

"As far as I know, but I don't track my guests' comings and goings."

Syd nodded. "What was the woman's attitude like, when she checked in?"

"Hmmm…" Mrs. Overlund's brow creased in thought. "She was quite pleasant, but her eyes seemed so sad. Beautiful, sad brown eyes."

Syd pursed her lips and wondered whether she should add suicide to the mix.

The two followed Mrs. Overlund to Cottage Number Three, adjacent to a silver Toyota Camry, a bike locked to its rear. Syd knocked on the cottage door.

Like Jeffers, she got no response.

Syd slipped on latex gloves and tried the handle.

It was locked.

Mrs. Overlund's duplicate key opened the door, and Syd's voice sang out, "Anyone home?"

Again, she got no reply.

Syd asked the two to wait outside, and she entered.

In the living room, a backpack rested on an overstuffed couch. A dozen or so empty beer cans lined the coffee table.

Syd moved into the bedroom. It smelled like sweat and sex. Two pillows were bunched at the head of the double bed, one on each side. It appeared as if a couple may have slept in it.

On the bed stand was a cell phone and a ring of keys that included a remote vehicle-entry fob. Scattered on the floor were a pair of biking shoes, lacy blue panties with a matching bra, a wrinkled t-shirt, and black Spandex biking shorts. On a Naugahyde chair, a duffle bag sat. Syd peered inside and saw folded women's hiking shorts and a crop top.

In the bathroom, women's toiletries surrounded the sink, but the lingering scent was definitely male.

Syd was so certain because of Eli. He'd used the same cologne and/or body wash.

Then, she remembered his vehicle and frowned.

Syd shook off her foolish thoughts and opened the still-wet shower door. Inside was a skinny bar of soap. A damp towel lay outside the shower on the floor.

Syd returned to the backpack and pulled out a billfold. From it, she removed a driver's license. The face of the dead woman recovered from Cave Point smiled up at Syd.

Her palms started to sweat as she read the info beside the photo: Carli Lacount, 5'1", 98 pounds, brown hair, brown eyes, Door County resident. Given her date of birth, she'd been a mere twenty-one years old.

Syd was excited to identify the victim, but also distressed. She knew what lay ahead.

Syd stepped outside, and her eyes connected with Sam's. "Good work." She handed him Carli's license. "I believe we have our victim."

"Oh, my..." Mrs. Overlund's voice and hands fluttered in tandem. "I need to sit down."

"Deputy," Syd said, "why don't you escort Mrs. Overlund back to the office? I'd then like you to interview the occupants of the remaining cabins to see whether they can provide any information about Ms. Lacount. I'll continue here."

"Yes, ma'am."

Syd re-entered the cottage and returned to the backpack. She removed and set aside three folded brown paper lunch bags. There was also an envelope of materials from Saturday's Century bike ride.

Back in the bedroom, Syd picked up the cell phone. It was still connected to its charger. There had been two calls that morning: an incoming one at 7:03 and an outgoing one at 7:44, both within the Northeastern Wisconsin calling area.

She tried the first.

It rang and rang, no pickup, no voicemail.

She called the second number. It went into the voicemail of a Woodbridge residence. Syd left a message for the party to return the call.

She'd have these two numbers checked, along with other recent calls made from or received by this cell.

The phone's contact list could also be critical, so Syd scanned it for any "Lacounts" or familial nicknames like "Mom" or "Dad."

Syd considered it strange when she found none.

She checked under the bed.

There were two discarded condom wrappers—additional confirmation—a male had been present.

Syd lifted the bed's tangled top sheet, which was twisted inside the blanket.

Her heart shifted into high gear.

The contour sheet was stained with splotches of blood.

Chapter 5

Syd phoned Marv at the park. "What's your status?"

"Just finished," he said.

"That's good. I need your help at the Solstice Cottages on Clark Lake. I'm here with Sam Jeffers."

Marv's voice was rough. "I gave him explicit instructions to call me."

Syd's mouth tightened. He'd confirmed her assumption.

While waiting for his arrival, she removed the key ring from the room. She was in luck when the remote entry button unlocked the Toyota Camry.

She checked the glove compartment. The car was registered to Carli Lacount and listed a Fish Creek address. This was different from the Egg Harbor one printed on her driver's license.

Other than a few CDs and an empty soda can, the interior of the car was clean.

Of the five keys attached to the ring, three were quite small. One of these unlocked the bike from the car rack, so Syd could pop the trunk.

Inside were only an ice-scraper/brush combo and some jumper cables.

She relocked the vehicle, then the bike, then headed off to locate Sam.

"Those two cabins," he pointed, "are rented to families with children. The parents remembered a young woman sitting at the communal campfire on Friday night, but nobody saw her last night. I'm heading over to the last cottage—Number Four. That couple's checking out today."

They approached a plump woman and her plumper husband. With a beet-red face, he struggled to repack their car.

Syd showed her badge. "Excuse me. Can either of you tell me whether you saw anyone from Cabin Three during your stay?"

As the woman shook her head, her husband glared at Syd. "Never saw a soul—but someone visiting the occupant stole our parking spot while we were at dinner last night. Was I pissed!"

"Sir, can you give me a description of that vehicle?"

"Shit, lady—it was too dark. All I can say is that asshole was lucky I didn't ram into the bike mounted on the back!"

* * * *

Since Deputy Jeffers knew the organizer for the Door County Century, he was off to secure a participants list. If Carli had ridden in it on Saturday, the owner of the notorious car might have, too.

Meanwhile, Marv and another detective arrived. Sweat darkened the underarms of Marv's blue short-sleeved shirt.

As children, Syd's brother and Marv used to gang up on Syd, but she fought back. In addition to the bug bites on his arms, Syd took pleasure in seeing some faded human bite marks left by her own juvenile teeth.

"Well, Detective Bernhardt..." Marv's voice was smug. "Don't you look refreshed."

"Don't bitch. Remember, you suggested I go home."

Syd led the two toward the cottage and explained what she'd found. She then left them to process the evidence.

She returned to the resort's office and asked Mrs. Overlund for a phone book. There was one Lacount listed, a "Frank" in Fish Creek, with two phone numbers. His address matched Carli's car registration. Syd tried the first phone number. It went into an answering machine.

She hung up and tried the second. A deep voice answered, "Triangle Shops & Café."

The name created an immediate picture for Syd and that god-awful zing of regret. Now, she recalled where she'd seen Carli. She was the petite waitress who'd worked at the Café.

It had been a favorite of Syd's and Eli's. They'd enjoyed chewing the fat with Frank—the establishment's owner—though Syd had never known his last name.

Her mouth had gone dry. "Is this Frank Lacount?"

"Speaking."

She swallowed hard. "This is Detective Sydney Bernhardt from the Door County Sheriff's Department."

"Well, Syd. Haven't seen you in here for quite a while."

"Sorry..." What else could she say? "Frank, this isn't a social call. I'm inquiring about a woman named Carli Lacount. Do you happen to know her?"

"Of course." His voice had turned cautious. "She's my daughter."

* * * *

Frank and his wife were to meet Syd at the Sheriff's Department. On her drive back, her gas gauge neared the red zone, so Syd pulled into a Sturgeon Bay station, just north of the canal that divided the county seat in half.

As she topped off her gas tank, Marv passed in his van. When she'd left the Solstice Cottages, he'd been finishing up. She screwed on the gas cap, grabbed her receipt, climbed back into her vehicle, and nosed it into the stopped highway traffic.

She cursed at the delay. Each hour, the canal bridge rose if any tall vessels needed to get through.

Syd phoned Gina. "When Marv arrives, try to detain him. I'm afraid he'll head straight into Sergeant Morrell's office to keep me from getting this case."

"I'll do the best I can, Syd."

Hanging up, she felt better. Then better still as the traffic began to move.

Everyone, other than Macho Marv, felt Gina, the department's administrative assistant, was an invaluable resource with a generous heart. On her daily coffee breaks she religiously knitted stocking caps for the hospital preemies, and she often brought in homemade apple strudel for everyone to share. From kindergarten on, Gina and Syd had attended the Sevastopol public schools together. With a slim sampling of thirty-five kids in their class, they'd been lucky to have each other.

Syd arrived at the department and passed through the door that led into the investigative wing. Gina sat front and center. A peasant blouse and beaded skirt covered her ample body. Her corn-silk hair was worn stylishly long on one side, and gigantic, multi-tiered earrings nearly touched her shoulders—*classic Gina*, Syd thought.

Gina gave Syd an apologetic shrug. "I did my best, but Marv wasn't up for my chitchat. He's in with Morrell, but you're to go in, too."

"Thanks for trying." Syd touched her friend's shoulder. "Were you able to print the photo I sent?"

"Yeah, it's on your desk. Damn—what a tragedy."

"Sure is."

In addition to Gina, Syd had another cheerleader in her corner, her boss, Sergeant Stuart Morrell. He'd worked for the department since the '70s, first as a deputy, then as a detective, and now as the head of detectives. Stu and Syd's daddy had been schoolmates and, in their teens, had launched the Soft Squeeze Accordion Band. They still played at local events.

Outside Stu's office, Syd could hear Marv's angry voice through the door: "You know, Sergeant, I've got far more experience than Sydney."

Asshole, she thought, knocking, then opening the door. Stu, a slender man with thinning hair he habitually tickled into place, was seated at his desk. Marv was still standing. Seeing Syd, he was clearly irritated.

Marv and Stu were like oil and water, and Syd could see this particular day was no different. She'd always admired Stu who was an advocate for the underdog, whether due to financial means, ethnicity, or sexual orientation. Marv, conversely, couldn't hold back his bigotry in each of the mentioned categories.

Syd ignored Marv and addressed the sergeant: "Gina said you wanted to see me."

Stu turned toward her. "Marv's been updating me on the situation. I understand the victim may be Carli Lacount."

"Yes, sir. Her parents will be arriving shortly to confirm this."

"If it's a homicide, do you think you're up to this? It'd be your first."

"I'm definitely ready." Her voice was firm as hardened concrete.

Marv snorted. "You've been a detective for just over six months. Work under me. I'll show you the ropes. The next homicide can be yours."

Syd calmly looked at Stu. "I found the young woman's body. According to standard operating procedure, this case should be mine."

"You weren't on duty," Marv wrangled, "so that doesn't fly."

She locked eyes with Marv. "Look, it's my—"

Stu pounded a fist on the desk. "That's enough!"

Syd and Marv both fell silent.

"This Cave Point death isn't the only critical case on our radar." Stu picked up a report. "Around 10:30 this morning, Deputy Bob Rudolf responded to a Sister Bay 911 call concerning a young girl by the name of Cassie Monroe. She and her mother reported a child-enticement incident with a similar m.o. to last Wednesday's. Like Jenny Tyler, Cassie was lured to a black sedan by a man wearing a clerical collar. Luckily, the mother noticed her daughter wasn't at her side and called out, causing the guy to flee."

"So," Marv raised one eyebrow, "this occurred in Sister Bay rather than Jacksonport?" His interest, like Syd's, had been piqued.

"Yes. Near St. Rosalia Catholic Church, right after the service let out. The description of the perp is a match: clean-shaven, between thirty and fifty—and again, in addition to the clerical collar, he was wearing a Brewers

28

baseball cap. I've put out a bulletin requesting any information from the public."

"It looks as if our pedophile has an itch that needs to be scratched." Marv frowned. "Not good."

Stu nodded. "First off, I know you're both working more than a dozen cases. Those need to be put on the back burner. Syd, your full-time focus will be on the young woman's undetermined death. But if I see that it's more than you can handle, I may change my mind. Understand?"

"Yes, sir." She held back a grin.

"Marv, for now you take the lead on these escalating child-enticement cases. But I want you both to utilize each other's expertise as you progress on your designated assignments."

"Sergeant…" Marv protested.

Stu raised a hand. "You know how important your case is, Marv."

Syd listened as Stu talked about the Crimes Against Minors task force, established in conjunction with the Sturgeon Bay Police. "In many instances," Stu reminded Marv, "our success has been due to your individual perseverance. We need you to catch this guy before we're dealing with a sexual assault, kidnapping—or worse."

Marv's chest had puffed out, soaking up Stu's praise—praise that, admittedly, he was due. He acquiesced to the sergeant's directive with sullen indifference. But his eyes shifted Syd's way as if to say, *See? I got the more important case.*

It was hard for Syd not to laugh at Marv's dramatics. Then again, what else could she expect from him?

No matter, though, she'd gotten what she wanted. The case was hers.

And she vowed to keep it that way.

Chapter 6

The Lacounts had arrived. Syd took a deep breath, then entered the lobby.

Frank's eyes found hers at once. *He's hardly changed*, Syd thought. Frank's carrot-colored hair was still unruly, but streaked with silver. He wore khakis and a green button-down shirt, the pocket monogrammed with the Triangle Shops & Café logo. A worry-line had replaced the teasing grin that had perpetually crossed his ruddy face.

Syd assumed the petite woman in a pale pink twin-sweater set had to be Frank's wife. She seemed calm, maybe a bit aloof. Her hand, with its beautifully polished red nails, rested possessively on Frank's arm.

Syd now had no doubt that the victim was their daughter. Though Carli Lacount looked nothing like Frank, she could have been a younger twin of the woman beside him: the same pixie haircut, the chiseled features, and the large doe eyes of Audrey Hepburn.

"Syd?" Frank's voice was unsure, like he was afraid to ask more, so instead he introduced Alice.

Her thin, dry hand slid into Syd's sweaty one. "I knew your mother." Alice tilted her head. "You look like

Grace: your auburn hair, your freckles. I'm sorry for your loss."

Syd was taken aback. Here she was, ready to inform them about their daughter's death, and Alice brought up Mama's. Syd stammered "Thank you" and pulled away.

"Can you tell us why you called us here?" Alice asked. "What has this to do with Carli?"

Apologizing for the secrecy, Syd opened the door and led the pair down the hallway. She ushered them into a sparse ten-by-ten room where the Lacounts took seats across from her.

Syd cleared her throat, dreading this part of her job. "This morning, the body of a young woman was found in the water at Cave Point. Can you identify her?" Syd opened her notebook and glanced at the frontal headshot. Rivulets of lake water ran from the victim's wet bangs and down her cheeks. *At least*, Syd thought, *she looks peaceful.*

Syd placed the photo on the table toward the Lacounts.

The color drained from Frank's face. A strangled cry of "Carli!" escaped his lips. His ample body shrank against his wife's and tears filled his eyes.

Alice sat wax-figure-stiff, eyes glued to her daughter's photo. With the tip of one finger, she stroked the image of Carli's face. "My poor, poor baby." Her voice was a disturbing monotone. Alice's dry eyes lifted. "How can this be?"

"I'm sorry for your loss." Syd echoed Alice's earlier words. "An autopsy will be performed later today to help us determine whether Carli's death was accidental or foul play."

Both Lacounts flinched. "This must be accidental," Alice said.

Syd shook her head. "It's too early to tell."

As Frank sobbed, Alice drew him close.

Syd let them console each other until Frank quieted. "I know it's difficult," Syd said, "but I need to ask both of you some questions."

"Of course..." Alice straightened up, her voice intense. "We'll do anything to help." She leaned forward, taking charge.

Syd removed a pen from her notebook's spiral binding. "Did Carli share her weekend plans with either of you?"

Alice nodded, her eyes jumping to Carli's photo. "She was staying on Clark Lake. For the past few years, she and some of her college friends rented a cottage there for the Door County Century weekend."

"Do you know who she was meeting this year?"

Alice placed her hand on Frank's. "Most of her friends had graduated from St. Norbert back in May, so Carli wasn't positive who all would be there. But she did mention one guy named Solly. I'm sure it's a nickname."

"Who else?" Syd's pen waited. "Her other friends might know this Solly."

Alice glanced at Frank's glazed-over eyes and flushed. "Other than Tina Kelsey, from Sturgeon Bay, neither of us had the opportunity to meet Carli's friends."

That's odd, Syd thought and frowned. During her college years, she'd often brought friends home for the weekend. Why hadn't Carli? "Can either of you think of anyone who would've wanted to cause your daughter harm?"

"Absolutely not!" Alice's eyes were sharp.

Frank mumbled his concurrence.

Syd was amazed that Alice was so strong. Frank,

conversely, was a wreck. Syd wanted to pat his back and tell him everything would be all right—just like she had with Daddy. Instead, she asked, "Did Carli have a significant other?"

"She's always been more of a casual dater, preferring to hang out with a group of kids." Alice's eyes took on a look of regret. "I wish Carli had found somebody special at college—my God—especially now." She raked her free hand through her hair. "But she didn't give it a chance. Of course, she insisted on driving home to work at the Café every other weekend. That didn't help."

Syd mentioned Mrs. Overlund's comment about Carli seeming sad. "Can you explain why she may have come across this way?"

A deepened sense of misery settled over Frank, who finally responded, "Carli seemed to be even more withdrawn lately, as if something was pestering her mind. We talked about it, didn't we, Alice?"

She nodded, biting her lower lip.

"What do you mean by even more withdrawn?"

Alice drew her face tight. "Right around the time we moved to Door County, Carli became very moody. That's when she quit sharing anything personal with me, yet for years she'd rarely let me out of her sight."

Syd frowned. "So you don't know what caused Carli's personality change?"

"I thought she blamed me for the move and was punishing me. But her clingy response seemed to say just the opposite. I didn't know what to think."

"Where did you move from?"

"Kaukauna, about twenty miles south of Green Bay. It's where I grew up and met Carli's birth dad, Joseph Kane."

Syd glanced at Frank. That explained why Carli didn't resemble him.

There was a wistful quality to Alice's words as she continued. She explained how she and Joe had met in high school, how they'd married, and soon after, had their son, Brian. Two years later, Carli had come along.

Frank's lips tightened when Alice said, "We had the perfect family—until Joe's fatal car accident. At that time, Carli was nine."

"So how did you two meet?" Syd tilted her head toward the pair.

Alice shared a look with Frank. "At church, we…"

He cut in. "I was a good friend of the family."

Alice nodded. "About a year after Joe's death, we married. Soon after, Frank adopted Carli and Brian." Her voice caught. "Fish Creek was to be our new start."

Syd turned back to Frank. "What was your relationship like with Carli?"

"I tried so hard to connect with her."

"Too hard." Alice shot him a reproachful look, then addressed Syd. "Carli was extremely close to Joe and didn't want anyone taking her dad's place."

Alice's comments bothered Syd. At the Café, Frank had charmed everyone. Why not his stepdaughter?

"Did Carli make friends after the move?"

"Very few," Alice said, "until she became involved in sports. Then she seemed to settle in. Her grades were good, and she especially liked working with numbers. That's why she majored in Finance at St. Norbert College."

"And Carli moved back here?"

"Yes." Frank nodded. "She shocked both of us. Carli had gotten two job offers and told us she was leaning toward a major insurance company in Milwaukee." Syd heard pride in his voice.

"Then, out of the blue, Carli called and asked if I would consider letting her work at the Café full time. She'd take on the bookkeeping responsibilities and fill in at the Café. Alice and I were stunned but so pleased. And, of course, we agreed."

Given Carli's apparently dysfunctional relationship with her parents, Syd was also amazed. She had to believe there was someone other than Carli's parents who'd drawn her back.

"As I remember," Syd addressed Frank, "you concentrated on the restaurant?"

He nodded. "One side of our building and the middle courtyard are dedicated to the Café. My younger brother, Luke, and his wife, Colette, lease the second side for their art gallery. Since the recent birth of their daughter, however, Luke's been handling it alone. The third side houses Alice's fashion boutique."

Alice had slid closer to Frank. It appeared as if she was never far from his side. Syd had also noticed, while Frank had been talking shop, the affable man she'd known had begun to resurface. But his desolation returned when he said, "Our plan was to have Carli own the entire complex within ten years."

"What about your brother and stepson, Frank? Were they okay with that plan?"

"Well, it's my business. Even if Luke didn't like the idea, I told him he'd have to deal with it." The animosity in Frank's voice was extreme, but it settled down as he talked about his stepson. "Instead of taking an interest in the business, Brian wanted to be an educator. He teaches math at Gibraltar High School and coaches cross country."

Frank lowered his head and ran his hands through his hair. "My God, Brian's lost his sister, and he doesn't even know."

At those words, tears gathered in Alice's beautiful eyes.

She's human after all, Syd thought and turned back to Frank. "Did Carli confide in Brian?"

"Some." He got a nod from Alice. "But Beth Halverson was Carli's best friend and the most likely candidate. The two have shared a condo since Carli graduated from college, although, I believe, Carli was making plans to move out."

Syd raised her eyebrows. "Do you know why?"

Frank shook his head. "You'll have to ask Beth." He provided Syd the address to Beth's Egg Harbor condo. It matched the one on Carli's driver's license.

"Did Carli move all her personal belongings to Beth's?"

"Yes." Alice nodded. "She took everything. I even insisted she take her bedroom furniture we'd moved here from Kaukauna."

"One last thing… I have to ask…where were you both this morning?"

Alice gave Syd a look of disappointment. "You're not suggesting we had anything to do with our daughter's death, are you?"

Syd flushed. "I'm just trying to understand the total picture."

Alice's large eyes didn't waver. "I was home until I drove over to the boutique at about 9:30 this morning."

"Can anyone verify that?"

She frowned. "Well, other than Frank, who left at about 7 a.m., I'm afraid not."

Syd turned to Frank. "Where did you go once you left home?"

He rubbed his head, trying to recollect. "I purchased

a Green Bay Press Gazette in Fish Creek, then I drove over to Champagne Rock Park to read it. Around 8:45, I left to attend the 9 a.m. Mass at St. Paul's Church."

Syd knew that sliver of a park, located between the mansions on Cottage Row. It was perched high on a rock overlooking the bay and two islands: Chambers and Adventure. Most tourists didn't even know the park existed.

"Where did you purchase the newspaper?" Syd asked.

"From the box on Main Street across from Julie's Café."

"Can anyone vouch for your time at Champagne Rock?"

He shook his head. "I didn't see a soul. It's the reason I go there. I like the solitude."

Syd frowned. Neither Lacount appeared to have an alibi.

Chapter 7

To maintain the chain of evidence, both Syd and Deputy Coroner Hutton followed the Baker Funeral Home hearse, transporting Carli Lacount's body to Green Bay.

During the forty-five-mile drive, the radio station broke the news of the "undetermined death of a twenty-one-year-old Egg Harbor woman." Syd knew the media wanted answers. This news was huge. Door County's livelihood depended on the tourist dollar. But the department had been unable to locate Carli's brother. Until that happened, her name would not be released to the public.

Syd's stomach sank as they pulled up to St. Vincent Hospital's emergency entrance. At one point, this building had been her home. She remembered how she'd felt so alone, as if nobody existed but pitiful her.

Wisconsin is a friendly state where even a passing stranger gives you a nod, a smile, or a "Good morning." But for the first six months, after Syd's hospital stay, she'd refused to meet people's eyes. Instead, she'd focused on her shoes when crossing the pavement, walking down a hall, or entering a room.

She now realized how far she'd come.

Hospital personnel met Syd and Hutton. The two then trailed behind the gurney carrying Carli's body bag toward the autopsy room. "You know, Syd, I remember a seventy-something Lacount woman from Chambers Island, who passed away from a stroke." There was a sparkle in Hutton's eyes. "I wonder if she's related to our victim."

"Why? Do you think her death could have any bearing on our case?"

"No." He shrugged. "Just curious."

Syd tilted her head, but he didn't elaborate.

They dressed in scrubs, then entered the autopsy room. Inside, a drip, drip, drip of water resonated from one of the stainless steel sinks. Surgical instruments were lined up on a nearby cart. Empty specimen jars inside a glass cabinet were ready to be filled and marked.

Dr. Susan Piper greeted them. "What's the Door County contingency bringing me this time?"

The two updated the forensic pathologist on the current situation. Under an impervious apron, she listened, attired in similar scrubs. She then covered her eyes with goggles before securing a bonnet over her hair. Lastly, she pulled surgical gloves into place and stationed herself beside the gleaming stainless steel table where the body bag had been placed.

Dr. Piper unzipped the bag, and Hutton helped her remove Carli.

Syd cringed. "She looks so small, so exposed, so clean… I'm worried Lake Michigan might have sucked all of our evidence away."

Piper and Hutton agreed.

As Syd began to take photos, her iPhone rang. She could see it was Marv.

Hutton offered to take over, so she could answer the call in the outside hall.

After the Lacounts' departure, Syd had asked Marv for his help. Even though she'd received a snide remark, he'd agreed to focus on two areas. First was to identify Carli's early-morning cell phone calls. Second was to uncover the owner of the "notorious" car.

"So, what's up?" she asked Marv.

"Since you're on that joyride down to the major metropolis of Green Bay, I've been diligently following your wishes. Of course, that's in between checking out alibis of all the locally registered pedophiles and sexual offenders that you and I had already started."

"Stop your moaning." Syd laughed. "So, tell me, what have you found?"

"Well, the call coming into Carli's phone at 7:03 was traced to the only public phone booth in Jacksonport."

Her eyes widened. "That's just ten minutes from Cave Point."

"Yep. Maybe it's a coincidence, but it's also within a few blocks of where our pedophile was reported last week. I'm on my way to check for recent prints. I'll also canvass the area to see if anyone noticed any phone booth usage."

"How about Carli's outgoing call to the Woodbridge residence?" Syd watched as a cart of covered meals was maneuvered out of a nearby elevator. Even hospital food smelled tempting to her.

"It was the unlisted residential phone number of Dr. Ellen Woodbridge. She's a shrink in Green Bay and is vacationing in Europe until later this week. Her backup will be contacting you."

"Thanks, Marv." Syd's tone was sincere. "Was Sam able to secure that list of Door County Century participants?"

"Yeah. I had him first check for anyone by the name of Solly—No luck. Now, I've got him calling the list of male cyclists. That's about 1,400, so it's going to be a major feat."

"When Carli's name is released to the media, someone is bound to come forward and speed up the process."

"I like your optimism," Marv said as Syd's iPhone beeped with an incoming call. She thanked him, pushed END, and answered the second call.

It was Dr. Robert Smith. "Detective, I'm sorry. There's no way to reach Dr. Woodbridge. Ellen's cell doesn't get international coverage, and she purposely didn't leave her itinerary. For once, she said, she didn't want to be called away from her much-needed vacation."

"In her absence, have you received any calls from a Carli Lacount?"

"No… Her name's not familiar. Ellen briefed me on those patients she figured might call, and Ms. Lacount was not among them. Ellen will be back on Thursday. I'll make sure she contacts you."

Disappointed, Syd hung up and took a short break to locate a vending machine. The one on the current floor didn't have granola bars. She frowned. The third-floor machine used to, but she wasn't up to revisiting her old haunt.

She'd have to pass *that* room.

Instead, she chose a less traumatic and appetizing option, a bag of pretzels, and gobbled them down, taking sips from the drinking fountain in between.

All the while she speculated: why was Carli's last outgoing call to a psychiatrist?

It was frustrating to know the answer could be on Dr.

Woodbridge's machine—but to access it, Syd would need a search warrant.

At this stage—without evidence that Carli's death was anything but accidental—Syd knew no judge would provide it.

Chapter 8

Syd entered the autopsy room. By the far wall she located Dr. Piper and Deputy Coroner Hutton. They were peering at a set of backlit x-ray films of skulls, which, Syd presumed, were different angles of Carli's head.

"Her cause of death was blunt force trauma," Piper was saying to Hutton. "And I estimate her time of death to be somewhere between 6:30 and 8:30 a.m."

As Syd listened to Piper's words, she passed Carli's covered body. Syd still bet Carli's death was around 8:07, based on Carli's wristwatch time.

"The skull was forcibly struck, or it struck something, nearly dead center within the parietal region. This caused that piece of bone to break loose." Piper pointed to the spot. "It then forced its way into the cranium to form these concentric fractures around the area."

Syd reached her side. "So, your findings verify, the rock outcrop, pooled with Carli's blood, could've been the fatal instrument that caused her death?"

"Yes." She turned to include Syd.

"You're positive she didn't drown?"

"I checked her lungs. There was no water in them."

43

Syd absorbed that fact. "I assume we can now rule out suicide?"

Piper and Hutton both nodded.

"Could you tell whether she'd been raped?"

"As we suspected, because of the lake water, both the victim's pubic hair and the area beneath her fingernails was clean. I swabbed all her orifices and also drew blood for a toxicology screen. Those samples were sent to the lab. I expect a call shortly with some preliminary results."

Syd nodded as Dr. Piper continued: "There was an overall swelling and bruising to her genitalia, and small suction hemorrhages on her breasts. However, both can occur in consensual intercourse."

"The doctor's finding concerning the victim's hymen is quite interesting, though," Hutton added.

Piper nodded. "Shortly before her death, it ruptured. Inflammatory reactions are still at the site of the tear."

That fact didn't necessarily surprise Syd. It backed up the blood splotches on the cabin bed sheets. To her, the surprise was that Carli had been a virgin at twenty-one. In this day and age, that was pretty rare.

"There were also injuries to the vaginal wall." Piper's eyes located Syd's. "This most often results from violent penetration. In consensual sex, this occurs only when the partner's penis is markedly larger than the vaginal opening."

Syd shook her head. "So you're saying we need to check the penis size of our suspects?"

"I bet you won't have to arm wrestle Marv for that honor." Hutton laughed and nudged Syd.

She jerked back. Her reaction frustrated her, for she knew she'd embarrassed this man.

Just then, the wall phone rang. Like Syd, Hutton

seemed glad for the diversion. They both listened to Piper's side of the conversation, and their awkward exchange passed.

"The lab found no trace of semen in any of the samples," Piper said, hanging up. "Of course, it could've been washed away by the lake. Or, consistent with what you found in the cabin, a condom may have been used."

"What about the blood work?" Syd asked.

"No drugs were found, and the alcohol was within the legal limit."

Syd returned to Carli's body and pulled back the sheet to expose the numerous torso incisions Piper had made. "Is there any evidence of a struggle?" Her eyes scanned Carli's naked body and limbs.

Piper joined Syd. "There are no bruises, abrasions, or lacerations to the lips. The teeth are also intact. However, you can see the recent bruising to both her right wrist and forearm, and to the top of her skull." She pointed out the spots.

The latter, Piper concurred, could have resulted from the wave action pounding Carli's head against the cliff wall. But the recent bruises to her wrist and arm could've meant another party reached out to grab or swing Carli to the ground.

Piper then pointed out some pronounced injuries to Carli's left elbow, the back of the same hand, and an abrasion to her left knee. "Based on their age, I'd say these, unlike the other bruises, probably occurred more than a dozen hours before her death."

They next discussed the random scratches on the fronts of Carli's thighs and hip bones.

"I understand, Detective, there were bushes along the water's edge where you believe the body entered the lake."

Syd nodded.

"These scratches are consistent with that type of foliage rubbing against bare skin. It looks as if her shorts were already down around her ankles as her body went through that brush."

Syd considered that fact as Hutton helped the doctor turn Carli's body.

"There are no scratches on the backs of her thighs or calves." Piper showed Syd. "That would've suggested forcible contact with the ground. But, notice the longer scratches on the buttocks and shoulder blades. These are at least four hours old, and they appear to have been produced by fingernails."

Syd contemplated the overall autopsy results. Even if the cottage sex had been rough, it could have been consensual. If it had been rape, the guy might've hidden his car better. Although, being a virgin, maybe Carli never wanted to have vaginal sex. Could this guy have forced himself beyond her limit? Was that why she'd called her psychiatrist? Had her bed partner heard her conversation and, after Carli left for her jog, worried about the ramifications and pursued her? Even if he hadn't meant to kill her, he would've known he'd been dealing with rape—something he might've attempted to hide.

Or had Carli said a friendly goodbye to her cottage bedmate, left for her run, and then been accosted by someone else? Possibly by the culprit who'd called Carli around 7 a.m. from the public phone booth and lured her to that spot?

Or, of course, her death could've been accidental. Running alone, Carli could've slipped, hit her head, somehow ripped her shorts while struggling to her feet, stumbled over the ledge, and transpired before reaching the water.

Syd had to admit, she had too many hypotheses, without enough firm evidence, to reach a conclusion.

She thanked Dr. Piper and Deputy Coroner Hutton for their work. Now, at least, Syd could provide the Lacount family with Carli's cause of death and release her body to them. But her *manner* of death was still undetermined.

That daunting task weighed heavy on Syd's slight shoulders.

Chapter 9

The bright moon dappled the tin roof of the Bernhardt Cherry Chalet. Syd made her turn and followed the winding drive toward her family's homestead. On both sides stood the orchards, comprised of 6,000 precisely spaced trees, blanketing more than eighty acres.

Back in the '50s, Syd's grandparents had pulled up their Pennsylvania roots to join Wisconsin cousins who'd raved about Door County's ideal environment for growing cherries. When her grandfather died, Syd's daddy had picked up the reins and also opened the retail roadside business.

Syd still found it amusing her grandmother had insisted on naming her only child "Monty" for the tart Montmorency cherries they cultivated. Due to Daddy's early-onset Alzheimer's, Syd's brother, Bobby, had now taken charge of the business. Daddy, however, continued to work at the Chalet. With his salacious wink and familiar chitchat, he remained the Bernhardts' premier authority on selling cherries in all formats: fresh, frozen, dried, jams, salsas, and juices.

Shadows moved in the front room as Syd climbed

the steps to the homestead's broad porch. In the ample foyer, she was met by Lloyd's wet nose. The faint smell of peppermint meant Daddy was near. His pockets always held a stash of red and white Starlight Mints. Syd found him next to the massive stone fireplace, squeezing his accordion, as her grandmother, on her upright piano, played a show tune from *My Fair Lady*. An open can of beer sat on a pile of sheet music, stacked on the floor beside her.

One of Syd's earliest memories was of hearing her grandmother singing "The Itsy Bitsy Spider" while walking her rough fingers up Syd's chubby arms. Ever since, she'd called her grandmother "Bitsy," and so had Syd's closest friends.

At eighty-two, other than Bitsy's periodic attacks of arthritis, she was undeniably spry. Always dressed for comfort, she wore a plaid work shirt and a feminine scarf. A denim skirt hugged her ample hips.

The music stopped, and the two turned.

Daddy's smile stretched from ear to ear. "What a pleasant surprise!"

Pleased, Syd gave him a peck on his scratchy cheek. *Today, must be a good day*, she thought.

Bitsy patted a spot on the piano bench next to her. "Sit your ass down, honey. You look like shit!"

"Thanks!" Syd laughed, then pointed at Bitsy's beer. "First things first." Ambling into the kitchen, she grabbed and opened one, then laid out the makings for a sandwich on the worn trestle table—the location where Syd's childhood had been centered.

It had been the destination for Mama's lavish meals, the stage where Daddy played his accordion while friends danced and clapped to their favorite polkas, where Syd and Bobby struggled over homework, and where family games of Sheepshead were played. It was where Syd still challenged Daddy to a round of cribbage—next to Mama's vacant spot. As a young girl, Syd had chided the two for laying cards to help her peg. Now, she did the same for Daddy, hoping to coax that sparkle back into his often-confused eyes.

Syd bit her lower lip, her beer and sandwich in hand, as she joined Bitsy on the piano bench. It was so unfair: Bitsy had to deal with her granddaughter's issues *and* her son's.

Daddy had rested his accordion in a corner and was now seated in a ladder-back chair, whittling a piece of cedar with his jack knife.

Bitsy addressed Syd. "We heard about the Lacounts' tragedy. Is that where you rushed off to?"

She nodded and took a much-needed gulp of beer.

"Everyone was concerned about Frank," Bitsy continued. "He's such a dear. But that ice-princess of a wife is another story."

"Bitsy!" Syd scolded, though the name fit Alice to a "t." "She's just lost her daughter."

"I understand. But Alice Lacount is an Arctic Cat, and I'm not talking snowmobiles. I bet she didn't shed a tear. Even your mama, our sweet Grace, called her that."

"Alice mentioned she knew Mama." Having demolished the sandwich, Syd wiped her fingers on a napkin.

"She certainly did. You tell her, Monty."

Under Daddy's chair, curls of cedar were making a mess on the wide plank floor. "Nothing much to tell. It was all untruths."

Syd found his eyes. "Tell me, Daddy."

"Well…a couple of years back, Alice Lacount

accused your mama of inappropriate advances on good old Frank."

"You're kidding!" Syd huffed. "That's a laugh."

"Sure is, but your mama wasn't the first to be targeted. I heard Alice even pointed those red vixen nails at her own daughter."

Syd gave a start of surprise. "Really?"

"Hey, now." Bitsy placed her hands on the keyboard. "That's enough talk of the Lacounts."

Hearing the opening chords, Syd rolled her eyes. Bitsy was not subtle with her hints.

While Lloyd howled and Daddy stamped his feet, Syd and Bitsy belted out "I'm Getting Married in the Morning." Syd knew it was far from pretty.

As she rose to go, Lloyd followed her lead.

"Night, Syd." Daddy stood to give her a hug.

Bitsy was sweeping up the wood shavings under his chair, but now she paused. "Honey, you be careful." Then, instead of giving Syd the expected hug, Bitsy swatted her on the butt with the broom.

Tonight, within this familiar room, Syd felt swaddled by the warmth of her family. Carli Lacount's death had given her a reality check. For two years, Syd had pitied herself as multiple tragedies had clobbered her in tidal waves.

Yet through it all, she'd known, she'd been intensely loved.

Maybe Carli was the one who could pull Syd out of her ugly rut.

Chapter 10

On Monday morning, Syd entered the department's investigative wing, pretending to be all put-together in a blue linen suit, tall heels, and an ornate barrette to secure her curls. On closer inspection, she knew others wouldn't miss the bags under her eyes, the residual left from another night of fitful sleep.

Late the previous evening, Brian Lacount had been notified about his sister's death, and the press had released Carli's name to the public. Syd expected a deluge of tips.

Gina waved her over. "A number of local residents have called. They drove past Carli while she biked in Saturday's Century. She appeared to be riding alongside a young man."

Syd was encouraged. "Did anyone recognize him?"

"Not yet."

"Damn!" Syd frowned. "But keep up the good work." She headed toward Deputy Jeffers' desk.

Sam looked up, a sheen on his cratered face. "I've made some headway with the Century list, but so far, I've come up empty."

Disappointed, Syd patted him on the back. "Appreciate the effort. Call my cell if you get a hit."

"Will do."

Monday was normally Marv's day off, but Syd stuck her head into his office anyway. There he was, peach fuzz sprouting on his chin and a portion of his skull. "Hey, Marv."

He looked up.

"I'm surprised you're here."

To Syd's relief, he gave her a slanted smile. "If Super-Syd could work yesterday, Marvelous-Marv can work today."

She laughed at hearing their childhood names. It felt odd having come to a tentative truce. She wondered how long it would last.

"I'll have to make it up to your bro', though." Marv rocked back in his chair. "I promised Bobby we'd go bass fishing on Clark Lake today."

At the mention of her brother, Syd remembered the Hobie-Cat, and told Marv about it. "You know Bobby's been looking for one. Why don't you let him know it's for sale? That may appease him."

Marv's eyes brightened. "It just might."

"So, how's your case going? Did you talk to that young girl approached by the possible pedophile?"

"Yeah." A look of frustration crossed Marv's face. "I asked Cassie Monroe to think hard about the priest and what he'd said. All she could remember was him asking whether she could provide him directions. The rest of his words were muffled by her mother's shouts. But Cassie's interview was insightful on one level."

"What's that?"

"You and I both interviewed Jenny Tyler, right?"

Syd nodded.

"I discovered Cassie is also petite with big brown eyes and brown hair cut in a pixie style."

Syd considered Marv's words, perplexed.

Both girls, it appeared, could pass for a younger version of Carli Lacount.

* * * *

Syd headed north on Highway 57 to interview Beth Halverson, Carli's best friend. In addition to the crackle of dispatch requests from her two-way radio, she listened to a music station. It took a news station break and led off with Carli's undetermined death. Syd knew her case was now the talk of the entire peninsula.

She reduced her van's speed as she entered Jacksonport. On her left, she noticed the phone booth adjacent to Harvey's Citgo and across from the Big Scoop Ice Cream Parlor. On Sunday morning, Marv said the latter had been closed, and no employees from the station had noticed anyone using the booth. Both the door handle and payphone's receiver had been suspiciously clean. The names of the Citgo customers, who had made credit or debit purchases during that time period, were being provided for follow-up.

Syd's foot hit the accelerator. There was too much to do.

She continued along Lake Michigan's shoreline until she reached the community of Baileys Harbor. At the sign for Halverson's Fishing and Dive Charters, she made a right. Under a tin roof, supporting a flock of seagulls, sat a weathered office adjacent to a dock. A ripe concoction of seaweed, dead fish, water, and sand fermented in the stagnant air.

For Syd, the strong odor released heart-tugging memories of summer days she'd spent with Eli...

The two of them had often headed out into the waters of Sturgeon Bay for a day of fishing in his dad's Bayliner. Gina had claimed there was "nothing more boring," so she'd opted to stay ashore.

The bay had been named for the sturgeon, revered by the Potawatomi. According to Eli, that species of fish could reach 200 pounds and a length of nine feet, which had helped the tribe ward off starvation. As waves lapped Eli's boat, their lines out, he talked to Syd about the Potawatomi mythological creature that brought good luck with sturgeon fishing—that was, until the white man discovered the money he could make selling its eggs, better known as caviar. Then, a fishing explosion made the sturgeon a rare species.

Syd and Eli had always been looking for their sturgeon. They'd caught northern, pike, walleye, and smallmouth bass, but never their illusive fish.

As Syd entered the charter office, she realized their dream would never come to fruition—and all because of her.

A beautiful young woman staffed the desk, her blonde ponytail pulled through the back of a well-worn pink Green Bay Packers cap. Slender but muscular, she was a postcard-perfect image of the Norwegians who'd lived in Door County for more than a century. The nameplate on her form-fitting tank top said "Beth."

Syd introduced herself, then said, "You must be Carli's friend."

She nodded and tears welled up in her crystal blue eyes surrounded by thick lashes.

Syd gave Beth's calloused hand, with nicely shaped nails, a firm squeeze. "I'm sorry for your loss."

She accepted the condolences. "Go ahead. Pull up a stool. My dad's out with a dive charter."

Syd arranged her skirt on the seat and slid her heels around the rung. To set Beth at ease, she mentioned her upcoming dive with Gina. Then Syd addressed Carli's death.

Beth's brooding eyes pierced hers. "It was accidental, right?"

"I'm sorry, but it's too early to tell."

Even though she said "I see," it looked to Syd as if her words had disturbed Beth.

Syd opened her notebook and slipped out the pen. "Can you tell me where you were between 7 and 9 a.m. on the morning of Carli's death?"

Beth seemed surprised. "Why, right here."

"Can anyone confirm that?"

"I believe I took at least one charter reservation during that time." She opened the log and slid her finger along the page. "The McConnell family was one, and then Mr. Johnson and his son were another."

Syd wrote down their names and numbers. "Can you tell me about your friendship with Carli?"

Beth tilted her head. "What would you like to know?"

"Well, for starters, how did the two of you meet?"

Beth's eyes took on a distant look. "It was in sixth grade." She did the mental arithmetic. "My God, that was a dozen years ago. Carli was the new kid who'd moved here from Kaukauna and had a negative attitude to boot. A bad combination, if you know what I mean."

"I do."

"There were about thirty kids in our class, and they were cliquey. I'm not one to follow the crowd, so I connected with Carli. I also convinced her to join the soccer team, never imagining she'd be so good. At that time, she was the youngest girl to make first string."

Beth's face shone with pride before it shifted into painful loss.

Syd studied her while listening to the scratching of seagulls doing a balancing dance up on the roof. Beth's reaction was what Syd normally saw from a parent or a significant other.

But of course, the two women *had been* best friends.

"After that," Beth continued, "Carli seemed to come into her own."

"How so?"

She shrugged and ruffled through some papers on the counter. "Being 'the star,' Carli became quite bold, almost to a fault, and began to intimidate people, both on and off the soccer field. It seemed important to her to be in control of every situation. She confided to me, her lack of control had caused her tremendous pain in the past."

Syd gave Beth a sharp look. "Did she elaborate?"

"No, it's something Carli never wanted to discuss, but her attitude caused a rift with some of the girls in our class. They hated how she needed to dominate every situation, whether in sports, in classroom presentations, or hanging out at a party. But this very same trait seemed to be a magnet for the guys. Carli had this disarming charm, plus a rather angelic look about her. Her mom encouraged her to date, and she did, a little, before shutting each guy down."

Syd frowned before moving on. "I understand Carli attended St. Norbert College. What about you?"

"College wasn't my thing." Beth shook her head, her ponytail bouncing. "I've always known I had a spot here."

"Did you stay connected with Carli while she attended college?"

"Yeah, she still came back every other weekend to work at the Café." Her eyes shifted to the cloudy panes of glass and gazed out toward the lake. "We'd try to connect then." Beth blinked hard.

"I take it you were pleased when she decided to move back?"

She nodded. "I'd purchased my condo, the August before, but my finances were tight. When Carli agreed to move in, her rent money helped cover my monthly expenses."

"Carli's parents mentioned her personal items were moved from their home to your condo. Can you provide me access, so I can look through Carli's things later today?"

Beth looked unsettled by the request. "Well, I work until about 5:30."

"What if I meet you at your condo at 6 p.m.?"

"I guess that'll work." Beth looked down. "But maybe you should know. Carli gave me her two-month notice on Thursday, the last night I saw her."

Syd had wondered whether Beth would volunteer that information. "Were you two at odds?"

Beth shifted on her stool. "Not really..." A flush appeared on her cheeks. "Carli claimed she needed her own space."

"Do you think she had a love interest?"

A frown formed on Beth's face as she twirled the end of her ponytail around her finger. "Maybe... Last Wednesday, I walked into the condo while Carli was on her cell. She was upset and crying. At seeing me, she seemed very uncomfortable and stepped out onto the balcony to finish her conversation."

Syd's heart quickened. "Do you have any idea who she was talking to?"

"I know I shouldn't have been listening, but I heard her mention the name 'Nick.'"

"Do you know who this guy might be?"

Beth looked grim. "I wish I did."

Chapter 11

The lush green foliage along the cooler eastern shoreline of the Door County peninsula was changing into vibrant shades of red, rust, and gold. The scenery was stunning, on Syd's drive back to Sturgeon Bay, yet she barely noticed, for she was considering Beth's words about Carli.

The two women had seemed to be very tight. Maybe too tight for Carli. Was this the reason she'd decided to move out? And who was this Nick? Syd assumed she'd be able to uncover his identity from Carli's cell phone records. Based on past history, it seemed Carli had not had much success with long-term romantic relationships. Since she'd been upset on the call Beth had overheard, had Carli been failing again? Could this Nick have been Carli's bike-ride partner rather than Solly?

Syd clutched the steering wheel and wondered: *Have we been chasing the wrong guy?*

Her iPhone rang.

"Hey, Sydney," Deputy Jeffers' voice boomed. "We may be in luck! I talked to Eric Ingersol. He lives in Green Bay, and he says he knew Carli Lacount. They spent

Saturday biking the Century together. And, by the way, he goes by the nickname of Solly."

"Good work, Sam!" That answered at least one of her questions. "What was Eric's reaction?"

"He was very upset and even volunteered to drive up to Sturgeon Bay for an interview. He's on his way now."

* * * *

Eric was seated in the same room where Syd had talked to the Lacounts.

She felt a sense of relief—Eric's cologne matched the scent in the Solstice Cottage's cabin.

Eric was a rugged kind of guy: over six feet, with a firm chin, deep-set eyes, and dressed in jeans and a button-down shirt. His upper lip was dotted with perspiration, apparently from nerves. Syd knew it was too cool in the room for the alternative. After introductions, she got down to business. "So, Eric, tell me about your weekend with Carli Lacount."

"I can't believe she's dead." He leaned on his elbows and trapped his fingers within his dark hair.

"I understand you biked the Century with her on Saturday."

"Yeah. I drove up that morning and met her for the start in Sturgeon Bay."

"Over the 100-mile route, you two had plenty of time to talk. Can you give me any highlights?"

"Well…we reminisced about our college years…we updated each other on mutual friends…" He hesitated. "Carli was a complex person, evasive, never one to share her problems. But on Saturday, she posed an interesting question."

Syd gave Eric a long look. "Okay?"

"She asked, if I had the chance to live my life over, is there anything I'd change?" Eric's thin lips tightened. "I've got to admit, my answer was pretty lame compared to Carli's."

"How so?"

"She said for more than a decade, she'd been concealing a secret that had altered her life."

Syd leaned forward. She wondered whether this secret was related to Beth's words about Carli's prior lack of control. "Did Carli provide additional insight, Eric?"

"I kept at her as we biked, encouraging her to open up, but she said she wasn't quite ready." His dark lashes blinked rapidly. "I felt honored that she'd even revealed that much to me."

Syd nodded. "What did you and Carli do after the bike ride?"

"I'd planned on returning to Green Bay, but Carli asked me to hang out with her at the cottage she'd rented for the weekend. Other years, many friends had done the same."

"So…" Syd held her gaze steady on his face, "did you end up spending the night?"

"I did." He squirmed. "But it was definitely Carli's idea, not mine. And, believe me—she was fine when I left at around 7:30 yesterday morning. She was stretching before her run, so she could make it over to the Café by 10:30 to waitress."

"Did you hear her cell phone ring early yesterday morning?"

His brow wrinkled. "I think I did."

"Do you recall Carli's conversation?"

"No, I'm sorry." He shook his head. "I fell back asleep until my cell's alarm went off."

"Why did you leave so early?"

"I'd promised to be back in Green Bay for Sunday brunch with my parents."

"Can anyone vouch for the time you got home?"

He frowned. "Not really. But on the way back, I did stop for gas in Dyckesville."

"Do you have a receipt showing the time?"

Eric considered before shaking his head. "I paid cash, and I'm sure I tossed the receipt in the trash." He hesitated, his eyes hopeful. "Maybe they have one of those cameras?"

Syd nodded and took down the make and license plate number of his car. She was now ready to ask a key question. "Eric…" She waited until his eyes landed on hers. "Can you explain why there was blood on the cabin bed sheets?"

"There was?" He looked confused. "Was there a lot of blood?"

"You tell me."

"I didn't know there was any!" He drummed his fingers on the table. "It could be from Carli's knee. On Saturday, she hit some gravel and took a spill. The sag wagon gave her something to clean the scrapes. Maybe the cuts started to bleed again?"

"It's possible." She owed him that. "I assume you and Carli had sex?"

"Yeah." Eric crossed his arms in a defensive gesture. "But Carli came onto me. I've got to admit, though, I've always been interested in her. She had this wide-eyed innocence about her, yet gave off these intense sexual vibes. Until this weekend, she'd rejected my advances, but Saturday night was different. It was almost weird—as if she was possessed."

Syd leaned toward him. "What do you mean?"

"Well, Carli kept saying she wanted to do everything and do it right." He looked worried. "You don't think I raped her, do you?"

"Did you know she was a virgin?"

His eyes widened. "My God! I had no idea." He analyzed this new piece of information. "I'm not an expert on this, but couldn't that also explain the blood?"

"Possibly." Syd settled back into the chair. "Did you use protection?"

"Yeah." He frowned. "I bet you found the condom wrappers under the bed. I meant to toss them." He looked concerned. "Do I need a lawyer?"

"It's your choice if you want counsel present."

"Are you charging me with anything?"

"At this point, Eric, I'm just trying to understand why Carli ended up dead."

"That's what I want to know, too." His voice caved in. "I truly cared for her. I was thrilled when Carli agreed to hook up again this weekend. Believe me, I want to help you in any way I can."

Syd saw pain in his face. She did believe him. Eric also agreed to be examined at St. Vincent Hospital. She couldn't help but smile. Marv was off the hook. A qualified professional would verify whether Eric's privates, when aroused, were indeed larger than Carli's vaginal opening.

Syd's next objective was to uncover the identity of this Nick. She asked Eric whether he knew anyone by that name who Carli might've known.

He thought hard, finally shaking his head. "Is this guy someone from college?"

"I don't know."

"You could talk to her former roommates. Carli

64

shared a rental house in De Pere with Tina Kelsey and two other girls. I'm not sure whether they've all graduated yet, but I've got Tina's cell number." He provided it to Syd.

"Eric, you already mentioned this secret Carli wouldn't share. Did she mention any recent concerns or problems?"

"Not specifically, but on the bike ride, and while having a few beers in the cabin, she seemed a bit down, like something was on her mind."

"Okay, Eric." She put him on the spot: "How about in bed?"

"Well, I guess, after she gave me her demands, we didn't do too much talking." He cleared his throat. "If you know what I mean."

Syd cocked her head with a wan smile. "All right, then how about Sunday morning? Did Carli say anything before you left?"

He nodded as tears sprung into his eyes. "She thanked me for spending the night and called it momentous. It marked what she called her 'rebirth.'"

"Rebirth?" Syd repeated, surprised.

"Yeah… I'm sure that's what she said. Then, when I got into my car, Carli motioned to me to put the window down." He choked back a sob. "She grabbed my face with both of her hands and gave me this passionate kiss. I drove away and checked my rear view mirror. Carli was standing there, hugging her body, this unbelievable smile on her face."

* * * *

Syd was "On the Road Again." This time she followed the Green Bay shoreline north along Highway 42 that passed through the small communities of Carlsville, Egg Harbor, and Juddville. All the while Syd analyzed Eric's interview.

He'd confirmed Beth's contention that Carli had possessed some secret she wouldn't reveal. He'd also solidified the Lacounts' concern about Carli's recent depression. But Syd wondered what Carli's "rebirth" meant? Until her night with Eric, had she been afraid to have sex? And knowing Carli had been a virgin, where did this puzzling Nick fit in?

Before leaving the department, Syd had retrieved Carli's cell phone from evidence and rechecked its contact list. There were no Nicks. Also, Deputy Jeffers had provided Syd a twelve-month list of every phone number coming into or going out of Carli's cell. Beth had mentioned the call Carli received from Nick on the Wednesday prior to her death. But that incoming call, Syd confirmed, had been made from the public phone near the Fish Creek Post Office and killed that possible lead. Syd then had skimmed her other recent calls. Beth had phoned Carli four times over the past weekend, but based on the seconds per call, it appeared as if Carli had never answered.

Within the last three months, calls had also been placed to and from Carli's family, Colette and Luke Lacount's residence, Dr. Woodbridge, Carli's hairdresser, Reuben's Garage, and the Café. But Carli's cell phone records hadn't revealed any Nicks.

Syd shook her head. She needed to talk to the Lacounts again. Maybe Beth's and Eric's new information would help them shed more light on their daughter's death.

For Syd, though, it was difficult not to think about Eric's feelings for Carli and imagine the night they'd spent together. Syd was ashamed to admit she was envious. But how could that be? She slammed the steering wheel with her palm. Carli was dead, and she wasn't, at least not physically. Emotionally was another story.

It had been such a long time since *she'd* given a guy a passionate kiss and an unbelievable smile.

Chapter 12

Syd followed the steep road down into the village of Fish Creek, nestled between a bluff and the waters of Green Bay. This resort village, initially established as a fishing community in the mid-1800s, was now the number-one destination spot in the peninsula. Original white clapboard buildings housed numerous shops and restaurants along Main Street. Syd took her time, always on the alert for jaywalking tourists.

During WWII, a German POW camp had been established near this site. Prisoners had worked on local construction projects. Among them was a portion of the Triangle Shops & Café, which Syd now approached.

Of course her eyes were also drawn to the Greek Revival Farmhouse on the opposite side of the street. The sign out front read *Eli Gaudet, Attorney at Law.*

Syd's eyes began to smart. Rather than pulling into the Café's parking lot, she drove on, trying to regain her composure as memories from her past attacked her...

Syd had been very attached to Eli's parents who'd met in 1966 after the Alger-Delta Cooperative Electric Association ran lines onto the Hannahville Indian Reservation.

Eli's dad, Leon, had been the harbormaster in Menominee, Michigan and was among the forty volunteers who'd wired homes on the reservation. One of those was Eli's mom's. "And it was love at first sight," Leon liked to say.

The two married and after a difficult pregnancy, Eli was born. When the harbormaster job opened in Sturgeon Bay, Leon leapt at the opportunity. The Gaudets purchased a home in the Town of Sevastopol where Eli started kindergarten. That year Syd's tight friendship with both Eli and Gina took hold.

During the next ten years, Eli's mom had four miscarriages. It was tough for Syd to see the constant stress in the Gaudets' household. But when Eli was a freshman in high school, joy erupted when his mom finally carried a baby full term. At the hospital, Syd and Gina were excitedly waiting with Eli when his dad delivered the tragic news. "Our baby girl was breech," he sobbed. "A volume of amniotic fluid entered your mom's bloodstream, which caused cardiac arrest. She's dead, Eli, she's dead, and so is our baby girl."

Leon's and Eli's grief was immense. Syd and Gina suffered too, not knowing how to provide Eli any comfort. His mom's death was what led his dad, formerly a teetotaler, to drink. Because Leon had felt incapable of handling his extensive work responsibilities, he luckily was able to secure the less-stressful harbormaster position in the small community of Fish Creek.

Eli was also forced to attend Gibraltar High School, but that didn't stop the three friends from seeing each other. Nearly every weekend, the two girls would pick Eli up in Gina's ancient Grand Marquis. The three would cruise the county roads, squeezed into the front seat. Gina would be at the wheel, Syd would sit on the hump, and Eli would be tilted on his left hip to her right, his arm slung loosely around Syd's shoulders. The car radio would be cranked up as Bryan Adams crooned "Have you Ever Really Loved a Woman?" Not until later did Syd grasp how very differently each of them had interpreted that song...

On Syd's right, she now passed the Skyway Drive-in Theater. The three friends had watched nearly every double feature there, crammed into the front seat of Gina's steamy car, swatting at mosquitos, and eating buttered popcorn. Of course, there were also the secret underage beer parties. An uncle of one of their classmates owned a deserted barn in the woods near Baileys Harbor where he would haul in half-barrels. Five bucks would buy you a cup. It was rumored that he paid off his Chevy truck loan with that little endeavor.

On one of those nights, Eli took Syd's hand and pulled her into the woods, away from Gina and the others. It was the first time they'd been all alone, and her heart started to pound. When Eli bent down and his lips touched hers, she felt this huge rush. They groped each other, all hands and mouths, two adolescents in heat. This was what she'd fantasized about for years, but hadn't known how to tell Eli. Yet, at that moment, she was also worried about Gina. A co-ed friendship of three was complex. Syd feared Gina might have feelings for Eli, too, and be devastated that Syd had betrayed her. But Eli believed, since Gina loved them both, she'd be happy for them. And—at that time—Syd thought Gina was.

From that point on, the daily separation between Syd and Eli made their weekend time together more intense. But they knew they wouldn't be apart for long. Unlike Gina, who was making plans to attend the technical college in Sturgeon Bay, Syd and Eli both chose colleges in

Milwaukee: UWM for her, while Eli received a four-year merit-based scholarship to attend Marquette University.

Syd spent her freshman year in a dorm on campus. It was one of the best years of her life. At that stage, her relationship with Eli was still quite innocent. She'd yet to sleep with him, so their togetherness was full of that incredible unsatisfied passion. But her sophomore year, that all changed. She moved into a charming but dilapidated Queen Anne Victorian on Murray Street with seven other students. Eli was one of them. Initially, the two of them had individual bedrooms. Syd's mama saw to that. But by mid-semester, Syd announced to her family: "It's beyond your control, I'm officially moving into Eli's room. We've made a commitment." Syd thought Gina would be happy for them. And she said she was, but Syd wasn't so sure...

Syd extracted herself from her thoughts and, now, more composed, turned back south, taking the scenic route through Peninsula State Park. To her right stood the Memorial Totem Pole commemorating Potawatomi chief Simon Khaquados.

In the seventeenth century, Father Allouez, who lived among the Potawatomi, documented his perception of his "native neighbors." It was eerie how his words mirrored Eli's personality. He was very intelligent, cordial, and inclined to good-humored teasing. When he set his mind to something, he rarely backed down. But unlike his ancestors, Eli had this carelessness streak.

Growing up, both Syd and Gina would tease him. How he'd lose every softball glove he'd ever owned. How he'd jump out of Gina's car so fast, he'd hit the door of the one parked alongside, and was forever paying off repairs. How they'd get out on the water in his dad's boat, and he'd realize he hadn't filled up with gas, so they'd have to call for a tow. It went on and on. But in college, when Syd started to live with him, she saw his carelessness not as comical but as a major flaw, something he needed to fix…

Syd now waved at a young woman walking a Golden Retriever along the state park's road, a sharp reminder of Eli's major incident. It occurred after the two of them had bought their first Golden Retriever.

Beau was beautiful, with a wild personality. One October afternoon, Eli rushed off to classes. Rather than locking Beau in their bedroom, as they'd both agreed, Eli left him in their fenced-in backyard. Syd returned home from the library, entered their bedroom, and bent down for her standard lick on the face.

But Beau wasn't there.

She searched the house and yard with that awful taste of fear in her mouth, certain someone had stolen him.

Then she discovered a low spot under the fence that contained dig marks.

She searched the busy neighborhood, as cars whipped by, frantically calling his name and listening for his familiar little bark.

Instead, she found his broken body on the side of the street, his nose still warm.

Syd hurled herself at Eli when he got home and pounded on his chest, repeating over and over, "You killed our Beau!" This time, she couldn't forgive Eli, even though she knew he was as devastated as she was. Syd threw all his belongings into the hall and wouldn't talk to him for weeks. Whenever they'd pass, he'd swear, "Believe me, Syd, nothing like this will ever happen again."

After both of them had suffered enough, she finally caved in.

For their remaining days in college, Eli's personality

flaw seemed to have vanished. He was attentive to that issue and continued to convince Syd he'd learned from Beau's death. The way Eli seemed to mature and handle that situation proved to her that—like his early ancestors, the arbiters for the tribes along the bay—he would make a fine attorney.

When Syd graduated with her degree in Criminal Science, Eli received his B.A. in Economics. While she had finished her college education, he still needed ninety more credits to earn his law degree.

It was difficult being back in Door County without him. In hindsight, though, it allowed Syd to concentrate on her new job as a deputy sheriff.

That was the prime reason, she believed, she'd been able to move up in the ranks to detective so fast...

At the Fish Creek exit for Peninsula State Park, Syd now turned left onto Main Street, only a few blocks from where her emotions were initially triggered.

When Eli had returned to this village, the price of real estate had sky-rocketed. As harbormaster, Eli's dad was provided a small waterfront office with a back-room apartment, so he could be close to the action. Even though Leon still maintained the home he and Eli had lived in during Eli's high school years, Leon preferred his small bachelor pad. After Eli earned his law degree, his dad insisted he move back into the Fish Creek home they'd previously shared. It was highly visible along the main thoroughfare, and a portion of its first floor would be the perfect location for his law office. After some affable resistance, Eli acquiesced.

Much to Syd's family's chagrin, she moved in too. "Those young people!" Bitsy had scowled. "In my day, there was a proper marriage first!"

Syd now turned into the parking lot across from the home she and Eli had once shared. Throughout her life, he'd been there for her—almost an extension of her.

But no more.

Syd climbed out of her van and advanced toward the Triangle Shops & Café, knowing she was solely to blame for that loss.

Chapter 13

Tantalizing scents of bakery permeated the vestibule that led into the Café's dining area. The space was decorated in cheery primary colors, but the atmosphere seemed subdued. The few tables within Syd's view were filled with couples, keeping their voices low. The one waitress she could see shuffled between tables, her head down. As difficult as it might seem, Syd realized, business must go on, even after the death of the staff's co-worker—and the owners' child.

A dead ringer for Eric Stolz approached Syd. In addition to this man's wavy copper hair, blue eyes, and a spattering of freckles across his nose and cheeks, Syd was drawn to his unshaven look. About her age, he wore a green polo shirt monogramed with the Triangle Shops logo. He tried to put on a good face, and dimples appeared. "Table for one?" To make sure he was correct, he peered over her shoulder.

"Not today." She introduced herself. "I'm here to see Alice or Frank Lacount."

He grimaced. "Frank told me about his meeting with you. Sorry, but they're not here." He cleared his throat. "I'm

Frank's younger brother, Patrick. Maybe I can help?"

Syd was surprised this man was Frank's brother. The two had to be at least ten years apart in age. The deep baritone, though, was nearly identical. "I understand your brother, Luke, works here, too."

"Yeah." His voice produced a "too bad" rumble. "He's actually my twin."

Syd regarded Patrick. It looked as if Luke wasn't winning any popularity contests with either of his siblings.

"Luke's over in the art gallery." He motioned that way. "I'm overseeing both the restaurant and the boutique today while Alice and Frank are at home. I'll give you directions to their place, if you'd like…"

"That would be helpful." As Patrick scratched a small map on a piece of paper, Syd asked, "How long have you worked here?"

"This is a new venture for me. In April, Frank kindly asked me to work here for a change of venue." He twisted his wedding band with his thumb. "My wife passed away from breast cancer last year."

"My God! How tragic for you. My mother also died from that dreadful disease." Syd looked away as she visualized her last moments with Mama. With eyes barely focused, their light growing weak, she'd smiled up at Syd and whispered, "All in all, sweetie, I have no regrets… How many people can say that?"

Syd knew she couldn't.

Patrick handed her the directions to Frank's home. For an instant, their fingers brushed. She felt a sense of connection—a shared pain. Her eyes lifted. "It's good you're here to help your brother through Carli's tragedy as, I assume, he's been helping you through yours?"

Patrick nodded. "Who would've thought? Since I

still own a restaurant in Saugatuck, Michigan, Frank's helped me out by lending me a car and also finding me and Blinker a place to rent."

"Blinker?"

"My Irish Setter." Patrick's face lit up. "I don't know what I'd do without him. He's also a great traveler on my bi-weekly trips across the lake to lower Michigan and back."

Syd smiled, picturing the combo: this copper-haired man with his silky-red-headed dog. The love for his canine told her something about Patrick. "Are you two taking the car ferry out of Manitowoc?"

"No." He laughed. "I fly a private plane, and Blinker's my co-pilot. This was not to be a permanent arrangement, but on our last visit, my Saugatuck business partner sweetened his previous offer to buy out my portion of the restaurant. I've been reluctant to do that, but with Carli's death, Frank wants me to reconsider."

A couple approached Patrick, their bill in hand. While Syd waited for them to settle up, she thought about her earlier interview with Frank. He'd insinuated Luke might not have liked the idea of Carli taking over the business. What would Luke think about his twin, newly arrived on the scene, now moving in on Carli's vacated territory—and with Frank's blessing?

The outside door closed behind the couple, and Syd refocused on Patrick.

"Did Frank tell you we're still investigating whether Carli's death was accidental or foul play?"

He nodded, his face troubled. "But I agree with Frank and Alice. It's got to be accidental. Who would want to hurt my niece?"

"That's what I'm trying to determine." Syd tilted her chin his way. "How well did you and Carli get along?"

He leaned back against the wall, his warm eyes trained on her. "We had an amicable working relationship. Until this summer, though, I'd never met either Carli or Brian. When Frank and Alice married, the two had a private wedding." Patrick gave Syd a sheepish look. "I hate to admit, I never made the effort to visit Fish Creek after that."

"So, what was Carli like?" Syd opened her spiral notebook and removed the pen.

He crossed his arms, considering. "Carli was very bright, but often moody. And this past week was one of her worst."

Syd pursed her lips. There it was again—that darkness in Carli's life. "Do you know why?"

"No." He shook his head. "She didn't confide in me."

Syd frowned. "How did your niece relate to her mom and dad?"

"Not overly warm, but always civil. She wasn't one of those huggy-squeezy girls, like some of the other waitresses who work here. Carli had her fans, though. A number of customers would wait nearly an hour for one of her tables to free up. But in general, Carli seemed to keep most people at arm's length."

The front door opened and a young couple strolled in. Patrick excused himself to seat them. Syd watched how he made them feel welcome. Big brother Frank had to think this sibling was an asset. But what did Patrick think of his two brothers? He'd already provided some insight, but she caught Patrick's eyes on his return and still posed the question.

He nodded toward her open notebook. "Is this on or off the record?"

She answered by flipping it shut.

"All right, then. Frank's a real gem and always has been. But Luke's another story." He gave her a tight smile. "I know twins are supposed to be close, but we've never been. If he weren't my brother, I wouldn't even like the guy. Let's just say, this summer has been interesting."

"What do you mean?"

"Well, although Luke's now married, he's still quite the ladies' man. Likes to flirt with any young female."

"Did he flirt with Carli?"

"Sure, but she did an admirable job of ignoring him." His eyes darted toward the gallery. "Maybe you should talk to Luke directly."

Syd sensed Patrick's reticence to tell her more. Rather than pushing him, she removed Carli's key ring from an evidence envelope and showed him the four unaccounted-for keys.

"This larger one," Patrick said, pointing, "opens the Triangle complex's front and back doors. And this small key is for the desk in the business office."

"Is that where Carli worked when she wasn't waitressing?"

He nodded.

"It would help my investigation if I could search the desk and any office computer."

Patrick looked surprised. "I'll need to run that by Frank first." He reached for the phone and gave his brother a call. Moments later, Patrick hung up and swung the office door open. "Go ahead. Frank said the computer probably hasn't been turned on since Carli last used it."

"Does it have a password?"

"Yeah, *triangle*." Patrick laughed. "You can see the kind of security we have around here."

* * * *

Syd checked the desktop computer. The only thing that looked questionable was its web history log. It appeared as if Carli had erased it before she'd left on her biking weekend. Was this for some particular reason—or standard operating procedure?

Syd opened the two large desk drawers. Everything was organized in hanging folders. She flipped through each. Nothing appeared to be personal. The same went for the top desk drawers to the left and right.

Lastly, she opened the top-center drawer. There was a yellow notepad stamped "Property of Carli Lacount." Written on the top sheet was a single phone number.

Syd recognized it at once. Why would Carli have written down Eli's cell number?

Syd had been relieved when the scent in the cabin had matched Eric's cologne, but could Eli have been there, too? Syd was certain she'd seen him in his vehicle near Cave Point, soon after Carli's death.

There couldn't be a connection—could there?

Syd returned to the vestibule, where Patrick was filing a bill. "Mr. Lacount?"

He looked up, his gaze leveled on Syd, a sparkle in his eyes. "That's too formal. Please call me Patrick." He smiled.

She couldn't help but return it and thought, *This twin likes to flirt, too.*

Patrick seemed pleased by her response, which made Syd's stomach sink. She knew it was a mistake, unprofessional. Besides, what guy in his right mind, once he *really* saw her, would ever be interested? She wiped the smile off her face, determined to get back to business.

He'd noticed her mood change. "Did you find anything helpful?" Patrick asked.

She thought about Eli's cell number, but shook her head. She then hesitated. "Can you tell me where you were yesterday morning, between 7 and 9?"

He gave her a curious look. "Why, right here." He gestured with both hands. "My kitchen duties start bright and early at 5 a.m. with food prep and baking."

"Were other staff or customers here at that time?"

"We opened at 7 a.m. Polly Adams and Tanya Cornell both arrived shortly before that to waitress. Our cook is Pete Argus. He joined me in the kitchen at around 6:30. And when I unlocked the front door, I believe two locals were already waiting."

"Can you provide their names?"

"Sure. One was Ruthie Arnette, and the other was Chad Werner. Before church, they often come in for a cup of coffee and a breakfast pastry. If you need more names, let me know. We get a constant stream on Sunday mornings."

Syd wrote the names down as a family of five entered. Patrick tousled the little boy's hair, then picked up some menus. They started for the dining room, and Patrick turned back. "Why don't you stop in again when you're off duty? I bet I could tempt you with a piece of my homemade cherry pie."

Syd smiled, unable to stop herself.

She couldn't lie.

This attractive man's attention felt good.

Chapter 14

Syd wove through the Café toward Luke's art gallery. Her eyes couldn't help but steal a glance at the table reserved for locals.

It was a terrible mistake. The color drained from her face.

Among them sat Eli Gaudet.

Syd had made a point of not stopping at the Café for just this reason. It had been twenty-three months since she'd last seen Eli. The reason for avoiding him was what kept her up at night. It made her ache with revenge to hurt him—and regret she felt this way.

In that initial year, Eli had tried to talk to Syd, first daily, then weekly, then monthly, until he stopped all together. At that point, Gina caved in and met Eli for a drink. What he conveyed to her made Syd honestly reconsider seeing him. But she vacillated too long, not knowing how to take the next step. Then six months ago, when Eli started to date, Syd realized she'd lost her chance.

She hated it. Even though she'd repeatedly told herself she was over him, Syd knew he was still in the back of her mind—and in her heart.

She wondered if it was the same for him.

At seeing Syd, Eli looked startled. He stood and blocked her way, gently grabbing her wrists. "Hello, Sydney," he said in his soft, sexy, slow drawl.

A rush of schoolgirl crush made her heart pound, her breasts tingle, and her groin ache.

Who was she kidding?

Eli gave Syd a tight smile. "Looks like I've trapped you, after all this time. I thought once Gina talked to you... When was that?" His voice now dripped sarcasm as his eyes penetrated hers. "Oh, I remember, wasn't it last November? I thought I'd hear from you, but I guess you didn't care enough to let me know you'd even considered what I said."

Distressed by his response, Syd tried to shake loose. "I don't have time for this." Her voice came out nasty. Her natural defenses had kicked into gear—though she knew she had it coming.

"Has this worked for you, Syd? Wiping me out of your life?" He attempted to push her blazer sleeves up. "I know you have scars." His thumbs began to rub her tender, vulnerable skin as she tried to pull away. "Well, I have scars, too." His voice broke. "You can't see mine, but they've been festering under my skin for nearly two years."

Tears filled his eyes. "I can't get over you, Syd."

"Well, I'm over you." She pulled free and tried to turn away.

He grabbed her shoulders and stared down at her. His fingers snagged her hair. The motion sprung the curls from her barrette, which fell to the floor. "Come on, Sydney, I dare you. Look at me!"

She did—and saw his tragic yet dear face: the wide violet eyes and the familiar squint lines, etched a little deeper. His raven hair, now cut short rather than secured at the nape, showed no hint of gray.

"Syd…" His voice wavered. "I'd give anything for you not to have been hurt."

"Leave me alone!" This time, she pushed against Eli's broad chest.

Defeated, he dropped his hands, threw some bills on the table, and marched out of her life—again.

Syd closed her eyes. Her body sagged. This time, she'd done it. She'd driven him away for good.

But she couldn't think about that now. She bent to retrieve the barrette, then secured it.

Patrick approached. "Are you okay? Was that guy hassling you?"

Syd shook her head. "I'm fine." She straightened her cuffs. "It's just somebody I used to know."

With purpose, she strode toward the gallery and drew a calming breath, still sensing Patrick's worried eyes.

Syd stepped through the archway where soft music played, evoking a welcoming sense of tranquility. Shoreline and pastoral scenes of Door County lined the walls.

She was surprised not to see a mirror image of Patrick. Rather than identical, this copper-haired fraternal twin looked more like Frank: both had distinguished Roman noses. But unlike his two brothers, Luke had the girth of an NFL player. He also had the permanently stained fingernails of a painter.

Syd admired artistic people. In addition to being inquisitive, like children, artists often immersed themselves into important causes. As a detective, she could relate to both.

Luke's crooked smile showed the same dimples as Patrick's. But the slight squint of Luke's eyes made her feel as if he was checking her out like a fine piece of art, or, conversely, a piece of meat.

"May I help you?" he asked, his deep baritone a match to both of his brothers.

Syd introduced herself. "I assume you're Luke Lacount?"

"That would be me." He gave a slight bow. "So, Detective Bernhardt, are you Monty's daughter?"

She nodded.

"I never would've figured his little girl would take on a man's job rather than working at the Chalet."

Syd was taken aback. "Well, Mr. Lacount, some might consider running a fancy retail shop to be women's work."

"Touché!" He dipped his head, ceding a point in his sexist game. "You must be here to discuss my niece's shocking death. I understand, from Frank, you're investigating whether it was foul play." He lifted his brow. Like his brothers, Luke seemed to be questioning the validity of that premise.

"That's right, but let's back up."

As he nodded, two young women wandered in.

Luke's gaze jumped to them. "Excuse me."

Syd watched him stroll toward his prey. She couldn't hear what he was saying to the twenty-something bleached blondes, but it made one of them giggle.

He returned and stationed himself in front of Syd, his eyes sliding down to the white cami covering her breasts.

She frowned at his disgusting behavior.

Her reaction made him laugh. "Okay, Detective. For the moment, I'm all yours."

Great! she thought. To regroup, she opened her notebook and removed the pen. "I'd first like a little history,

Mr. Lacount. Can you explain how you came to lease from your brother, Frank?"

"Let's see." He stroked his chin. "That was back in 2000... Frank was overseeing the construction of this building's two new wings, and I was living in the Fish Creek area. I'd purchased a defunct art studio with living quarters situated on ten acres off the beaten path."

Syd raised her eyebrows. "That sounds like a nice amount of land for a starving young artist."

"Inheritance money." He gave Syd a slippery smile. "It came from the sale of a portion of our parents' Door County estate."

"I'm confused. Frank said he was from Kaukauna."

"He lived there for a number of years before he moved to Fish Creek. But we all grew up in Chicago and spent many summers at my parents' vacation home here on Chambers Island. After Dad's death, Mother sold off a majority of the property and divided the proceeds between Frank, Patrick, and me. Frank used his portion to develop the shops and Café."

Luke gave Syd a conspiratorial wink. "I think Frank felt obligated to bring me into the business. But I also know he liked my work."

Luke ushered Syd over to a wall that featured his paintings. She had to admit they were quite good. Most highlighted recognizable lighthouses and historic communities within the county.

Syd turned back toward him. "So, you and Frank struck a deal?"

He nodded. "I split up my ten acres and gave him half. That's where he built his home. In exchange, I got the first five years in this gallery rent-free."

Like a vulture, Luke had been tracking the two

women. He now joined the favored one who'd carried a print to the checkout counter. As he completed the transaction, she deftly slipped him her business card. He pocketed it and gave her his signature wink.

Syd could only shake her head.

Another couple entered the gallery. Luke welcomed them, then sauntered back to Syd, at ease with his indiscretion.

She showed Luke the map Patrick had drawn. "Is your current home-and-studio still next door to Frank and Alice's?"

"Yeah, on this side." He pointed to the left.

"Based on that, I imagine you often saw Carli?"

"I wouldn't say that." He crossed his arms. "She and Brian were young when they moved here, and I was in my early twenties. Those first five years, I spent most of my time getting this gallery off the ground. The extra tourist traffic definitely worked to my advantage. Those chic Chicago girls, like the two who just left, would come up here with their daddy's money and an itch to have some fun."

A wolfish grin crossed Luke's lips. "I didn't mind fitting the bill in both categories." He gave Syd a good-old-boy nudge.

She backed away. "Is that how you met your wife?"

"Colette?" Luke rolled his eyes. "Her daddy certainly didn't provide *her* any cash. She was a waitress at the Café when I met her last summer."

Syd scrutinized Luke. Within a year, it appeared he and Colette had met, married, and had a child. Maybe an unexpected pregnancy had forced him into his new lifestyle.

"So, Mr. Lacount, how did you and Carli get along after she came back to work full-time at the shops?"

His smile faded. "I made the mistake of letting Colette work with Carli on the gallery's financial matters."

"What do you mean by 'mistake'?"

A vein in Luke's neck pulsed. "Well, at my insistence, Colette recently quit work to stay home with our daughter. Since then, Carli told me, on more than one occasion, I wasn't as adept as Colette at handling business matters."

Syd's eyes took in this angry man. Could Carli's criticism have made Luke upset enough to do something about it? Unlike other artists Syd had met, the only "important cause" Luke appeared to support was putting women in their place.

Syd turned back to Luke's paintings. "Isn't that a watercolor of Cave Point?"

She could see that she'd made him uneasy.

"Mr. Lacount, where were you the morning Carli died?"

"Well... in my studio." With one fingernail he picked at another, not meeting Syd's eyes.

Chapter 15

Syd followed Patrick's map toward the Lacounts' home. Finally, she had a chance to think about her confrontation with Eli. What a disaster! Seasick misery ebbed through her. She'd had her chance, and she'd blown it.

Near the north entrance to Peninsula State Park, Syd made a right. From there, she passed the road that led into the Ephraim-Gibraltar Airport, where 20 to 30 private planes took off or landed each day. She figured this was the airport Patrick Lacount used. A few miles farther down, she passed Luke and Colette Lacount's mailbox. About a quarter-mile farther was Frank and Alice's box. Syd maneuvered the long drive to reach a traditional-looking two-story house hidden in the woods.

She parked alongside a distinctive Triangle Shops & Café catering van. Primary-colored stripes were painted on each side of the white vehicle, and the custom license plate read TSCAFE1.

Syd had called the Lacounts to alert them of her arrival. With hunkered-down shoulders, Frank now answered the door and led her into the front room. Alice, all in black, sat on the stone fireplace hearth. Photos of Carli rested on her lap. Others were scattered at her feet.

Syd took a seat on a chair across from Frank and brought the Lacounts up to date. She ended with Eric Ingersol's comment about Carli's life-altering secret.

"This is so confusing." Frank wrung his hands. "I can't imagine what terrible secret Carli was keeping from us. Can you, Alice?"

She shook her head. "This whole thing is beyond me." Alice then handed Syd a photo. "This is from St. Anne's Camp."

"You mean the all-girls Catholic church camp that used to be located on Adventure Island?" Syd analyzed the pictured group of pre-teen girls standing by a cabin. She recognized Carli with her familiar pixie-style haircut. Next to her, a young girl with her hair in brown braids held up two fingers behind Carli's head to form bunny ears. Carli was the only one not smiling in the photo.

Alice nodded. "Carli attended St. Anne's with her best friend, Molly." Alice pointed out the girl with braids. "It was in July of 2000, right before we moved here, and about a year after my first husband's fatal accident." She hesitated. "I know his death altered Carli's life, but that's no secret."

Syd nodded. "I met with Beth Halverson. She seemed to be very protective of Carli. What's your opinion?"

"Beth was a good influence," Alice said. "Back in high school, lots of kids were getting into drugs and alcohol and having wild parties." She glanced at Syd. "You know how it happens in small communities."

"I do know." Syd's shoulders gave a guilty shrug.

"Beth didn't seem to go with the flow, so Carli didn't either. In turn, Beth may have hindered Carli's boyfriend status." Alice's large eyes held hers. "Beth seemed to be critical of the guys Carli met, and I think Carli listened. I always thought Beth was jealous that guys seemed to be interested in Carli rather than in her."

Syd frowned. This information didn't quite match Beth's recollection.

Now she launched a key question: "Do either of you know anyone named Nick?" Syd hoped the name might click with one of them since her own efforts had been unsuccessful.

The Lacounts looked mystified. Alice turned toward Frank. "I can't think of anyone by that name, can you?"

Frank slowly shook his head. "Sorry, Syd, neither can I."

A disappointed Syd let herself out of the Lacounts' home. As she did, Syd noticed a lanky young man climbing out of a black Prius and assumed he was Brian Lacount. Dressed in a blue oxford shirt and dress slacks, he was way over six feet tall. His dark hair and eyes matched both his mom's and Carli's.

Syd approached him and, holding out her hand, introduced herself.

Brian did the same. "I just finished meeting with the funeral director." He ran his hand down his distraught face. "Carli's service will be at St. John's tomorrow at 10 a.m. after two hours of visitation."

Syd offered her condolences and got down to business. "Brian, the morning your sister died, I understand you and your girlfriend were on Washington Island."

"Yeah. The two of us took bikes over on the 8 a.m. ferry. Shellie had her cell, but I didn't. The first I heard about Carli's death was when I returned home around 7 p.m." He shook his head. "What a shocker."

"Were you and your sister close?"

"I would say we were much closer when we lived in Kaukauna. Right around the time we moved, Carli became rather sullen and stopped confiding in me. I figured she was going through that girl-type puberty stage."

"I understand your family had a nice life in Kaukauna before your dad died."

"Did my mom say that?"

Syd nodded.

He frowned. "It was far from perfect. My dad was fooling around."

Syd's eyes widened. "He was?"

"Yeah. I never told Mom I knew, but I discovered Dad in bed with some woman shortly before he died. Dad talked to me about it. He said he'd made a terrible mistake and it wouldn't happen again. At that time, I wanted to believe him, but I also knew my parents argued a lot and seemed rather distant."

"Did Carli know about your dad's infidelity?"

Lines formed on Brian's brow. "She never brought it up, so I'm pretty sure she didn't."

Syd next mentioned Eric Ingersol's comment about Carli's life-altering secret.

"That's disturbing." Brian balled his hands into tight fists. "Maybe Carli did know about Dad, but how could his infidelity alter her life? I could understand if his car accident hadn't happened and our parents had divorced."

Syd nodded and leaned against Brian's car. "How did you handle the move to Door County?"

"It was hard to leave my friends, but my family exchanged our treeless lot near the smelly paper mills to live in this paradise." He gestured. "I can still remember how Frank built a tree house for us that first August."

"My brother and I had one, too, but the tornado of '98 destroyed it. Is yours still standing?"

"I think so. I moved to my own place, and I haven't been into my parents' back woods since. Let's go look."

They strolled down the tree-lined path until they reached a three-tiered tree house. The lifelike birds and flowers painted on the sides were faded, yet still showed obvious talent. "Which one of you was the artist?" Syd asked, surprised.

"Neither! We were lucky enough to have moved next door to a pro."

"Do you mean your Uncle Luke?"

"Yeah. I had loads of fun with him that August. But Carli never cared for him. She'd disappear whenever he was around."

"Do you know why?"

"She said Luke gave her the creeps."

Syd lifted her eyebrows.

"This path," Brian pointed toward it, "ends at his and Colette's home."

They headed back, and Syd's eyes caught his. "How did your sister get along with Frank?"

"Not so good." Brian frowned. "It bothered me that Carli never warmed up to him."

"Do you think there was ever any inappropriate behavior?"

Brian looked shocked. "You mean between Carli and Frank?"

"Yes."

"Well, I never saw anything." Brian looked upset. "Did you hear this from my mom?"

"Why do you ask?"

"She's always had this possessive streak. It's

probably because of my birth dad's behavior. The first year we were up here, Frank often had Carli go into the Café on weekend mornings to help him with the baking. I think he was trying to find some one-on-one time with her, but Mom didn't like it."

"Was your mom working at the boutique then?"

"No. That first year, Frank leased to Sally Renard. She now owns her own shop in Sister Bay."

"So, why did your mom take over that part of the business?"

"I know there were some arguments between Frank and Mom. The next season, Sally was out, and Mom was in. Carli also stopped going into the Café with Frank."

"When did Carli first start to waitress?"

"Around her freshman year in high school."

"How did that work out?"

"She liked waiting tables and got good tips, but I know there were a few tense situations."

"What do you mean?"

"Carli was having a hard time with Mom. I guess Carli heard her say some pretty nasty things to some of the local women."

"Like what?"

"You know," he looked at his feet, "something to do with Frank and that possessive streak. It embarrassed Carli, and she let Mom know. After that, the two moved even further apart."

Syd nodded, but wondered if there was more. "Can you tell me about any of the guys Carli dated?"

"I know a few from high school—Billy Rice, Jake Sabin. I believe they still live in the area."

Syd stopped to write down their names. "Anyone else?"

"Well, her last semester of college, I tried to fix her up with a teaching friend of mine, but she wasn't interested."

"Did she say why?"

"She said she was involved with someone." Brian's jaw tightened. "From the way Carli talked, I assumed the guy was married."

Maybe this was the Nick Syd had been looking for. She asked Brian if he knew anyone by that name.

He considered the question. "The only Nick that comes to mind is Nick Bogart. He just got a teaching job at Southern Door High School, and I believe he graduated with Carli from St. Norbert. Tina Kelsey, who lived with Carli, is his cousin."

Syd brightened at this information. It sounded like a good lead. "I've already talked to Beth Halverson. Is there anyone else Carli confided in?"

Brian cocked his head as they reached Syd's van. "Well, Luke's wife, Colette. Also Zach Newson. He's one of my math students at Gibraltar High, and he runs cross country for our team. Zach works part-time at the Café, and Carli mentioned how he often sought her out."

Brian crossed his arms and frowned. "Since school started, I know many of Zach's friends have been shunning him. This week, I'd planned to draw him aside at cross-country practice to find out why."

That was Syd's goal, too.

Chapter 16

Syd pulled into a restaurant parking lot across from Gibraltar High School. Buses were lined up outside. She could see her niece's ten-year-old Saturn, still in the student parking lot.

Syd texted Jules: *"Outside your school. Where are U?"*

In Syd's extended family, Jules was the creative one. At the age of four she got her first camera, and it, or its many successors, had never left her side. When she took photos, her eyes saw things differently than Syd's. For the past year Jules' obsession had been lines. She'd swoon over a crack in the sidewalk, the wrinkles on an aged arm, or the striations along a limestone ledge. She used Photoshop to enhance the imperfections and added her own palette of colors to pull you in.

Each year, Syd and Jules attended a few notable Wisconsin art fairs where she'd been invited to participate. As unlikely as it might seem, other than Gina, Syd shared more with her sixteen-year-old niece than she did with peers her own age. Apparently, Zach's and Carli's connection had been like that, too.

Jules texted: "At Peninsula School of Art."

"*Do U have time 2 talk?*" Syd texted back, knowing Jules' location was right around the corner.

"*Meet U outside in 10.*"

Syd stationed herself adjacent to the three-tiered Peninsula School of Art. While waiting, she placed a call to Southern Door High School and left a message for Nick Bogart.

Her niece emerged from the entrance and strolled down the brick path in tight jeans and a capped-sleeved flowered top. Jules' wavy brown hair nearly reached her waist. Syd could see the stud in her nose that her niece and Syd's brother were forever battling about.

Jules opened the passenger door. "Hi, Auntie, what's up?"

"Jump in." Syd smiled. "I'll drive you back to your 'beater' while we talk."

"Very funny. It's better than this 'Loser Cruiser.'" She slid in next to Syd and slammed the door. "So?" Jules' perfectly tweezed eyebrows formed two peaks.

"Do you happen to know Zach Newson?"

"Sure." She hesitated. "We've been friends since grade school." Her eyes widened. "My God! Did something happen to him?"

"No." Syd patted her hand. "Nothing like that." She told Jules what Brian Lacount had said about Zach's school friends shunning him. "Do you know why?"

"Yeah." Her body slumped into the seat. "Kids can be so mean."

Syd patiently waited, but her niece didn't offer more. "Come on, Jules. What's the scoop?"

With a resigned look, she blurted out, "Zach's gay."

Syd wouldn't say she was shocked. It had been one

of her guesses—especially since she'd had first-hand experience in her own recent history.

"He's also involved at the School of Art with me. Zach's into sculpture... And you've got to see some of his current pieces!"

She watched her niece's cheeks flush and Syd didn't ask more.

"This summer, Zach opened up to me. Since the age of twelve, he said he's been fantasizing about boys in our class rather than girls." She paused, her eyes finding Syd's. "You know how you probably pictured touching and kissing Eli before you two became an actual item?"

Syd gave a start, yet managed to nod. It also upset her to know—she still fantasized about Eli—and far more graphically than she'd done at the innocent age of fifteen.

"In August, Zach 'came out' to a number of his friends."

"So, what's school like for him now?"

"Well, he's good in cross country and, of course, the team uses the locker room. Zach said it's become a horror movie. Last week, I guess, he inadvertently became aroused in the showers."

"Oh, my."

"It sounds pretty awful, doesn't it?" Jules' lips formed a thin line. "Since then, he's been harassed. I told him I definitely support him, but, honestly, it's been awkward for me. And I'm a girl! I know some of the guys are afraid Zach's attracted to them, and if they support him, others will think *they're* gay, too."

Syd squeezed her hand. "I'm proud of you for being there for your friend. Life isn't easy."

Jules returned the squeeze and gave Syd a shrewd look. "You and I both know that."

* * * *

Syd dropped Jules off by her car and watched the cross country team take off. Since Zach was probably in the pack, Syd figured she'd have at least an hour before she'd hopefully be able to talk to him at the Café.

Within a stone's throw of the high school was the YMCA. Syd parked her van and alerted dispatch of her plans to run. She grabbed the duffle she'd packed that morning and proceeded toward the locker room for a quick change. Then, jogging down Fish Creek's main drag, she made a right into Peninsula State Park. Up ahead was the Sunset Bike Trail. It was heavily utilized, reducing the "lone woman" fear factor.

Syd turned onto the trail and settled into an easy pace, rehashing Jules' comments about Zach—how some of the guys at Gibraltar High were afraid he was attracted to them.

In Syd's case, she'd been too dumb to even recognize the signs…

Soon after Syd had returned from UWM and started at the Door County Sheriff's Department, she'd moved into her cottage. She'd been pleased when her parents had agreed to let her take out a loan to purchase the place. To celebrate, Syd had asked Gina over for dinner. That night, Syd was a little drunk and moony, talking about Eli, who was still at Marquette.

At dusk, she and Gina took a stroll through the cherry orchard, and Syd got choked up missing Eli.

Gina wrapped her arms around Syd and let her cry. As Gina's comforting body pulled even closer, she began to stroke Syd's hair. Then moments later, Gina let out a groan followed by what Syd shockingly believed was an orgasmic shudder.

Syd turned her head, stunned, and Gina's lips grazed Syd's cheek.

Mortified, Syd jerked away. "My God, Gina! What just happened?"

She looked flushed and ashamed. Tears filled her eyes. "You're so lucky you have Eli—somebody you love that loves you back."

Shaken, Syd sat down cross-legged under a tree and peered up at Gina. "What do you mean?"

"You're so naïve, Syd." Gina squatted; her Indian patterned skirt billowed out over the grass. "Can't you see I love you, too?"

"Well, of course you do. We're best friends."

"I know. But for me, it's far more than that." Gina abruptly stood and strode back toward the cottage, her skirt flying around her legs.

"Wait!" Syd struggled to her feet and gave chase. She found her friend sobbing in the driver's seat of her car. After extensive pleading, Syd convinced Gina to stay.

They settled into Adirondack chairs beside a lit bonfire pit and Gina began to discuss a subject she'd never broached before. "I was about thirteen when I started to question my sexuality. Erotic thoughts would cloud my mind whenever I was close to you. When I rubbed sunscreen on your back, or noticed the scent of your hair as we crammed for an exam, or in the Grand Marquis, when your bare leg would be squeezed against mine."

"Oh, Gina..." Syd touched her hand.

"I was so confused until I finally put a label to my feelings." Gina heaved a sigh. "But it seemed so unfair that I couldn't date the person I was attracted to. And, Syd, if I couldn't have you, what options did I have? I didn't see any of the girls in our class secretly flashing me signals."

Syd shook her head. "You should have told me."

"How could I, when I felt about you the way I did—and still do?"

Syd didn't know what to say. Gina had suddenly transformed into a new being. The day before, Syd had thought Gina was straight. Now she was gay. In high school, Syd had worried about Gina's hurt feelings when Eli and Syd had become a couple, but she'd never realized Gina had wanted to trade places with him—not with her.

Syd scrutinized her friend—who, admittedly, had never dated—her warm but troubled eyes, her beautiful clothes, and her stylish haircut. Syd shook her head. How could she have guessed?

With that thought still resonating in Syd's head, she reached the two-mile mark on the Sunset Bike Trail and pivoted to begin her return trip.

That same night, Gina told Syd she'd found a lesbian counselor at the technical college to confide in. "It felt so good to talk to someone who knew how I felt." This counselor had introduced Gina to other lesbians on campus. Among them was Myrna Simpson.

Gina gave Syd a shy smile. "She took me under her wing and showed me the ropes."

Syd had to ask. "Was this Myrna, like, your first?"

Gina looked down and nodded. "But all the while, I still visualized making love to you."

Syd blushed at her words and analyzed how they made her feel. Was she repulsed? Not really... "I'm flattered you want to love me in that way. But if you are totally honest, Gina, you have to know that can't be. Eli—my Eli—is definitely the one for me."

Gina sat beside the fire and poked logs with a stick, the light reflecting off her face.

Syd could tell her last words had finally sunk in. That night, Gina permanently shut the door on her "Sydney Fantasy" and moved on with her life.

Some of Syd's friends thought Gina's "coming out" might've hurt their friendship. It was just the opposite. Thanks to her admission, Syd realized how selfish she'd been. Rather than monopolizing every conversation with Eli-talk, she now encouraged Gina to discuss her own relationships.

That year, Gina reconnected with Myrna, who by then was working at Door County Memorial Hospital as an LPN. Gina later confided, "Myrna makes me happy in ways you never could."

The two women were now committed partners and very active in the Door County Lesbian, Gay, Bisexual, Transgender (LGBT) community.

Syd exited the trail, then the park, and slugged up the hill to the YMCA. In less than thirty minutes, she was presentable. She returned to her van and listened to her voice messages. One was from Gina, so she gave her a call.

"Syd, I forgot to tell you, Sara Cob, a friend from the LGBT community, called me last week. A woman had contacted her needing some legal advice. Sara asked if I could refer the woman to Eli."

"Eli?"

"Yeah. Even though he's not on your radar, you know he's still one of my closest pals."

"I know, Gina, and I'm glad."

When Gina told Eli she was gay, he'd called her Two-Spirited. In certain Native American cultures, the name is given to those individuals who are attracted to the same sex. The tribe believes such people have special gifts and are especially blessed. Eli had hugged Gina and said, "That's what I believe about you, too."

Gina now said, "I called Eli about Sara's request, but before I hung up, he asked about you."

Syd sighed and gave Gina the blow-by-blow details of the day's run-in. "What's wrong with me?"

Gina snorted. "Nothing Eli couldn't cure. What's it been? Two years? I think, all you need is some hot and heavy sex!"

Chapter 17

For the second time that day, Syd pulled into the Triangle Shops & Café parking lot, now better armed to confront Zach.

Inside, Patrick shook his head at her in mock disappointment. "Business again?"

"Afraid so." She smiled and glanced at the regulars' table, grateful to see no sign of Eli. "I understand Zach Newson works here. I'd like to talk to him, if he's here tonight."

Patrick's brow lifted. "Does this have anything to do with Carli?"

"I'm not sure."

He nodded and pointed out a cute kid with moussed blond hair. He wore glasses with fashionable designer frames and carried a tubful of dirty dishes.

"Grab a table in the courtyard," Patrick said. "I'll send Zach out with a cup of coffee, if you'd like…"

"That would be nice."

Syd found a seat at a bistro table. Soon after, Zach approached. He looked nervous as he set down the coffee and utensil setup. After introductions, he took a seat at her

104

request. "Zach, I understand you were friends with Carli Lacount."

A spasm of pain crossed his face. "We used to be."

"Did you often talk to her?"

He nodded. "We'd take breaks together."

"Did you confide in each other?"

"Maybe." He looked down.

"Just so you know, I talked to my niece, Jules Bernhardt." She gave Zach a kind smile. "I understand you're being harassed at school."

Inside him, something appeared to break. "Jules isn't like most of the other kids." His eyes brimmed with tears. "She's been really nice." Embarrassed, he wiped his eyes with the cuff of his shirt. "I assume she told you I'm gay?"

Syd nodded and took a sip of coffee. "Did you talk to Carli about this, too?"

"Yeah, over the summer." His eyes were now accusing. "She's the one who convinced me to tell my close friends. She said they'd accept me—that being gay was cool rather than a stigma."

"So, Jules said you told them?"

He nodded, scowling. "They first seemed to be really supportive, but when school started last week, everything changed."

"Did you blame Carli for this?"

"Yeah! If I hadn't listened to her, my life wouldn't be wrecked." Zach's lower lip jutted out.

"Did you try to talk to her about it on Sunday morning?"

"Sunday?" He shook his head, confused. "No. We had a shouting match last Wednesday. Since then, I'd been ignoring her." He removed his glasses and rubbed his eyes. "And now, I can't believe she's dead."

"So, Zach, where were you Sunday morning?"

His face screwed up in thought. "I know—I was out for a long run in Peninsula State Park."

Syd stared at Zach. Instead of getting in a run, she wondered whether he'd been getting even with Carli.

Patrick emerged through the doorway. In one hand he carried a tray that held a salad and a piece of pie. In the other hand he clutched a set of keys. He gave Syd a questioning look. "Any chance I can steal Zach from you?"

The teen gave Patrick a look of relief as Syd nodded.

Patrick handed Zach the keys. "I'd like you to make a delivery run similar to last week's. I've already loaded up Van #2 and signed it out. On the front seat is a printout of the restaurant stops in Baileys Harbor and Jacksonport along with their pie count."

Zach stood. "Sure thing." With haste he sprinted out the back.

Patrick leaned forward and placed the food in front of Syd.

She could feel the heat from his shoulder.

"I thought you might be hungry." He smiled at Syd.

She returned it. "This looks wonderful." She placed the napkin in her lap and picked up the fork. "I've hardly eaten all day."

"I figured as much." Patrick settled into Zach's vacated seat. "You know that guy who was hassling you earlier today?"

Syd was caught off guard, but managed a nod.

"I think he and Carli were seeing each other."

"Really?" Syd's fork stopped in midair.

"Twice last week, I saw her leave with him."

Syd was stunned. She could no longer dismiss Eli's possible connection to Carli's death.

He had to be questioned.

"How did your talk with Zach go?" Patrick changed the subject. "Did you discuss his issues since he 'came out'?"

Syd stared at him, startled he knew.

"Detective Bernhardt, I'm not naïve. Remember, I have a restaurant in Saugatuck. It's got an active gay community. Carli also told me that she and Zach had discussed the subject. You don't think that has anything to do with her death, do you?"

"I'm just following every path." She speared and ate the last cucumber slice, then moved on to the pie.

"Makes sense." Patrick leaned back, his warm eyes trained on her. "So, Detective, Luke told me your family owns the Bernhardt Orchards where we purchase most of our cherries."

Relieved he'd moved off the case, Syd dropped her guard. "I guess if I'm to call you Patrick, then you should call me Sydney." She smiled. "Or Syd. And, yes, that's my family's business. I bet you didn't know that one of our mature cherry trees yields about forty-eight pounds of fruit, enough for twenty-eight of your pies?"

"Well, I do now!" He laughed and watched her nearly lick the plate clean. He reached for it, brushing her fingers in the process—on purpose, it seemed to her.

An unexpected rush shot through Syd. As a diversion, she checked her watch, upset to see it was nearly six. She fished out a ten from her purse. "This should cover my meal."

Patrick put up his hands. "No way. It was my treat."

"If you won't take it, consider it a tip for Zach." She placed the ten on the table.

"I'll agree to that."

She stood to leave. "Thanks, Patrick, for all your help."

His eyes found hers. "Any time... Syd—ney."

The way he had rolled her name off his tongue, made her flush.

Chapter 18

At about ten after six, Syd arrived at Beth Halverson's condo complex. The units were built into a hill overlooking Egg Harbor with an exposed lower level. Beth had seemed a bit nervous that morning when Syd had mentioned her desire to look through Carli's personal items. For that reason, Syd had wanted to beat Beth home, so she couldn't potentially hide anything.

But Syd knew she was too late when the front door was opened by Beth, already changed into comfortable sweats. "Do you know anything more about Carli's death?" she asked.

"I'm working on it. Where can we talk?"

Syd followed Beth into the combined kitchen and great room. Sliding glass doors provided access to the balcony where, Syd assumed, Beth had overheard the conversation between Carli and the mysterious Nick.

They sat down at the kitchen table. "First," Syd began, "I discovered who Carli spent her weekend with." Syd briefly discussed her interview with Eric Ingersol.

Beth's thick lashes blinked rapidly, to keep her tears in check.

"Did Carli ever mention Eric to you?"

She shook her head. "I thought I knew Carli, but, obviously, I didn't. In addition to Eric, did you uncover who the Nick I mentioned might be?"

"Not yet." Syd removed Carli's key ring from its evidence envelope. "I'm still looking for the homes for these two keys." She pointed out the remaining large one and the smaller one.

"I believe the large key opens my front door." Beth took the key ring and they both proceeded to that location. She then slid the specified key into the lock to prove it. "I know Carli used a small key for her bike lock."

"That's already accounted for."

Beth tilted her head. "Carli had another bike that was stolen during her final semester of college. Maybe that last key is for her old lock."

"That sounds plausible, but I'll still see whether it unlocks anything within her belongings."

Beth nodded. "I'll show you where they are."

Syd followed her down a flight of stairs to the lower-level hallway. Syd could see a queen-sized bed through the first open bedroom door. "That's my room," Beth said. "Carli's is down the hall."

"Thanks, Beth. I can handle it from here." Syd's voice was firm, dismissing her.

Beth looked surprised, but said, "Okay," and started up the stairs.

Syd watched her for a moment, then headed down to Carli's bedroom. She stepped through the doorway into what could have been a teenager's abode, outfitted in white furniture stenciled with rosebuds. Syd was surprised Carli hadn't replaced the twin bed with a larger size—unless she'd planned on sleeping alone. There was also an attached bathroom and walk-in closet. An acoustic Martin guitar leaned against the bedroom wall.

Syd began her search by looking under both Carli's bed and mattress, but found nothing. On top of the nightstand was a half-filled glass of water, a pen, and a tissue box. Beside it were three used tissues. She opened the drawer, hoping to find a journal, but was disappointed.

There was nothing of interest in the dresser drawers, closet, or bathroom, so she moved on to the bookshelves and desk. Atop the latter rested a laptop computer and a printer, with an empty paper drawer. Syd booted up the computer. Luckily, a password wasn't required. She clicked on the browser icon. Carli's homepage was her Gmail account. Since her password had been stored, Syd was right into her correspondence.

The overhead bedroom light came on, and Syd jumped.

"Did you find anything?" Beth entered and handed Syd a can of soda.

"Thanks." Syd popped the top. "Nothing out of the ordinary."

"Are you sure I can't help?" Beth peered over Syd's shoulder.

"Well, there's one thing… Did Carli have a cold or allergies when you last saw her?"

"She never had allergies." Beth looked confused. "And I'm certain she didn't have a cold." Her gaze moved around the room and landed on the nightstand evidence. A faint blush crept up Beth's neck.

"You said Carli had given you her two-month notice the last night you saw her alive. Did you two have a falling out, Beth?"

"No." Her voice was adamant. "We didn't argue that

night. I just figured her decision had something to do with that Nick. But, who knows?" She threw up her hands.

"What did you discuss that night?"

Beth bit her lip as if trying to remember. "Well, we talked about that Jenny-something who was nearly abducted last Wednesday. Her family had frequented the Café."

Syd was surprised. "Carli knew Jenny Tyler?"

"Yeah…anything else?"

Syd scrutinized Beth's face. A few minutes earlier, she'd seemed eager to help, but now she looked as if she wanted to escape.

"No, that's good for now." She took a sip of soda and watched Beth retreat.

The laptop was disappointing. Other than the cleared web history log, like the one on Carli's work computer, Syd found nothing of interest. Since she could access Carli's laptop this easily, Syd knew Beth could've done the same. Syd kicked herself for her late arrival.

Carli's desk drawers both contained hanging folders that held important documents and bills. Her past life, Syd thought, looked to be in perfect order.

Last were Carli's bookcases. On two shelves were photo albums, their bindings marked by year. Syd pulled over the desk chair and took a seat. She first checked the albums prior to Carli's move to Door County. They included family vacations, birthdays, and holiday photos. Carli was often featured with her brother and a man who had to be her dad. There were two group cabin photos from St. Anne's Camp for '98 and '99. In these, both Carli and her best friend Molly were smiling.

But then Syd reached July of '99. The obituary for Carli's dad, Joseph Kane, had been glued to the page. The next photo skipped to the Christmas of '99. Carli stood beside a decorated tree with her mom and brother. Alice and Brian were both beaming, but Carli looked angry. By this time, Syd figured, Frank had been involved with Alice and was on the other side of the camera.

In 2000, the photos picked up. The family, Syd thought, was recovering from Joseph Kane's death. Syd flipped through the summer activities until she reached a blank page. The July 2000 photo, Alice had shown her from St. Anne's Camp, was not included. Neither were any subsequent ones until Christmas of 2000, when Carli's new family was pictured on a Christmas card.

The next several albums held photos from Carli's Gibraltar school and soccer activities. Syd paused to analyze one labeled "Junior Prom." It showed Carli with a cute guy.

The last album was quite slim and dedicated to Carli's St. Norbert college years.

Syd was disappointed. None of the photos in any of the albums had included the name "Nick" within the caption Carli had scrawled.

Syd leaned back in the chair. It appeared as if Carli hadn't documented two segments of her life: right after her dad's death and the span from July 2000 to that same Christmas. Syd wondered whether Carli's life-altering secret had occurred in either timeframe?

Syd also realized—she'd never found a home for that final, small key.

Chapter 19

Syd knew she'd find Marv at Al's Place. The Egg
Harbor pub, named for Al Capone, was within walking
distance to Marv's home. He'd been frequenting the pub
ever since his messy divorce. Marv's elevated testosterone
level had also ignited his frantic pursuit of any available
women. For that reason, Syd was relieved to find Marv
alone.

He'd just vacated his barstool and swayed as he
headed, she assumed, toward the downstairs bathroom
facilities. Syd watched his burly arm bump a high-top table
surrounded by a group of college kids, one of them African-
American. In the process, a pitcher of beer tipped over.

She stepped in, ready to appease the young black
man who was trying to have words with Marv. Given her
co-worker's inebriated condition, Syd knew that was a big
mistake.

At seeing her, Marv forgot the kid and gave her a
sloppy smile. "Well, lookie who's here!"

Syd wanted to grab a menu and jam it down Marv's
throat. Instead, she handed the kid some cash to replace the
pitcher. Then she negotiated a path to the staircase for Marv.

On the first step down, he nearly tripped.

"My God, Marv! At least use the handrail."

"Yes, ma'am." He turned and gave her a two-finger salute. "Sydney knows best."

She rolled her eyes and somehow managed to get him down the remaining steps and into the Gents' bathroom.

Syd leaned against the wall to wait, idly reading the captioned photos mounted on the walls. They pictured Al Capone and his Chicago mobster cronies. Door County's natural setting had been one of Al's favorite hiding spots. The photos were part of this pub's ambiance as was the adjacent door marked *Al's Escape Route*. Under the quaint village of Egg Harbor were tunneled caves. Historical records confirmed both Chief Tecumseh and Al Capone had utilized them for quick escapes from the law or other enemies. Out of curiosity, Syd tried the door handle, but it was locked.

She had been tapping her foot and finally knocked on the bathroom door. "You alive in there?"

Marv emerged, his shirt drenched. To his credit, it appeared as if he'd been splashing water on his face to sober up.

She gave him a dirty look. "I was worried you were sprawled out on the floor, anesthetized with alcohol."

He responded with a sheepish grin, and they both traipsed back upstairs.

At the polished wooden bar, Syd ordered a soda and offered to buy Marv the same. She was glad when he agreed and also ordered a burger.

"How about it, Syd? I'll buy you one, too?" Marv's voice was amazingly steady.

"No, but thank you. I already ate while talking with Frank Lacount's younger brother."

Marv appraised her, sloshing soda around in his mouth. "You had dinner with the guy?"

She ignored the comment, feeling heat rise in her cheeks. "Any progress on your case?"

"Well, I interviewed a number of St. Rosalia parishioners. None of them heard anything our pedophile said to Cassie, so I'm back to square one."

"That's too bad. You know the other little girl, Jenny Tyler?"

Marv nodded.

"She and her family knew Carli from eating at the Café."

"Duh…" He gave her an exasperated look. "Carli could've known half the county."

Syd realized he was right. "How are you doing with the registered pedophiles and sex offenders? Any luck?"

"Well, I'm getting on a first-name basis with our county's most upstanding citizens."

She laughed. "And what about your buddies' alibis?"

"I've got a few who have problems for one girl, but not both. Nobody's climbing the charts on my hit list, yet. But I've got a few choice guys I haven't tracked down."

"Any names I can help you with?"

"Hey, that's not fair." He squinted over at Syd through bleary eyes. "You can't expect me to remember their names in the state I'm in. But don't worry, I've got it covered."

"Okay, Marv, if you say so." Syd shifted on her stool, ready to address the real reason she'd stopped. "When I talked to Patrick Lacount, he mentioned his niece and Eli Gaudet might've been a couple."

Marv's eyes opened wide as he motioned to the bartender and pointed to his empty soda glass.

"Of course, you know my history with Eli. I'd owe you one if you'd interview him for me." She gave Marv a pleading look. "How about it?"

He shook his head. "Not a good idea."

She frowned. "Why not?"

"Remember that Hobie-Cat?"

She nodded, confused. "Did you tell Bobby about it?"

"Yeah, but guess who beat your bro' to the punch?"

"I have no idea."

"Well, this nice Mrs. Overlund told Bobby a young lawyer with these 'dreamy eyes' had already put some money down to hold the Hobie. Sound like anyone you might know?"

Syd's jaw dropped. "Are you saying it was Eli?"

"One and the same. I guess he stopped by on Sunday morning to see it."

"You mean, the morning Carli died?"

"Apparently." Marv clinked her glass. "So, we both need to talk to Mr. Eli Gaudet."

As much as Syd hated the idea, she knew Marv was right.

Chapter 20

That evening, in the darkness, the scent and sound of rain came through Syd's porch screens. She lay back on her ratty chaise lounge and sipped a glass of white wine. Lloyd snoozed by her side, and a boom box played a Mary Chapin Carpenter CD.

Eli had been in her thoughts for most of the day. It was hard to believe he had any connection to Carli's death. It was even harder to believe, after the way Syd had treated him for two years, he was not over her. His words from the Café encounter kept circling through her head: "I know you have scars, Syd. Well, I do, too..."

She closed her eyes. She'd told Eli, in no uncertain terms, she was over him...yet she knew that was a lie.

Why couldn't she let him back in?

Two years ago had been another lifetime. She and Eli had been living together ever since he opened his law practice to specialize in labor and employment cases with a focus on sexual harassment, wrongful discharge, and discrimination. Eli's older cousin, who resided on the Hannahville Reservation, had fought in Iraq. That first year, as a new attorney, Eli helped Robert and other Potawatomi vets recover state taxes the Department of Defense had erroneously deducted from their pay. More recently, Eli had made a name for himself by defending Roger Tromleau, a Sturgeon Bay teacher wrongfully accused of having sexual relations with a student.

Though still grieving Beau, Syd had finally relented and they'd rescued another Golden. Eli then set out to prove to her that nothing bad would ever happen to Lloyd. And the way the two loved each other, she believed that was true. Eli was ready for marriage, but she kept dragging her feet. In her mind, that major commitment meant the possibility of children. Given Eli's past unreliability, she still needed more time.

That first week of October, they'd reserved their favorite campsite in Newport State Park. At that time of year, they knew it would be nearly deserted. For Syd and Eli, that was a major draw—plus, the wilderness park allowed leashed dogs.

The three of them pulled up in Syd's car at the visitors' center on that Thursday, around 3 p.m. The woman behind the counter told them they'd be the only registered campers for the evening. Over the weekend, ten of the remaining fifteen sites would be filled.

It was a beautiful fall day in the high 60s as they unloaded their gear. By nightfall, the temperature would drop into the 40s. Syd realized she hadn't packed any gloves, but she found a work-issued pair in the trunk of her car.

It was a three-mile hike to their site. At the two-mile point, they crossed the blacktopped Europe Bay Road, then picked up the trail again. It was rough going as they backpacked through boreal forests and northern hardwoods, all at their peak of color. Fallen leaves covered many of the tree roots and boulders, creating a hidden obstacle course.

Even with hiking boots, they tripped, taking turns to catch each other.

Eventually, they reached their site, high on a sand dune overlooking Lake Michigan. They both knew the next morning's sunrise would be superb. Syd gave Eli a hug. "Imagine. This park is all ours!"

They unpacked their gear and pitched the tent, quizzing each other on various wildflowers that still populated the shoreline. Among them were Black-Eyed Susans. Eli said their root had been used by the Potawatomi to make a tea for curing colds. There was also the yellow-flowered Silver-Weed. Syd told him Bitsy gathered its leaves from May to October to make her own tea to help reduce her arthritic pain.

She then held up a roll of toilet paper. "This time, I remembered."

"That's my Syd." Eli wrestled her to the ground and pinned her arms behind her head. "Will you give?"

"No way!" She shook her head against the crackle of fallen leaves. "Not until you kiss me."

And he did, starting with her forehead, her eyelids, and then filling her mouth with his tongue. His big hands cradled her head, his fingers tangled in her hair. She buried her face against his shirt as Eli slipped his hands under her to unhook her bra.

Oh, God. She remembered how good it felt as his fingers touched her breasts, making a noise come from the back of her throat.

Eli responded by stripping off her blouse and bra, his lips finding her breasts.

Syd's hands pulled his head closer and released the twine from his hair. Its sleek blackness covered them like a shawl.

He pulled back, his lips shiny and wet. In the breeze, she felt the cool ring around her nipples.

Eli grinned wickedly and slid one hand down inside the front of her jeans. His fingers reached her wetness and disappeared within.

Syd reared her head back, at his probing touch, writhing in the leaves.

He pulled off her jeans. Then his mouth slid down her body and made a rest stop around her navel before it continued on its course—his tongue arriving in its new home.

When her body shuddered, Syd cried out, and tears came.

He slid back up and touched his fingers to her temples, wiping the corners of her eyes with his thumbs.

"I love you, Eli."

He gave her his slow and sexy smile. "I know."

Syd rested her face against his shirt, her naked thigh feeling the ridge beneath his jeans. She yanked off his t-shirt and buried her face into the heat of his smooth chest, listening to Eli's breathing. Syd turned her face into the hollow beneath his arm, scented by sweet sweat. Then she raced her tongue down his body, making him shiver.

He helped her pull off his jeans, and she reached between Eli's legs, wrapping her fingers around him, making him gasp. Jockeying her body, Syd positioned herself, so he could slip inside her. Syd's hips trembled as they both began to push and moan, faster and faster, tangled together, her back scooting on the bed of leaves and hemlock needles.

His shoulders blocked Syd's view of the sky as he reared over her, and they convulsed together, her arms and legs laced tight around his body, holding him close.

Eli was her best friend and her lover. With her head tucked beneath his chin, Syd couldn't believe he was hers.

Before Syd could crawl onto his lap to pull on her underwear and jeans, he brushed the leaves off her behind and laughed. "A pine cone left its imprint on your ass."

Syd shoved him. "Very funny."

She knew he'd left his imprint on every inch of her.

Chapter 21

Syd was startled by Lloyd's bark. It pulled her back from her intimate thoughts about Eli—the ones she'd relived far too often.

Lloyd inched his snout onto her lap and gave her his curved-lips smile.

"Okay, boy." She stood and opened the porch door as Lloyd dashed outside.

Syd poured another glass of wine, checked her iPhone for messages, and let him back inside. Both creatures of habit, she and Lloyd returned to their identical spots.

At Newport State Park, only Eli had brought his cell. When they discovered it was dead, Syd was upset. "For months, Eli, you've complained about your battery. How it wouldn't hold a charge. I thought you'd replaced it."

"Sorry," he said, rather sheepishly. "I should have…or at least told you to bring your cell."

"You've got that right!" Syd shook her head. This was disconcerting. His old habits seemed to be returning.

The air between them was tense as Syd made grilled-cheese sandwiches on the camp stove. But when Eli started to tease her about her cooking abilities, she couldn't help but smile...and forgive him.

With their camaraderie restored, the two enjoyed their meal.

Then it was time for a campfire. At the visitors' center they'd purchased wood. To find additional kindling, Syd headed off into the woods with Lloyd and shouted, "Eli, check the fire pit."

"Okay," he yelled back.

Each campsite had a well-utilized pit inside a metal ring, and Syd never knew what the last campers might've left behind.

She and Lloyd returned, her arms full.

In the pit, a couple of yards from their tent, she could see Eli had already made a teepee of wood. He stuffed the open areas with kindling she provided and lit it with a match.

The sun had set. The wind blowing off the lake chilled Syd. She slipped on a thick wool sweater, hand knitted by Gina, and layered it with one of Daddy's bulky hunting vests. She poured some wine in plastic cups before sliding her hands into her last-minute gloves.

On a rustic bench, she and Eli sat side by side, adjacent to the fire pit. Mesmerized, they watched the flames shoot up against the landscape of beach and open water.

"Come on." Syd patted Eli's leg. "It's time for some campfire songs."

"Nuh-uh." He chuckled. "I wouldn't subject you to my voice. But please," he nudged her, "go ahead."

In second grade, their teacher had singled Eli out, at their holiday concert, and told him to mouth the words to "Jingle Bells." Ever since, Eli had refused to sing. Syd, on the other hand, loved to. Tonight was no different. She started with "You are My Sunshine," moved on to "Kum Bay Ya," and finished up with "If You're Happy and You Know It, Clap Your Hands." Even though Eli's voice remained silent, he put his mitts together to accompany her.

As Syd's last notes hung in the air, Eli smiled. "I feel like Anishnabe, the first Potawatomi, who heard a woman's melodic song coming from across the Great Lakes." He tilted his chin toward her. "I believe she sounded just like you."

Syd laughed. "So tell me more."

"Well, Anishnabe crossed the water and discovered the voice belonged to a beautiful woman. Her father was the sacred Firekeeper who kept the council fire burning. Like Adam and Eve, she and Anishnabe formed the first union." Eli pulled her close. "Don't you think it's time for us, too?"

Instead of responding, Syd stood to busy herself. The fire had started to dwindle, so, using a stick, she first stirred the embers and then restocked the wood. She could feel Eli's eyes on her back, his question still awaiting an answer.

It was never to come.

A loud explosion shook the ground and lit up the night sky. It was a ball of fire—and Syd was part of it. A searing pain engulfed her arms. "Eli!" she screamed, then dropped and rolled.

He fell on top of her to smother the flames.

As Syd cried out, he picked up her writhing body and raced toward the water. Within the first five yards, Eli nearly tripped. Crying out in disbelief, he kicked at the jagged and scorched remains of an aerosol bug spray can, apparently buried in the fire pit, which had fueled the explosion.

In a frenzied dash, he covered the remaining twenty-five yards and gently placed Syd in the frigid lake. In the shallow water, he submerged her arms as she whimpered, "Why didn't you check?" It was like an out-of-body experience as she watched him remove what was left of her charred sweater sleeves from her ravaged arms. It appeared her gloves were flame resistant as was Daddy's vest. Miraculously, the latter had kept the fire away from her face.

The cold water numbed Syd's body and gave her temporary relief. But now their earlier solitude seemed a curse. Without Eli's cell, there was no way to get Syd proper medical attention.

"My God!" Eli knelt beside her, ignoring the cold water that soaked through his jeans. "What can I do?" He put his head in his hands.

Her quiet sobs weren't giving him the answer. Syd kept thinking, because of him, she was suffering this excruciating pain. If he'd checked the fire pit, like he said he would…if he'd told her to bring her cell, rather than his…if… if…

She floated on her back, her butt bumping against the sandy bottom, her anguished face bobbing in the light of the moon. Syd couldn't think about what he'd done to her. She'd deal with that later. Instead, she needed to focus on her damaged arms. How could she remove herself from this water and get back to civilization without suffering immeasurable pain? What had they brought that could help her? She knew they had a First Aid kit, but it only contained a small tube of burn ointment.

Syd turned her face toward the shoreline and spotted the clump of Spotted Joe-Pye. Earlier, she'd pointed it out to Eli. From July to September, the weed bloomed with pink flowers. Now, only clusters of lance-shaped leaves remained. They'd discussed how the leaves could be used in poultices for healing burns.

His eyes followed hers.

"Use the Joe-Pye," she whispered.

New resolve replaced the desperation on Eli's face. He first called Lloyd into the few inches of water to sit by her. "I've got to make a short trip back up toward our gear. But I need your help. Pick out one of those campfire songs. It's important, Syd. You need to keep singing, so I know you're okay."

"I can't."

"Yes, you can." His words were firm. "If I'm willing to, so can you." He cleared his throat. His deep voice, a bit shaky and way off-key, filled the night air: "Kum bay ya, my Lord, kum bay ya…"

In her appalling situation, knowing what his negligence had done to her, Syd couldn't appreciate his sacrifice.

He prodded her. "Come on, Syd." He started again. And after two more lines, she took him out of his own misery, her feeble voice joining his.

"That's my girl!" He kissed her forehead, making her cringe at his assumed intimacy. Syd forced herself to continue singing as he scrambled to his feet. She then watched him lope across the beach. His encouraging shouts sounded weird in her ears, located just below the water line.

Syd's weak voice repeated the same line over and over. The chant actually soothed her. So did the wet-smelling dog against her cheek.

Eventually, Eli returned to the beach, their cooking pot filled with fresh Joe-Pye leaves along with his backpack and their campfire stove. From the backpack he removed some clothes, two kinds of towels, the First Aid kit, some matches, and a bottle of water.

Syd's voice finally faltered as she watched Eli set the

campfire stove on the beach and light it. Squatting on his haunches, he added the bottle of water to the pot of torn leaves and brought it to a boil.

By now, Syd's teeth were chattering. In the freezing water, she knew her body temperature must have dropped several degrees. In addition to the burns, she was dealing with hypothermia.

With things in progress, Eli stood. He spread out a beach towel, then entered the water, a determined look on his face. "It's time, Syd. Let's get you out of here. But please, prepare yourself. It's going to hurt like hell."

She gritted her teeth as he gathered her body in his arms and lifted her out. The mild breeze attacked her arms and triggered excruciating pain, making her moan.

Eli laid her down on the towel, his gentle hands stripping her naked. With a second beach towel, he patted her body dry and used it to cover her up. After guiding Syd's legs into fleece jogging pants, he yanked cotton socks over her feet.

He then refocused on the cooking pot and removed it from the stove, briefly floating it in the lake water to cool the leaves. He placed the mixture between layers of homespun dishtowels and wrapped them around each of Syd's damaged arms, securing the poultices with white medical tape. Over her head and shoulders, he finally slid one of his sweatshirts to cocoon her arms inside. "Okay, Syd." He lifted her quivering chin. "That's all I can do. Let's get you inside the tent, so you can warm up. Then I'll go for help."

As he picked her up, Syd begged, "Please, Eli, don't leave me."

"I know you're tough," he said, carrying her up the sandy incline toward their gear. "But I'll make better time without you." With each step, the exertion made his breathing heavier. "Remember how difficult the footing was...even in daylight? And now the woods are pitch black."

Within the restrictive sweatshirt, Syd tried to lift her arms to pound on his chest, but the pain jolted through her body, and she choked out a scream. She continued to sob, pleading over and over, beseeching Eli not to go, though she knew he was right.

Syd sank into herself, not realizing they'd reached the tent until Eli zipped her into a sleeping bag. Lloyd's warm, but damp body squeezed in beside her.

Syd recoiled when Eli kissed her wet cheeks and used his thumb to wipe away her tears. "Syd, I know you're in terrible pain, but try to sleep. I promise, I'll be right back."

She was filled with confused emotions. This bad situation had occurred because of Eli. Yes, he'd worked hard to concoct some temporary relief for her. But because his cell was dead, he'd had no other option. If the situation had been an accident, or her fault, words of gratitude would've been sliding off her tongue. But instead Syd said, "Just go."

Then, she went into shock.

Chapter 22

On her chaise lounge, Syd shivered. She knew she shouldn't regurgitate that painful night, but she couldn't help herself. She walked to her bedroom and slipped inside the fisherman sweater Gina had recently knitted to replace the damaged one Eli had removed from her body. She then returned to the back porch.

Syd had regained consciousness in St. Vincent Hospital's ICU, her parents at her side. They said Eli had hiked out to Europe Bay Road. Instead of following the additional two miles of trail, he located a farm house about a mile down the paved road. From there, he called 911. An ambulance from Sister Bay picked him up, so he could lead the medics to the campsite.

When they reached Syd, she was still passed out. The medics, she understood, placed her on a stretcher and Eli along with Lloyd followed them out. Once she was loaded into the ambulance, Eli and Lloyd took off for Syd's parked car and drove to her parents' home. Eli left Lloyd with Bitsy, then he and Syd's parents headed to Green Bay.

For weeks, other than immediate family, Syd wasn't allowed any visitors. Mama said Eli had camped out in the waiting room whenever he wasn't working, but Syd refused to see him. She also refused to return Lloyd. He was her dog as much as Eli's. Syd couldn't bear the thought that something might happen to him as it had to both Beau and her.

Before that night, Syd believed Eli had changed. He'd been proving it to her. But this time, she couldn't forgive him.

Throughout her life, Syd had been self-conscious, upset her hair was too curly, her bottom teeth too crooked, her knees too fat…but her second-degree burns were the ultimate. She felt like a monster. That feeling, and that dreadful night, and her terrible pain, and the man who caused it, consumed her waking hours and dreams.

There were a number of surgeries, agonizing dressing changes, and weeks of physical therapy. During that time, Syd religiously exercised her arms to keep the skin stretched. Once she regained total use, she was truly thankful.

It took five long weeks before Syd was discharged from the hospital. At her family's insistence, she moved back into her childhood bedroom. By then, per her detailed instructions, her parents had removed all of her belongings from Eli's house.

After that fateful night, Syd's return to life was slow. On medical leave from the department, she became insular and distant. But then… Mama was diagnosed with cancer. Her amazing strength and openness about her disease shocked Syd out of her own daytime self-pity, but her nightmares continued.

It was Gina who began to acclimate Syd back into the real world. An important first step, Gina insisted, was for Syd to regain her independence. So, Syd moved back into the cottage she'd rented to a friend ever since she'd moved in with Eli.

Syd knew she'd changed and couldn't resume the life she'd left. That included her relationship with Eli.

Gina supported Syd by turning on him that first year, but after that, Gina finally gave into Eli's begging. He wanted her to help him understand why Syd wouldn't talk to him. Gina was the one who told Syd: Eli confessed he'd screwed up by not replacing the battery in his cell. But, he maintained, Syd's burns were not his fault. Eli told Gina over and over, as Syd went into the woods to gather kindling, he thought she yelled out to him: "I checked the fire pit." So, he *didn't* check it.

"Think about it, Syd," Gina said. "You told me, you yelled, 'E-*li*, check the fire pit.' Doesn't that sound nearly the same? He wasn't careless. It was just miscommunication—with a tragic result."

For a year, Syd had believed Eli was totally at fault. Now it seemed he wasn't. That was hard to wrap her mind around. A number of times she picked up her cell to call him, but she didn't know what to say. The longer she put it off, the more awkward it became. It appeared as if she didn't believe what Eli had told Gina.

The months ticked away, and Syd heard Eli had started to date. She was sick knowing she'd lost her chance. He'd given her the opportunity to repair their relationship, but she'd let him down.

Syd realized the way she'd handled the situation was wrong. Whether they would have ended up together or not, she'd acted as if Eli didn't exist, didn't matter. And Syd knew that wasn't what people did who'd been as connected as they'd been.

She returned to work because it gave her structure.

Instead of staying in bed, she showed up at 8 a.m. to perform her patrol duties. Vehicular infractions, traffic accidents, and shoplifters filled her days. But at 6 p.m., she'd drive home and sink back into her familiar depression.

Gradually, with the support of her family, Gina, and the eager-to-please Lloyd, Syd's world began to improve. She dove back into her job, and it paid off with a promotion to Detective.

Some things, though, didn't change. Syd continued to keep her scarred arms hidden from everyone but Bitsy.

Now inside Syd's back porch, even with Lloyd's warm head resting in her lap, Syd felt so alone. She leaned back against the chaise and let Mary Chapin Carpenter's poignant words embrace her: "We've got two lives: One we're given, and the other one we make."

Sure, she'd been given an imperfect life. But in retrospect, it was far better than that of so many others—one of them being Carli Lacount.

Lloyd's body twitched as he dreamed. Oh, to be a dog, Syd thought, and dream happy chipmunk-chasing dreams, rather than the miserable ones that continued to haunt her...

Syd scratched Lloyd behind the ears. She knew the time had come for her to stop pushing people away—and to admit to one, in particular, she might have judged him wrongly—if he'd even listen to her. To do this, however, she'd have to expose her scars. And not just the hideous striations that covered her arms, but the ugly damage that had seeped into her soul.

Was she strong enough?

Maybe, she thought, just maybe...

Syd took a deep breath... brought the darkness into her lungs...and let it go.

Chapter 23

Syd arrived at Southern Door High School on Tuesday morning. Carli Lacount had now been dead for forty-eight hours. In the secured vestibule, Syd noticed the telltale odor of industrial cleaning supplies. She showed identification through a sliding window, and she was buzzed into the office area. Nick Bogart had agreed to an 8 a.m. meeting.

A dumpling of a man with Buddy Holly glasses crossed the office threshold. If Syd used Eric Ingersol as a barometer, this guy didn't appear to be Carli's type. But you never knew.

"You must be Detective Bernhardt." He offered her his hand.

"I am." She shook it and noticed his other hand was not wearing a wedding band.

"I'm surprised you want to talk to me about Carli Lacount." He blinked back tears. "Her death is so sad, such a shock."

"Yes, it is. Would there be a private place where we can talk?"

Nick ushered her into an empty conference room where they took seats.

"So, Mr. Bogart." Syd opened her notebook. "I understand you met Carli Lacount through your cousin, Tina Kelsey."

"Yeah, during my freshman year of college." He pushed his glasses back up the bridge of his nose.

"Did you see her socially?"

"No...nothing like that." He blushed. "But I wish it could've been more. We just spent lots of hours together—driving back and forth between school and Sturgeon Bay. Even though Carli had a car on campus, when I was driving home for the weekend, she'd beg a ride from me." He sighed. "She was shameless about using people to get what she wanted, but I guess that was just one of her quirky charms."

"What else can you tell me about Carli?"

Nick rubbed his chin, thinking. "Well...we were in some finance classes together. I was surprised when she seemed inhibited around the 'cool' guys, yet was assertive and confident around the women—and the nerds." A sardonic smile crossed Nick's lips. "Like me." His face then shifted. "I also believe Carli might've had some kind of panic disorder."

"What do you mean?"

"I remember one time when she showed up for class, not realizing we had a big exam, and began to hyperventilate. She located a brown lunch bag and began to breathe into it. She seemed rather embarrassed afterward, but it did the trick and helped subdue her attack."

Syd nodded. Carli's backpack contents now made sense. "So, Nick, when you and Carli drove home from college, where did you drop her off?"

"At the Target store in Sturgeon Bay."

"Did you ever notice who picked her up?"

"I often saw either a Triangle Shops van or a dark-colored Jeep."

"Who was driving the Jeep?"

"It was always parked too far away, so I couldn't see. But I asked Carli. She said it was somebody I wouldn't know."

Syd raised her eyebrows and made a note.

"Oh, and there was one other occasion when I saw a different vehicle. It was about four months ago, right before we graduated. Carli and I were driving home, and, just south of Sturgeon Bay, there'd been an accident that stopped traffic. Carli's cell rang. It must've been her ride, because Carli explained why she was going to be late. When we pulled into the Target lot, she asked me to drop her off near the store's main entrance. I thought that was odd, knowing her ride was probably in the lot. However, I did as she asked and then pulled away. But before exiting the lot, I decided to circle back to pick up a few items at Target. Carli didn't see me, but I saw her next to a silver BMW. She was bending down to kiss the driver. After Carli placed her duffle in the trunk, she climbed into the passenger side, and the car drove away."

"So you couldn't see the driver?"

Nick shook his head. "It was too dark."

Syd was disappointed. "Can you be more specific on the date and time when this occurred?" She showed him her iPhone calendar.

He squinted. "It would've been the last Friday in April. We got to Target around 6 p.m., so the call came in around 5:45. That weekend was the last time I talked with Carli."

"So you didn't call her cell last week?"

"No." He looked confused.

Syd frowned. "Well, thanks, Nick."

He nodded. "I couldn't get off for Carli's funeral today, but Tina should be there. She's pretty broken up about Carli's death. I know my cousin liked rooming with Carli, especially during her senior year."

"What do you mean?"

"The two shared a bedroom. But Carli would go home every weekend, so Tina and her boyfriend took advantage of Carli's absence."

"Every weekend?"

"Yeah. If Carli didn't hitch a ride from me, Tina said Carli would drive home alone."

Syd contemplated Nick's words. The Lacounts, as well as Beth, had said Carli had come back to Fish Creek every other weekend.

Where had she been spending the alternate ones?

* * * *

Syd arrived back at her family's homestead and noticed storm clouds moving in. Bitsy and Daddy were waiting on the front porch, dressed for Carli's funeral. But Syd didn't see Lloyd. His sharp ears normally heard her vehicle from nearly a mile away. Often he dashed down the driveway to meet her.

Bitsy opened the van's front passenger door, and Syd smelled the pungent scent of skunk in the humid air. With Daddy's help, Bitsy boosted herself into the seat. Then Daddy settled into the rear.

"Where's Lloyd?" Syd wanted to confirm he was inside. He hated thunder and lightning.

Bitsy shook her head. "You tell her, Monty."

"Well, Syd, I'm sorry to say he had another skirmish

with Mr. Skunk."

"Oh, my God!" Syd sighed as she drove down their road. "Not again! Did he get a bath?"

"Yep. Used a whole case of tomato juice. But I'm afraid it's far from doing the trick."

Bitsy agreed. "Lloyd's still a stink-a-roo, so we had to put him in the shed. I laid down his blanket, though, so he'll feel secure if a storm comes up."

Syd gave Bitsy's hand a squeeze. "What would I ever do without you two?"

As Syd made a left, she spotted three wild turkeys alongside the shoulder and slowed down. Just then, her iPhone rang. She could see it was Gina.

On Syd's return trip from Southern Door High School, she'd called Gina and asked her to review Carli's cell phone records for that incoming call from the BMW owner.

"Syd," Gina said, "I have two things for you. First, that particular call you asked about was made from a pay phone located inside the Target store."

A "Damn!" slipped out of Syd's mouth, and Bitsy gave her a dirty look. "So what else do you have?"

"You're heading over to the Lacount funeral, right?"

"Yeah, I'll be there in fifteen minutes."

"Good. When you arrive, you're to talk to Patrick Lacount. There seems to be some trouble related to his niece's funeral."

Chapter 24

Syd turned into the parking lot of St. John the Baptist Church. Next to a Triangle Shops van was a forest-green Jeep. Syd was excited. Her eyes now scanned for the silver BMW, and she noticed a possibility in the last row of parked vehicles.

Syd knew she had to talk to Patrick Lacount before the service, but she first needed to check this other car. She persuaded Bitsy and Daddy to go in without her.

Syd maneuvered her body between parked vehicles until she reached the silver car. When she saw the VW Passat logo, her shoulders deflated. The BMW was still unaccounted for.

Syd returned to her van and used its mobile data computer to check the Jeep's registered owner. Moments later, she headed toward the church entrance contemplating what she'd discovered.

The Jeep was Beth Halverson's.

The packed church vestibule smelled like a greenhouse. Syd scanned the crowd for Patrick Lacount and located him beside Alice and Frank. All three flanked Carli's closed casket and a photo collage, propped up on an easel.

Syd's eyes connected with Patrick's, and a tight smile crossed his lips. He motioned to her, and she followed him down a hall. They entered a compact room, reserved for family. Along one wall, a buffet table was laid out with a coffee urn, platters of both pastries and specialty cheeses, and a bowl of fresh fruit.

Patrick closed the door and turned toward Syd. "We had a dreadful shock this morning."

"What do you mean?"

"About an hour before the visitation was to begin, Ralph Baker delivered Carli's casket to the church from his funeral home. But when he opened it, for our family's private viewing, the casket was empty."

Syd's eyes widened. "Did Ralph bring the wrong casket?"

"No. He said it was Carli's. He was scrambling, trying to determine what happened. Then he returned to the funeral home, just to make sure. But Ralph's already called me back and confirmed her body is not on his premises." Patrick ran his hands through his hair. "Syd, what does this mean?"

"There must be a logical explanation. I'll talk to Ralph and get to the bottom of this."

Patrick reached for her arm. "We'd appreciate it." And he gave it a squeeze.

Syd's normal reaction would be to jerk away, but she didn't. Instead, she took a calming breath. "How are Alice and Frank coping?"

"They're very distressed." Patrick dropped his hand and began to pace. "Carli's death was bad enough...and then this. Friends were arriving at the church, and Frank didn't know what to do. I pulled him aside and asked whether he wanted to cancel the arrangements. I volunteered to stand outside the church and send people home. But after we weighed the pros and cons, Frank decided it would be easier for all concerned if the family proceeded with the visitation and service."

Patrick's feet halted, and he slumped against the door. "When the casket was empty, both Frank and Alice wanted to believe Carli was still alive and had somehow opened it to escape."

"How terrible for them." Syd bit her lower lip. "I probably made a big mistake having them identify Carli from a photo. Brian's the only family member who physically saw her."

"It's not your fault." He again laid his warm hand on her forearm. "How could you ever know this would occur?"

Syd raised her eyes to his. This basic human contact was something she'd been rejecting for two years. As she struggled to figure out how to respond, she heard a knock.

Patrick appeared reluctant to remove his hand, but he did, to open the door.

Ralph Baker entered. His black suit and old-fashioned bow tie had both seen better days.

"Mr. Lacount," Ralph wrung his hands, "I can't tell you how sorry I am about this unfortunate situation."

Patrick gave him a thin smile. "I've already filled in Detective Bernhardt, so I'm going to excuse myself and let you two talk. Feel free to have a cup of coffee." He nodded that way, then locked his eyes on Syd's as he closed the door.

She was already ruffled. The last thing she needed was caffeine. She offered to get Ralph a cup, and he gratefully accepted. They sat down on folding chairs at one of the three circular tables. "The last time I saw you, Mr. Baker, was at St. Vincent Hospital in Green Bay. Can you please walk me through what's occurred since?"

"Certainly." He held his cup with nervous fingers. "After Miss Lacount's autopsy, I drove her body back to the funeral home and embalmed her that same night."

Ralph took a sip of coffee. "The Lacount's son stopped over yesterday to make the arrangements and to pick out Miss Lacount's casket. He also provided her funeral attire and a recent photo. After our meeting, I dressed Miss Lacount, styled her hair, to hide her injury, and applied makeup." He hesitated. "She did look beautiful, if I may say so, but of course, no one will know." That reality brightened his cheeks.

Syd nodded, empathizing with his discomfort. "Did you work alone?"

"No, my assistant helped."

"Your assistant?"

"Yes, Jason Potter, my sister's son." Ralph opened his mouth to say more, but then shut it.

"Mr. Baker?" Syd raised her eyebrows.

He bit the inside of one cheek and sighed. "Well, about three months ago, I decided to give Jason a second chance. He'd worked for me in the '80s, right out of high school, but at that time I had to let him go."

"Why was that?"

"He was rather scatterbrained and frequently late for work." Ralph frowned. "Jason often used his computer as his excuse, claiming he'd been so engrossed in a game, he'd lost track of time. When he moved back this summer and was looking for work, I gave him another chance. I thought I'd made the right decision, but, recently, he's been back to his old tricks. That's why I first talked to Jason when today's disaster occurred. I thought he'd screwed up, but he assured me he hadn't."

Syd made a note to talk to Ralph's nephew. "When did you place Carli in the casket?"

"Last night, around ten. Then Jason and I loaded it into the hearse. Of course, I locked both it and the air-conditioned garage. Two months ago, I had Jason mount a surveillance camera on a light pole outside the garage that sends streaming video to my PC. I just watched it back at my office. I had Jason fast-forward through the ten hours Miss Lacount's body was in the hearse. But neither of us saw anything unusual." Ralph handed Syd a DVD. "I had Jason burn that specific timeframe."

"I appreciate it, Mr. Baker, but I'll still need to talk to Jason and have one of our detectives review the original footage."

"I understand."

"When did the hearse arrive this morning at St. John's?"

"Jason and I pulled into the lot at 7 a.m. The visitation was to start at 8:00, and I wanted to make sure the family had enough private time with their loved one, prior to the public viewing."

"Let's walk outside, Mr. Baker. I'll have you show me the cars that were here at that time."

"Okay." He gulped down the last of his coffee. "I'll try."

In the parking lot, Ralph pointed out the Triangle Shops van, Brian Lacount's black Prius, and Beth Halverson's green Jeep. The three vehicles, parked side by side, were the closest to the hearse, which occupied a Reserved parking spot. "Mr. Baker, who was inside the church when you arrived?"

Ralph scratched his chin. "Well, Father Matthew, and Carli's immediate family. Patrick Lacount was also there, but he was busy setting out the food in the room we were just in. There was also a young blonde woman who was quite broken up."

Syd nodded. That had to be Beth. "How long were you away from the hearse?"

"About ten minutes. Jason and I first checked the church's inside surroundings to decide on the best casket placement."

"Was your nephew always in your sight?"

He thought hard. "Honestly, I don't know. But the two of us returned to the hearse with Patrick Lacount." Ralph looked sheepish. "I think I locked it while I was in the church, but I'm not positive. By that time, one of the other pallbearers had also arrived in that black SUV." He pointed it out. "I believe he was Frank and Patrick's brother."

"Luke Lacount?"

"Yes, that's it. He said his wife and daughter were coming later, in a separate car."

"Who carried the casket into the church?"

"Frank's brothers assisted Jason and me." Ralph hesitated. "Thinking back, the casket did seem rather light. But then, Miss Lacount was quite petite."

"When you'd returned for the casket, had any of the vehicles in the lot disappeared?"

"Not that I noticed."

Syd watched latecomers arrive and realized there seemed to be no logical explanation for Carli's strange disappearing act. In Syd's mind, this might have pushed Carli's manner of death from undetermined to homicide. If so, Syd sensed the person responsible for Carli's death had a morbid need to steal her body as some kind of trophy. Since Syd had arrived at Cave Point, soon after Carli's death, there might not have been enough time for the perp to take her body.

At least Ralph had provided Syd a short list of candidates: Beth, the immediate Lacount family, and the two Lacount twins. Of these, three had validated alibis for the morning of Carli's death.

Deputy Jeffers had contacted both charter reservation parties Beth had provided. They confirmed they'd called the Halverson Charter office and Beth had taken their bookings at the specified times. In addition, Carli's brother had definitely been on Washington Island that morning. And both the staff and customers, Patrick had named, confirmed he, indeed, had been at the Café.

When Deputy Jeffers told Syd about Patrick, she'd experienced a sense of relief. But now she also told herself: *You can't have tunnel vision.*

Carli's murder and her body's disappearance could be two separate acts, carried out by two separate individuals.

Chapter 25

Back inside the church vestibule, Syd approached Patrick and explained the situation. "During the funeral service, I'd like to conduct a search inside each of the four vehicles."

He was incredulous. "Do you think one of us took Carli's body?"

"I hope not." Her lips tightened. "I'm just doing the job you requested."

He grudgingly nodded. "Well, here are the keys to the Café van." Patrick removed them from his pocket and placed them in Syd's hand. "It's what I arrived in with Frank and Alice. But you'll have to ask the others for their permission."

Syd located Carli's brother, who was talking to a distraught young woman. She was pointing a finger at a photo within the collage. Tall and willowy, she was close to Brian's six-foot-plus height, but whereas he was muscular, she looked fragile. Dressed in a skintight black mini-skirt, stiletto heels, scads of bracelets, and a low-cut ruffled red blouse, she seemed to be attired for a dance club rather than a funeral. She was pushing an umbrella stroller that held a fussy baby. The little girl reached out for an approaching man—none other than Luke Lacount. The woman, Syd thought, had to be his wife, Colette.

Syd watched Colette's response to Luke: her shoulders faltered, she dropped her hand from the photo and appeared meek. Luke gave her a once-up-and-down as he had Syd during their encounter at his art gallery. But instead of a wolfish grin, Colette was awarded a sneer.

Luke bent down to give his baby girl a peck on the cheek. With that duty accomplished, he turned away, ignoring them both.

Syd wanted to talk to Colette, but that would have to wait. Instead, Syd touched Brian's arm.

He turned. "Detective Bernhardt, Patrick told me he discussed our disturbing situation with you."

She nodded and explained her need to search his car. "May I have your permission?"

Like Patrick, Brian gave her a shocked look but handed over his car keys. He then turned to Luke, who'd been eavesdropping. "What about it? Can you provide yours, too?"

Luke swung his keys in front of Syd's eyes. "Go at it, Detective. I've got nothing to hide."

* * * *

Fifteen minutes later, Syd completed her search of all three vehicles. Carli's body was still missing. All that remained was Beth's Jeep.

Syd peered into its windows, but couldn't see behind the rear seats. Before returning to the church, she hiked around the perimeter of the parking lot and checked behind bushes and within tall brush, but found nothing unusual.

Back inside the church, Syd entered the empty nave. The service had started. As a white-robed Father Matthew recited a prayer, she slid into the last pew rather than joining her family. The muted cries of a baby reached her ears. The source appeared to be the child of Luke and Colette Lacount.

Syd focused on the small white casket placed near the chancel. She assumed the pallbearers had carried it there during the processional hymn. She was sickened by the horrendous implications surrounding the fact it was empty.

What must the Lacounts be feeling?

Father Matthew sat down as Brian Lacount positioned himself behind the podium for the reading. His steady voice began, "Justice shall flourish in his time..."

It seemed an appropriate mantra for Carli.

Seated, a few rows up, Syd noticed Beth Halverson. Her shoulders were shaking, and one hand covered her mouth to mute her sobs. She suddenly stood and rushed down the aisle.

Syd followed. Out in the empty vestibule, she could see the front door closing. In pursuit, Syd reached it and stepped outside. "Beth!" she shouted.

Already next to her Jeep, she fumbled for the key to open it. Rather than acknowledging Syd, Beth climbed in.

Syd dashed toward the vehicle to block Beth's exit.

Backing up, Beth nearly hit Syd.

She lowered her window. "What do you want?" Beth rubbed her red eyes.

"I know you were present when Carli's casket was opened. May I please search your Jeep?"

Beth screamed: "You think I have her body?" Her anger had replaced her anguish. "That's disgusting." She slammed the steering wheel with both palms and then turned off the Jeep. Beth climbed out, her eyes shooting bullets at Syd. "Enjoy yourself!"

Syd released the rear seat behind the driver's side and located a metal lockbox marked with a "Halverson Fishing and Dive Charters" label. It was about an 18-inch-cubed container, similar to the fireproof safe she kept at home, and certainly not large enough to hold a body. Syd walked around to the passenger side and opened that door, then released the second back seat. She sifted through a pile of fishing gear, a sweatshirt, mud-covered tennis shoes, and food wrappers.

Again—no body.

Syd emerged from the cramped vehicle, a sincere apology on her face. "I'm sorry to have put you through this."

Beth gave Syd an "I told you so" nod and climbed back into her Jeep. She then squinted up at Syd. "So, somebody actually stole Carli's body?" Her voice registered disbelief.

"It appears so." Like Beth, Syd was more than confused.

"What are you going to do?"

"That's a good question." Syd took hold of the open door, so Beth couldn't close it. "I saw your reaction in church. Would you like to talk?"

"I doubt whether you or anyone else could fix my messed up life."

"Well, Beth," Syd sighed, "I'm working on mine. Maybe I can help you, too."

Syd was momentarily optimistic when Beth hesitated…but then she scowled. "Now is not the time or the place." She restarted the Jeep, and Syd reluctantly released the door.

Beth slammed it shut, and Syd watched her drive away, sensing the same vibes she'd gotten the day before when Beth discussed Carli.

Even so, Syd was no closer to understanding what had happened to Carli—or her body.

Now Syd needed assistance.

* * * *

The first squad car pulled up, and Deputy Ed Jones climbed out. "Toller will be here in about ten minutes with the cadaver dog."

The most likely spot for someone to have hidden Carli's body, Syd and Jones agreed, was to the south, near the cemetery.

"I'll be your point guy, Syd. In addition to searching for the body, we'll be on the lookout for anyone suspicious, trying to beat us to it."

"Thanks, Jones. I'll leave this in your hands."

For what seemed the umpteenth time, Syd entered the church. Inside the sanctuary, she finally slid in beside Bitsy and was startled to see Eli and his dad seated directly across from them. Of course, Syd told herself, the Gaudets would be here for Frank.

But, for Eli—maybe it was more.

Syd was sure he'd seen her enter the pew, but Eli didn't acknowledge it. What else could she expect?

Marv had left Syd a message that Eli had agreed to talk to them at 3 p.m.

She was not looking forward to it.

People stood for communion. Syd refocused and checked each row. She didn't see Zach, but then, this was a school day. Eric Ingersol was on the aisle. He whispered to the blonde beside him, possibly Carli's St. Norbert roommate. Syd also noticed a Gibraltar High School letter jacket on a guy too old to be in school.

As the service ended, the Lacounts followed Father Matthew down the aisle. The congregation stood to be released by row, and Syd whispered to Bitsy, "Sorry, I need to talk to the Lacounts again."

"Don't worry about us." She chuckled. "Some neighbors are here. We can get a lift home." She gave Syd a peck on the cheek and wrapped her arm into Daddy's.

Syd gave her a thankful smile and butted into the departing queue, averting her eyes away from Eli.

In the vestibule, Syd spotted Father Matthew, who had baptized her eons ago. Because he was a priest, Marv had immediately checked the Father's alibis for the child enticement cases and had ruled him out. She now approached him. "Sorry, Father, for dashing out during the service."

"I understand, Syd. What an unfortunate situation for the Lacount family: first the death of their child and then her body vanishes. I wish I could provide you some help, but I'm clueless."

"Do you remember seeing Frank at your Fish Creek Mass on the morning of his daughter's death?"

"Hmmm…" Father Matthew considered her question. "Can't say I saw him, but I did notice Colette Lacount standing in back with her baby. Colette and Frank often sit together."

Syd next located the exhausted Lacount family in the room reserved for their use. Alice stood alone by the window. Patrick was playing host, preparing plates of food for his brothers and Brian. The three had all taken seats around one of the circular tables. Apparently, Colette had returned home with the baby.

Patrick gave Syd an expectant look. "Do you have some news?"

"I'm sorry. I wish that were the case." As she explained the actions she'd taken, Luke had this weird smirk on his face, as if he was glad she'd come up short.

Alice focused on Syd, her face tense. "Please find my daughter."

Brian helped his mom take a seat next to Frank, who choked out, "Syd, we need some answers."

"Believe me." She placed a hand on his shoulder. "I understand."

Syd felt as if she was letting everyone down.

Chapter 26

In the vestibule of St. John the Baptist Church, Syd looked for the guy in the Gibraltar High School letter jacket. He was part of a group stationed by the photo collage. Syd approached him and introduced herself. "Were you possibly a high school classmate of Carli's?"

"Yeah, I'm Jake Sabin."

Syd was pleased to find one of the guys Carli had dated. "Would you have time to talk later today?"

He looked confused. "I guess you could stop by the Bayside. I tend bar there, and that's where I'm headed now."

As Jake took off, Eric Ingersol, along with the blonde, emerged from the sanctuary. He made eye contact with Syd. "Were you able to check the security tape at that Dyckesville gas station?"

She nodded. "As a matter of fact, one of our deputies stopped there this morning. I'm happy to say your alibi checked out."

Eric looked relieved.

Syd turned toward the blonde. "Could you be Tina Kelsey, Carli's college roommate?"

She looked surprised and nodded.

"Could we talk?"

Tina gave a nervous shrug. "I guess."

To achieve some measure of privacy, the two women returned to a vacated pew, and Syd got right to the point. "While you and Carli attended college, did you see her experience any sort of panic attacks?" As an example, Syd mentioned the one Tina's cousin, Nick, had seen.

She blew her nose with a damp tissue. "Well, I do remember one episode."

Syd nodded encouragingly. "Okay."

"It was quite late. Carli and I were walking home from the library, and we could hear footsteps behind us, speeding up, putting us both on edge. I even got out my pepper spray." Tina's hand went to her mouth. "It's not legal, is it?"

Syd smiled. "Don't worry. Just tell me what happened."

"Well, Carli began to hyperventilate. When this guy reached us, she nearly fainted. It turned out to be a friend from one of my classes. I'd left my scarf at the library, and he'd chased us to return it. After that, when Carli planned to stay late, she'd drive her car to the library."

Carli's panic attacks, Syd realized, could be the reason she'd been seeing a psychiatrist. In a couple days, Dr. Woodbridge would return, and Syd should know.

Syd switched directions. "Tina, do you know Beth Halverson?"

"Sure. Back in high school, I played soccer with both Carli and Beth. She was Carli's best friend."

"Do you think they were tighter than that?"

"What do you mean?"

Syd took the plunge. "Is there any chance Carli was gay?"

Horror filled Tina's eyes. "No way! All through college I roomed with her. I would've known."

Rather than debating the issue, Syd apologized for upsetting Tina and moved on. "Other than your cousin, do you know whether Carli knew anyone special named Nick?"

Tina hesitated. "I promised Carli I wouldn't tell, but now that she's dead, I guess it's okay... She told me she'd been seeing someone from Door County named Nick, who was still married."

Syd was thrilled. "Did she tell you Nick's last name?"

As Tina shook her head, a "Damn!" escaped Syd's lips.

* * * *

Outside the church, Syd got an update from Deputy Jones.

Carli's body was still missing.

They next discussed Ralph Baker's assistant.

"I'll drive to the Sister Bay funeral home," Jones volunteered, "and interview Jason Potter while you talk to Jake Sabin. We'll touch base afterward."

"Thanks, Jones."

Syd arrived in Fish Creek and parked outside the Bayside Tavern. She entered the popular establishment filled with the scents of hoppy beer, fried food, and pizza. There were three high-topped tables filled with couples eating lunch and a few locals nursing drinks. A red canoe embossed with the Leinenkugel Brewing Company logo hung from the ceiling over their heads. In the past, this bar had been frequented by Eli's dad. Syd was relieved when she looked over at Leon's usual stool and found it empty.

Behind the bar, Jake Sabin was restocking liquor. He

was quite buff with hair the color of Guinness beer. Seeing her, he said something to a waitress and waved Syd over to a stool located away from prying ears.

She talked over a Counting Crows tune coming through the sound system: "Thanks for taking the time to meet with me, Jake."

"What can I do for you?"

As he got her a soda, Syd explained, "I'm still looking into Carli's death. Back in high-school, I understand, the two of you dated."

A cynical smile crossed his lips. "Not for long. But I've got to say, Carli made a lasting impression."

"How so?"

"Well, all the guys thought she was this cute, sexy thing with an attitude. And as far as we knew, she'd never dated anyone. That became my personal challenge." He poured himself a soda. "I was in the same English class as Carli and Beth Halverson. It butted into our lunch period, so I encouraged the two girls to join us at the jocks' table." He took a sip, then chewed on a piece of ice. "Of course, I managed to sit next to Carli. It took a few weeks, but she finally agreed to go out with me."

"How did that work?"

"Okay, for a while."

The music had changed to a Bob Dylan song. "Can you elaborate?"

He reluctantly nodded. "Initially, we hung out at some weekend parties. Everyone was shocked when she'd openly make out." He gave Syd a wry look. "I guess I enjoyed the limelight."

"Did it move beyond that stage?"

"Not at first. Beth always seemed to be there, and she'd drive Carli home. But I eventually persuaded Carli to go to the Skyway Drive-in—with just me. That's the night she freaked out."

"What do you mean?"

He frowned. "Well, this is sort of personal."

"Come on, Jake, I need to know. Carli's past issues could be important." Syd gave him a rueful smile. "I'm not *that* old. I remember what kids do at that age."

"Okay." He moved in closer and lowered his voice. "I imagine you know how most guys were fixated on that 'Bill Clinton thing'?"

"You mean, convincing girls a blow job wasn't having sex?"

His eyebrows shot up. "Yeah, you get my drift."

"So, what happened that night?"

"Well, Carli and I were heated up. I'd brought along a bottle of Jack we'd been sipping. Carli seemed to be enjoying herself, even letting my hands travel to off-limit places. But when I unzipped my jeans and began to coach her head down, she went crazy. She began to shake and scream and jumped out of the car. I tried to locate her, but I couldn't. I later heard she'd jogged the two miles home."

"Hmmm…" Syd contemplated his words. "Did you two ever discuss that night?"

"No. She avoided me like the plague."

Syd nodded. "I understand Carli also dated Billy Rice."

"Yeah." Jake picked up a rag and began to wipe down the bar. "Billy went to Prom with Carli in May, about a month after our last date. I think they saw each other until about mid-July. Billy and I were playing summer ball together, and he told me the two had split up. We compared notes. I discovered Carli had flipped out with him under circumstances similar to mine."

Jake laughed. "That fact helped repair both our egos."

Chapter 27

Syd felt queasy as she approached Eli's Greek Revival Farmhouse. She parallel-parked in front to wait for Marv, and her cell rang.

"Hey, Syd," Deputy Jones said. "By the time I arrived at the Baker Funeral Home, Jason Potter had taken off, and his uncle wasn't sure where to find him. But listen to this. I checked to see whether Jason had any priors."

"Does he?"

"He sure does! He's on the registered sex offender list."

"You're kidding!"

"Nope. Back in '89, he was arrested in Sister Bay for attempted child enticement and exposing himself to a ten-year-old girl. At that time, our department also located kiddie porn on his home computer."

Syd's heart raced as fast as a hawk swooping down for a rodent or snake. "In Jason's '89 case, was the young girl's physical description listed?"

"Sorry, I don't have those details. But based on this information, I contacted Marv."

"Had he talked to Jason?"

"Nope. He's one of the registered sex offenders Marv was still trying to track down. Jason's last known address was his mother's place in Sister Bay. Marv said he'd previously contacted her, but she'd kicked Jason out and didn't know where her son was living. Based on that, I've just issued an Attempt-to-Locate to find out."

"Good work, Jones." Syd hung up, but then scowled at Marv's profile as he drove past and parked two spaces in front of her.

On Eli's front walk, she nudged Marv. "If you could've remembered the names of your elusive sex offenders at Al's last night, I might've snagged Jason Potter this morning."

"You had to rub that in." He twisted his mouth. "And here I'm doing you a favor by mediating this interview with your old flame."

They climbed the steps to the porch, and Marv opened the front door for Syd. She entered the familiar foyer and noticed Eli had come up in the world. There was no need to press a button beside a locked door. The entrance was wide open, and an actual receptionist greeted them. She was a brunette with a pleasant face. Syd noticed a wedding ring, but that didn't faze Marv.

"Hello, Miss…" He gave her his Marvelous smile.

She returned it. "It's Mrs. Greenwood, but you can call me Sandy."

Marv introduced Syd and himself.

"Mr. Gaudet should be here shortly," Sandy said. "A preliminary hearing ran long in Sturgeon Bay. But while you wait, can I offer either of you a beverage?"

They both declined.

Marv pointed to a food takeout box stamped with the Triangle Shops & Café logo. "It must be nice having the Café right across the street."

"It's very convenient. In the past, Carli Lacount even offered to deliver our food." She looked down. "Her death is so tragic."

Syd and Marv exchanged a glance before he asked, "Was Carli here for anything other than deliveries?"

Sandy's eyes shifted. "I'm not at liberty to say. You'll need to discuss that with Mr. Gaudet."

Syd was disappointed to find she wasn't as chatty as some. But Syd was also pleased that Eli had hired a woman who wouldn't betray his confidences.

Syd and Marv sat down in black leather chairs that flanked a credenza covered with magazines. Like the receptionist, the furniture, Syd noted, was new and added a modern motif to this familiar historical setting where hand-carved scrolls adorned the massive fireplace's oak façade. But the Oriental rug had not been replaced. She rested her spiked heels on it and flushed, remembering how she'd lain there, naked, when Eli and she'd made love in this very room. In that era, the foyer bell had come in handy.

Eli entered the parlor and Syd's heart lurched. His face was professionally composed, but his hair looked wind tousled.

God he looks good, Syd thought. She noticed a cowlick she'd never seen when he'd worn his hair long. She had the urge to smooth it down, which, of course, would just be the prelude to more…

"I'm sorry I kept you waiting," Eli addressed them both.

Marv stood and shook Eli's outstretched hand. "Long time no see."

"It has been, Marv. I believe it was when you testified at the Tromleau trial."

Marv squirmed. He'd been assigned to investigate the sexual misconduct accusations against the Sturgeon Bay teacher whom Eli had cleared.

Syd managed to stand, and Eli reached for her hand. She was afraid to touch him, but she did—and felt weak in the knees. She yanked her hand away.

Marv rolled his eyes, enjoying her discomfort.

"Let's talk in my office." Eli gave her a tight smile. "I bet you remember where it is, don't you, Sydney?" He swept out his arm. "I'll let you lead the way."

Their meeting, Syd realized, might be even worse than she'd expected.

She entered Eli's office, located in the sun room at the rear of the house. They all sat down, Eli behind his desk. He leaned on his elbows and clasped his hands under his chin, then addressed Marv. "So, what can I do for you?"

He opened his mouth, but Syd butted in. "So, Eli." She crossed her arms over the rapid pounding in her chest. "Tell us about your relationship with Carli Lacount."

He reared his head and fixed her with his astute eyes. "Relationship?"

Marv kicked Syd's foot. It wasn't going the way they'd planned. "Let's back up here." His eyes bounced between Syd and Eli. "Can you first tell us where you were the Sunday morning Carli died?"

Eli tipped his head toward Syd. "You did see me, didn't you? I thought that was you, sitting in the front seat of the squad near Cave Point. I believe your hair was wet."

She flushed. "Very observant. So, why were you there?"

"Well, Mrs. Overlund from the Solstice Cottages gave me a call on Saturday. She said Carli had checked in for the weekend and had mentioned I was looking for a

Hobie-Cat. So on Sunday morning, I drove over to check out the boat."

Syd nodded. "And did you see Carli?"

"No, I never did. I just talked to Mrs. Overlund." He pointed toward his back yard. The Hobie was pulled into a gravel driveway. "I picked it up early this morning before I cleaned up for Carli's funeral."

"I'm confused."

"What's so confusing, Syd? Carli was a good friend. She knew I wanted a boat. She told Mrs. Overlund to call me. It's what good friends do. My being there on the morning of Carli's death was purely coincidental. I didn't even know she'd died until later that night."

"So, Eli," Marv interjected, "were you and Carli *more* than good friends?" He gave Eli a wink. "You know what I'm getting at."

Eli shook his head as if Marv was crazy. "No, nothing like that."

"Well, then what?" Marv barked. "Sandy out there didn't squeal or anything, but I could tell from her eyes, Carli had been here for more than sandwich deliveries."

"You both know I can't divulge any legal dealings she might've had with me." Eli stood as if dismissing them.

"Sure, you can." Marv looked up at him and rubbed his slippery head. "Carli's dead. Your client/attorney privileges went down the drain when that occurred."

"That's not necessarily so."

"What are you saying?" Syd asked as she stood, taking Eli's hint.

"Let's just say, you and I might have a mutual friend who could possibly provide more insight."

"Gina?"

He shrugged. But he didn't say no.

On Syd's way out, her eyes tried to connect with Eli's. She had to believe, if they could just sit down and talk, like two mature adults, they could iron out the past two years. But when he didn't give her any sort of sign, a rush of disappointment surged through her. Syd felt as if she were on the other end, getting a dose of what he'd been going through, back when she wouldn't talk to him.

In the waiting area, Syd noticed a woman. Her blonde hair was perfectly coiffed, her clothes tastefully simple, yet obviously expensive, as if purchased from the elite stores on Chicago's Michigan Avenue.

Marv and Syd stepped into the foyer, but her eyes darted back. Eli emerged from the sun room, and, rather than a handshake, he leaned in toward the woman for a kiss. She slid her long fingers, with their French-manicured nails, into his thick black hair and smoothed down Eli's cowlick in an intimate fashion—just like Syd's fantasy.

She was stunned.

Marv noticed and pushed Syd out the door.

Over the past twenty-four hours, non-platonic thoughts of Eli had undeniably crossed Syd's mind. The day before, he'd claimed he wasn't over her...but after Syd's negative response, his feelings appeared to have changed. Since his admission, she'd never considered he might be in a relationship with anyone other than Carli. And he'd managed to convince Syd he hadn't seen Carli on the morning of her death. Syd had stupidly imagined—if she ever got the opportunity to admit to Eli she might have judged him wrong—her confession could reopen the door for them.

That was obviously not the case. Instead, Syd was back to where she'd started.

Across the street, two Triangle Shops catering vans

were being loaded by the copper-haired man who'd also been in Syd's thoughts. At seeing her, Patrick Lacount waved and shouted, "Are you going to be at the ASSIST benefit tonight?"

Syd nodded and shouted back, "I am."

"Great!" He beamed at her. "We're catering it. I'll see you there."

She finally cracked a smile.

Chapter 28

Syd got in a short run, then used the YMCA facilities to shower. Knowing she'd be short on time, Syd had packed formal attire for the ASSIST Benefit.

She arrived at the Peninsula School of Art dressed in a figure-flattering black dress with a low-scooped neckline. Of course, the dress had long sleeves.

ASSIST was a non-profit organization that helped more than 500 Door County domestic-abuse victims and their families each year. Twice a month, Syd volunteered by answering calls on their twenty-four-hour hotline.

Within the octagonal room with its walls covered in local art, a cash bar was set up next to the large spread of heavy hors-d'oeuvres. Many representatives from law enforcement were present as well as an array of local business owners.

"Hey, Syd."

She turned and got a big hug from Gina's partner attired in her unvarnished fashion. Myrna was what some might consider the stereotypical dyke. Beneath a black sport coat, her white blouse was tucked into cargo pants, and her cropped black hair was extra spiky for the occasion.

Gina joined them in her flowing multi-tiered skirt and a red cardigan sweater. For a few minutes, the three chitchatted. Then Syd transitioned into her recent meeting with Eli.

"Gina, he insinuated you might have insight into how he and Carli were connected. I assume it has something to do with a legal matter. So, what gives?"

She screwed up her face. "Honestly, I have no idea... Wait, unless it's related to that call I made to him per my friend Sara's request."

"Didn't you say she knew a lesbian couple who needed some legal advice?"

"Yeah, but I don't know the couple's identity." She turned to Myrna. "Hon', do you have any idea?"

A crafty smile formed on Myrna's lips as she slid her arm through Gina's. "No, but since it's Sara, I bet I can find out."

Syd looked at her friends. "Do either of you know whether Carli swung your way?"

Myrna shook her head. "She's never been in our circle of acquaintances."

"I agree," Gina said. "But then, consider me. It took years before anyone knew I was gay. Maybe it was the same for Carli."

Someone whispered in Syd's ear: "You look beautiful tonight, Detective."

She spun around and found herself face-to-face with Patrick Lacount. He'd changed into a charcoal sport coat with a starched white shirt, open at the neck—and he smelled good. Not like the bar soap she'd just used at the YMCA.

"Hey, Patrick, you don't look so bad yourself."

Gina's eyebrows went up.

Syd knew she'd hear about this later.

Patrick thanked Syd again for her efforts related to his niece's death, then asked, "Can I buy you a drink?"

She smiled. "A white wine would be nice."

The two angled toward the bar where they joined Marv, already waiting for a beer. Patrick put in his request, and Syd made the introductions.

Nodding Patrick's way, Marv continued to scarf down a plate of food.

As Patrick handed Syd a glass of wine, she felt his arm slide around her back, giving her a surge of cautious pleasure. Even though Syd could read surprise in Marv's eyes, she didn't pull away.

Patrick's arm felt good.

The sound system crackled, and a cultured female voice said, "May I have your attention?"

On an elevated stage, the blonde female from Eli's office stood.

Eli was off to the right of the platform. But instead of looking at her, his eyes had located Syd. They then darted to Patrick—a hurt look on Eli's face.

Syd was terribly confused.

"Welcome, everyone. I'm Angela Grafton, the national chairperson for ASSIST. I want to thank you for being here tonight, but more importantly, for all you do to…"

Syd tuned out her polished words, and her eyes drifted back to Eli.

His were still boring into her.

Syd knew she'd been caught in the act. Agitated, she looked away.

At the close of Angela's comments, the audience applauded. Syd stole another glance at Eli and panicked. He was headed her way. Sandwiched between Marv and Patrick, his arm still around her, Syd had no escape.

That's when Marv's cell rang.

He listened. "Shit. I'm on my way." Marv turned to Syd. "Come on. We've got to go."

She'd never felt more relieved.

* * * *

Syd followed Marv down the hill to St. Paul the Apostle Catholic Church, located across the street from the south entrance to Peninsula State Park. This was the area from which eleven-year-old Megan Hanson had been reported missing. Dispatch had told Marv, her mom had already arrived at the church, and her dad was en route from his job in Sturgeon Bay.

A Wisconsin Amber Alert had been issued and a roadblock established on the only highway leading off the peninsula.

As the two detectives approached Megan's distraught mother and friends, Syd passed Marv a piece of gum. Luckily, neither of them had finished their first drink.

"If I would've known earlier," Mrs. Hanson said between sobs, "it might have made a difference."

Syd assumed Marv was thinking about the elusive Jason Potter, just as she was.

While Marv talked to Mrs. Hanson, Syd knelt down to talk to Megan's friend, Wanda. "Can you tell me what happened, honey?"

With a quivering lower lip, she said, "Megan walked to St. Paul's for choir practice with me, Tara, and Kim." She pointed at the other girls, who were cowering together. "In front of the church is where we saw a man with this puppy."

Wanda hung on to the black Lab's leash. "Megan stayed behind to play with it while the rest of us went into the church." Tears filled her eyes. "None of us even noticed Megan didn't come in until practice ended."

"How come you still have the puppy?" Marv joined the conversation. He slid on gloves to check the dog's tags.

"When we came outside to look for Megan, we found the puppy, tangled up in a bush. I sent Tara back inside to tell our choir director."

Marv turned to Syd. "He's the one who placed the 911 call. The emergency operator told me the puppy had been reported missing before Megan was."

At those words Mrs. Hanson's sobs grew louder.

Syd tried to console her as Marv gave the frisky pup to a deputy, who'd arrived on the scene.

Marv bagged the dog's leash and collar, in hopes that some evidence might still be recovered: a hair, a print on the tag, or anything else to identify the perp.

Syd wasn't optimistic.

"Honey," she addressed Wanda, "can you describe the man?"

"I didn't see his face." Tears rolled down her cheeks. "When we left Megan, he was scratching the puppy's tummy."

"How about his hair color?"

She rubbed her eyes with the back of her hand. "He was wearing a Brewers cap, so I couldn't see."

Syd turned to the other girls. They also hadn't seen his face or hair—just his cap.

"What about his clothes?" Syd asked Wanda.

"I can't remember." Her shoulders slumped.

"I can," Kim whispered. "He was dressed all in black."

"What do you mean?"

"I thought it was weird. It was so warm out, but he had on a ski jacket, zipped tight to his chin."

Syd frowned. "So, you couldn't see his neck?"

"You mean, like, was he a priest?" Kim asked.

Syd nodded, surprised.

"My mom heard on the News that we were to watch out for a guy like that. I guess if he was a priest, the jacket was hiding his collar."

"My God!" Mrs. Hanson's voice broke. "I told Megan to be extra careful, too." She looked ready to collapse. "Do you think that's the man who took her?"

"Ma'am…" Marv's arm reached out to support her. "I'm sorry, we just don't know at this point."

Syd was sickened. Even though many Door County children had been cautioned to report anyone fitting the description of a priest, this particular pedophile had outsmarted them.

He'd changed his m.o.

Chapter 29

In Door County, there were about fifty registered sex offenders. Eighty percent of them lived in Sturgeon Bay. Over the next five hours, Syd and a newly-established six-deputy taskforce, headed by Marv, formed teams and knocked on the doors of the same sex offenders Marv had previously contacted. They met back at the department at 2 a.m., frustrated, for neither the roadblock nor the Amber Alert had turned up any promising leads. And all but three of the offenders were accounted for.

Jason Potter, notably, was among the absentees.

As they parted ways, Marv's tired eyes found Syd's. "I have a gut feeling, if Jason doesn't want to be found, there must be a reason."

She nodded. "I'm in your camp."

Syd fell into bed around 3 a.m. and promptly began to toss and turn. Readjusting her pillow, she cringed, thinking about Megan's parents and what they must be going through. Marv had secured a recent photo of Megan. It was eerie. She was petite, her brunette hair cut in a pixie style, and her eyes, big and dark.

Just like Jenny and Cassie.

And just like Carli...

Syd rolled onto her right side as images of Eli and Patrick now began to surface. Gina had phoned Syd and told her: "The way you dashed off, the two ended up in each other's faces. The situation was quite tense until that 'fancy bitch' from ASSIST joined Eli. She was hanging all over him, Syd. He didn't seem to reciprocate, but, then, we both know he's never been one for public displays of affection." Gina said she'd drilled Angela for information. Chicago was her home base, but she also owned a Fish Creek three-season condo.

Syd buried her face in the pillow. She didn't want to think about Angela and Eli. How he'd keep her warm in his bed, in the upcoming winter months, as he once had Syd...

* * * *

On Wednesday morning, Syd awakened, exhausted from lack of sleep. She made a pot of coffee, poured a cup, and ambled out to the front stoop with Lloyd. He still smelled pretty ripe.

With a sigh, she told herself it was already mid-week and she'd made little progress on Carli's case. More disturbing was that Megan had now been missing for fifteen hours. Syd knew most abducted children, who are later found murdered, have died within the first three hours.

While Marv's taskforce would continue to focus on Megan's case, Syd was to remain on Carli's. The information Jake had provided, about her reaction to both his and Billy Sabin's oral-sex overtures, made Syd believe that Carli could've been sexually abused.

But if so, then by whom?

And did this have any bearing on her death?

Back in the kitchen, Syd picked up her iPhone and called Brian Lacount. When he answered, she first told him the status of his sister's case and then got to the point. "Your mom showed me a photo of Carli's best friend from Kaukauna. I believe her name was Molly. Would she still live there?"

"It's Molly Vincowski. Her family lived next door to us on Pine Street. I don't know if she or her parents still live there, but her dad's name was Dennis."

"One more thing, Brian, at Carli's funeral, Colette Lacount seemed upset when she looked at the photo collage. Do you know why?"

"Well, Colette—at that time she was Colette Riley—also grew up in Kaukauna, and she attended St. Peter's Cathedral with us. After she moved here, she and Carli became quite close—I think I mentioned that."

Syd was startled. "Did someone from your family provide Colette her job at the Café?"

"I think Frank arranged it. He would've been the one who hired the summer help."

Syd disconnected and gave Colette's residence a call. She answered with the sound of a crying baby in the background. "I'm glad you contacted me, Detective, but it's not a good time. Could you stop over tomorrow morning when Luke's at the art gallery?"

Syd was surprised at Colette's response. She was glad Syd had called, and she wanted to talk—without her husband present. Interesting...

* * * *

Syd knocked on the Vincowskis' front door at around 10:30 a.m. When she'd called Mrs. Vincowski, she'd said Molly was on maternity leave from work. Now, Syd noticed an SUV with a baby seat in the back parked in the driveway. She hoped Molly might be inside the home, too.

Syd could see why Brian had liked moving to Door County. His old house, to her left, was flanked by a row of nearly identical bungalows. A crow flying sideways would have a hard time squeezing through.

A young woman with straight brown hair, fanned across her shoulders, answered the door, a tiny baby over her shoulder.

"You must be Molly." Syd smiled and introduced herself. She admired the infant before following Molly into the living room. A large portrait of Jesus was displayed over a floral-print couch. A drab carpet covered the floor, and a Siamese cat was curled up on a worn velvet chair.

A plumper and grayer version of Molly entered. On an ottoman, she placed a tray. Its contents filled the room with the scent of hot coffee and warm cinnamon rolls. Gloria Vincowski and Syd made their introductions while Molly disappeared to put her baby down.

"Please," Gloria said, "help yourself."

Syd did and thanked her, then settled into a rocking chair. They discussed Carli's untimely death until Molly returned and joined her mom on the couch.

Syd asked Gloria, "How long were you and the Kanes neighbors?"

"They already lived here when we moved in. Molly was two at the time."

"And did Frank Lacount move into Alice's home after they married?"

"No. In the spring of 2000, he moved up to Door County, and later that summer, Alice and the kids joined him. That's when they were married. But it seems weird to hear you call him Frank Lacount."

"What do you mean?"

"Well, he was Father Frank to us until he left the priesthood to marry Alice."

Syd was shocked. "Frank Lacount was a priest?"

Gloria tilted her head and nodded.

"Was he the priest at your church?"

"Both Father Frank and Father Milton were. Frank worked with the youth at St. Peter's."

Molly pulled out a group photo from her son's diaper bag. "I thought you might like to see this." She handed it to Syd. "This is our first communion class. Here's Carli." She pointed to a petite girl with a big grin on her face. Then she slid her index finger over to a man dressed in black robes. "That's Father Frank."

Syd stared at the photo of a much thinner Frank, a white clerical collar around his neck. "Did the kids at St. Peter's like Frank?"

"Oh, yes. Father Frank was cool. He started up a computer lab, so we could put out the St. Peter's Youth Newsletter. We also built a website where kids could sign up for volunteer activities."

"Was Colette Riley in that group?"

Molly looked surprised. "Yes, but how do you know her?"

"She used to work at Frank's Café, and now she's married to his brother."

Her eyes opened wide. "Colette had a real knack for computers, so Father Frank put her in charge of the lab." Molly now seemed uncomfortable, but she continued: "In addition to being smart, though, Colette had a reputation."

"What do you mean, Molly?"

She looked over at her mom, a bit embarrassed. "Colette was considered to be, you know, quite 'easy' from middle school on."

"Hmmm…" Syd didn't know what else to say, so she turned back to Gloria. She was giving her daughter a disapproving look. "Was there ever any sort of scandal in your parish when Father Frank was there?"

Gloria seemed taken aback. "You mean, like those stories about priests?"

Syd nodded.

"Nothing I ever heard about."

The cat stretched and then leapt from the velvet chair, slinking over to Syd.

"Mom, don't you remember the inappropriate emails Carli got in the computer lab? I think it was the spring before her family moved."

Gloria scrunched up her brow, trying to recall.

"What kind of emails, Molly?" Syd slid her hand over the cat's glossy back. It looked up at her with bright blue eyes.

"I don't remember, exactly. Just that Carli didn't like them. She showed them to Father Frank, and, after that, they stopped."

Syd made a note, then addressed Molly: "I understand both you and Carli attended a camp on Adventure Island, right before she moved."

Molly nodded. "We'd gone to St. Anne's Camp for the past few years and always had a great time. But that last summer wasn't the same."

"Why was that?"

"I know there was a lot going on in Carli's life, but near the end of camp, she stopped participating in any activities. She only wanted to lie on her bunk."

"Was there anything you can point to that would've caused that change in Carli?"

Molly turned toward her mom. "Remember? There was that girl from another cabin that disappeared?"

Gloria nodded. "I was quite upset. I believe that's the reason the camp was shut down."

Syd frowned. "Do you know what happened to the camper?"

"I don't think they ever found her. I believe the officials thought she might have drowned."

"Did you know the girl?" Syd asked Molly.

"Not really." She thought for a moment. "I think her name was Leslie…" Her forehead creased. "Leslie Gorman. It rhymed with Mormon, one of the religions we discussed at camp."

"Did Carli know her?"

"I don't think so."

About five years earlier, Syd and Eli had kayaked the two and a half miles from Fish Creek to Adventure Island. Next to a flock of blue herons, they'd tied up at a deserted camp dock. Syd remembered how they'd hiked along the shore and thought it looked like a ghost town. There, among the birch and cedar trees, the nine cabins and the big log lodge had all been boarded up.

At that time, they hadn't known why St. Anne's Camp had closed down.

In retrospect, Syd realized: she and Eli might have paddled right over little Leslie's grave.

Chapter 30

Syd entered the investigative wing's conference room. It had been taken over by Marv and his taskforce.

Megan Hanson's disappearance was nearing twenty-four hours. In addition to the official work in progress, a number of neighborhood canvasses had been launched in the communities where the abductor had chosen his targets. Marv had assigned deputies to supervise the search efforts in each locale. Hundreds of volunteers had shown up. Everyone was looking for any evidence to help uncover Megan's whereabouts.

"It's like hunting for a needle in a haystack." Marv shook his head at Syd. "I just wish we could find Jason Potter and either finger him or rule him out. He, or whoever abducted Megan, could be anywhere in the Door, including the islands."

"Well, I may have another lead." Syd crossed her arms. "Guess who used to be a priest?"

Marv gave her a frustrated look. "I'm in no condition to figure that out."

Syd paused for effect, then said, "Frank Lacount."

"You're fucking with me."

She shook her head, pleased at his reaction. She then told him about her talk with the Vincowskis. "Did you work on Leslie Gorman's disappearance in 2000?"

Marv leaned back in his chair. "I was new on the job. It was the sergeant's before he was promoted." He looked perplexed. "But how could that old case have any connection to yours or mine?"

"I'm not sure whether it does, but I'd like to talk to the sergeant about it."

Marv lumbered to his feet and followed Syd. She knocked on Stu's slightly ajar door, and he waved them in.

Syd explained Carli's connection to Leslie.

"That's very interesting." Stu looked up at the ceiling. "Leslie's case has never been closed. Without a body, it's difficult."

Syd slid into a chair across from him. "Could you review the case for my benefit?"

"It's a tough one to forget." Stu eyed Marv. "I know you remember it, too."

Marv was leaning against the door frame and grunted his agreement.

"It occurred," Stu began, "on a Monday night in late July of 2000, during the final week of Leslie's camp session. She'd gone to sleep in her cabin, but her bunk was empty in the morning. Nobody thought much of it until all the campers were called to breakfast and Leslie didn't show up. The camp staff searched the general area without any luck, then called us in. It was very mysterious. We didn't find any evidence of foul play. Since her cabin was about an eighth of a mile from the water's edge, we hypothesized that Leslie could've gotten up to use the latrine and become disoriented. But nobody could figure out why she would've entered the water."

"Was there any medical history, like seizures?"

"No, she was perfectly healthy."

"What about her state of mind? Could she have been committing suicide, for instance, swimming out too far and succumbing to fatigue?"

"Not one person we interviewed believed she would've taken her own life."

Syd crossed her arms. "Were there any males who worked at the camp?"

"Just one of the directors. I believe his last name was Paulson. He and his wife had supervised the camp for five years. Prior to St. Anne's, they'd worked in the same capacity at other camps, and nothing suspicious had ever been reported."

"How did the camp receive their supplies?"

"They were delivered by the *Spartan*, the boat that still transports people and supplies to Chambers Island."

"Didn't Fred Parson captain that boat, even back then?" Syd had met Fred years before, through Eli's dad.

"Yes. He's done it for more than twenty-five years. When Leslie disappeared, I talked to Fred. The last time he'd delivered supplies was the week before she'd gone missing."

"I'm sure you conducted a search?"

"Yes, an extensive one. We even transported cadaver dogs over from Fish Creek to scour the entire island. It took more than a dozen people over a week to cover the forty-three acres. Much of it was forested. We also had scuba divers search the nearby waters, but to no avail."

"At that time, other than the camp, Adventure Island was uninhabited, wasn't it?"

"Yes."

Syd shook her head. "You've got me stymied."

"That's how I felt. I'll get the records pulled, so you can take a look. I'm sure I haven't recalled all the details." Stu slouched in his chair. "It's been difficult. Leslie's parents continue to call, believing she might still be alive."

Syd looked at Marv. He'd been trying to behave, but she knew it was impossible for him to hold back his disdain for their boss. He rubbed some lemon on the cut. "As I remember, Sergeant, it remains our only unsolved disappearance in the county."

Stu gave him a smug look. "Well, let's hope you have better success with Megan Hanson than I did with Leslie Gorman." Stu hesitated, as if something had clicked. "Leslie's face is still cemented in my mind. In the records, you'll see she looks very similar to the photo of Megan. And, Marv, you told me Megan looks a lot like Carli Lacount. Maybe there's a connection between the three cases. Why don't you check whether any other young Wisconsin girls, with similar characteristics, have gone missing over, roughly, the last fifteen years?"

Marv nodded, his lips tight. "You know we've been looking for Jason Potter. After serving ten years for child enticement, he was released in June of 2000 and returned to Sister Bay."

Syd's eyes widened. "That's one month before Leslie Gorman went missing."

"Bingo…"

* * * *

Marv followed Syd's vehicle as they turned into the Lacounts' driveway. Because Frank Lacount had been a priest, he'd also become a definite person of interest in

181

Marv's case. Syd had called the Café, and Patrick had told her that Frank should be at his home.

The catering van with the TSCAFE1 plate was the only vehicle in sight. The two detectives got out, and Marv knocked on the front door. When nobody answered, they walked around the back but found no sign of Frank. The recent rain had made his backyard boggy, and the odor of rotting leaves, wet moss, and worms hung in the air.

"Look." Syd pointed at some footprints. They led toward the path through the woods. Carli's brother had told Syd the trail ended at Luke Lacount's home.

"Let's go find the guy." Marv eyed Syd. "Maybe he's up to no good." He began to stride down the skinny path.

She jogged to keep up, thankful she'd worn a blue pants suit with flats.

Suddenly Marv stopped, and Syd plowed into him. "Do you see Frank?" she whispered.

Marv's voice was low: "Well, I see some guy up ahead with scruffy hair."

Syd stuck her head around Marv's massive body. "That's him."

Frank wore a faded Packers sweatshirt over a pair of jeans. Work boots were on his feet. But what jolted Syd was the shovel in Frank's right hand.

"Let's see where he's headed," Marv whispered, excited. "Maybe he'll lead us to Megan."

The two crept along, single file, trying not to alert Frank to their presence. But when a massive pine snake slithered out of the weeds, Marv instinctively blurted out "Fuck!" followed by "Great! Now Frank sees me."

Marv started to announce himself, but, from behind

his back, all Syd could hear was the pounding of feet and a banshee scream.

Syd's heart leapt into her throat as Marv reached for his Glock.

Then came the sound of metal against bone.

Marv's huge body crumbled...exposing Syd.

Chapter 31

Syd faced what looked like a deranged Frank.

He swung his shovel back and forth, and she ducked.

"My God, Syd, is that you?" He dropped the shovel to the ground.

Syd looked down at a stunned Marv. A grapefruit-sized bruise had bloomed on his forehead.

Frank was beside himself. "I thought this guy was the one who'd attacked Carli, and now he was after me."

"Frank, he's Detective Robbins."

"My God, I'm sorry." Frank began to cry. "I've been so distressed about Carli... I—I know I overreacted."

Marv rubbed his skull and a flurry of "Fucks" spewed from his mouth.

Syd was certain Marv would like nothing better than to arrest Frank for assault. But, like Syd, Marv knew they'd been trespassing.

Frank wiped his nose and eyes with his sleeve. "I'll get you a cold pack and some Ibuprofen from the house." He put out his right hand to help Marv up, and Syd noticed it was blistered.

Marv shoved Frank's hand away and struggled to his feet on his own.

"You okay?" Syd asked Marv.

"My head hurts like hell." He eyed his attacker. "What the hell were you doing with that shovel?"

"I was just returning it to Luke's shed."

Marv's voice was nasty: "And what were you using it for?"

Frank seemed distressed by his reaction. "I laid some pavers in my back patio area. The physical work helped me take my mind off Carli's death."

Syd pointed at the blisters. "What happened to your hand, Frank?"

"Oh, this," he mumbled. "I had a run-in with some poison ivy. But that's the least of my worries." His miserable eyes darted between them. "So, why are you here? Do you have news about Carli?"

"Frank, we need to talk."

Marv picked up the shovel and led the way back to the house, still rubbing his bruise.

When they reached the back yard, Frank pointed out the pavers he'd just installed—about a ten foot square area.

Syd knew Marv had to be thinking what she was thinking: *Megan could be buried here.*

Syd followed Frank inside the house to retrieve the ice pack, Ibuprofen, and a glass of water. Then, the two of them returned to the outside deck to join a seated Marv. He placed the cold pack on his ugly bruise and winced, then slugged down three pills with a gulp of water.

Frank looked embarrassed. "Make sure you send me any medical bills."

"Fuck! Let's just drop it!"

Frank cowered at Marv's harsh words.

Syd put her hand on Frank's arm, ready to address the reason for their visit. Earlier, she and Marv had agreed she'd take the lead. "Frank, why didn't you tell me you'd been a priest?"

He looked startled. "Why, Syd, there was no reason to." He took a deep breath. "My previous life has no connection to Carli's situation."

"I'm not so sure." Syd frowned and pulled her hand away. "I talked to Mrs. Vincowski and Molly about your years at St. Peter's Cathedral. I understand Colette was part of the youth group."

He nodded.

"So, how did she end up here?"

"She'd been raised by a single mom who attracted one abuser after another. I'd been trying to steer Colette along a different route, so when I moved to Door County, we kept in touch through emails. After her mom basically drank herself to death, I offered Colette a summer job. I was so pleased when she accepted and also enrolled at the technical college. But then," Frank frowned, "she met Luke."

"When you started the St. Peter's computer lab, I understand there were some questionable emails targeted at Carli."

Frank nodded sheepishly. "But once I spammed out the non-registered youth-group emails, the problem disappeared." He looked down at his hands. "I was wrong in not reporting the issue, but Colette begged me not to. She didn't want the lab shut down."

"Can you recall the general content of the emails Carli received?"

He stroked his unshaven chin. "The author seemed to know a lot about her physical appearance, yet never said anything suggestive or threatening." He leaned toward Syd. "Do you think those old emails could have any bearing on Carli's death?"

"I don't know, Frank."

The sound of a pesky woodpecker filled Syd's ears. From Marv's expression, she could tell the noise was exacerbating his headache, so she quickly moved on. "Were you still a priest when you first moved to Fish Creek?"

"Yes." Frank ran his hand through his shaggy hair. "Leaving the priesthood to marry Alice was a big step. The spring of 2000 I prayed on my decision at the Holy Name Retreat House on Chambers Island."

"Luke said your parents had a home on Chambers Island as well?"

He nodded. "Back in the '20s, Mother's dad had purchased Hemlock House from a Chicago investment firm whose vision was to develop elite summer homes. Only three were actually built. Mother was living at Hemlock House that spring of 2000 until she passed away in June."

Marv finally asked: "Does anyone currently live there?" He was still pressing the cold pack to his head, though he seemed to have calmed down.

Frank shook his head, and his shoulders relaxed in response to Marv's friendlier tone. "We considered leasing it, but because of its size, condition, and remote location, we didn't even try. However, since Patrick's been back, the two of us have been renovating it."

Marv readjusted his body in the chair. "When you stayed at the retreat house on Chambers Island, did you utilize the *Spartan* launch Fred Parson captained?"

"Yes. That's when I discovered Fred had started to spend quite a bit of time with Mother at Hemlock House, soon after Dad passed." A brooding look crossed Frank's face. "She was in her late sixties, and he was in his mid-fifties. But Mother was still a beautiful woman with a commanding presence."

Syd scrutinized Frank, then asked, "During the summer of 2000, did you ever accompany Fred over to Adventure Island?"

"As I recall, each Sunday he'd motor me or one of the other priests to St. Anne's Camp to officiate the outdoor church service."

Syd lifted her brow. "Did you do the July service at Carli and Molly's 2000 camp session? You know…the one from the photo Alice showed me."

"I did, but I was disappointed when neither girl showed up." He paused. "Afterward, I believe I got Carli's cabin number from someone and walked over, but it was empty. One of the girls from an adjoining cabin told me the girls in Carli's cabin had gone on a backpacking trip to another part of the island, or something like that. So, I just returned to Chambers Island with Fred."

"Did you know a girl named Leslie Gorman who attended that camp session?"

Marv, like Syd, watched Frank's face closely.

"That name sounds familiar." His head tilted as if to jog a memory. "Was she a friend of Carli's?"

"No." Syd hesitated, wondering whether he was putting on a good show. "Tell me, Frank, do you remember anything disturbing that happened during the summer of 2000?"

"Well, as I said, my mother died." Then, an uneasy look crossed his face. "A little girl disappeared from Carli's camp session, too, didn't she?"

Syd nodded. "That was Leslie Gorman."

"That's probably why I recognized her name." Frank

shifted in his chair. "Did they ever find her?"

"No, Frank, they didn't." Syd's eyes penetrated his. "Do you have any idea where Leslie might be?"

He looked shocked. "Absolutely not!"

"How about Megan Hanson?" Syd stared at him a beat longer. "I assume you heard she disappeared yesterday in the vicinity of your business."

"What are you saying?" He placed his head in his hands. "You think I had something to do with both Megan's abduction and Leslie's disappearance more than a decade ago?"

"Do you still have any clerical collars, Frank?"

He sighed. "I'm sure I do, but they're packed away with the other relics from my past life."

Marv leaned forward. "Where were you yesterday afternoon, around 4:00?"

Frank closed his eyes. "I know this won't look good, but I was right here, all alone. After Carli's funeral, Brian returned to his house, and my brothers and Alice all left for the shops at around 2 p.m. She'd taken some special orders for customers on the Saturday before Carli's death and needed to call them in. I just couldn't return to work. Carli's funeral and then our pretense that she'd actually been in her casket..." He shook his head. "It all just did me in."

Syd again placed her hand on Frank's arm. "I want to believe you. But to verify your story, it would help if we could conduct a search of your vehicle, home, and grounds."

He raked his fingers through his hair. "Go ahead. Do whatever you need. I have nothing to hide."

Syd turned to Marv. "Are you up for this?"

"Yeah." He removed the ice pack and gingerly felt the bruise. "I think the lump's gone down some, and my headache's better, too."

"Well... that's one good thing!" Frank stood up.

The detectives followed him to the same catering van Syd had searched at Carli's funeral. This time she used a powerful hand-vac to capture any trace evidence from the vehicle's floors and seats.

The detectives next searched the garage and house. In particular, they looked for a Brewers cap or for any sign of Megan, but they were unsuccessful.

Frank, finally, took them down into the basement. It had two entrances, one from the kitchen and the other from the back yard.

Syd pointed to the door that led outside. "Do you keep that locked?"

"Rarely." Frank then showed them a dusty old trunk, pushed into a corner.

Marv raised the lid. The contents were in disarray.

Frank looked upset. "I'm positive I neatly packed this about a dozen years ago. And, honestly, Syd, I've not opened it since."

Among the contents were some musty robes, a number of crosses attached to chains, and rosary beads. There were a few well-worn Bibles, other religious books, plus a packet of clerical collars. These were in a cellophane wrapper, ripped open along one edge.

Syd turned to Frank. "Was this sealed when you packed everything away?"

He sighed. "I can't remember last week, much less twelve years ago."

Marv lifted the packaged collars. A yellowed newspaper clipping dated July 25, 2000 was exposed.

Frank's stunned eyes met Syd's.

The headline read: "A search is on for Leslie Gorman, a ten-year-old camp attendee."

Chapter 32

Marv and Syd talked before splitting up. He'd already radioed in a request. Three of his taskforce deputies were now en route to assist him with the outside search at the Lacounts.

"Marv, don't you think Frank's reaction to the newspaper article looked genuine?"

"Yeah, it did, but I still want to search his five acres—and dig up those newly installed pavers. I have to prove to myself that Megan's not buried there."

"I agree."

"And, don't you tell a soul I got smacked on the head by an old guy carrying a shovel!"

Syd laughed. "My lips are sealed."

"Speaking of Frank, did he have that poison ivy on his hand when you interviewed him on the morning of Carli's death?"

"No." Syd frowned. "I'm certain he didn't. Why don't you have a naturalist accompany you on your search to see whether you can locate the plant?"

Marv nodded. "Maybe Frank used his shovel in some spot he decided not to mention."

On the drive back to Fish Creek, Syd thought about the possible suspects for Megan's disappearance. If neither Frank nor Jason Potter panned out, their perp could be someone who'd entered Frank's basement. During the summer of 2000, Frank said he'd met people from Fish Creek and also at the retreat house who'd watched him transform into a lay person. If someone other than Frank had disturbed his trunk, that individual could be setting Frank up as a suspect in both Megan's and Leslie's cases.

And it still seemed feasible that these cases were linked to Carli's death.

Marv was in the process of placing Frank's entire storage chest into evidence. Hopefully the department's techs might find some useful prints or trace evidence on the items inside. Marv had already dusted for prints on the latch and on the outside basement door handle. Both had been unusually clean.

Syd reached the Triangle Shops & Café. Rather than stopping to talk to the other Lacounts, she first drove two miles farther and turned down the street toward Fred Parson's home. Syd wanted to ask him about the summer of 2000 when he'd piloted his boat to the islands of Chambers and Adventure.

Fred's fieldstone home was located next to the small bachelor cottage where Eli's dad lived.

At the sight of Eli's Honda, parked in that driveway, Syd's heart lurched as if jolted by an electric shock.

From just in front of Fred's house, she could see the Fish Creek Municipal Dock—and Eli. He and Leon were helping a boater tie up to a transient slip.

Syd should have figured Eli might be in the vicinity. Any free moment he got, he'd be on or near the water.

Eli shaded his eyes and saw Syd, confusion on his face.

Hers, she was sure, showed embarrassment. It looked like she was stalking him.

She climbed the stairs to Fred's house and knocked, but nobody answered. Instead of returning to her van, Syd took a deep breath and strode out onto the dock toward Eli. He was now loading his own boat with fishing gear.

"Eli, do you have a few minutes to talk?"

He turned and crossed his arms over his chest. "Are you serious?"

Syd nodded, and her words began to flow as she explained her regret at pushing him out of her life. "It doesn't matter who did or didn't check the fire pit," she confessed. "The point is—I know my burns were an accident. I've wasted two years trying to place blame. But what's the point? It doesn't make any difference. My burns happened, and I can't change that. Once I recognized that fact, I knew I needed the support of my family and friends."

Syd's eyes had filled with tears. "And you've been both to me. This may be the wrong time to tell you this, but I had to let you know how much I've missed having you in my life. Can you forgive me? Can we at least be friends?" Her eyes implored his as she wiped away her tears with the back of her hand.

"Friends?" Eli said, his lips tight. "Is that what you want, Syd?"

She nodded.

Eli's dad yelled, "Hey, son, can you lend me a hand?"

Eli hesitated, before shouting: "I'll be right there." Then he turned back to Syd, still frowning.

Her heart sank. "I'm sorry. I thought you'd accept my apology. But apparently…"

"Eli," Leon yelled again, "are you coming?"

Eli gave Syd a frustrated look, then turned on his heel.

She couldn't just stand there, hoping he'd come back. So she returned to her van and put it into gear. As Syd sped off, she thought she'd feel relief, but she only felt worse. She'd refused to forgive Eli for two years, and it appeared as if he wouldn't forgive her now.

Syd didn't know what the future would hold.

All she really knew was that—finally—she'd done the right thing.

* * * *

Syd entered the Café and her eyes located Patrick in the dining area. He was wiping down a table with one hand and setting up an adjacent table with the other.

He noticed her and approached. "Well, Syd, it's nice to see you after your abrupt exit last night."

She forced a smile. "Are Alice and Luke still here? I'd like to talk to them."

"Sorry, you just missed them."

"Damn!"

Patrick laughed. "It sounds like you've had a rough day." He checked his watch. "It's after five. Let me buy you a glass of wine to replace last night's."

It *had* been a rough day, and her encounter with Eli had just put it over the top. Syd shrugged and said, "Why not?"

"Great!" Patrick placed a hand on her elbow and escorted her to a table. He headed off for the wine and spoke to one of the waitresses. She removed her apron and positioned herself at the front of the restaurant to handle any new arrivals. Moments later, Patrick returned with two glasses.

"I heard about that little girl who was abducted." He sat down across from Syd. "Is that why you dashed out last night?"

"Yeah. We believe it happened around 4 p.m., just before I saw you loading up the van for the ASSIST benefit. Is there any chance you noticed anyone suspicious?"

His face took on a pensive look. "No, nothing out of the ordinary. Is that what you wanted to discuss with Alice and Luke?"

"Yeah. Do you know where they both were at about that time?"

"Sorry. I was so busy getting ready for the benefit, I wasn't keeping tabs."

Syd nodded, taking a sip. "I visited old friends of Carli's in Kaukauna. I was surprised to discover Frank had been a priest."

"You know, it's been so many years, I tend to forget."

A waitress brought over some plates and an order of bruschetta. Patrick smiled up at her. "Thanks, Mattie."

"This was not necessary, Patrick."

"I assume you're hungry, like me?"

"Yeah." Syd smiled. "And it looks great."

As they both helped themselves to the colorful appetizer, Syd's eyes caught his. "I understand you and your brothers grew up in Chicago."

"We did." He took a bite, then wiped his mouth with a napkin. "My parents married when they were in their forties. It was the second marriage for both, although neither had any children from their first. I'm certain, only Frank was planned. Mother was in her fifties when Luke and I were born."

"Wow! That must've been quite a shock."

He smiled and nodded.

"Luke said you spent summers on Chambers Island?"

"Yes—or at Rose Cottage, another summer home my parents owned in Saugatuck. Dad had a private plane, which made the weekend Chicago commutes to either summer home quite feasible. When Luke and I graduated from high school, my parents sold their Chicago home. From May to October, they decided to live solely at Hemlock House and winter in Florida. But that first spring, Dad passed away. I was lucky enough to inherit both Rose Cottage and Dad's private plane."

"Is that why you own a restaurant in Saugatuck?"

He nodded. "The summers my family spent there, I worked in that restaurant's kitchen with the chef. That's where I found my calling. I attended culinary school, where I met my wife, and the two of us bought the restaurant from its original owner. After Dad's death, his plane made it easy for me to fly across the lake to visit Mother."

"Frank said she died in June of 2000?"

"Yes. I think her death was especially hard on Frank. One of the reasons he'd decided to launch his business in Fish Creek was to be able to see Mother more often. But he'd been up here only two weeks when she passed away."

"That's too bad." Syd took a sip of wine, then reached for another piece of bruschetta. "Frank says the two of you have been fixing up your parents' Chambers Island home."

Patrick's face glowed as he nodded. "I'd love for you to see it. I'm boating over there on Saturday afternoon with Blinker. Is there any chance you could come? That is, assuming you don't mind dogs."

She laughed and told him about Lloyd.

"Well then, bring him along, too!"

It sounded so appealing. Before Syd could think of a reason to decline, she said, "I'd love to."

"Okay, then." He grinned. "It's a date."

A date? she thought. Her palms started to sweat. *She hadn't had one of those in years.*

Chapter 33

At the break of dawn on Thursday, Syd arrived at Dr. Ellen Woodbridge's Green Bay home, situated along the Fox River Trail. She'd contacted Syd late the previous evening. Rather than trying to tell her about Carli's last phone message, Ellen had felt it would be better if Syd heard it firsthand. Ellen was booked all day but said if Syd arrived by 7 a.m. she'd skip her run. Syd had offered to arrive even earlier, so the two of them could both exercise while talking business.

On her drive down, Syd had listened to a CD rather than the radio. It depressed her to hear about Marv's and her cases, neither of which seemed to be going anywhere. Carli Lacount had now been dead for four days, and Megan Hanson's disappearance was going on thirty-eight hours.

Dressed in running shorts, a long-sleeved dry-fit running top, and Nikes, Syd rang the doorbell. Ellen greeted her in similar attire. The doctor was about Syd's height and weight; her dishwater-blonde hair was tied back into a ponytail.

"Detective Bernhardt, please come in." She swung the door wide open. "I'd like you to listen to Carli's message before we take off. I'm glad my machine doesn't have a call limit. Her message is quite long."

Syd followed Dr. Woodbridge into her kitchen, filled with the scent of coffee. Ellen poured two mugs and started the message:

"Hi, Ellen, it's me, Carli. I know I'm only supposed to use this number in an emergency, but after my incredible experience last night, I couldn't help myself." Carli gave a breathy giggle.

"You know how I mentioned the weekend I'd planned? Well, this guy I've known from college is the only one who showed up. For years, I could tell Eric was attracted to me, but because of my past fears, I pushed him away. But this weekend, that all changed.

"I made that breakthrough we discussed. Being with Eric, close to his warm and very male body, his strong arms around me, protecting me, I experienced an intimacy and an arousal I never fathomed. Maybe I'm discovering who I am—who I truly want to be. Maybe I can be happy again."

Listening to Carli's melodic and clear voice, laced with rapture and hope, Syd felt so sad. Carli's words sounded like those Syd might have spoken when Eli and she had first explored each other's bodies and beliefs. But for Carli, the journey had come to a crashing halt. Syd found Ellen's pained eyes as Carli's voice continued:

"I wish you'd answered your phone. I wanted to tell you about the physical contact, how scary it was at first. But rather than feeling out of control, I took charge, like you told me to. I told Eric what to do and showed him what I wanted. He seemed so pleased, and he certainly responded.

He told me he'd never met a girl like me—that I was unbelievable."

In Syd's mind's eye, she could picture little Carli standing outside the Solstice Cottage, where she'd spent the night with Eric, talking on her cell and blushing with emotion.

"I trusted Eric. For the first time, I let a man make love to me, knowing he wouldn't hurt me. And it was so different from being with a woman."

Syd nodded slowly. She'd been on the right track.

"I was able to get past my phobia." Carli laughed. *"Actually, more than one time. Not once did I ever feel the urge to breathe into my paper bag. It's the first time since... Well... I think I'm ready to tell you everything at Friday's appointment. But right now, I'm heading out for a marvelous run!"*

Syd's eyes met Ellen's. In two very different ways, they both had a tie to Carli. Her words had made her death much more personal to Syd.

Ellen looked at her watch. "Are you ready for a four-miler? I'll fill you in on any relevant details, so you can catch the bastard that killed Carli."

The women first jogged through Ellen's backyard to reach the Fox River Trail. The water was peppered with fishing boats, their occupants squeezing in a peaceful hour before heading off to work. As the two adapted to each other's pace, Syd looked over at Ellen. "Why did you begin to treat Carli?"

"She decided to seek some therapy related to her conflicted feelings about her sexuality."

"Carli mentioned being with a woman. Was she involved in a lesbian relationship?"

"Yes. But it wasn't totally satisfying for her." Ellen dodged some goose droppings. "A healthy lesbian feels positive about her sexual identity. That did not define Carli. She told me she wanted to be 'normal' like most women she knew. This included the wide spectrum of heterosexual intimacy."

Syd related Jake Sabin's conversation about Carli's panic attacks in high school.

Ellen nodded. "I believe that's about the timeframe when she became involved with her female friend. Carli said it had started with physical exploration, then moved into a romantic commitment."

"Did she mention her partner's name?" Two women roller bladers glided by.

"No. And I understood from Carli, they'd both been careful to keep their relationship hidden."

Syd frowned, but assumed it was Beth. The two of them veered left to pass an overweight male jogger, plodding along. "Have you worked with other sexually confused women?"

Ellen nodded. "Often, these clients grew up with the perception that their moms were weak and inadequate, so they identified with their safe and strong dads. But, I've also had clients engage in a lesbian lifestyle as a result of sexual abuse and the subsequent fear of the male gender. I believe that was Carli's case."

Syd nodded and used the back of her sleeve to wipe the sweat off her brow.

"We're all socially conditioned by such things as our

family's culture, our education, and the media. Sexual abuse is another form of conditioning. If Carli did suffer from abuse, as a survivor, she could've been attracted or repulsed by things that had nothing to do with her natural self. I told Carli, being drawn to a woman, or being sickened by certain male behaviors, didn't define her sexual orientation. If Carli's lesbianism was not authentic, and if she did want to change, I told her it was possible for her to do so."

The women had reached the two-mile turnaround point. Ellen headed toward a water fountain and bent down for a drink.

"On Carli's phone message, she mentioned Eric, a guy I've already interviewed." Syd linked her fingers behind her head with elbows out and stretched. "Did she ever mention a guy named Nick?"

Ellen straightened and brushed water from her lips as Syd bent down to take her turn. "Not that I can recall. But in her last session, Carli did provide me a hint about her past."

Syd straightened. "Really?"

Ellen nodded, and they both turned north to retrace their steps. "She said she believed her conflicted sexuality stemmed from a specific event, and because of it, and her subsequent response, a little girl named Leslie probably died."

Syd was jolted by Ellen's words. "So, Carli thought she caused this young girl's death?"

"Apparently, but Carli also said she was taking some steps to make amends."

Chapter 34

At around ten on Thursday morning, Syd arrived at Colette and Luke Lacount's cedar shake home and Luke's studio. To save time, Syd had showered at the YMCA, then dressed into a black pants suit.

Marv had left her a frustrated message. His own prints had been the only ones discernible on the clerical collars' packaging and the newspaper article. Nothing else of significance had been located in Frank's chest. In addition, the vacuumed contents of Frank's van and the search on his land—including the ground beneath his newly installed pavers—hadn't provided any evidence that pointed toward Megan. The naturalist had discovered a number of spots covered in poison ivy, but nothing had appeared to be disturbed in the area surrounding it.

All in all, Marv didn't consider Frank to be a top candidate for Megan's abduction. Even so, Syd was still keeping him on her radar for Carli's death.

Colette answered the door. She looked disheveled, her dark brown hair pulled up on top of her head in a messy bun. In the background, Syd could hear the cries of a baby, along with rhythmic music. Dressed in a black long-sleeved spandex top and cropped yoga pants, Colette emitted the scent of sour milk. Sweat dripped down her neck, and her feet were bare. Even though she chewed gum, the faint odor of alcohol was evident on her breath.

"I've been trying to do an exercise DVD, but Anna's not cooperating." Colette sounded flustered. "She's a colicky baby and regurgitates nearly everything. I'm sorry. I know I stink. It's all I hear from Luke."

"Don't worry. When my niece was a baby she had the same issue. The scent brings back fond memories."

"Well, come on in—if you can stand the screaming."

Syd followed her into an open-concept family room and kitchen. Colette used the remote to turn off the DVD. She appeared to be in good control of her faculties. On the hardwood floor, an exercise mat was positioned in front of the flat-screen TV. Shelves on the adjoining sides housed photos, books, and a number of trophies. Anna, secured within a crank-up swing, was definitely not enjoying herself.

"Can I hold her?"

Colette nodded. "But it'll be at your own risk."

Syd lifted out the baby, her head covered in silky brown fuzz, and placed the little girl against her body. Syd had been with Molly's baby and now Colette's. Both women were far younger than Syd—a reminder of her screwed-up life. Patting Anna's behind, Syd rocked back and forth, and the baby's wailing dropped down a notch. "So, Luke's working today?"

"Yeah." Colette frowned. "He likes to keep me cooped up here. I guess both Anna and I cramp his style." She filled two glasses with ice water and placed one within Syd's reach.

Syd's eyes followed Colette's. Beside a liberally stocked wet bar stood a highball glass, filled with melting ice.

Colette's cheeks flushed. "Carli's death has been on my mind, so I'm glad we can talk." Colette grabbed the glass, dumped the ice in the sink, and placed it in the dishwasher.

Syd pretended not to notice. "Father Matthew said that you attended Mass at St. Paul's the morning Carli died. Other than your daughter, were you there with anyone?"

"Luke won't attend, so I often sit with Frank. But, that morning, Anna was fussing, so I stood in the back. I don't know whether Frank was even there."

Syd nodded. "Luke said he was in his studio. Is that right?"

Colette paused to think. "Well, he was there when I left at around 6:30 a.m. I made a trip to the supermarket in Sister Bay before church. Luke told me he'd be at the gallery when I got home, so I looked for his SUV at the Triangle Shops on my return trip. I didn't see it. But he often parks in the back."

Syd frowned. It looked as if both brothers' alibis were still shaky. "At Carli's funeral, I noticed your distressed reaction when you looked at the picture collage. Can you tell me what that was all about?"

Colette winced. "I'd rather not. I assure you, Detective, it has nothing to do with Carli's death."

"Why don't you let me decide?"

She shook her head like an obstinate child.

Syd decided to drop it—at least for now. "Brian told me that you and Carli had been friends."

"Yeah. She was two years younger than me, so back in Kaukauna I didn't know her that well. But when I worked here last summer, Carli was waitressing full time, and we often hung out together."

Colette paused to walk around the counter to check

on her daughter. "You're a miracle worker, Detective, Anna has dozed off. Let me put her down." She gently extracted her daughter from Syd's arms and left the kitchen.

Syd moseyed over to the family room shelves and checked out a few trophies. They were all male division awards, dating back a number of years, for such things as windsurfing, sailing, kayaking, and snowmobiling.

Syd was startled when she heard Colette say, "I think it's rather immature for Luke to still flaunt such things. Don't you?"

Syd turned toward her and shrugged.

"Luke hates the idea of getting old."

"Don't we all?" Syd smiled. "What attracted you to him?"

"Last summer, Carli and I often got a drink after work at the Bayside Tavern. That is, if Jake wasn't bartending. For whatever reason, Carli couldn't stand the guy."

Syd didn't comment. "That's where I saw Luke in action. On the nights Carli and I stayed until closing time, we'd often see him take some young girl home. I was envious. So I was flattered when he zeroed in on me." She shook her head. "Both Carli and Frank warned me about Luke—but I didn't listen. I was so stupid and got pregnant." A pained expression crossed her face. "He wanted me to abort, but I couldn't. Even though Anna's not an easy baby, she's one of the best things that's happened to me."

"Had you ever met Luke prior to your move to Door County?"

"No, but he told me, years before, he'd noticed me."

"What do you mean?"

"Luke said he used to drive his mom to Kaukauna when Frank periodically did the church Mass. But rather than listening to the service, Luke said his eyes would roam. That's when he claimed to have first seen me. In addition to being tall for my age, I'd developed early and looked far older than my peers."

Syd considered Colette's comments. If Luke had noticed her, had he also noticed Carli?

She followed Colette back into the kitchen where they both took seats at the counter.

"So, tell me, Colette. Was marrying Luke a good decision?"

Tears sprang into her eyes. "It was a big mistake. I've always fallen for the type of guys my mom clung to. When I moved here, and started at the technical college, I thought I could be different." Colette grabbed a tissue from a box on the counter and blew her nose. "But once Luke and I got married, I dropped out of school to assist him at the gallery."

"How did that arrangement work?"

"It was rough, right from the beginning. But Alice recognized that fact and befriended me."

Colette's comment made Syd see Alice in a different light. "Did you see much of Carli during her last year of college?"

Colette hesitated. "Well, I saw her when she came home on weekends to waitress."

"You said you and Carli hung out together?"

Colette nodded and took a sip of water.

"Did she ever talk to you about her sexual orientation?"

Colette nearly dropped the glass, her eyes wide at the question. "What are you asking?"

"Can you tell me whether Beth Halverson and Carli were an intimate couple?"

Colette remained silent.

"Help me here. I could understand your reluctance to breach Carli's confidence if she were still alive. But she's not."

Colette looked down, not meeting Syd's eyes. "Yes, Carli and Beth were a couple."

Syd had finally confirmed her suspicion. "Okay, then tell me, how were they getting along during Carli's last year of college?"

Colette frowned. "Carli was questioning their relationship."

"What do you mean?"

"She felt she'd settled for Beth without exploring other options. That included the entire male gender."

Syd nodded. "Did Carli ever discuss her St. Anne's Camp experiences with you?"

Colette looked surprised. "That's the reason I wanted to talk to you. Last week, Carli brought up her 2000 camp session. I think it was on the Wednesday before she died. She told me about this little girl named Leslie who'd disappeared from camp. I was shocked when Carli said she felt she'd been responsible."

Syd tightened her lips and thought about Dr. Woodbridge's similar revelation. "Did Carli mention anything more?"

"Not about that specific incident. But we discussed Jenny Tyler, the little girl Carli knew from the Café, who'd been the target of that weirdo wearing the clerical collar. Carli said she was fearful history might be repeating itself. Based on that, she said she'd decided to take some action."

Syd's pulse quickened. "What kind of action?"

"I don't know."

Syd frowned. "Did you tell anyone else what Carli said?"

"Well, I know I told Luke. He wanted me to find out more, but I never got the chance."

You certainly didn't, Syd thought, disturbed.

Because a few days later... Carli was dead.

Chapter 35

At the end of Colette's driveway, Syd waited for a black sedan to pass. Alice was at the wheel. Rather than returning to Fish Creek, Syd decided to follow her. They both turned down Alice's drive, then Syd parked and got out to meet her.

Dressed in designer jeans and a trendy over-blouse, Alice was distraught as tears streamed down her face. She choked out, "Tell me you've found Carli's body."

Syd was shocked. In their prior meetings, Alice had seemed emotionless and unapproachable.

"I'm sorry. I haven't. But I assure you, your daughter's death and her body's location are my top priorities."

Alice looked beaten. "I tried to go in for a full day of work, but I couldn't." She wiped away her tears. "Joyce Baxter stopped in. First, she expressed her condolences. Then, with that out of the way, she wanted my help to pick out the perfect attire for her daughter's wedding. I just cracked. Courtney and Carli were high-school classmates. I know Carli and I weren't close, but that doesn't mean it hurts any less." She hugged her body. "It actually hurts more. What mother wants to outlive her child—and suffer from so much regret?"

"What do you mean, Alice?"

Her thin lips quivered. "It's been years since I told Carli I loved her." She stifled a sob. "That I was so proud of what she was making of her life. That no matter who she chose to love—I'd still love her."

She collapsed on the porch steps and put her head in her hands. "And now, on top of that, I couldn't even whisper those words to Carli in death. I wanted to leave work today and go kneel down beside her grave. But, of course, that's not possible. Instead, all I can think is some monster is doing something awful to my little girl's beautiful body—desecrating it in some perverted way." From deep within Alice, a cry of agony escaped.

Syd sat down beside her and cautiously placed a hand on Alice's arm. "When you said, 'no matter who Carli chose to love'—what did you mean?"

Alice lifted her head and looked into Syd's eyes. "I've always had a feeling Carli and Beth were linked beyond friendship... Was I right?"

Syd nodded slowly.

Alice let out a heart-wrenching moan. "As a mother, I should've broached the subject, but I didn't want to believe it. Those unspoken words created a barrier that kept us at odds. But then I met Eric Ingersol at Carli's funeral. He was so handsome—so much a man." Alice's shoulders faltered. "He told me he'd cared for Carli for years, and when he left her on Sunday morning, he believed the feeling was mutual."

Alice shook her head. "My God, it's so sad—and confusing. What do you think drove Carli to Beth? Or, was my daughter bisexual?" She flushed. "I guess I don't even know what that means. Maybe Carli explained it in her diaries."

Syd blinked at her. "What diaries?"

"Didn't you find them?"

"I found a number of photo albums. Is that what you mean?"

Alice shook her head. "Ever since Carli's sixth birthday, she recorded her thoughts in a diary. I gave Carli her first one." She offered Syd a sad smile. "I remember its pink plastic cover, decorated with poodles. From that birthday on, Carli always asked for a new diary. At thirteen, she purchased a lockbox with her waitressing money. She stored all her special mementos in there. That included her diaries."

Alice's eyes found Syd's. "I'm surprised you didn't find her lockbox at Beth's."

Syd frowned and remembered just such a box in the back of Beth's Jeep, marked "Halverson Fishing and Dive Charters." Could that be Carli's? Maybe Beth had moved it there before Syd had arrived at her condo. Then, by sticking the label on it, she'd successfully diverted Syd's attention. "I'll talk to Beth."

"Thanks. I'd love to have Carli's diaries back."

Syd nodded. "Tell me, Alice, did Frank mention we'd searched your home and property?"

"Yes." She stood, collecting herself. "I know Frank was upset." Alice started to busy herself, deadheading the red geraniums in the window boxes. She spun back toward Syd. "I was, too. But we talked about it and resigned ourselves to the fact, you were just doing your job."

"Did Frank also mention the newspaper article we found? The one about Leslie Gorman's disappearance from St. Anne's Camp in 2000?"

"Yes. He said he was certain, he hadn't put it in his chest." Her eyes signaled confusion. "So, who did?"

"That's what we're trying to discover... Do you remember that incident?"

Alice nodded and used two hands to scoop up the dead debris, then dumped it into the mulch. "The camp contacted us." She stared into the distance. "I also remember asking Carli whether she knew that girl."

"How did she react?"

Alice refocused on Syd. "Distressed. But if I'd been at camp and another camper had disappeared into thin air, I might've felt the same." She cocked her head. "Do you think that old disappearance has anything to do with Carli's death?"

"I'm considering it."

"Really?" Alice recoiled in surprise, then sat back down on the steps.

"What was Carli like after she returned from that camp session?"

"The previous two years, Carli had talked about her fun experiences for days. She'd never been homesick. But that last camp session was different. And now that I think about it, that's when she started to cling to me, not wanting me out of her sight, yet not telling me why."

Syd nodded and took a deep breath. "I need to ask. Did you ever feel there might be anything inappropriate going on between Frank and Carli?"

She squirmed. "No. But I hate to admit, I was jealous of my own daughter. Frank kept trying to win Carli over, paying more attention to her than me. It seems so petty now, and I know my behavior hurt Carli's and my relationship." Alice hesitated. "Frank's a good man. He never would've done anything to harm Carli."

"What about Frank's brothers?"

Alice ran a hand through her short-cropped hair. "Well, Patrick's only been around since May, but he's been a godsend to the whole family—especially since Carli's death. The two seemed to get along quite well. Luke, however, is another story." She looked in the direction of his home. "Over the years, Carli seemed uncomfortable whenever he was around. But so was I. Carli managed to keep her distance from Luke, but in her new capacity, she had to deal with him."

"Frank told me, on the afternoon following Carli's funeral, you returned to the Triangle Shops. Can you confirm that?"

"Yes. Luke drove me in, and then Patrick drove me home before he headed over to the ASSIST Benefit."

"On that afternoon, did Luke work the same hours as you?"

"No. He didn't even come in. On the drive over, he tried to persuade me to join him at the Sunset Bar to 'drown our sorrows.' But I told him, that wasn't my thing."

Syd scowled. Luke's name kept popping up.

She now had another stop to make.

Chapter 36

Syd pulled out of the Sunset Bar's parking lot and headed back toward Sturgeon Bay. She'd just had an interesting conversation with Vern Campbell, the rotund owner of the dingy tavern, who claimed to work there twenty-four-seven.

"Of course," he'd told Syd, "I know Luke Lacount. He's one of my best customers." But Vern had also been positive—Luke hadn't stopped in since Carli's death.

If Luke hadn't been at the Sunset Bar or at the Triangle Shops, on the afternoon following Carli's funeral, where *had* he been? Syd drummed her fingers on the steering wheel. She knew Megan had disappeared during that timeframe. Luke had also lived in Door County when Leslie Gorman went missing in 2000. Was there a chance he was responsible for both abductions? Syd knew he could get easy access to Frank's basement. Maybe Luke was attempting to frame his big brother for his own evil deeds.

Syd then considered Carli's death. Luke could've met her years ago in Kaukauna and initiated those inappropriate emails. Maybe they'd escalated into an episode soon after Carli arrived in Fish Creek. Had she recently accused Luke, and he'd been forced to silence her? On the morning of Carli's death, Colette confirmed, Luke had been in his studio at 6:30 a.m. But he could've departed right after his wife, then placed the call to Carli from the Jacksonport phone booth at 7:03 and discovered her whereabouts.

Syd's thoughts flitted back and forth between Marv's case and hers. Were they looking for separate perps? Or could Luke be the prime suspect for both?

* * * *

Syd entered the department's investigative wing, and Gina waved her over. "Are you up for a drink after work tonight? By then I should have some information about Carli's connection to Eli."

At the mention of his name, a nauseous feeling settled in Syd's stomach. But she pasted on a smile. "Just name the place."

"Let's make it Hero's Pub." Gina grinned. "The atmosphere may add to the conversation."

Syd laughed. They'd be meeting at a gay bar.

She stuck her head into the conference room.

Marv was rubbing his forehead, still an ugly shade of purple, as a guy from his team finished giving him an update.

"Any news on Jason Potter?" Syd asked.

"No." Marv frowned. "But I've got everyone and their brother looking for him."

Syd gave him a resigned nod. "Do you remember the DVD? The one Jason burned to prove the Baker Funeral Home didn't lose Carli's body?"

"Yeah, what about it?"

"I had one of our techs meet with his uncle. The original video footage was recorded directly to a zip drive. Since it couldn't be located at the funeral home, I assume Jason pocketed it before he disappeared."

"Fucking great!" Marv put his head in his hands as if he couldn't take any more bad news.

Syd tried to lift his spirits and told him about Luke Lacount.

His eyes brightened. "Sounds as if he could be a viable suspect. I'll ask for round-the-clock surveillance on the prick. We don't want to lose him, too."

At Sergeant Morrell's door, Syd knocked and then entered. "Did you reach Leslie's parents?" Syd had asked Stu to contact them to see if Carli had called them to "make her amends."

"Yeah." He shook his head. "Carli didn't contact them."

Syd frowned, disappointed.

"But here's Leslie's cold case." He nodded toward a box on his desk. "See if you can find something I missed."

Syd dropped the box in her office. Before digging in, she raided the snack machine and poured herself a cup of stale coffee. Marv and the other deputy passed her on their way out.

Back in her office, Syd removed Leslie's photo from the case file and placed it next to Carli's. Their resemblance was uncanny. Syd walked over to the darkened conference room. On the table was Megan Hanson's abduction case, in addition to both Jenny Tyler's and Cassie Monroe's unsuccessful ones. There was also a folder containing Marv's research on similar Wisconsin cases over the past fifteen years.

Syd took all the folders back to her office and added

Megan's photo to her lineup. Leslie, Megan, and Carli could be sisters. There was no photo of Jenny or Cassie. But based on Marv's comments about Cassie's physical description, and Syd's memory of Jenny's, Syd knew they, too, resembled Carli.

There had to be a connection.

Syd began to read Leslie's file from cover to cover until she reached the interview of Susie Peterson, a twenty-year-old counselor. On the night of Leslie's disappearance, Susie had seen a guy in a kayak.

Syd shot upright in her chair. He'd been wearing a Brewers cap.

Susie had said she couldn't tell his age, but his arms had been muscular.

Syd had seen Luke's kayak trophies. He would've been about twenty in 2000. Luke currently had muscular arms, so he probably had them back then.

In Leslie's file, there was also a list of about one hundred campers, designated by cabin. Syd noticed Carli Kane was not in Leslie's. But Syd took a short intake of air upon reading a name that was.

Elizabeth Halverson.

Beth was at St. Anne's, too? Syd shook her head. *And in Leslie's cabin?*

Syd read, with interest, the interviews from Leslie's and Beth's cabin mates. Then Syd opened the research file, Marv had been working on.

In addition to Leslie Gorman's detail sheet, there was one that included two African-American sisters who'd disappeared from Milwaukee in 2007. Syd bet their disappearance revolved around one parent kidnaping their children from the other and was not connected to their case. One other little Caucasian girl, who had disappeared from the Madison area in 2010, looked promising. She had short dark hair with large brown eyes, but looked a bit chubby.

Since Syd now considered Luke Lacount to be a possible suspect in Megan's abduction, she left a note for Marv to check the Chicago area—Luke's original stomping grounds.

Syd skimmed through Cassie Monroe's unsuccessful child-enticement case and, lastly, picked up Jenny Tyler's. Deputy Borat had been the first responder, and his report was in the folder. Marv and Syd had interviewed Jenny the day after the incident. At that time, she'd only remembered how the "priest" had complimented her on her looks. But in Borat's report, Jenny had also recalled the priest saying, "I bet you like Popsicles."

Syd leaned back. *Popsicles? How sick...* Coming from a pedophile, that probably was a reference to oral sex.

Syd reached for her iPhone and called Jenny Tyler's home phone number, listed in the file. Her mother answered.

"Mrs. Tyler?" Syd reintroduced herself. "I understand your family knew Carli Lacount."

"We did. Her death was such a shock, especially since Carli had just stopped over to talk to Jenny."

"Really? When was that?"

"I believe it was last Thursday, the day after Jenny's incident."

"Do you know what they discussed?"

"I know Carli conveyed how relieved she was that Jenny was safe." Syd heard a muffled voice in the background, and Mrs. Tyler said, "Jenny's right here, and she's willing to talk to you, if you'd like?"

"That would be great."

The phone was switched, and a youthful voice said, "Hello?"

"Honey, can you tell me what you and Carli discussed last week?"

"Well, what my mom already told you, but there's one other thing."

"Yes?"

"Carli asked me whether the priest had mentioned Popsicles. I was so surprised and told her he had."

Syd's heart thumped faster. "What was Carli's reaction?"

"Her face turned white. Then she hugged me and said it would've been all her fault if I wasn't safe."

* * * *

Syd entered Hero's Pub and located Gina. She was leaning against the bar, squeezed in between a schoolmarmish woman and a rugged gal, her boots caked with dried manure.

A few ladies were checking Syd out, but when she touched Gina's arm, they disappointedly moved on to other possibilities.

Gina gave Syd a broad smile. "Let's find a private spot. Gals around the bar are discussing your case and Marv's. They don't need additional gossip to spread. Oh, and I've already ordered us some chicken quesadillas."

"That's perfect."

The two women jockeyed through the crowd. Gina carried a basket of chips and a bowl of salsa. Syd followed with two margaritas. In a back corner, they located a quiet table and settled into chairs.

Syd first told Gina about her disappointing talk with Eli.

"I'm proud of you, Syd. Maybe your talk didn't turn

out as you would've liked, but at least the ball's back in his court."

Syd realized she was right. "So, tell me." She dipped a chip into the salsa. "Did Myrna discover why Eli might've been representing Carli?"

"Did she ever!" Gina paused for effect. "Guess who was a lesbian?"

"Carli Lacount."

Gina's jaw dropped.

"Or at least, she'd been living as one. But what has that to do with Myrna's news?"

Gina perked up, ready to impart some information Syd *didn't* know. "Well, Carli was one of the women in a problematic sexual encounter."

Syd squinted at Gina. "I'm confused."

"Carli knew my friend, Sara, was active in the LGBT community, so Carli had sought her out for some guidance about her incident." Gina popped a chip in her mouth and chewed.

"When did it occur?"

"The weekend before Carli's death. She and another woman had gone to the Packers pre-season game. On their drive back, they'd stopped at a bar, and the two had been dancing to the jukebox music. With all the excitement and booze, Carli told Sara, she and the other gal had been turned on and headed for the women's bathroom to do something about it."

"But how could Carli's sexual encounter have anything to do with Eli?"

"You'll see." Gina gave Syd a slow, appraising look as she sipped her margarita. "According to Sara, Carli said the women's one-stall bathroom facility was locked, but the men's was ajar, so they decided to use it. When Carli closed the door, it automatically locked. Carli later discovered, the establishment's patrons accessed the two bathrooms with individual keys, returned to the bar area when the facilities were available. Since the men's key was still behind the bar, Mr. Gordon, an eighty-year-old man that used a walker, had his grandson secure it. The two then opened the men's bathroom door and stumbled into Carli and the other woman. Mr. Gordon apparently collapsed on top of his grandson, who also fell and hit his head on the ceramic floor."

"My God!" Syd nearly dropped her drink.

Gina nodded in agreement as the bartender delivered the quesadillas and told them to "Enjoy!"

As both women picked up a pie-shaped wedge, Syd asked, "I assume Carli went for help?"

Gina snorted and threw her head back. "Yeah—after she pulled up her jeans and panties. When Mr. Gordon and his grandson entered, the other woman was kneeling on a Packers blanket, her face in Carli's crotch. When Carli talked to Sara, the Gordon family had already hired an attorney who'd contacted Carli. He'd told her, Mr. Gordon had suffered a heart attack and died on the way to the hospital. His grandson had been treated for a concussion and relayed the restroom specifics to his parents."

"Wow!" Syd shook her head and reached for another chip. "Did the family press charges?"

Gina nodded. "Since Eli had helped other clients with gay discrimination issues, Sara recommended that Carli talk to him. Because Carli knew Eli, Sara had first called me to feel him out."

"Did Sara identify the other woman?"

"Nope." Gina took her first bite of quesadilla.

Even so, Syd had to believe it was Beth.

Chapter 37

In a mid-thigh jogging jacket, Syd sped into a parking spot in front of Beth's condo. It was Friday morning—five days since Carli's death and two and a half since Megan Hanson disappeared. Syd had reached Beth the previous evening, and she'd reluctantly agreed to talk at 7 a.m. The problem was, Syd had overslept and hadn't even had time for a shower.

Beth now opened the front door dressed in jeans and a stripped knit top. Her pretty face was not friendly. "I hope you can tell me you've located Carli's body."

When Syd admitted she hadn't, Beth huffed and motioned Syd in. "Well, let's get this over with. I assume you like coffee?" Beth pointed at two mugs already poured.

"Thanks, I do," Syd said cautiously and selected one, then followed Beth through the sliding door to the outside balcony. They took seats on patio chairs placed on either side of a table.

The anger in Beth's eyes faded as they focused on the distant Village of Egg Harbor, perched on a bluff that dropped into the expansive waters of Green Bay. "I love the view from here. It helps me forget my screwed-up life."

Syd looked at Beth's profile. The breeze blew strands of hair into her face, and her thick lashes fluttered to keep tears at bay.

"I know you're hurting." Syd reached over to touch Beth's hand and noticed, since Monday, Beth's fingernails had been bitten down to their nubs.

Beth didn't pull away. Instead, she turned toward Syd. Pain lined her face.

Syd gave Beth a compassionate smile. "I know how important Carli was to you."

"You do?" Her voice cracked.

"I know your love for Carli went beyond friendship."

A sob escaped from Beth. She pulled away to cover her face with both hands, her blonde hair spread across her shoulders. "How did you know?"

Syd took a few moments to explain, unable to see Beth's reaction, then Syd finally asked, "Why did you and Carli keep your relationship a secret?"

Beth lifted her head and used both hands to dry her eyes. "Carli's the one who didn't want anyone to know. She claimed it was due to her Catholic religion—and mine. But the real reason, I think, was that Carli was still confused about her sexual identity. Until she resolved that issue, she didn't want anyone to know, especially her mom." Beth reached for her coffee with a shaky hand and took a sip, then set it down.

"That's too bad." Syd gave her a sad smile. "I talked to Alice yesterday. I believe she would've accepted Carli for who she was."

Beth ran her hands down her distressed face.

"Tell me, Beth, when did your attraction to Carli first begin?"

She stood and leaned against the balcony rail, her

back to Syd. "It was the summer before my freshmen year of high school. Carli and I went swimming at the dunes, and we were fooling around in the water, as girls do. But that day was different. Every time I brushed against Carli, this warm feeling would shoot through me. I remember even swimming off on my own, and, you know..." She turned toward Syd, her face flushed.

A middle-aged guy on a noisy lawn mower came into view.

"Did Carli begin to feel the same way about you at that age?"

Beth shook her head. "Not until our senior year, after her attempts with guys had failed." She settled back into the chair and wrapped her hands around her mug, now eager to share. "I'll always remember the night of our first kiss. We were coming home from a soccer meet and sitting side-by-side inside our team bus. Like other teammates, Carli was dozing. Her head was resting on my shoulder, and her breath was soft against my ear." Beth's voice had turned husky. "I had this incredible urge to brush my lips against Carli's, but I kept thinking, *God, if I do, please don't let me be wrong.*"

Suddenly self-conscious, Beth looked at Syd. "I'm sorry. I shouldn't be telling you this."

"Believe me, Beth. I can relate." Syd decided to share her own experience with Gina in the cherry orchard.

Beth listened intently.

"Am I right in assuming your outcome with Carli was different than ours?"

"Oh, yes." Beth appeared to be more at ease now knowing Syd had been down a similar road.

"So, did you take the plunge and kiss Carli?"

"I did." Her voice was shy. "And the kiss gave me the most amazing rush—especially when Carli opened her eyes and gave me this sexy smile."

Syd laughed as Beth demonstrated.

"Carli then slid down low in our seat and kissed me back." Beth's face glowed. "That was it. That kiss started our intimate relationship." She reached for her coffee and, sipping, scrunched up her nose. "I need a warm up." Beth stood. "How about you?"

"Sure." Syd followed her back inside and handed Beth her mug. "I assume your relationship with Carli continued while she was in college?"

Beth nodded. "With lots of stressful planning." She filled Syd's mug and handed it back. The two then returned to their seats on the deck. "During Carli's first three years of college, we secretly met at the charter office on the weekend nights she'd come home to waitress. But then I purchased this condo last August, and we met here. On the alternate weekends, when she wasn't working, I picked Carli up in Sturgeon Bay. Of course, she had her school work, but other than that, the two of us could spend nearly every minute together." Tears sprang into Beth's eyes. "Those were the best months of my life. I felt as if we were finally a couple, and I could envision us living like that forever." She looked down. "But I guess Carli couldn't."

"What changed, Beth?"

"Well, during Carli's last Christmas break, just like the ones before, she stayed at her parents' home." Beth lifted her head and frowned. "That's when I believe she met someone new—possibly the Nick I told you about. Right before her last semester of college, Carli told me she wanted to take a break from our relationship, so she could figure things out."

"I bet that was rough on you."

"It was." Her face sagged. "After that, the only time I

saw Carli was on the weekends she worked at the Café. I would purposely stop in, and she'd be friendly enough, but our intimate relationship was on hold. I'd kept reminding Carli, I'd purchased this condo with her assurance she'd move in with me, once she graduated. Even though Carli continued to keep her distance, I know she felt guilty. That's why she took the permanent job at the Café and made good on her commitment."

"How did that make you feel?"

"I was thrilled. I thought I could win her back. But..." Beth slumped in her chair. "But I was mistaken. Carli made it immediately clear, her bedroom was off limits. Then, in mid-August, we sat in this exact spot. She told me she'd never had the opportunity to date other people, and it was something she regretted. Even so, Carli said it was wrong for her to have started an affair back in December." Beth's eyes took on a wounded look. "Just as I'd feared."

Syd nodded in sympathy.

"She claimed I'd been too demanding, too dependent on her, and she needed out." Beth shook her head in disbelief. "But she agreed to live here for her committed year—on the condition our sleeping arrangements would remain separate."

"But, didn't you say, Carli had given you her two-month notice on the Thursday evening before her death?"

She closed her eyes and nodded. "It was one of the best and worst nights of my life."

"How so?" I asked as three mourning doves landed on the deck railing and started to coo.

"Well, Carli arrived home from work with a case of beer and announced she wanted to get drunk. I was surprised, but I needed no encouragement to join her. Ever since our August talk, things had been uncomfortable between us. That night, Carli slugged down two beers, then opened a third. That's when she told me she'd stopped over to talk to that Jenny who was nearly abducted."

"Did Carli talk about any other similar situations?"

Beth looked confused. "No, just Jenny's incident."

Syd eyed her carefully. "Did Carli mention a girl named Leslie Gorman who attended St. Anne's Camp in 2000?"

Beth looked surprised. "Carli didn't mention her, but I recall the name. She was in my cabin that summer, right before sixth grade. I remember a sheriff talking to all the campers after Leslie disappeared."

Beth squinted up at Syd. "I take it you already knew I attended that camp?"

Syd nodded. "How well did you know Leslie?"

"I met her at St. Anne's."

"Did you get along with her?"

She looked down at her hands. "Good enough."

"I read in the case file you two didn't get along. That there was some pushing going on."

"Well, Leslie constantly teased me. Back then, I was still wearing an undershirt rather than a bra like the other girls in my cabin. Maybe I did push Leslie, but it revolved around that petty issue."

Syd stared at Beth a beat longer. "You told me you met Carli at Gibraltar Middle School, but didn't you meet her at that camp session?"

Her mouth dropped open. "Carli was at St. Anne's, too?"

Syd nodded. "You both attended the July 2000 session."

Her eyebrows shot up. "Well, that's news to me. There were more than a hundred girls at the camp. There's no way I would've known them all. Carli hadn't even moved to Door County yet, had she?"

"No."

"It's odd Carli never mentioned St. Anne's. I'm sure I did at some point." She sounded a bit defensive.

Syd wasn't sure whether Beth was being truthful, but she let it go. "What else did you and Carli discuss while drinking that case of beer?"

Beth hesitated. "You know how booze can loosen you up?"

Syd nodded.

"Well, Carli's mood seemed to lift. It was as if she was her old self." Beth's voice caught. "That's when I inadvertently slid my arm around her. But rather than rejecting me, I was stunned when Carli instead responded, and I mean *really* responded. We made the most amazing love—what I'd been praying for since December." Her face glowed with emotion. "But as I lay beside her, in the dark of my bedroom, elated about our renewed connection, Carli said she needed to tell me something."

"Go on." Syd gave her an encouraging nod.

Beth's blue eyes registered confusion. "It was about a bar incident she said she'd been involved in. Carli said there might be a lawsuit. And since she didn't want to put me through any embarrassment, she was breaking her earlier commitment and moving out. What we'd just experienced, she said, was her goodbye gift to me." Beth dug the stubs of her nails into her palms. "Carli went into her bedroom and locked the door. I kept pounding on it. I wanted her to explain this incident. I knew it could be fixed. But she refused to let me in. Eventually, I slunk back to bed and cried myself to sleep. In the morning, I figured we'd talk. But when I awakened, she'd already left for work."

Beth put her head in her hands and sobbed, "I never saw Carli again."

Syd placed her hand on Beth's shoulder.

She looked up with miserable eyes. "Do you know anything about this bar incident?"

Syd hesitated, then admitted she did. "I assumed you were the other woman."

Beth's neck jerked back. "What do you mean?"

Syd watched Beth cringe when she described the incident. "Do you have any idea who attended the Packers game with Carli?"

"I don't." Her eyes were wild as she rose. "I think I've talked enough."

"I appreciate your candor, Beth." Syd also stood. "But I've got one last question for you. I understand, from Carli's family, she kept a number of diaries stored in a lockbox. You know I didn't discover that container in her bedroom." Syd's eyes targeted Beth's. "Can you take me to it?"

Beth looked agitated. "I was just trying to protect Carli, to honor her wishes. I didn't want her family to read about our relationship when Carli had kept it a secret."

"I understand, but I need to read those diaries. They could help solve her death."

Beth sighed in resignation, then turned and slid open the patio door.

Syd followed Beth into the kitchen where she opened the utility door to the garage. The lockbox, still marked with the "Halverson Fishing and Dive Charters" label, sat on the cement floor, a hammer beside it. Syd could see the container's condition had been altered.

"I tried to bust into it." Beth's face was pinched tight. "But that damn lock wouldn't let loose."

"Could you please pick up the container?" Syd motioned that way.

Beth hoisted the lockbox off the floor as Syd removed Carli's key ring from her jacket pocket.

The remaining small key slid into the lock, turned, and—to Syd's relief—opened the box.

Chapter 38

Syd traveled past farms anchored by modern and historical barns, a number of art galleries, and the occasional bed-and-breakfast retreat. All the while, she mulled over Beth's interview. When Syd had disclosed the details of the bar incident, Beth had appeared to be shocked and hurt. Or had she played dumb? If she'd known, could her jealously have driven her to kill Carli?

Syd knew most murder victims were killed by their spouse or significant other.

Yet Deputy Jeffers had described Beth's alibi as airtight.

Syd shook her head. Nothing made sense.

Two routes led to her cottage. The back route was a rutted lane packed with gravel that meandered through the cherry orchards. The distance was short, but the path was hard on her van, so she drove a mile past it to the second route: the road next to the Bernhardt Cherry Chalet. In the parking lot, Daddy was loading a box full of goodies into a customer's car. Syd tooted her horn.

She continued up the lane and approached her family's homestead. Bitsy stood by the sturdy clothesline from which hung the living room's Oriental rug. Using a broom handle, she was beating it to death.

Syd considered joining Bitsy. It could relieve some of Syd's frustration about Carli's case. "You make me feel guilty," she shouted. "I haven't cleaned my place in over two weeks."

"You're never there," Bitsy called back. "How dirty can it get?"

She had a point, Syd thought. Still, Lloyd's telltale fur balls had populated the nooks and crannies.

Bitsy pointed the broom at Syd. "Or, were you giving me a hint?"

She shrugged and gave Bitsy a wistful smile. Syd realized, she was a bit like Carli, shameless about using people to get what she wanted. But in this case, Syd knew Bitsy would derive extreme pleasure from helping her out.

Syd lugged Carli's lockbox into the front room of her cottage and placed the box atop the oak tavern table. To counter the stuffiness of her small abode, she opened all the shades and windows.

Syd had phoned Gina to tell her she was going to work from home. This would be a treat, something Syd rarely did. Now, there was no reason to jump into the shower. She also didn't need her gun and holster, so into the safe they went.

Lloyd had been dancing around her legs. Syd gave him a scratch behind the ears and put him outside, then started a pot of coffee. Her stomach growled. She checked the refrigerator and screwed up her nose. Other than leftovers that needed to be tossed, it was bare. Instead, she grabbed a granola bar, then sat down and opened the lockbox.

Inside were the remnants of Carli's life: three dried corsages from special events, a stack of youth newsletters from St. Peter's Cathedral, various medals from soccer, a large yellow envelope marked "Research," and of course her diaries. Before Syd dove into her primary interest, she opened the yellow envelope.

Her mouth dropped open.

Inside were three missing person detail sheets with photos: Leslie Gorman, the young Madison girl who disappeared in 2010, and a girl named Cynthia Butler, who disappeared from a Chicago suburb in 2002.

It was disturbing, yet not surprising, to see from Cynthia's photo that she looked like the other girls. Syd recognized the Internet address on the top line of each sheet as the URL for the public database for Missing and Exploited Children. The pages had been printed at around 6 a.m. on the Friday before Carli's death.

Syd leaned back. Carli must have been doing this research in her locked bedroom while Beth was in her own, sunk into a deep sleep fueled by depression and booze.

Also within the envelope was a sheet of notebook paper. Carli had divided it into four titled quadrants: Wisconsin, Michigan, Illinois, and Minnesota. In the Wisconsin quadrant, Carli had listed the 2000 and 2010 dates, along with their matching case numbers. In the Illinois quadrant, she'd listed two cases: Cynthia Butler's in 2002 and a second Chicago one in 2006. The Minnesota quadrant also had two cases listed: one each from 2004 and 2008, in Rochester and Minneapolis, respectively. The Michigan quadrant was blank.

Syd checked the envelope again. There were no matching sheets for the additional three cases. When she'd searched Carli's bedroom, Syd had noticed that the printer's paper drawer had been empty. Maybe Carli had run out before she printed the missing case sheets.

Syd analyzed the quadrant chart. The six cases all fell within the even-numbered calendar years. They began with Leslie Gorman's 2000 disappearance and ended with the Madison, Wisconsin case two years ago.

Syd got a sick feeling as it struck her: Megan Hanson's disappearance fit perfectly into this pattern.

Syd used her iPhone to send an email to Marv. She told him to check the four new cases and carefully typed in their numbers. To make sure he saw her message, Syd also texted him.

Carli had told Colette she'd been taking some action after talking to Jenny Tyler about her close call. Had this research been Carli's initial step? But how was this connected to Carli's death? Had the "priest," who first approached Jenny, been worried Carli might identify him? Had he been forced to kill her, so he could pursue first Cassie and then Megan? Carli said she'd been fearful history was repeating itself. Hopefully, Syd would find some reference to that comment in Carli's diaries.

Syd called Lloyd back inside, thankful his skunk scent had nearly disappeared. Then she carried a stack of Carli's diaries out to the screened-in back porch, along with a cup of coffee. On top was the pink plastic diary decorated with poodles. Sunlight streamed through the screens and filled the space with warmth. Other than the tinkling of a bamboo wind chime, the only sound was the chirping of birds coming from the lilac bushes that bordered the yard.

Syd lay back on her well-worn chaise lounge, and Lloyd plopped down on the floor beside her. Then she proceeded through each year of Carli's life.

Syd read about her crushes on boys and her affection for her dad. He'd taught her to play his Martin guitar, possibly the one Syd had seen in Carli's bedroom. There were a number of entries that covered Carli's despair at the loss of her dad, but no mention of his affair. Her writings began to include Father Frank's presence in the home. Carli seemed pleased, but then started to question why he was there so often. That was when she referenced the weird emails.

Syd reached the 2000 St. Anne's Camp entries. Carli wrote about her camp director, Thomas Paulson, and his wife, Dorothy, calling them "awesome"—especially Thomas. Each evening, Thomas had played his own Martin guitar at the campfire sing-a-long. "I told him, I'd inherited my dad's, and Thomas was impressed." Carli had drawn a smiley face. "I knew the chords to 'He's Got the Whole World in His Hands,' so Thomas asked me to play his Martin at tonight's campfire. Way cool!"

Syd flipped the page, and the next entry skipped forward to August. Carli now lived in Fish Creek. This seemed odd. Syd stretched the binding apart and realized a page had been ripped out. She now was certain something had happened at camp.

The missing diary page fell within the timeframe when Leslie Gorman disappeared.

Chapter 39

Syd scowled in frustration and returned to the lockbox container on the chance the missing page was crumpled up inside. There wasn't so much as a gum wrapper, a post-it-note, or even a paper clip.

Her iPhone vibrated with a text message. Syd figured it was from Marv, but her stomach knotted at seeing Patrick Lacount's name. She'd managed to push her impending "date" out of her mind, but now realized it was less than twenty-four hours away.

Patrick's text said: "Looking forward 2 Saturday. Let's meet at Fish Creek Marina at 1 p.m. K?"

Syd stared at his message and shook her head. She couldn't do this.

She began to text back: "Sorry, not going 2 work." She positioned her finger to hit SEND, but then stopped. Hadn't she made a pact with herself to move forward with her life? And accompanying Patrick to Chambers Island wouldn't commit her to anything, right? In turn, he could potentially provide some additional insight into his family, especially Luke. Patrick's twin, Syd noted, was apparently behaving, otherwise, either Deputy Brighton or Deputy

Denton, who had been assigned to Luke's round-the-clock surveillance, would've alerted her.

What tugged at Syd, however, was that Eli's dad might be at the marina on Saturday and see Patrick with her. But why should she care? Eli, after all, was seeing Angela.

Syd used the backspace key to wipe out her words, then typed: "Sounds great!" And before she could change her mind, she hit SEND. A giddy feeling took hold of her. Syd poured another cup of coffee, shaking slightly from either nervous anticipation or too much caffeine. She returned to the porch where Lloyd lifted his head at her movement and settled back down.

Syd forced her thoughts back to Carli's life and was immediately sucked in by an August 2000 diary entry. It mentioned her new Uncle Luke. "His voice gives me the chills," Carli wrote. She also said she'd been having nightmares. They'd continued until school began and she made a new friend, Beth. Apparently, she'd been telling Syd the truth—at least about that.

Unlike the contents of the earlier Kaukauna entries, Syd didn't see any Door County middle-or high-school ones that mentioned crushes on boys. Instead, Carli was focused on soccer and her need to control her life. But her attempts at the latter seemed to be unsuccessful. She and her mom were constantly at odds about Frank and about Carli's non-existent dating life. She eventually wrote: "I've had enough of my mom's bitching. I finally agreed to go out with Jake."

For the first few dates, Carli sounded optimistic. She seemed to enjoy Jake's kisses and the feeling of belonging. But then, the drive-in movie incident occurred, and she wrote: "The sight of his ugly dick made me gag." This entry was followed by a month of nightmares that relived that experience until she gave Billy Rice a chance. "He swears he won't try anything that will make me uncomfortable." But when Billy broke his promise, Carli wrote, "That sleazy prick. He's like every other guy. Especially those you believe you can trust."

Syd considered Carli's last words. Had she trusted someone at St. Anne's Camp who broke that trust? It appeared as if she'd been on a first-name basis with the camp director, Thomas Paulson. He'd let Carli play his guitar. Had their relationship moved beyond that point? Syd made a note to locate him and stifled a yawn. The warmth of the porch was making her drowsy.

She skimmed the next few pages. Carli was suffering from another bout of nightmares. Syd yawned again, fighting to keep her eyes from drifting shut. Then she reached the entry about Carli and Beth's first kiss. "It turned me on," Carli wrote, "because it can't lead to where Jake's and Billy's did..."

* * * *

Syd's eyes popped open, and she sat up straight. She heard the *vroom* of a vehicle engine, and her heart started to race. She must have dozed off, and the sound had startled her awake.

Lloyd scrambled up on his haunches and began to bark, further unnerving Syd. If the vehicle had belonged to one of her family, he wouldn't have made a peep.

She climbed to her feet and reached for her Glock. "Damn!" she cursed under her breath. It was in the safe. Adrenalin surging, Syd hustled into the kitchen and heard a spray of gravel hit the front porch as the vehicle beat a retreat.

A ripple of fear streaked through Syd. Whoever had been outside had taken off in a hurry.

She reached the living room and opened the front door. In both directions, she craned her neck. No vehicles were in sight, but a cloud of dust filled the air along the rutted back route.

With a chill, she wondered: *Was someone watching me while I slept?*

Of course, Syd knew, that was silly. There were a number of employees who worked with Bobby in the orchards. She tried to convince herself that one of them had merely driven by.

Syd and Lloyd returned to the porch, and her tension dissipated. She settled back on the chaise and kicked off her sandals. It wasn't long before she was engrossed in Carli's diaries once again.

Syd had reached the entry that detailed Carli's first intimate experience with Beth. Late one night, the two girls had met at the Halverson Fishing and Dive Charters' office. To help them relax, Carli wrote: "I secretly secured a bottle of wine from the Café. Then we took our time, first touching each other in every conceivable place, afraid to move into territory neither one of us had explored before. Until dawn, we kissed, licked, and sucked each other in spots neither of us had imagined."

No wonder Beth had hidden Carli's diaries from her parents! Syd thought and padded into the kitchen to fill a glass with ice water. She needed to cool off—in more ways than one. In the process, she also filled Lloyd's water bowl. He lapped it up, then returned to the porch with Syd, her arms filled with Carli's remaining diaries.

Syd skimmed through the rest of Carli's high school years, not finding any reference to her 2000 camp experience. The college entries, when Syd reached them, were few and far between. The summer before Carli's senior year, when she worked at the Café, she wrote about her friendship with Colette. It was also evident Carli was beginning to have second thoughts about spending her life with Beth. "She's smothering me," Carli wrote.

Syd saw no mention of Carli's earlier nightmares—or the mysterious Nick.

During Carli's last semester of college, she wrote about staying at her parents' home and often taking the path through the woods to talk to Colette. But Carli made no reference to where she'd been spending her alternate weekends. Beth had confirmed they hadn't been spent with her. So, where had Carli been going?

Syd returned the journals to the lockbox, disappointed by what she *hadn't* found.

She finally picked up the St. Peter's Cathedral Newsletters from Carli's earlier years in Kaukauna. Understandably, they seemed rather amateurish. Syd located the Youth Editor's name—and then read it again, stunned.

It was Nicolette Riley.

Chapter 40

Syd's relaxed day had come to an abrupt halt. She looked through her interview notes and realized she'd never asked Colette about the mysterious Nick. Now, Syd wanted to put her on the spot.

Colette had provided Syd her cell number, which Syd now called. She was relieved when she heard a tentative "Hello..."

Syd's voice was assertive: "Hi, Colette. This is Detective Bernhardt. I'll be up your way in thirty minutes. Tell me where I can meet you to talk."

"I'm...I'm not home..." Her words were slurry. "Alice is watching Anna, so I can have some 'me' time." She gave a crazy laugh.

"I'll drive to wherever you are." Syd figured they'd be meeting at some bar but discovered she was wrong when Colette singsonged, "I'm at the beach, taking in the sun."

"Nicolet Bay, inside Peninsula State Park?"

"Nuh-uh, guess again."

Syd was not up for this. "How about the public beach in Ephraim?"

"Ding, ding, ding!" Colette's obnoxious laugher filled Syd's ear. "You win the prize."

* * * *

The beach would've been deserted if not for Colette. She was seated on a striped towel, attired in a sexy string bikini. A plastic 1-liter thermos was by her side, a straw sticking out from its top.

Syd yelled out a greeting and watched Colette clumsily reach for a beach cover-up. Drawing nearer, Syd saw bruise marks on the backs of Colette's arms. They disappeared as she donned the cover-up and flipped her hair over the top. She then picked up her drink and took a long suck on the straw as if steeling herself for their talk. In an attempt to stand, she lost her balance and keeled over onto her towel, laughing hysterically.

Syd settled down beside Colette and purposely knocked over her beverage. As the dark mixture seeped into the sand, Syd caught a whiff of rum and Coke. "I'm so sorry." She feigned embarrassment.

Colette's uncontrollable mirth turned into tears. "I'm such a mess."

"Look who's talking?" Syd placed her hand on Colette's arm. "I haven't showered, I haven't slept, and I haven't had a relationship in two years."

Syd managed to get a small smile from Colette as the tears, running down her suntanned cheeks, began to dwindle. She wiped her nose with a sandy hand. "So, did you find out what happened to Carli?"

"Not yet, but I'm working on it." Syd opened a paper bag that contained deli sandwiches and sodas. "It's a perfect day for a picnic. I'm hungry. How about you?"

Colette gave her a sheepish nod.

Syd popped open the cans, then wiggled their bases into the sand. She removed a turkey sandwich from its plastic wrap and watched Colette do the same. Her fine motor skills were not working quite like Syd's.

Both of them ate as their eyes focused on the water. Screeching seagulls landed on the beach. They kept their distance, but their keen eyes remained glued to the sandwiches. The women gave in and tossed them small morsels of bread. When the sandwiches were gone, the gulls rose, as one entity, and flapped away to the nearby dock in search of their next handout.

Now that Colette had something in her stomach, other than the sticky liquid that had left its mark in the sand, Syd was ready to get down to business. "This morning, I went through a number of items Carli had saved from her past. In addition to her diaries, I discovered some St. Peter's Cathedral Newsletters and noticed the Youth Editor was Nicolette Riley. That would be you, am I right?"

Unaware of Syd's intentions, she readily nodded and took a sip of soda.

Syd got right to the point. "Were you and Carli having an affair?"

Colette spat out "*What?*" along with a spray of soda.

As Syd described Carli's frequent visits to Colette's home, fabricating some intimate details along the way, Colette shrunk into herself. Syd ended with the bar incident and the potential lawsuit. "Today, I talked to Beth, and she confirmed, she was not the other woman. It was you— correct?"

Colette's eyes had glazed over with a caged-animal look.

"Were you the driver in the silver BMW who picked

Carli up at the Target store during her last semester of college?"

She still didn't know what to say.

Syd touched her arm again. "Colette, I need to know."

The human interaction finally made her break. "Yes," she sputtered. "I picked Carli up in my BMW, and then in the SUV we bought after trading in that car. Are you satisfied?"

Syd tightened her lips. "When did your affair begin?"

Colette took a swig of soda, probably wishing it was stronger. "During Carli's last Christmas break. I was pregnant and Luke was turned off by me. It was very lonely spending my first winter up here. And Carli was questioning her relationship with Beth."

Colette looked at Syd sideways. "Back in Kaukauna, I experimented with a string of boys—plus a few girls." She shrugged. "So, I guess one thing led to another. My involvement with Carli just happened. Nobody was suspicious when she took the path over to my house. After all, we were friends. We met on my days off when Luke was at the gallery."

"Did your relationship continue after Carli returned to school?"

She nodded. "We arranged to see each other on the alternate weekends, the ones she'd previously reserved for Beth. I'd pick Carli up in Sturgeon Bay, and we'd drive fifteen miles south to Brussels, where we'd stay at my Aunt Janelle's. She's a bit hard of hearing, and her guest bedroom has twin beds, so I'm sure my aunt never knew what was going on."

"How did you explain your weekends away to Luke?"

"He knew I was visiting my aunt—and Mara."

Syd gave Colette a questioning look. "Mara?"

She hesitated. "Mara's not really a secret. Everyone in Kaukauna knew I got pregnant in high school. Once she was born, I had to make a decision. My mom was in no condition to help me raise my baby, so, rather than putting her up for adoption, Aunt Janelle offered to take her, and I agreed." Colette's face lit up. "You should see Mara now. She just started kindergarten, and she's so bright and beautiful."

"She must take after her mom." Syd patted Colette's hand, hoping her children might be the incentive she needed to change her life. "When did you tell Luke about Mara?"

"Soon after our wedding. I thought she'd be able to move in with us, but Luke was livid. He claimed he never would've married me if he'd known."

Her face hardened. "Of course, he refused to help raise 'my bastard.' So I told Luke, whether he liked it or not, at least once a month I was going to Brussels to spend a weekend with her."

Colette picked up the discarded sandwich wrap and began to crinkle it with her fingers. Her angry eyes located Syd's. "Luke loves the arrangement," she snorted. "Those weekends, he tells me, are even better than his bachelor days before he was 'forced to marry' me."

They both noticed a young smiling couple step out onto the beach. An infant sat in the mom's backpack-style baby bag. A second child held onto her daddy's hand. On their faces was that fresh aura of an unlimited future. Syd could see the envy in Colette's eyes.

It probably was in hers too.

She turned back to Colette. "When did your affair with Carli end? Or, had it?"

With difficulty, Colette refocused on Syd. "It ended about a month before Anna was born. At that time, Carli and I decided to call it quits, but we maintained our friendship. I think, by having the affair with me, Carli realized it wasn't just Beth who was wrong for her, but being solely with women."

"I'm confused. If you and Carli were no longer sexually involved, how did the recent bar incident occur?"

"Well…" Colette shook her head, hard, "it shouldn't have. One of Carli's Café customers had given her two pre-season Packers tickets. I'd never been to a game, so I was excited when Carli asked me to go with her. We dropped Anna off at my aunt's on our way to Lambeau Field. Then, because Carli was the designated driver, I managed to take advantage of the opportunity and definitely enjoyed myself." She gave Syd a guilty look. "After the game, I pressured Carli and made her stop at a bar south of Brussels."

A crimson flush crept up Colette's throat. "That's when everything got out of hand."

Syd pulled her legs up to her chest and hugged them with her arms. "Were you contacted by Mr. Gordon's family about the lawsuit as Carli was?"

"Yeah." Colette frowned. "After I got the letter, I gave Carli a call. She was very upset about both that issue and Jenny Tyler's close call with that pervert. While we talked, Beth arrived home, so Carli told me she'd stepped out onto the balcony for some privacy."

Syd nodded. "Did Luke ever find out about your relationship with Carli?"

Colette's eyes widened in horror. "Absolutely not! But if this lawsuit becomes public knowledge, I don't know what he'll do." Her flush deepened. "When you arrived, I could tell you'd noticed the bruises on my arms." She released a gush of air. "Luke enjoys roughing me up to show me *he's* in control. And that goes for the sex, too. It's very sick and demeaning. He kept a box of photos hidden inside his studio that depicted all sorts of perverted sexual acts. The heterosexual ones he forced me to do, and still does—but there were also photos that showed animals, implements, and even children."

"Children?" Syd's adrenalin kicked in as she thought of Megan. "If Luke has child pornography in his possession—that alone is grounds for me to arrest him."

"I know, but when he discovered I'd found his stash, it disappeared. He said I'd look like a fool if I reported him. It'd be his word against mine, and who would believe a 'drunken bitch' like me over an 'outstanding citizen' like him?"

Syd scowled. She wanted to squish the despicable man with the heel of her shoe. "Colette, you know I can help you get a restraining order against Luke."

"I realize that, but I believe I can handle him." She slipped on her flip flops. "Earlier today, I finally made the decision to leave Luke."

"Good for you!"

"My aunt knows how bad my marriage is, and how I hate to be separated from Mara. If I move to Brussels, Aunt Janelle's offered to help me with Anna, too. That way I can go back to the technical college and make something of myself."

"That sounds like a wise decision." Syd's eyes undoubtedly shined with approval—yet she was still concerned for Colette's safety. Luke enjoyed abusing her. And what about other females—including little girls? Colette's confession had elevated Luke up another notch in Syd's prime-suspect list for both Carli's death and Megan's disappearance.

Colette got to her feet, this time with relative grace.

Syd was not as successful. One of her legs had fallen asleep. "Yesterday, you wouldn't tell me why you were so upset at Carli's funeral. Was it because you were lovers… or was there something more?"

Colette's face turned ugly as she balled her hands into fists. "I said it has nothing to do with Carli's death."

"Please, Colette, let me be the judge." To give her a moment to consider, Syd bent down to pick up Colette's towel, thermos, and the trash. Then she handed Colette her belongings.

She nodded curtly and mumbled, "It's disgusting."

"What is?"

"Well, if you *have* to know." She gave Syd the evil eye. "My mom refused to disclose my birth dad's identity, even when she was failing. She'd only tell me he was dead, and I should just forget him. But of course, I couldn't." Colette stuck her big toe in the sand, her mouth tight. "But after Mom's death, Aunt Janelle gave me a box of Mom's stuff. In it, I found my birth certificate listing my dad's name, and also some pictures of him with my mom."

Her desolate eyes met Syd's.

"Go on." She nodded.

"Well…at the funeral, I saw the photo of Carli's original family. When I lived in Kaukauna, I'd never met Carli's dad, since he didn't attend church. But this week, I put two and two together."

Colette took a deep breath. "In the photo, I recognized Alice's first husband. Carli's dad was mine, too. It made me physically ill. Brian and I are only a few months apart in age. That means my dad was screwing both my mom and Carli's at the same time. Plus, I'd been 'doing it' with my half-sister."

Her voice lowered to a whisper: "Isn't that incest?"

Syd gave her a sad smile, not knowing what to say. Syd's recent life had been an emotional mess, but it dimmed in comparison to the young woman beside her. Collette had made many mistakes, but her decision to leave Luke was an excellent one.

Syd just hoped Collette would follow through— before it was too late.

Chapter 41

Syd pulled up alongside Deputy Brighton's unmarked vehicle. "So?"

As expected, he said, "Nothing's been going on with Mr. Luke Lacount. His black SUV is still parked behind the Triangle Shops. But if he follows yesterday's schedule, he'll be tooling out of here soon." Brighton scowled. "Last night, he left at around 5 and drove to the Sunset Bar where he stayed until 10. Afterward, I would've loved to have pulled the guy over for a DUI, but that would've blown my cover."

"I almost wish you had." Syd shook her head. "He abused his wife soon after. She also said he's been in possession of kiddie porn."

"That bastard! Should we arrest him now?"

"I'd love to, but we can't. His wife's not ready to press charges. It also sounds as if the porn's long gone. That leads me to our other prime suspect in Megan's disappearance. Do you know whether Marv's located Jason Potter yet?"

"He's still at large, slithering around in the underbrush somewhere."

"I figured as much."

Syd entered the Café, relieved to see Frank rather than Patrick. Their impending excursion still filled her with mixed emotions.

The last time Syd had seen Frank, she and Marv had searched his home. But he seemed to have put that aside as he approached her.

"I understand Beth gave you Carli's diaries." Frank sounded rattled.

Syd was surprised. "How did you know?"

"This morning, right after you left Beth's place, she called Alice and apologized for hiding the lockbox. Then Alice and Beth had a real good talk." Frank's face looked grim. "It's heartbreaking to know Carli felt she couldn't talk to us about her most serious relationship."

Syd gave Frank a tight smile.

He shuffled some menus in his hand. "Did you find anything in Carli's lockbox that has any bearing on her death?"

Syd wasn't sure how to answer Frank's question. There'd been the "Research" envelope, Carli's questionable relationship with her camp director, and the missing diary page, but Syd only said, "The contents provided some leads."

It looked as if her words had piqued Frank's interest, but he remained silent as Luke sauntered over.

"Hey, big bro'." Luke talked over Syd's head. "Is this little lady boo-hooing to you about her lack of progress on Carli's case?"

Frank gave him a dirty look.

Syd's was scathing.

Luke looked pleased at her reaction. "I told Frank, here, it was too bad that macho male detective, who searched Frank's house, wasn't put on Carli's case rather than you. I bet he would've solved it by now."

A couple came in, and a look of relief crossed Frank's face. He excused himself to seat them.

Syd leveled her eyes on Luke and took a calming breath. "Tell me something, Mr. Lacount. Back in August of 2000, was there some reason Carli told her brother you gave her the creeps? Have you been hiding something Carli finally called you on? Were you forced to shut her up?"

Luke's face exploded with red, nearly matching his hair. "Don't you wish you could pin Carli's death on me, so you could be the top Deputy Dog?" The metallic gleam in Luke's eyes drilled into Syd. "Sorry, sister, that's not going to happen."

"Then tell me, Mr. Lacount, where were you on the afternoon of Carli's funeral, when Megan Hanson disappeared?" Syd longed to mention his former stash of child porn, but Luke would've known Colette was Syd's source.

"You're really hard up, aren't you?" He slicked down his unruly hair and puffed out his massive chest. "I know you asked my pal Vern at the Sunset about me. But he told me he must've been confused, 'cause now he recalls seeing me in one of his back booths, downing a pitcher of PBR with a pretty young thing."

Luke shoved past Syd. "I've got no time for your damn guessing games. It's a Friday night and the perfect time to prowl, so I'm out of here. And where I'm headed, there's no room for women like you."

He made a belligerent gesture in Syd's direction and strutted out the door.

* * * *

Syd entered her cottage, still trying to cool down from Luke's distasteful words—more convinced than ever—he could be the man in both her case and Marv's.

Inside, she noticed the scent of lemon and finally cracked a smile. Bitsy had taken her hint.

Syd had picked up a frozen pizza. As she turned on the oven to preheat it, she remembered the St. Anne's Camp director. Syd took a seat in front of her laptop and Googled Thomas Paulson. A guy who worked for the Peace Corps looked the most promising. She followed the link and read his bio. Syd believed she'd found him. Since the fall of 2000, he and his wife had been working in Western Samoa, more than 6,000 miles from Fish Creek. Syd knew Stu had interviewed Paulson the day after Leslie disappeared, and he'd looked clean. His record since then appeared to be the same. As Syd mentally removed Paulson from her suspects list, her iPhone rang.

"Hey, Syd," Marv said. "Although you keep managing to elbow your way into Megan's abduction case, I appreciate your surprising text and email. How'd you ever uncover that Carli had been researching these six particular disappearances?"

Syd gave him an update and included the information about Luke Lacount.

Marv huffed. "Well, I'll have one of my guys follow up on his 'pretty young thing' and Vern's sudden memory change."

"Don't you think Carli's research proves our cases are connected?"

"Looks that way." Marv sounded disappointed. Syd knew he was thinking: *We're back to share and share alike.*

His attitude irked her. Teamwork was critical, especially in this case. Megan's young life was still on the line.

Admonishing Marv would do no good, so Syd bit her tongue and asked, "Did you check whether the other missing girls that Carli had been researching looked similar to her?" As the oven beeped, Syd walked over to the counter to unwrap the pizza.

"Yeah…it was weird. For all of them, but one, I pulled up the case photos and saw a sweet little girl with short brown hair and dark eyes staring out at me as if pleading to be found."

"Are you saying one photo didn't match?" Syd slid the pizza into the oven and set the timer.

"No—just that I didn't get a hit on the Rochester, Minnesota case number. Can you verify it for me?"

"Hold on." Syd opened the lockbox. She expected to see the yellow "Research" envelope right on top, but it wasn't. She searched the entire container, but still couldn't locate it.

That's odd, Syd thought. With Lloyd on her heels, she scoured the house, but again, it was nowhere to be found. All the while, she could hear Marv's irritated shouts coming from her iPhone. She finally put it to her ear. "I think someone removed the 'Research' envelope from my cottage."

"Did you lock the door?"

"I'm sure I did. But Bitsy cleaned this afternoon, and she often brings my dad along." Syd shook her head. "I assume you know what *that* means."

He moaned. Syd knew her brother often complained to Marv about Daddy's memory loss.

"I'll check with Bitsy and call you back." As Syd hung up, she thought about the vehicle that had sped away earlier in the day. Based on her recent conversation with Frank, she knew, by that time, Beth had already told Alice she'd given Syd the lockbox. In turn, Alice had told Frank. Syd had no idea who else might've known.

Bitsy answered on the third ring.

"First," Syd plopped down in a chair, "thanks for spiffing up my cottage. I really appreciate it. But is there any chance you threw away a big yellow envelope?"

"No, honey, I'd never do that, though I did pitch out your moldy leftovers and restocked your fridge. This time, though, it's not a freebee. You owe me fifty bucks."

"Thanks." Syd laughed. "What about Daddy? I assume he was here with you?"

"He was, although his only work contribution was to scratch Lloyd behind the ears. But I'll ask him." She muffled the phone and then came back on. "Well, your daddy says he wasn't at your place today." She huffed. "That I must be confused."

Even though Syd bet Daddy had gotten curious and misplaced the "Research" envelope, she still asked Bitsy, "Did you see any vehicles drive past your home or mine today?"

"Well, I saw your brother's truck, and there was also one of those Triangle Shops vans. They often drop off a supply of their pies that we resell."

That spooked Syd. Had the driver been her peeping Tom?

Syd thanked Bitsy and called the Chalet.

Bobby's wife answered.

"Hi, Helen. Bitsy said a Triangle Shops van made deliveries today."

"Bitsy's mistaken, Syd. We didn't get any pies today."

Syd frowned. Daddy could be mistaken, but not Bitsy.

Syd hung up and next called Deputy Brighton. "Where are you?"

"I'm outside the Sunset Bar on the lookout for our mutual wife beater."

"You know the two Triangle Shops catering vans?"

"Yeah."

"Did either leave their premises today?"

"Sure. Both were on the move."

"Did you see who was driving?"

"No..." His voice sounded sheepish. "But I should've, right?"

"Shit, yes!" Frustrated, Syd hung up. Brighton wasn't the sharpest cookie in the department, but this was inexcusable. However, the answer to her question could be logged at the Café. Their policy, it appeared, was to sign out the vans. But calling the Café was risky. The driver might answer.

As Syd twirled a strand of hair around her finger and contemplated that dilemma, Marv called back. "What's been taking you?" he asked.

Syd explained the situation.

"I'll let you off the hook, this time. I think I found the correct case number for the Rochester, Minnesota girl. In the Missing and Exploited Children's database, the last two digits of Katie Malsack's case number were transposed. When she disappeared, her physical description and age matched that of the other five girls."

"So...it looks as if Carli was on the right track."

"Fuck, yes. Our pedophile's been doing this for more than a decade. And, guess what? I may have a lead on Jason Potter. It looks like he's been living the nomad's life, camping out at one of the state parks. My guys are checking every campsite in the county."

"That's great, Marv!"

"Yeah... I'm feeling good about this. If Jason pans

out, you won't have to worry about the Lacount brothers—
and I mean *all* the brothers. Y'know, you've been discussing
Luke and Frank, but what about that Patrick? I saw you two
at the ASSIST benefit. It sure looked as if you'd been
schmoozing with the guy. You know it's not smart to get
involved with someone who could be a suspect."

Syd hung up admitting Marv was right…but then,
her intuition usually was, too. She sensed Patrick was a
good man. She knew he wasn't responsible for Carli's death,
and there was no evidence linking him to Megan's case or
the other young girls' disappearances.

The stove timer went off, and Syd removed the pizza
from the oven, cut it into slices, and placed two on a plate.
She poured a glass of wine and sat down at the table.

Lloyd's head slid into her lap. It was comforting, but
at times like this, Syd really missed Mama.

She was the one Syd would've gone to for advice.

Chapter 42

Amid the scent and sound of popping kettle corn, Syd helped Jules assemble her photo racks. All the while, Lloyd lounged in the sun. This Saturday art and craft event at Lakeside Park in Jacksonport was normally a big success. But with Megan's disappearance and Carli's potential homicide, locals and tourists alike might stay away.

Syd's iPhone rang. She could see it was Marv.

"Hey, Syd! I finally located the sucker! He was in Peninsula State Park, right under our noses."

A surge of excitement whipped through Syd. "Do you mean Jason Potter?"

"You got it. And by the way, he drives a black sedan. A deputy is delivering him to the Baker Funeral home for a 10 a.m. interview."

"Good work, Marv!" Syd looked at her watch. She'd still have ninety minutes to help Jules. "I'll meet you there."

"Trust me, Syd, I can do this without you. It might be better man-to-man."

Syd knew what he was trying to do. "I told you, I'll be there."

He grumbled, "Well, of course, Sydney knows best."

She hung up as Beth Halverson approached. Syd had noticed her family's fishing and dive charter booth. Even though Beth's blue eyes seemed friendly, Syd got a wary feeling. Beth knew she'd read Carli's journals by now. But with Jules present, that was something Syd couldn't discuss. When Beth reached Syd, she introduced her niece.

Jules began to show Beth her "Line Photos" ranging from parallel rows of summer corn to wavy lines formed in the sand of a local beach. Syd's eyes, however, were focused on one specific photo within the group. It showed a line of bicyclists, dressed in bright, skintight apparel, pedaling by the Big Scoop Ice Cream Parlor—and a parked white van.

The primary-colored stripes and Triangle Shops logo jumped out at her.

Syd gave Jules a questioning look. "When did you take this?"

"Why, last Sunday morning. I was at this park for the sunrise. Then I took that photo, and a few others before I met Mom and Dad for the 8 a.m. Mass at St. Michael's."

Syd's mouth dropped.

Beth seemed just as shocked. "This was taken the morning Carli died?"

"Wow!" Jules said. "I didn't realize that."

Syd managed to nod, considering the implications.

The Triangle Shops van was parked right across from the phone booth where Carli's last incoming call had been made.

* * * *

On Syd's drive to the Baker Funeral Home, she kept thinking about her niece's photo. Jules had told Syd she'd review others she'd taken in that vicinity to see whether she could provide Syd additional insight.

Of course, Syd couldn't assume the driver of the Triangle Shops van had called Carli from that phone booth and subsequently caused her death. But when Syd had talked to each of the Lacounts and Zach, all had denied being anywhere near that particular location on the morning of Carli's death.

Someone was lying.

Then Syd considered the van Bitsy had seen when the "Research" envelope disappeared from Syd's cottage. Could she be lucky enough to discover the driver, or drivers, had logged their names on the Café's sign-out sheet? She decided to text Patrick, the only one she could trust. Syd pulled off the road and onto the shoulder: "See U at 1. Between U and me, did anyone sign out the Triangle Shops' vans yesterday or the AM Carli died?"

Syd was back on the road when she got his response: "Zach did yesterday for Sister Bay. Nobody did last Sunday. Please explain later."

Even though Zach had checked out a van on the day the "Research" envelope disappeared, Brighton had told Syd both vans had been on the move. She was betting the Sunday driver had also driven the second van Brighton saw.

Inside the funeral home, Syd was met by Ralph Baker. He nervously directed her past a casket-display room to reach his nephew's small office. Marv was leaning back against the inner doorframe, taking up nearly half the space.

Jason, who had to be in his forties, was seated at his desk. He politely stood when Syd entered and offered her the remaining chair before they both sat down. With a baby face, a full head of dark hair, and bright pink cheeks, Jason was quite handsome. His long fingers looked as if they were itching to slide onto the comforting domain of his desktop computer's keyboard. Beads of sweat stood out on his forehead, and stains had formed under the arms of his light yellow shirt.

Behind Jason was a shelf where he'd lined up a collection of PEZ candy dispensers: Minnie Mouse, Wonder Woman, Betty Boop... This didn't surprise Syd. Pedophiles often have child-like hobbies and collections targeted toward the gender they prefer.

Marv didn't beat around the bush. "I understand, Jason, that you like little girls."

Jason's face registered shock. "Oh my, no! That was ages ago and just a terrible mistake." Fear had filled his eyes. "I thought you were here to discuss Miss Lacount's missing body."

"We'll get to that," Marv snarled. "Did you snatch Megan Hanson like you tried to do with that other young girl, back in '89?"

Jason looked confused. "I don't know what you're talking about."

"Where were you last Tuesday afternoon between 2 and 4 p.m.?"

Jason thought for a moment. "Why, that's right after Miss Lacount's funeral." Then he scowled. "I was distressed. My uncle had basically accused me of losing her body. Because I didn't feel welcome at the funeral home, I decided to chill out for a few days at my campsite." His cheeks brightened. "Please understand, my living arrangements are temporary."

Marv squinted at Jason. "Y'know, Peninsula State Park's entrance is mighty convenient to St. Paul's Church."

Again, Jason looked perplexed. "What are you getting at?"

"Marv," Syd butted in. "Why don't we back up?" She smiled at Jason, playing the good cop.

He gratefully refocused on her rather than the hulk.

"I understand you were paroled in the spring of 2000. Can you step us through your job history from that point on?"

"Why, certainly."

Jason's recollections were somewhat vague, yet it seemed as if he was trying to be accurate. Overall Syd was disappointed. Even though there were gaps between Jason's various jobs, at first glance, the locations and date combinations didn't seem to match the cases Carli had been researching. And as for the initial July 2000 date, when Leslie disappeared from St. Anne's Camp, it sounded as if he had an excellent alibi. For the whole month of July, Jason claimed he'd been hospitalized for a blood infection he'd picked up in prison.

But Marv was not ready to give up. He squeezed behind the desk and peered at Jason's computer screen. "I understand you have a taste for kiddie porn. I'd love to see it."

Jason glared up at Marv. "You're wrong."

"I see…just another mistake. Are you saying you don't like cute little girls with short dark hair?"

"Definitely not! I've always preferred blondes." Realizing his mistake, Jason quickly stood. "I want you both to go. I don't know any Megan, and, from the video-camera feed, you already know I didn't take Miss Lacount's body."

"I'm not so sure about that," Syd interjected.

Jason's head swiveled back her way.

"I hear you're a whiz on the computer. Did you doctor that footage?"

"Absolutely not!" The pink in his cheeks had spread

to his chin, neck, and even his ears. He rummaged through a knapsack by his desk and pulled out a zip drive. "Here's the original streaming video." He placed it in Syd's palm with relish. "You'll see I'm right."

"Then tell us," Marv demanded. "Where were you last Sunday morning at around 8 a.m., when Carli Lacount died?"

Jason lifted his face toward his adversary and gave him a Cheshire-cat smile. "That's easy. I was at St. Rosalia's for Mass. You can ask any of the mothers who attended with their pretty blonde daughters. Every Sunday, I get the evil eye."

Chapter 43

Syd had always prided herself on Lloyd's obedient behavior. But as he jumped down from the open van door, and she told him to "stay," he gave her his curved-lips smile and dashed.

Syd was shocked.

Then she saw where he was headed.

At the end of the Fish Creek Dock stood Eli. Light reflected off the water and made him glisten—his hair, his eyes, the sheen of light sweat covering his bare chest. Syd had been worried about seeing his dad.

This was far worse.

Over the past week, after two years of separation, Syd had encountered Eli numerous times. Each meeting had stirred her emotions. This, she realized, would be Lloyd's first reunion. With a northerly breeze blowing into the harbor, Syd was sure he'd caught Eli's scent as soon as she'd opened the door.

The two had been devoted to each other. Perhaps Syd had been selfish to separate them—but now was not the time to address that.

"Lloyd!" she yelled and averted her eyes from Eli's.

"Come." When he didn't respond, she called again. When he *still* didn't respond, the boaters along the dock began to focus their eyes on the negligent owner. Among them, about three boats down, was Patrick with his Irish Setter.

Eli was not helping matters. From a distance, Syd could see him rubbing Lloyd's coat from nose to tail using both hands. Eli lifted his head and looked at her, his eyes hesitant. That was when Patrick yelled, "Hey, Syd, do you need some help?"

Eli suddenly understood. *He* was not the reason for their visit. His hurt eyes landed on Patrick, just as they had at the ASSIST Benefit. Eli gave Lloyd one last tummy rub and sent him back her way.

Syd's shoulders sagged. She couldn't understand Eli's reaction. The last time they'd talked, he'd seemed to reject even her request to be friends. And then there was Angela Grafton. Syd could still picture him giving her that kiss.

Lloyd loped toward Syd. In an attempt to hide her distress, she lifted her hand to give Eli a small wave of thanks.

He'd already turned away.

A sick feeling of discontent settled into the pit of Syd's stomach. But, for Patrick's sake, she forced a smile as she and Lloyd approached him. "Nice boat," she said, taking in the sleek lines of what she estimated was a twenty-three-foot Boston Whaler. "But, more importantly, nice dog."

"Yours, too." Patrick smiled, shielding his eyes from the sun. "I'll take credit for Blinker, but not for the boat. I'm lucky Frank lets me use it."

Patrick helped Syd climb into the spotless white launch, then offered her a seat beside him at the central console. This time Lloyd obediently waited. On Syd's command, he cleared the chrome railing and began to sniff Blinker's behind.

Their laughter released the tension. Both dogs seemed to be good-natured, and they settled down on the deck, ready for the excursion. Syd's eyes darted back toward Eli. Thankfully, he was busy talking to another fellow.

Patrick maneuvered Frank's boat out of the harbor and gradually picked up speed. They reached a comfortable 18 to 20 knots per hour and headed northwest toward Chambers Island, about seven and a half miles from Fish Creek. Once Syd could no longer see Eli, she relaxed and popped open two cans of soda.

"What was your text all about?" Patrick asked, accepting the beverage.

"Oh, it was nothing." She shrugged, purposely being vague about the catering vans.

Patrick still seemed curious. Instead of elaborating, however, Syd tipped her face toward the sun and let its warmth release her tension from the past week.

"Okay, then tell me what's up with that guy on the dock."

Her eyes shot open. "I told you before," Syd said evenly, "he's just someone I used to know."

"Well, it looks as if Lloyd knew him pretty good, too?" Patrick lifted his brow.

Syd didn't respond.

He placed his left hand over hers as his right continued to steer. "I can see you don't want to discuss this subject, but at some point, I'm going to get it out of you." He gave Syd a sideways glance.

She didn't remove her hand. Instead, she enjoyed the forgotten sensation and concentrated on Patrick's words. He was talking about some point in the future. Syd stole a glance at his profile against the blue sky. She couldn't compare this man's freckled skin, firm chin, and dimples to Eli anymore. Patrick was his own man.

The thought scared her. She was spending the day with a full-fledged man, and it somehow felt like something she'd never done before.

Syd had grown up with Eli, from kindergarten on, and even though he'd matured into a man, whenever she looked at him, she still saw that fresh-faced boy she'd first come to love.

But the copper-haired guy beside Syd, his thigh now pressed against hers—he was no boy.

* * * *

The sandy beaches and thick forests of Chambers Island came into view. This island had always held a mystique for Syd with its beautiful inland lakes, shipwrecks, and rumors of bootleggers and pirate caves.

Patrick entered the marina adjacent to the dock, still leased to the Catholic Diocese for its retreat house. When Syd's cell vibrated, she turned away from Patrick to read Marv's incoming text: "Potter's alibi 4 Carli's death checked out. Video footage 4 body snatching did 2."

Syd frowned, though this confirmed her assumption. She now hoped her excursion would provide additional insight into the Lacount family. They remained the prime suspects on her list. For the moment, Jason would remain on Marv's. Over the weekend, he'd told Syd, his team would analyze each of the missing girl's cold-case files they'd received from the other states. Their goal was to find a connection to Jason, or to Luke Lacount, or to some other guy, who had yet to appear on the radar.

Patrick tied the Whaler up in a transient slip. The four then headed toward an old Ford the Lacounts kept parked near the dock. Patrick located a magnetized box under its front left fender and removed a key. Once the dogs had scampered into the back seats, Patrick and Syd slid into the front.

They headed down a shaded graveled road toward his parents' summer home, situated on the edge of the 350-acre Mackaysee Lake.

"So," Syd prompted, "tell me about your summers here on the island."

"I have to admit, they were exciting when I was a child." Patrick removed his sunglasses and set them on the dash. "Frank was still around, and, even though he was ten years older, he'd often play with Luke and me. We three would pretend to be pirates, stranded on the island. We'd camp out on the beach and leap from dune to dune."

Syd opened her window to let some fresh air in. "It sounds like lots of fun."

"It was for us, but not for Mother." His hands tightened on the steering wheel. "Dad still worked in Chicago, so he was rarely around. Although he would promise to fly up on weekends, he seldom did. We three boys were Mother's primary companionship."

"Since Frank was older, I bet he was of some help."

"Yeah, in Dad's absence, Frank provided Mother with the emotional support she needed to deal with Luke and me. Frank also became her confidant and sympathizer. Late in the evening, they often played chess and took walks in the garden."

Syd contemplated his words. "I can see how lonely it might've been for your mom, out here, on this sparsely populated island."

He nodded. "But it became far worse when Frank left for seminary. That's when Luke started to act out." Patrick's eyes narrowed. "He got his kicks from vandalizing vacant vacation homes, and he'd purposely pick a fight with anyone who would use 'our beach.' Mother didn't know how to handle him. She'd try to ground him, but he'd just talk back and then disappear for days. He was a good outdoorsman, so it became a game for him. The only punishment that seemed to control him was when Mother would lock him in her dressing room."

Patrick turned to Syd with a look of embarrassment. "I can still remember his muffled screams and curses as he'd kick the door, begging her to let him out. She'd eventually release him, and there'd be a few days of peace. Then the two would go at it again."

Syd frowned, disturbed by Patrick's words. "How did you handle your twin's issues?"

"I did the best I could, but my efforts were doomed. You see, Luke felt I'd betrayed his trust and blamed me for his punishment. Because of that, he ignored me." There was a slight tremor in his cheek. "Dad was never around, and Frank was at seminary. The only person I could turn to was Mother."

"Hey, Patrick." Syd gave him a nudge. "It looks as if you turned out just fine."

"Well, thanks." He gave her a crooked grin and reached for her hand.

Chapter 44

The carved sign for Hemlock House appeared. Patrick made a left turn onto its gravel driveway, and Syd could immediately see why the house had been given its name. Tall hemlocks surrounded them. Through the open window she breathed in the scent of the forested floor of crushed needles, similar to the aroma of their poisonous plant namesake.

Syd was a bit unsettled: Patrick's mother had raised her boys on this estate filled with the scent of poison.

As they broke into the light, Syd sucked in her breath, stunned. For straight ahead, perched on the shore of a magical lake, was a fairytale castle. She wasn't sure what she'd expected. She'd always thought her parents' home was special, but compared to Hemlock House, it was a tarpaper shack. Spread across nearly two city blocks, the mansion was truly spectacular with its tall turrets, pitched gables, thatched roofs, and stunning cupolas.

Once they were inside this wondrous home, Patrick gave Syd a tour. In each room, he highlighted the work Frank and he had completed: the newly plastered walls, the refinished hardwood floors, and the fresh paint that had replaced ancient wallpaper. The spacious kitchen was outdated and missing a stove, yet Patrick's face lit up as he explained their plans to renovate it.

Upstairs were six bedrooms and four baths. For the best view of the lake, Patrick took Syd into the master bedroom suite.

Furtively, she looked for the infamous dressing room.

When Patrick had mentioned it, she'd felt Luke's discipline had verged on child abuse. But, in addition, the room's name still made Syd's hackles rise. It conjured up the sterile hospital room in which she'd suffered anxiety and pain whenever her burn dressings had routinely been soaked off and changed.

Patrick's mother's dressing room was a windowless space, Syd noted, about the size of a solitary-confinement cell. There were built-in drawers and cabinet panels decorated with raised moldings and ornate handles. On the inside of the entrance door, Syd could see potential kick marks. Picturing a young Luke in action gave her the chills.

She considered whether this secluded room had planted the seed for his current behavior.

They walked down a back staircase with their dogs in the lead and entered what Patrick called the solarium. Its domed ceiling was painted with frolicking cherubs and supported by two stories' worth of windowed walls. This was the only room that appeared to have been completely refurbished with high-end wicker furniture in muted stripe patterns. There was even a baby grand piano off to one side with a number of photos displayed on top.

"I'd love to see those." Syd headed that way, and Patrick followed. There was a cute shot of the three boys dressed as pirates with eye patches. Another one showed the beaming trio as they held up their catch of the day. Off to the side was a wedding photo, old but in color. The groom's carrot-colored hair stood out.

"Those were my parents, Rose and Peter Lacount."

Syd looked at Patrick's mother and took a deep breath. Her physical characteristics were so familiar: the petite frame, the short bob of brown hair, the big, dark eyes...

Patrick noticed Syd's reaction. "What's wrong?"

"Don't you think your mother, at that age, looks like your late niece?" Syd tried to catch Patrick's eyes, but they were analyzing the photo.

"I notice some resemblance." His voice was cautious. "But, couldn't you say that about anyone who has Carli's stature and coloring?"

"I guess you're right," Syd admitted—but the likeness still bothered her. She picked up a framed photo of Rose with her three sons. She sat in a chair, within this same room. "I assume that's Frank?" Syd pointed to the eldest boy, a teenager whose hand rested on his mother's shoulder, close to her breast.

Patrick nodded. "And Luke's the one trying to wiggle out of her lap." He then pointed to the last child, off to her left, whose small hand tugged on the fabric of her skirt. "That would be me."

"Earlier this week, you said your mother died in the summer of 2000?"

"Yes. In early June. She'd had her first stroke a few months prior, so her second wasn't totally unexpected. Like my brothers, I was able to get to the island and spend a few days with Mother before she passed." He snagged his bottom lip with his teeth and looked out toward the gardens.

Syd placed her hand over his.

The corners of Patrick's mouth lifted slightly. "Let's

get some air." He called out, "Blinker!" and both dogs lifted their heads from the tiled floor. "I'll show you the rest of the grounds." Patrick opened a French door that led outside, then took Syd's hand.

Accompanied by their inquisitive dogs, they strolled along a brick path. Weathered statues of Greek gods and goddesses stood guard by an ornate fountain that no longer operated. As they chatted, Syd continued to think about his mother. She seemed to have put her mark on her sons. For Luke, it had been her abusive punishment. For Frank, it had been their strange adult relationship. And for Patrick, it had been her companionship and comfort when his twin had ostracized him. Syd didn't know what it all meant.

Underneath a grove of hardwood trees, they paused at the Lacounts' private cemetery. One of the large granite tombstones was Rose Lacount's. She'd died on June 6, 2000, at the age of seventy-six.

They continued their hike along graveled paths that meandered through the Hemlocks. They passed a gazebo, a tool shed, and what appeared to be an old garage. Lloyd strayed from the path and nosed around its foundation, badly in need of repair.

"Maybe you should call him back, Syd. There's poison ivy in this area."

She thought about Frank. Maybe this was where he'd come in contact with the three-leaved devil.

They circled back and arrived at a limestone beachfront boathouse. Transom windows, located about twelve feet up the back wall, brought in natural light. The boathouse also had a stairway that led to the top flat platform, surrounded by an alabaster railing.

"We often ate meals up there," Patrick said, "because of the great view."

"Can we go see?"

He hesitated. "Well…why not? But, again, watch out for the poison ivy." He pointed to a nearby patch.

Along with their dogs, they climbed the stairs, and Syd looked out across Mackaysee Lake. Both Lloyd and Blinker raced around, acting quite hyper—understandable, with the water right in view.

They returned to the beach and released them. Both dogs charged into the lake. "Did you bring a swimsuit?" Patrick's eyes caught Syd's. "We could join them."

"I didn't think to bring one," she lied. Other than scuba diving, with a wetsuit that covered her arms, Syd hadn't gone swimming for almost two years.

They tossed sticks into the water for their dogs to fetch, and Syd's eyes followed the shoreline. About a half mile away, she could see children running across the sand. Their excited voices carried over the lake: "Olly, Olly, Oxen, Free!"

Syd couldn't help but envy them. They seemed to be playing hide and seek, just as she had as a child.

It had been so easy then—so carefree.

Again: "Olly, Olly, Oxen, Freeeeee!"

With those words, Syd knew anyone in hiding could come out—without suffering, without penalty.

Chapter 45

Just before dusk, Syd and Patrick headed back toward the Lacount mansion.

"I'm famished," he said. "How about you?" Then he suddenly leaned in for a kiss.

Even though his warm lips felt far different from Eli's, the sensation was good. Syd pulled away, feeling giddy, and grabbed his hand. "Are you going to cook for me?"

"You saw the sad state of the kitchen, didn't you?"

"Yeah." She gave him a questioning look.

"Well, instead, I've planned a dinner over our campfire grill."

His words made the hair on the back of Syd's neck stand up, and she jerked away.

"What's wrong, Syd?" He put his arm around her and pulled her body close. "Is it because of what happened to you?"

She was shocked. "You know?"

"I don't know the details, but Frank told me your arms were burned."

Syd had never considered Patrick might know. But now that he did, she felt immeasurable relief.

"I'm sorry, Syd. I should've been more considerate. Let's go back to Fish Creek and get something to eat."

"No." She shook her head. "It's about time for me to face my fear."

From the house, Patrick brought out a skillet of fresh perch filets he'd caught during the week. All the while, Syd tried to keep her anxiety in check.

He first prepped the logs, under the grate, with crumpled newspaper. Then, before lighting a match, he turned back to Syd. "Are you sure this is okay?"

She took a deep breath, then nodded.

As the pit burst into flames, she shuddered. Syd wasn't sure whether she'd ever feel comfortable in this environment. But she'd taken the first step.

She looked over at the man who was helping her deal with her fear and felt a rush of affection for him.

* * * *

As they docked in Fish Creek, Patrick placed his hand over Syd's. "How about grabbing a nightcap at my place?"

"Oh, Patrick, I don't know." Even though she'd figured he might ask, she still was not prepared.

"Come on, Syd. Just one glass of wine."

Against her better judgment, she agreed. Because the night was cool, and Lloyd still had a mild skunk odor, Syd decided to leave him in the van with fresh water and dog chow.

She followed Patrick up the steep flight of stairs to his flat, located above a Fish Creek retail shop. Once inside, Patrick opened a bottle of white wine and poured two glasses.

Syd gravitated toward a framed photo of a woman, displayed on a bookcase. "Was this your wife?"

"Yes, that's Rachel."

Syd turned back toward Patrick. His eyes held a deep sense of loss.

She figured the picture had been taken prior to his wife's chemotherapy, since her blonde hair was still full and long. Her face looked kind and sweet. *How sad*, Syd thought. *She died so young.*

Patrick led the way out to the deck that faced the harbor and handed Syd her wine. The moon was nearly full and provided ample light by which to see. On a wooden bench, they sat side by side, his shoulder inches from hers. Syd swirled her glass and took a sip before placing it beside her. She then leaned back, with closed eyes, and listened to the waves lap against the shore. She was edgy, thinking about what might come next.

"You know, Syd, you're the first woman I've taken an interest in since Rachel died."

She opened her eyes.

Patrick set down his glass and dipped his head to meet hers.

Syd responded, swaying in closer, and felt his warm lips, the urgency of his tongue, the cool breeze in her hair.

Patrick slid his hands into her curls and snapped open the clip. His lips moved across her cheek, around her ear, and down toward her neck. Syd could feel his hands investigating from the other direction, attempting to remove her gauzy blouse.

"I can't," she whimpered and pulled back.

His eyes found hers, his voice husky: "Why not?"

"Because…because I've been burned."

Patrick's eyes didn't waver. "Syd, I know your

physical appearance is probably important to you. It was for Rachel when she dealt with her mastectomies and hair loss. But none of that made me love her less. You must realize that, too, because of your own mom."

The truth of Patrick's words hit Syd. Yet she still hesitated, looking into his eyes…wishing they were Eli's.

"Syd, how can I help?"

"I don't know." Her chin sank to her chest. "I believe what you're saying. And I wish I could feel beautiful. But I can't. My scars are so ugly."

"Well, so are mine."

She lifted her head. "What do you mean?"

"I had my appendix taken out here." He pointed to his lower abdomen, a teasing look in his eye. "And then, a hernia repaired on this side." He placed his hand to the left of his groin.

Syd gave him a small smile.

Encouraged, he returned it. "If I show you my scars…" He positioned his hand by the fly of his jeans. "Will you show me yours?"

She couldn't help but laugh and slapped his hand away.

Still petrified, she took a deep breath and let Patrick pull her blouse over her head. Rather than horror, though, she saw only passion in his eyes.

"My God, Syd." He shook his head. "You think you're not beautiful, but you're so wrong! You glow in the moonlight." He began to massage her bare shoulders, his eyes watching hers. His hands slid down across her lace-covered breasts, his fingers pausing at the front clasp. "I understand, Syd, if you're not ready."

She placed her hands over his. "I don't know. I haven't done anything like this in two years."

"Well, it's nearly the same for me. Maybe it's time we both did." His lips touched hers in a long, slow kiss. Syd could smell the lingering scent of wood smoke in his hair. When they broke apart to breathe again she hesitated and, with trembling fingers, released the clasp herself.

Syd closed her eyes and felt his light touch against her nipples. She moaned as they responded. He continued to gently rub one as his other hand moved to her right palm. Then, light as a feather, his fingers journeyed up the uneven striations of that arm, giving her goosebumps. Syd opened her eyes, enjoying the multiple sensations. He continued along her right shoulder blade and paused for a moment to caress her neck, then traveled down her left, damaged arm until he reached that palm. With both hands, he brought it to his lips.

Syd's breath caught in her throat. "I don't repulse you, do I?"

"Of course not. To me your scars symbolize the pain you must have endured. Your pain…and your perseverance."

"That's what my Grandmother Bitsy tells me." Tears filled her eyes. Then suddenly self-conscious, Syd wrapped her arms around her naked upper torso.

Sensing her discomfort, Patrick reached for Syd's blouse and helped her back into it. He stood and grasped her shoulders, willing her eyes to look up at his. "Syd, believe me, it's not that I don't want you. I definitely do. But I know you took a big step tonight. I'm willing to take this slowly."

Syd was so grateful that Patrick understood.

He handed Syd her wine, then picked up his own and settled back down beside her. His free arm slid around her shoulders.

As they talked about their lives, both present and past, Syd tried to focus on Patrick's face and words.

But it was difficult.

Her eyes kept straying to the Fish Creek Dock's distant lights. Syd wondered whether Eli was out there. It was impossible, she knew, simply impossible to separate her past from that of her first and only love—Eli.

Her Eli.

Chapter 46

Syd woke in the near light, still dressed in her clothes. For a moment she was disoriented. But then she remembered. She and Patrick had polished off two bottles of wine, and, of course, she'd been in no shape to drive. She smiled to herself. He'd been quite the gentleman insisting she take the bed.

She tiptoed into the living room past Blinker. The couch on which Patrick had slept was empty, but that made perfect sense. He'd already be at the Café for his busy Sunday morning.

She headed down the stairs in her wrinkled attire. Her mouth felt disgusting, her hair was a rat's nest, and she needed a shower. She thought about Patrick's kind, freckled face. Was she moving too fast? Before she'd slipped back into her blouse the previous evening, she'd felt a real physical attraction. But could she take the next step when she still wished he was someone else?

Syd didn't know.

But she did know, thanks to Patrick, something had changed. She felt lighter as if she'd discarded the protective armor she'd been wearing for two years.

Outside, a cool breeze blew off the harbor, and Syd shivered. On the main drag of Fish Creek, a few shop owners stood outside, watering plants, changing sale signs, and chatting. Syd imagined much of that chat was about Carli and Megan. One had worked in the community, and the other had been abducted from it—nearly four and a half days ago.

The previous evening, before Syd had crashed, Patrick had accompanied her downstairs to check on Lloyd. She now clicked her van's keyless entry, called his name, and heard not Lloyd's bark but a familiar human voice calling hers.

Syd turned to see Eli, and her heart dropped into her belly. His hair looked damp from a shower, and his eyes were clear and bright—quite a contrast to hers.

There was concern in his voice as he reached her: "Are you okay?"

Syd felt the color rise in her cheeks. "Why wouldn't I be?"

"I picked my dad up from the Bayside last night, and when I heard a dog's constant barking, I traced the sound to your van."

Her muscles tensed. Lloyd probably had caught a whiff of Eli again. Now, in addition to appearing as if she'd just climbed out of bed with another man, Eli had to think she was a negligent dog owner—as she'd previously accused him of being.

"Okay, Eli. I get it. So, are you spying on me?"

"Of course not." He gave her an exasperated look. "I'm headed back to my dad's to make sure he shows up for work. On the way, I decided to check on Lloyd—in case something *did* happen to you."

"Well, you can see I'm just fine."

His lips tightened with disappointment. "So, the guy didn't even walk you to your van?"

Syd glared at him. "It's not what you think." She didn't know why she was defending herself.

"I know you're a big girl, Sydney, and you can do whatever you want. But what's all this bullshit about being just friends? After your speech on the dock—which, by the way, I appreciated—you dashed off while I was helping my dad, so I couldn't even tell you. Then I thought I'd have a chance when I saw you yesterday—till I realized you were with that guy from the Café."

His eyes looked hurt. "I can't believe you'd start up with someone you know so little about before giving the guy you've spent nearly your entire life with another chance."

"How can you say that?" Syd threw back. "I saw Angela Grafton run her hands through your hair before you two kissed. That didn't look like any brother-sister act."

"You're wrong!" He shook his head. "Why didn't you ask rather than assume? The two of us called it quits months ago." He stared at Syd, and his tone turned bitter: "So how *was* that guy from the Café? Was he better in bed than me?"

His words ignited her. "Wouldn't you like to know?" She stomped over to her van, climbed in, and started it. Then she put it into reverse, backed up, and steamed past him.

What a mess! Syd pounded the steering wheel. Eli had accepted her apology, but now he thought she'd slept with Patrick. And she'd thought Eli had been sleeping with Angela.

They'd both got it all wrong.

Chapter 47

Syd arrived at the paved public boat ramp on White Fish Bay at 1 p.m., a swimsuit under her clothes. She and Gina had been planning their dive to the Ocean Wave scow schooner for months.

As Syd waited, she thought about the Sunday family breakfast she'd managed to get through. While lying through her teeth to Bitsy and Daddy about where she'd been the previous night, Syd's mind had continued to playback her disastrous encounter with Eli—just like it was now.

Syd tried to refocus on pleasurable thoughts: the cloudless sky, the fantastic, luminescent blue-green lake, and the unseasonably warm temperature—all perfect conditions for the afternoon's dive.

But it was difficult.

She removed a water bottle from her cooler, and her iPhone rang. Assuming it was Gina, Syd was surprised to see the caller was Jules.

"Hey, Auntie, I'm over at the Peninsula School of Art, and I found another photo from last Sunday that might help you."

"That's great!" Syd swatted away a deer fly.

"In this one, I can read the van's license plate reflected off a store shop window. It's TSCAFE3."

Syd's head jerked back. "But I—I thought there were only two catering vans."

"Zach's with me. I'll go ask him."

Before Syd could say "Wait," Jules muffled her cell. A moment later, she came back on. "Zach believes the third van's been in for service since before Carli died—possibly at Reuben's Garage."

Syd kicked herself. That particular phone number had been listed in Carli's cell records.

* * * *

Gina pulled up, all alone, her uncle's boat in tow. She gave Syd a shrug, knowing she was ten minutes late. For once, Syd didn't mind. It had given her time to call Reuben's Garage, where she'd left the owner a message to contact her as soon as they opened Monday morning.

"Where's Myrna?" Syd asked.

"She was called into work, but said she'd be here in spirit. She insisted we call her when we enter and exit the water."

Syd frowned. On their last dive, Myrna had stayed topside to tend their boat. That was the same job she'd volunteered for on this dive.

"I guess we can scrap the whole adventure," Gina said, but her pleading eyes said just the opposite.

Syd knew Gina had been looking forward to this dive, and so had she. Against her better judgment, Syd agreed to proceed and elicited a broad smile from Gina.

Back in 1869, the *Ocean Wave* was en route to White Lake, Michigan to deliver twenty-three cords of stone for a harbor-improvement project. The scow apparently hit a piece of floating timber that created a major leak. The crew and captain survived, abandoning ship before the schooner sank. Now, the *Ocean Wave* was located nearly four miles off shore, in approximately 110 feet of water. That was about as deep as recreational divers, like Syd and Gina, should go.

As they motored toward the schooner's coordinates, using the boat's GPS, Syd turned around to admire the peninsula's scenery. That's when she noticed a white van pull in beside their parked vehicles.

A bad feeling came over Syd. Could its driver be keeping tabs on her?

"Okay," Gina said as they bounced over another watercraft's wake, "I know you've got work issues on your mind, but what's the scoop on your so called 'date' with Mr. Patrick Lacount?"

Syd turned back, laughing, ready to share selected details—though not her latest confrontation with Eli.

It was just too painful.

* * * *

As they neared the *Ocean Wave's* dive buoy, Gina stopped the engine. Syd reached out to grab on, and Gina tossed her the rope.

"Nuh-uh." Syd shook her head. "I'd feel better if you tied your uncle's boat up rather than me."

"All right." Gina laughed. "Then you raise the dive flag."

Syd nodded. When they were either in the water or planning to be there soon, the flag signaled their presence to other boaters.

After they finished their designated duties, it was time to gear up. They first assembled the tanks, regulators, and air hoses, then attached them to their jacket-style buoyancy control devices (BCD).

Gina stripped down to a bikini and exposed her familiar tattoos: the monarch butterfly on her right shoulder blade and the sprinkling of yellow stars near her belly button. She grinned. "Notice the new addition?"

Syd laughed. "How could I miss it?" A spiral of roses circled her left forearm. "MYRNA" was inscribed below it.

Syd admired Gina's tattoo, then took a deep breath. "Maybe I'll beat your artwork for once."

Gina reeled back, astonished. "You got a tat?"

"Not exactly." Normally, Syd would've made Gina turn her back, but instead, Syd took another deep breath and pulled off her t-shirt to reveal her damaged arms.

Gina appeared shocked—not from the sight, but from Syd's unveiling. "It looks as if that Patrick did some job on you!" She grinned. "I hate to agree, but your full-arm tats do outshine mine."

Tears filled Syd's eyes as she gave her best friend a hug.

With that major reveal accomplished and Syd's emotions back in check, she finished undressing. After the two of them tugged on their wetsuits and dive boots, Gina picked up her cell and called Myrna.

"Yes, hon', I promise to check in as soon as we resurface." Based on their dive depth, the water temperature, and the amount of air in their tanks, Gina had calculated they'd be able to stay under water for a maximum of sixteen minutes.

Myrna's voice was so loud, Syd could even hear her

response: "I'm serious, Gina. You *must* call me within a half-hour—or *I'll* be calling 911!"

Gina rolled her eyes. "Aye-aye, Captain!"

They finally secured their weight belts, slipped into their equipped BCDs, inflating them slightly, put on their masks, letting their snorkels dangle off to the side, and strapped on their fins.

"Ready?" Gina asked.

"Ready."

They placed their regulators in their mouths and back rolled off the side of the boat to enter the lake.

As Gina and Syd descended, they followed the dive buoy rope down and breathed steadily through their mouths. In the crystal-clear water, they could see an abundance of fish—everything from bait-sized minnows to 20-inch walleyes...

Eventually, they reached the scow.

It was amazing! The deckhouse was exposed, so they could swim inside, and the jib boom and bowsprit were still standing. On the latter, a bird-like creature with red eyes and extended tongue was crudely carved.

Attached to Gina's wrist was her underwater camera. As she posed Syd near the bowsprit, Syd heard the muffled sound of a motor and looked up.

Another boat had joined theirs.

Syd assumed the curious boater didn't understand the meaning behind the dive flag. When the boat took off, Syd felt much better and shoved her concerns aside.

They reached their time limit. Then, utilizing the buoy rope, the women began to ascend. But not too quickly, otherwise their bodies would fail to rid themselves of the nitrogen that had settled into their tissues and bloodstream.

When they were about forty feet from the surface,

Syd looked up. *My God!* she thought. *Where's our boat?* Its hull wasn't visible in any direction. She was certain Gina had tied it up securely, so the rope had to have been frayed in a spot and snapped.

But then...Syd remembered the interested boater. Maybe its propeller accidentally severed their tie-up line. Or, far worse, the boater could've intentionally cut it.

As Syd's stomach churned, she pointed up and exchanged a concerned look with Gina. Even though she, like Syd, probably had the urge to speed toward the surface, they both knew that would've been foolhardy. Instead, they forced themselves to maintain the same slow and steady ascent pace. In addition, at about fifteen feet from the surface, they paused for their three minute safety stop to slowly eliminate any excess nitrogen from their bodies.

Finally, their heads broke the surface.

"What the hell?" Gina sputtered as their eyes located the runaway boat.

"My God, Gina—it has to be more than two football fields away!"

The wind had come up, and the waves were choppy. Even if they were Olympic gold medalists, Syd knew neither of them could swim fast enough to recover the boat.

To say she was worried was an understatement.

"Let's not panic," Gina said as they inflated their BCD's. "I'm sure it won't be long before Myrna starts to worry and follows through on her threat to call 911."

"You're right." Syd gulped down a mouthful of water. "Thank God for Myrna!"

* * * *

It was near dusk when a Coast Guard cutter approached, towing the two women's launch and calling out their names from its loudspeaker.

Next to the dive-site buoy, Gina and Syd repeatedly shouted, "Over here!"

Since they often used the Coast Guard's professional services, they both knew Captain Phil Singer, who pulled up beside them.

Syd beamed. "Am I glad to see you!"

"Singer, I could hug you," Gina added as both women giggled with relief. They were lucky to have been wearing wetsuits. Other than being extremely fatigued, they had no physical issues.

Singer shook his head at them. "You two should've known better."

They could've made excuses, but, politically, it was better to say, "We're sorry" and accept their deserved reprimand.

Syd gingerly followed Gina up the dive ladder of her uncle's boat, then the two snuggled into dry towels and collapsed inside. As they waved their thanks to Singer and his crew, Gina grinned and broke out two beers from her cooler. "What an adventure!"

Even as Syd clinked her beverage to Gina's, Syd continued to worry. They'd verified a portion of their tie up rope had still been attached to the dive buoy. But it had been hard to determine whether it had been a fray snap or a clean cut. Nevertheless, Syd thought about the boat that had cozied up to theirs.

Had its owner intentionally set their launch adrift?

If the answer was "yes," then how had that boater located them?

A shiver ran through Syd as she remembered the white van.

Chapter 48

The temperature had dropped, and it was starting to drizzle, yet Syd kept her van windows down on her drive home from the boat launch. She liked the scent the rain made as it hit the dusty, winding road. Beyond that, the fresh air helped combat the lulling sound of the windshield wipers. Exhausted, she was finding it difficult to keep her eyes open—especially since the two-way radio air traffic was unusually silent.

Syd's iPhone rang, startling her. It was Bitsy. "How was today's dive, honey?" she asked.

"Very interesting..." Syd told her about their misadventure, but downplayed the tenuous hours they'd spent in the water.

"Daddy and I are just leaving for dinner at Bobby's, but there's a surprise for you on our porch."

"What kind of surprise?"

"You'll see!" Bitsy's voice bubbled over like an excited child's anxious to show off a new bike.

Syd hung up dreading any additional excitement after her previous night's emotional reveal, that morning's run-in with Eli, and, the icing on the cake, flipping her flippers for more than three hours. Syd was done in. Ever since she'd helped Gina secure her uncle's boat to its trailer, Syd had been fantasizing about a hot shower, a bowl of steaming soup right out of the can, and collapsing into bed.

But those thoughts faded as bright headlights appeared in her rear-view mirror. The vehicle behind Syd was approaching fast and not using its dims. She squinted into the blinding light and tilted her mirror into the night driving position.

"Damn!" A chill ran up her spine. The vehicle on her tail was a white van.

Syd attempted to see the driver or license plate—to no avail. To encourage it to pass, she slowed down, but the van sped up.

Then, unbelievably, she was jolted by a shocking impact. The extreme force snapped her neck forward, then back, and her iPhone catapulted onto the passenger-side floor.

"My God!" Syd breathed out. The vehicle had actually rammed her van.

Syd gripped the steering wheel with her left hand and reached for the two-way radio transmitter to place an officer-in-trouble call.

Her gut constricted. The cord had been cut—apparently the reason for the radio silence.

Syd now knew the driver behind her was not fooling around. This was a planned attack.

She floored the gas pedal. *Damn it*, she thought, fuming. *I'm fighting back!*

In her job, she usually was the chaser, not the chase. As her speedometer hit 75, Syd knew she should be focused on the slick and narrow road. But, instead, her eyes kept checking the rearview mirror.

A sickening wave welled up in her throat. Even at

this reckless, white-knuckle speed, she was not outdistancing the vehicle behind her.

Up ahead was the final curve. Syd squealed around it. *At last!* She breathed a sigh of relief—the Bernhardt Chalet was within a stone's throw.

But that thought was dashed from her head as she was struck again—hard.

Syd's heart plunged, and she gasped for air.

Her tires caught loose gravel on the shoulder and began to spin and spin...out of control.

"My God!" Syd panicked as she headed for the drainage ditch, its precarious angle making her tilt.

For a fraction of a second, Syd believed she could right her van.

She was mistaken.

As if in slow motion, it rolled over and over, her forehead slamming against the steering wheel...

* * * *

"That's my girl..."

The soothing voice entered Syd's dream and sparked a memory of belonging to someone.

Lips brushed her forehead.

She tipped up her own lips to find them—and discovered her tongue had a memory, too.

Syd opened her eyes. Shocked and disoriented, she pulled away.

Eli was just as stunned. He was sitting on the edge of the road with Syd in his arms, Lloyd hovering beside them. The flashers and headlights of Eli's car were both turned on. Sweat shone on his temple, and his face looked gaunt. "My God, Syd! Are you all right?"

She touched her wet cheek. "I think I'm bleeding."

He gave a relieved laugh. "It's just Lloyd's slobber. You have a goose egg on your forehead, but your air bags and seat belt probably saved you. I've already called 911."

"You shouldn't have." Syd used his body for support and attempted to stand. "I'm just fine." But her head felt light, and she fell back into his arms.

"I don't get it." She squinted up at him. "Why are you here?"

"Bitsy told you she had a surprise." He brushed the hair from Syd's eyes. "I guess...that would be me." He gave her a cautious smile. "I felt terrible about this morning's exchange and stopped by to apologize." His mouth twisted. "I guess we're both getting good at it."

"You've got that right!"

He laughed. "After your family left, Lloyd and I stayed to wait for you. But then his ears perked up, and he streaked down the driveway. I followed him in my car—and found you."

"Of course you heard my van, didn't you, boy?" Syd wrapped her arms around Lloyd, and his wet nose nuzzled her ear.

"What happened here, Syd?"

She told him about the crazy white vehicle. "I have to alert the department to check out the two vans at the Triangle Shops and also a third one that's potentially at Reuben's Garage."

"Reuben's? Isn't that owned by Reuben Jacoby?"

Syd nodded.

"I'm pretty sure he's related to Carli's friend, Beth Halverson. Maybe an uncle on her mom's side."

"Really?" Syd considered the implications. "We need to drive there right away."

"You need medical attention first."

"I said I'm okay." Syd glared up at Eli. "Are you going to help me, or not?"

"You're beautiful when you're defiant." He ruffled her hair. "Head lump and all. It looks as if your feistiness is back." His eyes found hers. "It's one of the qualities I love best about you. I...I realize I was way out of line this morning." He gave her his infectious grin. "Come on. How about it? Truce?"

"Okay," Syd huffed. "Truce—but only because I need your help."

A medivan arrived, so Eli got his way. Syd had a slight concussion, but that was it.

Before she and Eli started north toward Baileys Harbor, he managed to find her iPhone. It had flown out of the van, but, amazingly, still worked. Syd called Dispatch and provided details about her hit and run, then asked them to tow her vehicle into the evidence garage. A squad car was also being sent to the Triangle Shops & Café to check for damage to their vans.

Eli helped Syd into his car. As he chauffeured her north toward Reuben's Garage, her eyes kept sneaking a peek—not quite believing that Eli was beside her, and Lloyd was in the rear.

Just as it used to be.

* * * *

Eli and Syd turned into the front lot of Reuben's Garage and drove around to the back. Luckily, that lot was lit. There were about a dozen parked vehicles, but Syd's eyes were drawn to the only white van. And sure enough—TSCAFE3 was on its plate.

Eli pulled up behind it, and the two of them jumped out. They sprinted around to the van's front end where Eli placed his hands on the hood. "The engine's still warm, Syd!"

It was too dark to see, so she used her hands to feel the front bumper and discovered some major dents. "This has to be it!"

Eli pointed to the lock inside the passenger window. "The van's open."

"Why don't you enter from that side so we don't destroy the driver's prints?"

Eli nodded, then climbed in and leaned over the console. "Syd…" His voice was muffled. "The van keys are under the floor mat." He crawled back out and checked the adjacent vehicle. "This car's unlocked, too, and the keys are under its mat."

Syd checked the car next to her. It was the same. "Shit!" Her eyes caught his. "Anyone could've driven this van."

"But at least you have probable cause to tow it into the department's garage."

She nodded. "Hopefully, there'll be some evidence to link it to the driver who was out to hurt me and—more importantly—tie it to Carli's death."

Syd's cell rang. She listened to Deputy Borat's report and frowned as she hung up.

"What's wrong?" Eli asked.

"The two other Triangle Shops catering vans are parked behind the Café. And there's no visible damage to either vehicle."

Eli looked perplexed. "Shouldn't you be happy that *this* van is probably the one you're looking for?"

"Yeah. But all three Lacount brothers are working

tonight. And, according to a number of patrons, they've been there all evening."

Syd shook her head. "It's like I'm back to square one."

Chapter 49

Monday morning Syd awakened to the sound of the wind rattling the wood-shingled siding of her cottage. It was now eight days since Carli's death and five and a half since Megan disappeared.

Famished and still dressed in the sweatshirt she'd pulled on after her dive, Syd couldn't remember how she'd ended up in bed. She did recall having heard Eli's voice periodically wake her to make sure she was okay, per the medics' instructions. Syd had expected to count on Bitsy for that. It was just like Eli to have spared her the worry.

Bitsy had to have been thrilled to see his vehicle parked outside her cottage when she and Daddy got home. Syd would have to set her straight.

Or would she?

She still had no idea.

Syd took a hot shower to relieve the aches from the previous night's accident. A slow run, she knew, could also help work out the kinks. Syd toweled off and debated whether to leave her arms uncovered, but a cold front had apparently moved in since the outside thermometer read only 52 degrees. A long-sleeved zip-up top and Capri running pants was the appropriate attire.

Her stomach grumbled. That can of chicken noodle soup was still calling her name. She also had toast with peanut butter, a cup of coffee, and a big glass of milk. She was lucky—a full stomach never hindered her run.

Lloyd had been pacing, still attuned to her previous night's danger. As the two of them headed for the door, her iPhone rang.

It was Stan, one of the techs from the department. "I have some results from that white van, Syd. Inside, we found a number of human hairs in a variety of lengths and shades: red, gray, dark brown, and blond. Some were from the deceased, Carli Lacount."

Syd considered the van's possible drivers: the Lacount brothers, Alice, and Zach. "What about fingerprints?"

"There were a number throughout the vehicle. But the most interesting print was the one I discovered on the driver's inside door handle. A portion of the unidentified print was captured within a spot of blood that belonged to Carli Lacount."

A spurt of adrenalin shot through Syd. "You're saying the print was not Carli's?"

"Correct."

Syd was psyched! The most likely scenario was that Carli's killer had Carli's blood on his or her hand. The print's owner could also be responsible for Syd's hit and run. As she let this all sink in, Lloyd settled down on the floor. "Stan, you said the hair evidence was in various lengths, right?"

"Yeah. The most notable were the strands of blond hair from two different sources. One length was quite short, and the other was more than a foot long."

Syd's lips tightened. She wondered whether the long hair could be Beth Halverson's. The van *had* been parked at her uncle's garage.

But why would Beth have been inside the Lacounts' catering vehicle?

Syd told Stan about the metal lockbox in her office. "See if you can lift some prints from it that might match the bloody one you found."

She knew that could take some time, so she roused Lloyd and they started off on their run, her iPhone on her hip.

* * * *

As the beach path veered back into the wooded trail, Syd continued to jog toward Cave Point. The sound of the wave action grew louder and louder. She'd decided to take a chance and had followed the same course she'd run the morning she'd discovered Carli's body.

Moments later, she could see the limestone ledge jutting out high above the lake. But this time, someone was sitting along that dangerous edge.

Syd stopped dead in her tracks, surprising Lloyd.

She squinted at what appeared to be a woman, dressed in jeans and a form-fitting Norwegian sweater. A blonde ponytail was pulled back through the strap of a pink Packers cap.

Could that be Beth Halverson? Syd wondered.

She and Lloyd moved closer.

Then closer still.

It *was* Beth! A drum of panic beat at Syd's throat. Just then her iPhone vibrated. Thankfully, she'd put it on mute.

Syd pulled Lloyd off into the woods to take Stan's call. "What do you have?" she whispered into the phone, her eyes fixed on Beth through the branches.

"You know that print on the door handle?" His voice was excited.

"Yeah?"

"It's a match to a number of those on the lockbox."

Syd's pulse had already been speeding. Now it was going through the roof.

Was she looking at Carli's murderer?

Was Beth the one who had chased her van and set Gina and her adrift?

And if so, then how did Beth tie into the other missing girls?

Syd didn't know. But she told Stan: "Send some squads to Cave Point, ASAP!"

Chapter 50

Lloyd and Syd resumed their cautious approach, her muscles tense, her heart pounding like a hammer. Thankfully, Beth still seemed unaware of their presence as she swung her legs forward and back, in rhythm to the waves.

All Syd kept thinking was: *What if she's armed?*
What if she hears us and turns?
What if...

Syd shook her head. Without protection, she knew she should wait—but she just couldn't. She had to take this chance to talk to Beth one-on-one, like they'd done on Beth's deck just a few days before.

Finally, Syd took a deep breath and called out, "Beth?"

She turned, her eyes vacant. Syd watched for any hand movement toward a weapon. When Beth's arms remained limp, intense relief swelled through Syd.

But she was still on guard.

"Are you okay?" Syd asked as she and Lloyd reached her.

Beth released a horrendous sigh, and tears filled her eyes. "How can I be? Carli's dead."

Lloyd sensed her distress and angled over to Beth's left side.

"Down," Syd commanded, and he obeyed.

Averting her eyes from the precarious drop, Syd carefully seated herself on the ledge to Beth's right. Syd scanned Beth's body and finally relaxed. In her snug-fitting clothes, there was no way she could be hiding a weapon.

With that danger out of the way, Syd slipped her arm around Beth's heaving shoulders to console her. "You know I've been trying to solve Carli's death for more than a week?"

Beth nodded as tears ran down her cheeks.

"My current assumption is that one person is responsible for both Carli's death and Megan Hanson's abduction. But maybe that isn't so. Is there anything you could help me with, here?" Syd felt Beth tense up.

"Have I been barking up the wrong tree?" Syd squeezed Beth's shoulder. "Carli's dead. I wish we could change that, but we can't. However, Megan could still be alive. Is there something—anything—you could tell me, to help us locate that little girl?"

Beth opened her mouth, as if to say something, then shut it again.

"Beth... Please..."

She bit her lip. Then, just barely, she nodded. "They—they aren't one and the same."

"What do you mean?"

"I'm..." She let out a whimper. "I'm the one who hurt Carli."

Syd's heart accelerated again. "Tell me, Beth... Please tell me what happened."

She leaned into Syd and released an anguished sigh. "It's so hard."

"I know. But you'll feel so much better if you get this off your chest."

Beth started to sob in earnest.

"Did you talk to Carli on the Friday before her death?"

"No," she choked out. "I wanted to, but she didn't answer her cell."

Lloyd placed his head in her lap.

Syd could see this was a comfort as Beth slipped her fingers into his silky coat.

"I wanted to talk to Carli about her decision to move out, so I drove up to the Café. But Frank told me she'd taken the afternoon off. He also told me, to tell her, he'd checked the schedule for the weekend she'd requested, and yes, Carli could borrow one of his vans to move her stuff." Beth turned to Syd. "My heart just broke. She wasn't backing down."

Syd let her cry. Some hikers passed behind them, but Beth didn't even seem to notice.

When Beth's tears had dwindled, Syd proceeded. "In Carli's cell records, I saw that you called her a few times on Saturday."

"Yeah, but she never picked up. So on Sunday morning, I decided to do her a favor and drive the Triangle Shops van back to Fish Creek. She's the one who'd brought it into my uncle's garage for repair work. But on the way to the Café, I noticed the Century mileage markers on the pavement. That's when I realized Carli had probably spent her weekend doing that ride."

Syd nodded.

"Other years, she'd stayed on Clark Lake, but I wasn't sure where. So, I turned around and headed back in that direction."

"Did you make the call from the phone booth in Jacksonport?"

"Uh-huh. On the spur of the moment, I saw the booth and decided to call Carli from a number she wouldn't recognize. This time, she answered."

Beth closed her eyes. "If she hadn't, she might still be alive." She gave a tortured cry.

Syd sympathized by patting Beth's shoulder. "How did Carli respond to your call?"

"She was peeved and complained that I'd bugged her all weekend. That this proved—I'd never stop trying to control her."

"Yet she agreed to meet you?"

"Yeah, she finally yielded to my begging, and we picked Cave Point."

"Did you park in the public lot?"

Beth nodded. "I got there around 8 a.m."

"I'm confused. Isn't that about when you took a fishing charter call?"

"Yeah. I'd forwarded our office number to my cell, so I took the reservation before I hiked along the trail to meet Carli."

Syd frowned. Clearly, Beth's alibi hadn't been as solid as they'd thought. "Did you two argue?"

She nodded, her eyes bleak. "Carli told me our relationship was definitely over. That she'd slept with this guy, Solly, and it felt good. Much..." Beth's face twisted into an ugly grimace. "Much better than with me. I called her a slut, figuring she'd also been sleeping with that Nick, and started to push her." Beth's eyes were wild.

"So what happened next?"

"She told me to 'stay the fuck away' from her and jogged off."

"Did you follow?"

"Yeah," she huffed. "I couldn't end our relationship like that! Carli was fast, but I was faster. I eventually caught her arm and yanked it so hard that she stumbled and fell."

Beth placed her head in her hands. "My God! I actually heard Carli's head crack... But I didn't mean for this to happen. I kept kissing Carli's face, willing her to open her eyes... But it was hopeless. She didn't respond."

"Why didn't you go for help?"

"I could hear some hikers approaching, and I panicked. I knew Carli was dead—and I was the one responsible."

"Did you put her in the water?"

She nodded. "I didn't know what else to do. I was able to sling her body over my back and push through the brush, but her shorts got caught. I untangled them just in time to drop her body into the lake, and I ducked down to hide."

"When did you take the second charter reservation call?"

"Right after I got back to the van." Beth shook her head. "I was in no state to take it, but, somehow, I did."

With nostrils flared, she looked at Syd. "How could Carli have said those hateful things to me, especially after we'd made the most amazing love just two nights before?"

Syd didn't know what to say.

"Then, this week, you told me about Carli's lawsuit." Beth's voice had turned accusing. "Knowing she'd had sex with another woman was the worst. I was flooded with despair—I even thought about ending my own life."

She blew air out in disgust. "I should have. Instead, I almost killed you."

"Why *did* you target me, Beth?"

"Well, at the Art Fair, you and your niece were discussing that photo that showed the third Triangle Shops van. Then, yesterday, I was at the charter office where the after-hour calls are routed for my Uncle Reuben's garage, and I heard your message. I knew you were closing in."

"But how did you know where to find me?"

"That first Monday, when you interviewed me, you mentioned you and your friend were going to scuba dive on Sunday to see the *Ocean Wave*." Beth looked out toward the choppy water. "I knew which boat ramp was closest to that site, so I drove to it and waited down a side lane. But I couldn't believe my luck when you didn't bring along a third party to tend your boat."

"Did you cut our tie-up line and also my two-way-radio cord before you chased my vehicle?"

"Yes, I admit, I did try to hurt you—but Carli's death was an accident. You've got to believe me... I really loved her. The night after Carli's funeral, I cried myself to sleep, reading her diaries—"

"Wait, Beth... Are you saying you read them before you gave them to me?"

She gave Syd a curt nod. "When I couldn't hammer open Carli's lockbox, I located a duplicate key taped to the bottom of her desk drawer."

"Did you rip out a particular diary page?" Syd held her breath.

Confused, Beth shook her head.

Syd was truly vexed. "Well... was there anything in the lockbox you removed?"

"I dumped the contents out on my bed, but I put everything back inside."

"Everything?"

She nodded. "Other than some candy wrappers and such that had been mixed in."

Syd felt a glimmer of hope. "What did you do with that trash?" As she waited for Beth's answer, Syd's ears perked up. She could hear the sound of sirens.

Beth heard them, too.

"Beth?" Syd prompted again. "Is that trash still at your house?"

Beth managed to refocus on Syd. "No, I threw it into my condo's dumpster."

"Could it still be there?"

"I don't know."

Out of the corner of Syd's eye, she watched Deputies Jeffers and Larson break through the trees, their guns drawn. She motioned to them to lower their weapons, then turned back to Beth. "You know you need to come with us, don't you?"

"Yeah…" Beth's voice was filled with resignation.

Syd scooted back from the edge and stood. "Now," she implored, helping Beth to her feet, "can you tell me where you hid Carli's body?"

Beth whipped her head around. "I've already told you… I didn't take Carli's body!"

Chapter 51

Sergeant Morrell waved Syd into his office. "Great job!" He beamed at her. "From the video monitor room, I watched you take down Beth's written confession for both Carli's death and your hit and run."

"I'm sure you also heard that Beth didn't take Carli's body."

"Yeah." He frowned. "I was surprised."

"So was I. Based on that, I believe its disappearance must be linked to the abductions of Megan Hanson and the other young girls. I know the Lacount family members are no longer suspects in Carli's death, but they have to stay on the list for her body snatching and the abduction cases."

"They're actually the *only* suspects we currently have," Stu said, sounding frustrated, "now that Jason Potter didn't pan out."

She nodded. "Marv told me." When Syd had arrived at the department, she'd received a number of pats on the back and "well-dones" from other detectives and deputies. Most surprising were the accolades she'd received from Marv, especially after he'd just informed her: "Potter was a fucking dead end!"

Stu now steepled his fingers. "Tomorrow, I want you to join Marv's team to locate Megan."

Syd crossed her arms and gave him a defiant look. "I'm not waiting until tomorrow."

"Syd, listen to me. I saw your van in our garage. You're lucky to be alive. Take the day off."

"No way." She leaned on his desk with both hands. "But I do need some wheels. Larson's checking Carli's dumpster for her missing diary page as we speak. If the garbage has already been picked up, I'll be visiting some sort of landfill site."

Stu sighed and rolled his eyes. "Go talk to Gina about a loaner van. And let me know when you contact the Lacount family about Beth's arrest. I need to send out a press release."

In the kitchenette, Syd filled a Tupperware container with water, then returned to her office and placed it in front of Lloyd. Rather than wasting time by dropping him off, she'd had Deputy Jeffers drive them both back to the department, along with Beth, who'd been secured in the rear.

Syd now placed a call to the Café and Alice answered.

"I've got some news about Carli. Will you be at the Triangle Shops if I arrive there in, say, thirty minutes?"

Her voice was intense: "Just tell me, Detective."

Syd raked her fingers through her messy hair. "Okay, but, please, brace yourself." She took a deep breath. "Beth Halverson has been charged in Carli's death."

Syd heard Alice's sharp intake of air. "My God! I can't believe it."

"I know. Beth claims it was an accident. And I tend to believe her. But she still acted in a reckless manner." Syd explained the circumstances to Alice. "I'm assuming the State will be charging her with Homicide by Reckless Conduct."

"It's all so awful... " Alice moaned. "At least, though, I can now bury my daughter."

Syd cringed. "Sorry—I wish that were the case. Carli's body is still missing."

* * * *

It was close to noon. Syd's stomach was rumbling and she would've loved a shower. A quick wash-up in the ladies' restroom would have to do. But as she rose from her desk chair, her iPhone rang.

"Detective Bernhardt, this is Zach Newson."

Surprised, Syd asked, "How are you doing?"

"Not so good. I just stopped at the Café to pick up my check, and Alice told me about Beth Halverson's arrest. Wow! It's hard to imagine." He cleared his throat. "But there's something I should've told you about Carli."

Syd hesitated. "Does it concern her sexuality?"

She heard Zach's huge sigh of relief. "Yeah, then this will be easier. A few minutes ago, Luke Lacount approached me. He seemed awfully friendly, so I knew he was after something. He said he understood I'd been having a rough time at school after 'coming out.' At first I was shocked he knew, although, by now, probably everybody in Fish Creek does, too. Anyway, he asked me whether Carli was gay."

Syd frowned. "What did you say?"

"Well, I lied and told him I had no idea. But I don't think he believed me. Luke's face looked so ugly and mean. One of his hands was slapping this envelope into the other."

"What kind of envelope?"

"Well, it was from that attorney's office. You know...the one that's across the street from the Café."

Syd felt nauseous. Luke had somehow gotten hold of the lawsuit information that concerned Carli and his wife.

Syd thanked Zach, hung up, and immediately called Deputy Brighton.

He growled, "I'm sitting outside that dirty dog's place of work right now. This time, I'm watching both his vehicle and the vans. Don't worry about Colette Lacount. I know what to do."

Syd hoped to God that was true...

Chapter 52

Lloyd lifted one eyelid, then closed it as Syd left her office to finally hit the bathroom and vending machine. Afterward, she entered the conference room to join Marv, who was on the phone.

Tacked to bulletin boards, on the four walls, were the photos of the seven young girls who had disappeared. Below each photo, Marv had identified the channels he'd pursued with his primary focus on Megan Hanson.

Syd cringed as she spun around—circled by so many innocent faces—their features similar to Carli's. This was the work of a monster—a vile creature—one that didn't deserve to walk this earth. Syd tried not to imagine the trauma these children had suffered—but it was impossible. She could only pray that all of them—any of them—were still alive.

Marv hung up, his eyes brilliant. "I think I've uncovered something major." He gave Syd his itching-to-tell-her smile.

"So tell me." She managed to refocus and took a seat at the conference room table, stacked with the case files.

"I may have discovered a tie between the missing Chicago girls and each of the Lacount brothers."

"What do you mean?"

"I reviewed all these files." He motioned to the stacks. "It appears the other departments followed a similar protocol to ours, similarly leading nowhere. Of course, I had the unique advantage of recognizing these cases might be linked, so I considered why our perp picked Madison, Chicago, Minneapolis, and Rochester—all urban locations with medium-to-large populations. Maybe our perp traveled there for business reasons."

Syd nodded.

"In particular, the two disappearances in Chicago caught my attention as they occurred in the same week, but in different years. I wondered whether some kind of convention had been held."

"That makes sense."

"In these files," he placed his hands on two stacks, "the Chicago PD had also followed that line of inquiry for both cases. They uncovered that the same Midwest Travel Show was held at the McCormick Place on the two dates the girls had disappeared. They didn't know who they were looking for among the exhibitors and attendees…" He raised his eyebrows. "But I did. I called the Chicago Chamber of Commerce and got the name of the travel show's event coordinator—and she just called me back."

Marv gave Syd a satisfied look. "I hit the jackpot. An exhibitor's booth had been secured by all three Lacount brothers for both of those years."

Syd's mouth dropped open.

"Their booth focused on vacationing on both sides of Lake Michigan and included Frank's and Patrick's restaurants, paintings of the two areas done by Luke, and lodging accommodations from which the brothers would get a fee for referrals."

"Wow!" Syd looked at the two Chicago photos, on the north wall. "So, you're saying Jill Cabot and Penny Ransack both disappeared during the travel show's timeframe, but in different years?"

"Yep. The event coordinator also confirmed a travel show had been held in Madison, Minneapolis, and Rochester, during the timeframe when the other girls went missing. She's now checking whether the three Lacounts staffed a booth at each of those locations as well."

For the past week, Syd had been tying Carli's death to the disappearance of her body. But Beth's arrest, for just the former, had changed everything. Once again, Syd's eyes briefly landed on each of the photos that surrounded her. Whoever had taken these girls had an unnatural attraction to Carli's physical features...

Or was that true?

Syd considered Rose Lacount, the matriarch of the Lacount family who had looked so much like Carli. If one or more of the brothers was this monster—responsible for both the abductions and Carli's body-snatching—then Rose was the most likely connection.

Syd frowned. Instead of considering only Frank and Luke, she now had to include Patrick as well.

It looked as if Marv had been reading her mind. "I told you before, Syd, it's not smart to get involved with a potential suspect."

"Let's avoid the carping."

Marv gave her a smug smile.

Syd told him about Rose Lacount and the vibes she'd gotten when Patrick had discussed his mother's relationship with each of her sons. "I believe Deputy Coroner Hutton authorized her autopsy back in 2000 and, from his reaction, something wasn't quite kosher."

Syd called Hutton from the conference room's speaker phone and asked him about it.

"Well, Syd, as I recall, the autopsy request was issued by Rose Lacount's younger sister for health preventative information. I also seem to remember one of the Lacount sons thinking it wasn't necessary, and he tried to fight her. But Rose had made her sister the executor of her estate."

"Do you remember which son was against the autopsy?"

"Sorry, Syd, I don't. It was too long ago. But that's not the reason this case sticks out in my mind. And it's also not due to Rose Lacount's cause of death, which was a stroke. It's what the pathologist discovered when he routinely swabbed her mouth. Between her lips and teeth, he found traces of semen."

Syd and Marv exchanged a shocked look.

"I remember chuckling with Dr. Johnson about it. Here was a woman who'd suffered a second stroke and was still willing to perform oral sex on her partner. We both agreed we'd take her as a spouse any day!"

Marv laughed, enjoying the adolescent joke.

Syd shook her head. "I won't honor that comment with my own, Hutton." Then she hesitated. "Frank Lacount told me that his mother had been seeing Fred Parson."

"The guy who captains the Fish Creek to Chambers Island boat?" Marv asked.

"Yep," Hutton chimed in. "Both Dr. Johnson and I knew the guy. We didn't want to embarrass him by bringing it up. The sexual activity hadn't affected Rose Lacount's cause of death, so it was just dismissed. I don't believe the swab was even saved."

Syd frowned. "Well, thanks for your help." She hung

up and turned to Marv. "Maybe Hutton didn't want to approach Fred Parson, but I'm going to." Syd looked up his phone number and placed the call—disappointed when she was forced to leave him an urgent message to return her call.

Marv leaned back in his chair. "Well... let's see where we're at. First, we already know, both Frank and Luke Lacount were in this vicinity when Leslie Gorman disappeared...but what about Patrick?" He raised his brow. "I'd like you to find that out." Marv gave Syd a wry look. "Maybe your involvement with the guy will pay off after all."

She ignored his remark. "Well, I do know, Patrick was on Chambers Island the week his mother died—but so were Frank and Luke."

"What date was that?"

Syd checked her notes. "Rose Lacount died on June 6, 2000."

Marv nodded. "Did Patrick mention any other visits to Door County that summer?"

"No, but maybe we can verify that." Syd turned her chair and angled herself underneath a small desk that housed a communal computer. "I'll Google the closest airport to Saugatuck, Michigan."

Marv waited as Syd's fingers played the keys. "Okay...it appears to be Benton Harbor. Maybe Patrick filed a flight plan."

Syd returned to the speaker phone and dialed the airport. After being passed to a few parties, she reached Bob Wilson, who manned the desk for private charters and planes. Syd explained the reason for her call.

"Sure, I know Patrick Lacount. He rents an airplane hangar from our facility. Let me locate the log for 2000."

Syd and Marv waited patiently until Bob came back

on the line. "Okay, Patrick Lacount filed a flight plan for his Bonanza Four-Niner-Niner-Charlie-Foxtrot on June 4, 2000 from Benton Harbor to the Ephraim-Gibraltar airport."

The two detectives nodded. Since Patrick's mother had died on the sixth, this appeared to be a match.

"Did Mr. Lacount file any other flight plans to Wisconsin that summer?" Marv asked.

Bob took a moment before he said, "Not that I can see. But if the weather is good, a pilot can fly under Visual Flight Rules, so they don't need to file a plan."

Syd thought about the other girls' disappearances and looked at Marv. "You know, Patrick might have flown his brothers to each of those Midwest Travel Shows."

"That makes sense." Marv gave Bob each of the girls' disappearance dates.

Within his logs, Bob was able to locate the flight plans Patrick had filed, to the Gibraltar-Ephraim airport within a week of each date—and then a second leg to each city Marv had provided.

Syd couldn't control her excitement. "My God, Marv!" She grabbed his arm. "You were spot on!"

"Yeah." He grinned, basking in her praise.

Then the corners of his mouth drifted down. "But the million dollar question remains: which brother is our fucking mark?"

Chapter 53

In Syd's loaner van, Lloyd rode shotgun. Syd, still in her jogging clothes, pulled into a landfill site near Carlsville, parked next to Marv's vehicle, and climbed out. They'd been lucky. Monday was the trash pickup day for Beth's condo complex, and the entire contents of the truck containing Beth's dumpster trash had already been segregated for their perusal.

Marv eyed the mound. "Since this is your baby, Syd, I'll give you the honor of climbing into that mess and tossing out the bags. At least it won't make you smell any worse than you already do."

She slammed him in the gut. "Very funny."

Syd slipped on gloves and gingerly entered the garbage, trying not to step on anything too disgusting. In Beth's written confession, she'd told Syd to look for a white garbage bag with yellow pull ties.

Syd managed to locate about two dozen bags fitting that description. She tossed them out, and Marv dumped each bag onto the grass. He then began to search through their contents, one pile at a time.

As she climbed out to join him, she looked down at

her ruined running shoes and silently vowed to submit a request for a replacement pair.

From the contents of the sixth bag, Marv removed an envelope. "This must be it, Syd! It's addressed to Beth."

Syd's heart pounded like a fist on a locked door as the two of them separated out food wrappers and kitchen garbage from the other contents. What remained was junk mail, paper clips, a scotch tape holder, post-it-notes—but no diary page.

Syd was overcome with disappointment. "I was so sure it would be here."

Marv shook his head in disgust. "Now we've got to pick up this mess!"

Syd refused to give up. She eyed the pile of Beth's trash they'd previously separated. It contained banana peels, toilet paper tubes, damp paper toweling, coffee grinds, ice cream wrappers...and something else. "Look, Marv!" She pointed.

"Now what?" He crossed his arms and frowned.

With shaky fingers, Syd extracted a fully intact Popsicle wrapper. Of course its sexual connotation stuck out in her mind. It felt bulky, so she peered inside. "My God, Marv!" Syd slipped out a folded page and smoothed it open. Then she lifted her eyes.

"I can't believe it! We actually found the missing diary page."

He reeled back, astonished. "Well what are you waiting for? Read it to me!"

And she did:

Tuesday, July 28, 2000
Dear Diary,
It's been two days since I last wrote. I didn't know if

I could, but I had to tell someone before I ripped out this page and hid it.

I feel so icky, so dirty, and all because I can't tell.

On Sunday night, our cabin returned from an overnight camping trip. After dinner, we were all tired and turned in. But sometime in the night I woke up and needed to pee.

I shook Molly's arm, but she said she was too tired to walk with me. I really needed to go, so I took her flashlight and headed out alone.

The moon was nearly full, and up ahead I could see the lights of the latrine. But to get there I needed to walk through the woods. I tried to turn on her flashlight, but it was dead. I thought about turning back, but I really needed to pee, so I kept my eyes on the latrine and walked carefully.

It got easier to see as I got closer. But that's when I heard footsteps behind me and a man whisper, "Hello, Carli," really scaring me—even though his voice sounded familiar.

I turned around and could see a priest's collar and something pulled tight over his face. I wet myself looking up at this monster. He grabbed me and covered my mouth and nose with his hands to stop my screams. I was sure I was going to die.

He pulled me into the woods as I kicked my legs and swung my arms. Finally he stopped and promised to let me go if I did one favor for him.

I didn't want to die, so I nodded my head and quit fighting.

He took his hands away from my face, but used one to hold my wrist. I could hear the sound of a zipper. He forced me to kneel and I did. Rocks and sticks scraped my knees.

"I bet you like Popsicles," he said, and pulled my head toward his private area, telling me to suck.

I didn't want to die, so I did. It was so gross, so sick. He moaned like my daddy used to when I'd scratch his back. The monster's hands forced my head into that spot until something warm filled my mouth, and I gagged. He told me I had to swallow, and I did. It was so, so sick.

He patted my head, as if he cared, and said, "If you tell anyone, Carli, I'll kill your mom."

Dad's already dead. I can't let Mom die, too, so I swore to him I'd never ever tell. That's when I heard voices coming through the woods. I'm sure he did, too, because he yanked me up and disappeared.

I ran into the latrine where I usually plug my nose. But this time I turned on the light and closed a stall, then forced my face into that hole. As I heard the girls enter, I gagged myself. But the smell was so bad, I turned my head and threw up on the wooden seat.

The girls knocked on my door, but I told them to go away. Swimming in my dinner, I saw this milky stuff and two curly red hairs. The monster knew my name. He has red hair. His voice did sound like Father Frank's. Was he the man who'd made me do that awful thing? Was he the man who'd said he'd kill my mom if I told? But how could this be? He's about to marry her.

I stayed in the latrine until morning, afraid to go out into the dark. I swished water in my mouth a billion times, trying to wash the taste of him away.

But I couldn't.

When a bunch of girls came in for their early morning wash up, I finally returned to my cabin and crawled into my bunk.

I tried to forget. But I couldn't.

I kept remembering his smell, his taste, my fear.

All I could do was to repeat, over and over, in my head: "I'll never, ever, tell. Mom will be safe…"

Then, last night, another camper named Leslie disappeared.

I'm sure the monster got her. And it's all because of me.

Please, God, forgive me… I just couldn't tell.

Chapter 54

Syd followed Marv's van up Highway 42 and thought about Carli's life-changing event—and the bastard that caused it. It appeared as if Carli had blamed herself for Leslie's disappearance. Although that must have been difficult for Carli, Syd could see why the threat to Carli's mother's life had been far worse. But more than a decade later, when Jenny Tyler was approached by the same monster, Carli's adult sense of duty had finally overridden her painful non-action.

This time, she wasn't going to let him get away with it.

But who *was* Carli's molester?

Was it Frank, as she'd initially feared? Or was it one of her uncles impersonating her stepdad? Syd could attest to the fact that all three brothers' voices sounded nearly identical.

And what must Carli have felt when she discovered that five additional young girls had gone missing since Leslie? Had Carli blamed herself for their disappearances as well?

Syd thought about Alice's strained relationship with

Carli. If only Alice had known about the terrible burden her daughter had been carrying. Carli had been put in an impossible position. She'd felt obliged to keep silent in order to protect her mom, yet she also must've blamed Alice for having to do so. Even though Beth had been responsible for Carli's death, the real monster in Carli's life was still out there—enjoying his freedom.

And that made Syd sick.

About a half mile south of Egg Harbor stood Fred Parson's A-frame office building. He'd called Syd back and agreed to meet at this location. In addition to captaining the *Spartan*, Fred was a part-time commercial real estate agent. He worked out of a shared office where he also kept his public and private excursion records.

Syd cracked the window for Lloyd, scratched his scruff, and promised to walk him when she returned. She joined Marv and the two entered the building where an assistant directed them to Fred's office. The robust man with a beautiful mane of white hair stood to greet them. The deep-set blue eyes within his craggy face looked pleased to see Syd. "Where have you been keeping yourself?"

She gave him a tight smile and introduced Marv. The three took seats.

"What can you tell us, Fred, about the summer of 2000, as it relates to the Lacount family?"

He seemed surprised by Syd's question and rubbed his chin. "I get my years mixed up, but I'm pretty sure that's the summer Rose died."

Syd nodded, and Marv chimed in, "I heard, you two might've been a couple."

Fred laughed. "Gossip sure travels. I did enjoy Rose's company and was sorry when she passed. She was a sharp woman who played a mean game of chess."

"Were you two romantically inclined?" Syd probed.

"Well, I may have given her a peck on the cheek, on occasion, but nothing more."

Syd shared a look with Marv.

He nodded, his face grim, and turned back to Fred—to dig deeper. "Did you see Rose during the last few days of her life?"

"No, I'm sorry to say, I didn't. Like many Wisconsin veterans, I attend an annual event in Milwaukee the week after Memorial Day. When I returned, I heard Rose had suffered her second stroke and already passed. But I was able to make her memorial service."

Syd was confused. "Wasn't it held that same week?"

"No." Fred shook his head. "Apparently, some of Rose's Chicago relatives couldn't make it to Chambers Island for her interment in June, so her gravesite memorial service was held some time later in July. I'm not sure about the date, but I do remember it was maybe two days before that little girl from St. Anne's Camp went missing."

Syd caught her breath and exchanged another look with Marv.

He shifted in his chair, trying to control his excitement, and asked, "Do you know whether Rose's three sons all attended her service?"

"Well, I remember Frank being there, but I'm not sure about his brothers. I still have the *Spartan* passenger log for the 2000 season. Let's see."

Fred pulled the specified log from a shelf and flipped the pages until he first located Frank's name in the month of May. "He was still a priest at that time, and he stayed at the retreat house for that month and on and off during that summer. But I also met him at his mother's home once or twice during those weeks before her death."

Fred then turned a few more pages and reached the first week of June. "While I was in Milwaukee, my cousin filled in for me. Both Patrick and Luke Lacount, it appears, made a couple of trips back and forth to the island the week Rose died."

Fred then turned to the month of July. The two detectives crowded over his shoulder to see the names. On Friday July 24, 2000, Luke Lacount was listed as traveling from Fish Creek to Chambers Island.

Then, on Tuesday, July 28—the day after Leslie disappeared—his name appeared on the return trip log.

There were no entries for Patrick Lacount.

Chapter 55

In the parking lot, Syd discussed their findings with Marv. "It's disgusting, but I bet the semen in Rose Lacount's mouth came from one of her sons."

"I agree…and it could be from any one of the three. Though at first glance, it does look as if Patrick Lacount may not be a suspect in Leslie's July disappearance."

Syd felt a sense of relief, but wished the same was true for Frank.

"Of course, this is not proof positive Patrick didn't attend his mother's service," Marv back-pedaled. "He could've used a private boat to reach the island."

"I know." Syd thought about their recent excursion in Frank's boat. "But I'd still wager, if Patrick attended, he'd have first landed his plane at the Gibraltar-Ephraim Airport, like the week his mother died. Then, Luke would've picked him up, and the two would have traveled over to the island together." Syd paused. "But, Marv, Chambers Island has a grass airstrip, too, doesn't it?"

"You're right. Several islanders use it in the summer."

Syd frowned. Once again, Patrick was back on their Suspects list.

Marv checked his cell and looked up, disappointed. "Nothing yet from the Midwest Travel Show coordinator. We know Patrick filed a flight plan into the cities where each young girl went missing. I'd like to know if both of his brothers were with him at each location. It could help eliminate one of them if they weren't."

"It might be risky, but I could call Alice. She'd probably know."

"Go ahead, Syd." Marv grimaced, shaking his head. "The seconds are ticking away on Megan's life—that is—if she's still alive."

When Syd had conveyed the news about Beth's arrest to Alice, she'd been extremely upset and said she was going home. That was where Syd tried her now.

Alice answered, her voice sounding flat.

Syd first asked Alice how she was doing, then said, "I understand, Frank and his brothers staffed a booth at a number of Midwest Travel Shows. Did all three always attend?"

"Well, I believe so…"

Syd nodded at Marv, who frowned.

"…but why are you asking me about those travel shows?"

"Oh, it's nothing." Syd now wished she hadn't called. If Alice talked to Frank about this conversation, he might mention it to his brothers, and the guilty party among the three would realize Syd was on his trail. She tried to cover by asking Alice, "How is Frank doing since he heard about Beth's arrest?"

"Like me, he's very distraught and wanted to spend some time out on the water by himself. That worried me, so I asked Patrick to accompany him."

"Are they out in Frank's boat right now?"

"No. He called a few minutes ago. They were still making a few van deliveries and would arrive at the dock around 3:00."

Syd checked her watch. It was almost 2:30.

"But I also told Frank that Luke was trying to hook up with them. I was surprised when he knocked on our back door and seemed rattled. Apparently, he'd walked through the woods from his house."

Syd tensed up. "What did he want?"

"Luke said he'd driven home for a late lunch, and, afterward, his SUV wouldn't start. Since he didn't want to leave Colette without a vehicle, he asked if he could borrow my car. That's when I told him Frank and Patrick were going out in the boat."

A cold fist had closed over Syd's heart. "So, did you give Luke your car?"

"Yes, about an hour ago."

Syd hung up, suffused with fear and anger.

"What's going on?" Marv asked.

"Hold on." Syd called Brighton. "Are you on the road outside Luke and Colette's home?"

"I'm even closer than that." He sounded pleased with himself. "I crept up to the house about thirty minutes after Luke arrived. Everything seems to be quiet inside."

"You idiot!" She couldn't help herself. "Luke's not even there! Get inside the house right now, and check on Colette and her baby."

Syd hung up and told Marv about the current situation. "I hope to God Colette's okay."

Marv nodded, his face grim.

"Since all three Lacounts should be arriving at the Fish Creek Dock around 3:00, why don't I meet you there, Marv?"

"Sounds like a plan. It's about time we corralled the whole bunch for a showdown."

As Syd climbed into her van, Lloyd started to whine. "Okay, boy, I know, I promised."

It was about a ten-minute drive to Fish Creek, so Syd had a few minutes to spare. She drove into Egg Harbor and parked on a side street adjacent to Harbor View Park. While searching for anything within the unfamiliar vehicle to use for poop patrol, Syd heard the two-way-radio crackle.

An All-Points-Bulletin was being issued for the arrest of Luke Lacount.

Syd shuddered. Something *had* happened to Colette.

As Syd searched for Brighton's number, her eyes did a double take. One of the Triangle Shops catering vans was parked behind Al's Place, directly across the street.

Her adrenaline kicked into gear. Maybe she could apprehend Luke before he left Egg Harbor. Syd radioed for backup, and Dispatch confirmed Deputy Ed Jones was in the vicinity. His expected arrival time was ten minutes.

Under a navy rain jacket, Syd had retrieved from her office locker, she'd secured a department-issued gun, handcuffs, and backup credentials.

With sweaty fingers, she now grabbed the Glock...and she waited.

* * * *

Only three minutes had passed. There was still no movement at Al's, and Lloyd's whines had escalated into attention-grabbing barks. Syd decided to take a chance and give him some relief.

She holstered her gun and ran around the van to let him out. He loped into the park and immediately lifted his

332

leg. Syd called him back, still keeping an eye on Al's—and a rash of panic swarmed over her body. Luke had stepped out onto the back stoop with Frank and Patrick at his heels.

As Luke paused to scan the area, his cruel eyes lit on Syd's. He shoved his brothers backward and followed them inside.

"Damn!" Syd cursed out loud. She was no better than Brighton. If she hadn't been standing outside her van, Luke wouldn't have seen her.

Now, everything had changed.

Syd knew the staff and patrons inside Al's could be in danger. She couldn't wait for backup.

She glanced over at the park. Lloyd hadn't heeded her call. He was still having a jolly old time, sniffing around and marking his territory. Syd called again, but a squirrel caught his eye and he took off, high-tailing it in the opposite direction.

Syd had no choice—she had to leave him—and convinced herself: *He'll be just fine.*

She locked the van, sprinted across the street, and drew her gun. Displaying her credentials, Syd announced herself and pushed through Al's back door.

Two waitresses hovered around a guy sprawled out on the kitchen floor, rubbing his jaw.

Syd's voice was urgent: "Are you all right?"

"Yeah." He managed to sit up. "I was decked before my keys were taken."

"The keys to your car?" Syd was worried the Lacounts were escaping through the front.

"No, to the building."

One of the waitresses squeaked, "I saw three men heading down the stairs toward the bathroom."

Syd frowned. That seemed like a big mistake. Luke

had to know he'd be trapped with his brothers.

She dashed through the nearly empty bar. One guy was hunkered down, and the bartender had his back turned, his eyes glued to the TV. Neither would've noticed if the President had strolled through.

Syd stole a look down the stairs, where she'd followed Marv a few days before.

She was confused. The area was empty. However, the door labeled *Al's Escape Route* was halfway ajar.

Syd had no idea where the tunneled caves under Egg Harbor might lead, but the Lacounts had to be headed that way.

She pummeled down the steps, her gun still drawn.

Her heart pounded madly as she took a cautious glance inside the dark gloom.

Suddenly the door banged against her hand and she lost her grip. Her eyes wide, she watched her Glock skid under a chair, out of her grasp. As she lunged for it she felt a push from behind.

My God! she thought, as she stumbled forward.

Then the door slammed shut—enveloping Syd in darkness.

Chapter 56

Panicked, Syd felt around for the door handle, and her stomach spasmed when she heard a key turn in the lock.

She took a deep breath and slid her hands along the doorframe to locate a light switch. A dangling low-wattage bulb turned on. Beyond that, she saw what looked like the advertised limestone tunnel that led to who knows where.

Syd pounded on the heavy metal door, over and over, but nobody seemed to hear. She pulled out her iPhone, but the reception was nil. She took a deep breath, and told herself that one of the wait staff, or Deputy Jones, had to be looking for her. It was terrible to know the Lacounts were getting away, possibly armed with her gun.

She also thought about Lloyd and felt nauseous. He could be wandering near traffic. Or even—God forbid—dead, like Beau.

Syd waited and waited, pounding and shouting, getting more frantic by the minute. She couldn't just hang out and hope someone would come. She decided to try the tunnel.

After the first turn, the light from behind her disappeared. The glow from her iPhone's screen didn't help much, so she slid the device back into her pocket.

Like a blind person, Syd skimmed the walls with her fingertips and took baby steps. She kept cringing as her face touched what felt like spider webs…then another…and another…certain that all species of bugs were now crawling in her hair and down her neck.

She forced herself forward until she saw a faint glimmer of light up ahead.

The clammy walls were getting tighter as she kept moving toward the light, ducking as the ceiling closed in. Within the constricted space, she was starting to hyperventilate.

Syd finally reached a boarded-up wall. Thin lines of outside light were sandwiched between the slats. She pounded against the barricade, but it held firm.

Her shoulders deflated. *There is no escape here*, she thought.

Then she heard the muffled sounds of barking. *Lloyd's* barking—she was sure of it.

"Thank God!" she choked out and continued to pound and yell amidst his barks. Hopefully, either her shouts or the disruptive dog, with no owner in sight, would attract attention.

Finally, a voice came through the slats: "This is Deputy Jones from the Sheriff's Department. Is someone in there?"

"Jones!" Syd screamed, overcome with emotion. "It's me, Sydney Bernhardt! Damn, am I glad you're here!"

* * * *

Deputy Jones stood in the basement hallway of Al's as Syd wiped tears, grime, and crawling insects off her face, hair and hands.

"You look like hell!" He laughed. "And by the way, your Golden is locked inside my squad."

"I could kiss you—but first things first." Syd got down on her hands and knees and, amazingly, there it was—her Glock—still under the chair where it had slid. Obviously, the Lacounts hadn't noticed she'd dropped it.

Syd retrieved it and stood back up, elated she wouldn't have to explain that particular screw-up. "Now we need to find the Lacount brothers. When you arrived, did you see a white Triangle Shops van heading north out of town?"

"No…but some tourists did. They said they were nearly hit by it. I told them I'd follow up, but my first concern was you."

"Well, thanks for that." Syd squeezed Jones' arm. "Now we've got to locate that van."

They raced up the stairs, exited the building, and jogged toward his squad. Jones opened the passenger door and Lloyd jumped out.

"You've got some dog, Syd."

"I know I do." She bent down to give Lloyd a big hug, but she made it quick. They were losing time.

Syd clicked open her van and secured a magnetic beacon on top. Then she and Jones climbed into their separate vehicles and headed toward Fish Creek, their sirens and flashers going off.

Syd tried Marv's cell, but it went into voicemail. Worried, she left him a quick message then reached for the radio. "This is Detective Bernhardt requesting backup at the Fish Creek Dock."

"Two squads will be there in fifteen minutes."

"That's too late! How about a Coast Guard cutter?"

Syd was relieved when Dispatch replied, "The Bluebird is in close range."

* * * *

Deputy Jones and Syd made the ten-minute drive to Fish Creek in five. Coming down the hill, they continued straight toward the municipal dock. When Marv hadn't answered his cell, Syd had hoped he'd been detaining the Lacounts. But she was perplexed when neither Marv nor the Lacount brothers were there. Frank's boat slip was also empty.

Agitated, Syd scanned the immediate area, but could not locate the Triangle Shops van. She jumped out of her vehicle to talk to Jones, and he lowered his window. "I'm thinking the Lacounts may have split up, and Marv could be on one of their tails. You know where the Ephraim-Gibraltar Airport is, right?"

"Yeah." Jones nodded.

"Now that Luke Lacount is on the run, he could've forced his brother to fly him off the peninsula. But I don't know whether Patrick's plane is at that airport or over on Chambers Island. So, let's do this. You follow the Ephraim-Gibraltar Airport option, and I'll tackle Chambers Island. I'll also keep trying Marv."

"Will do," Jones said, and took off, his siren on and lights still flashing.

While talking, Syd had left her van door open. She now realized Lloyd had jumped out, and he was surging down the dock. She shouted his name as her eyes searched the area to find a boat to launch.

And…who did she see but Eli, standing by *his* boat—precisely where Lloyd was headed.

Syd locked her van and ran toward them. "Did you see Frank Lacount's boat leave the harbor?"

Eli frowned. "Well, hello to you, too. I thought you'd have taken the day off, but I guess not."

"Sorry, but this is urgent. What about Frank's boat?"

"I just got here, and the slip was already empty, but there was a Whaler motoring out of the harbor. Most likely it was his." He cocked his head. "Are you chasing after that Patrick again?"

"I can't believe you!" Syd shook her head, exasperated. "How about Marv? Did you see him?"

"Nope."

"Okay, I need your boat."

"What?"

"Don't ask questions. Just give me the keys."

"Well, wherever you're going, Sydney, I'm going, too."

Eli took the helm of his twenty-eight-foot Mako, mounted with twin 250-HP outboard motors. Syd knew she should lock Lloyd in her van, but that would take extra time, so they both scrambled into the boat.

Once Eli pulled out of the harbor, she had him gun it toward Chambers Island. Then Syd gave Marv's cell another call. This time, he answered.

"Where the hell are you, Marv?"

"I kept waiting, but when neither the Lacounts nor you showed, I got worried—especially after I heard the APB for Luke's arrest and Dispatch's request for help at Al's. I kept trying your cell, but when you didn't respond, I sped up to the Café. I thought I'd gotten your instructions wrong. But, shit! I just listened to your voicemail. I must've been trying your cell when you left me your message."

"Where are you now?"

"Back at the Fish Creek Dock. Where the hell are you?"

"I'm in Eli's boat, headed for Chambers Island."

339

"You've got to be kidding."

"I had no choice. Frank's boat had already left the harbor. But a Coast Guard cutter should arrive at the dock within minutes. Have them motor you toward Chambers, and be on the lookout for Eli and me. Given the cutter's speed, you'll probably beat us. I don't know who's in Frank's boat, but it could be all three brothers. I assume they're heading for the Chambers Island Marina where Patrick keeps a car. After that, I'm not sure whether they'll be driving to Hemlock House or the airstrip. Patrick's plane may be tied up there." Syd finally stopped for air.

"Anything else?" Marv sounded pissed at having to take orders from her—on *his* case.

Syd ignored his attitude and instead asked about Colette.

"After you called Brighton, he entered the house with probable cause and found her on the floor. She was in bad shape, but she managed to tell him that Luke was her abuser."

"God, I hope she pulls through."

"She should. She's critical-but-stable. An ambulance took her to Sturgeon Bay Hospital. Alice Lacount accompanied Colette and took charge of her baby, who, thankfully, was unharmed."

Knowing Colette was in good hands, Syd now focused on the Whaler up ahead. Eli's boat was by far faster than Frank's. Even though it had a good lead, Eli's was making decent gains. Using his powerful binoculars, Syd verified—all three men were in Frank's boat.

She saw something else, too—something that made her shudder.

One of the three brothers was pointing a gun at the other two.

Chapter 57

For the past thirty minutes, Syd and Eli had gradually been closing the distance between his boat and Frank's. In addition, the Coast Guard cutter was fast approaching, with Marv onboard.

Syd had given Eli an update on the day's events, then she'd fallen into silence, too keyed-up to make small talk. But it was reassuring to have his quiet and confident presence at her side. Lloyd must have felt the same: his head was resting in Eli's lap.

Syd now noticed Frank's boat veer off the course. "Shit, Eli—the Lacounts are heading north along the point rather than going into the marina."

"It looks that way." He frowned. "I bet their target's the harbor on the other side of the point. There's a beach in that vicinity with access to the airstrip."

The weather had taken a turn for the worse. The waves were choppy, breaking over the boat and soaking the three of them. Eli kept easing up to reduce the spray. Syd kept telling him to go faster.

They motored around the point and entered the harbor. Up ahead, Syd watched the Whaler drive right up onto the beach. She now was certain the Lacounts were headed for Patrick's plane. But was this Patrick's choice? Or would he be piloting under duress, a gun pointed at his head?

Eli began to motor in, his propeller partially raised. When they reached water shallow enough for them to wade and Lloyd to swim, Eli cut the engine and secured his boat with an anchor.

As they sloshed past Frank's boat, Syd scoped out the area. Mature evergreens stood on either side of what she assumed was the end of the open grass runway. But from the beach, it was impossible to see over the natural shoreline vegetation.

The Lacounts' footprints didn't head straight up into the open area. Instead, they first zigzagged to the left, and then to the right of center, more than twenty yards each way before doubling back.

Syd was perplexed. Had the brothers been looking for something before heading for Patrick's plane?

Her cell rang. "What's up, Marv?"

"We should be there within five minutes."

Syd hung up, knowing that might be too late.

Her eyes found Eli's. "I'm going to follow the tree line and try to stop the plane."

He shook his head. "You know at least one of the brothers has a gun, right?"

She nodded.

"I don't want to lose you again." Eli grabbed her hand. "You've got to wait for Marv."

"What makes you think you even have me back?" Syd spat out, then began to struggle. He wouldn't release her, so she finally gave up.

Eli frowned at her and turned away, calling out, "Lloyd!"

He bounded over, his tail wagging—not acting stupidly, like her.

"I'm sorry." Syd kicked at a piece of driftwood with her disgusting shoe. "I didn't mean what I said."

Eli didn't respond, and a knife of regret pierced her heart. She'd messed up again.

Since the air between them was heavy, Syd concentrated on the Coast Guard cutter finally pulling up beside Eli's boat.

The wind had changed direction and now whipped at them from the open field. But Syd was confused. Instead of the fragrant scent of pine, the pungent scent of gasoline filled her nostrils...

Then, at lightning speed, flames raced along the beach grass, framing the shoreline, to create a wall of blazing heat.

"My God!" Fear rose in Syd's gut. Now she understood the reason for the footprints. One or more of the brothers must have poured gasoline along the beach perimeter, then ignited it to create a roadblock.

Lloyd whimpered as both Eli and Syd recoiled from the fire. "That goddamn fire...again!" she shouted and took a deep, cleansing breath. "It's not getting me this time!"

A wildfire can spread rapidly from its original source. The Lacounts' rash act, Syd knew, could well destroy the entire island's natural beauty and wildlife. Some Coast Guard cutters were equipped to handle shoreline fires, but theirs were not.

Chambers Island, however, did have a tanker truck, so Syd urgently punched in 911 and reported the blaze. As Syd hung up, she could see that Eli felt useless, too. Neither of them could do anything but watch until the fire truck arrived—hopefully in time.

Marv jumped out of the cutter and chugged through the water to reach her side. "So what the hell happened?" he asked, out of breath.

Syd gave him a quick update.

He rubbed his fading bruise and scrutinized the shoreline. "Okay, what's the plan?"

Syd blinked at him, at a loss for words.

He gave her a tight-lipped smile. "It's clear to me you know what you're doing. And you certainly know these guys better than me. So how should we handle the situation?"

Still startled by his words, Syd hesitated, overcome with a mixture of emotions: a sense of pride, weird warmth for this big oaf of a guy, and that nagging regret over her recent behavior with Eli.

Syd's eyes flicked between the two men. "Okay, Eli, you stay here with Lloyd while Marv and I fan out on the beach. I'll take the right tree line, and Marv, you take the left. When the flames abate, we'll move in together…" But as the deafening sound of a plane engine filled their ears, they all looked skyward.

Barely clearing the fire, a private plane with "499CF" painted on its wings soared up into the blanket of gray clouds.

"Damn!" Syd let out an anguished cry, knowing the aircraft was Patrick's. "We're too late."

"Hey, listen." Eli tilted his head. "Isn't that the sound of a siren?"

"Yeah." Marv nodded. "At least the tanker is almost here." As smoke continued to fill their lungs, Marv turned to Syd and tried to be optimistic. "Maybe all three Lacounts weren't in that plane?"

"Maybe." She rubbed her stinging eyes and stared at

the flames. The heat prickled her damaged arms as they continued to wait.

From the island side, streams of powerful water began to squelch the flames.

Marv pointed toward the right tree line. "It appears that area of the beach has stopped burning."

Syd nodded, batting away hot ash. Then she took another deep breath. "Let's go."

Eli's hand darted out to grab hers. "Be careful, Syd."

Relieved by his gesture, she gave his hand a tight squeeze, then released it.

Syd and Marv jogged toward the charred section of grass, then, using the trees for protection, they got their first glimpse of the airstrip. Stationed in the center was the fire truck, still extinguishing flames. Behind it was a wind sock, and further inland, a few private planes were tied down.

But the real attention grabber was what looked like a body, crumpled up in the grass, about thirty yards from four parked cars.

Syd's eyes connected with Marv's. "We know Patrick's flying the plane, and Luke's on the run to escape abuse charges—"

"And probably more."

She nodded. "That has to be Frank."

"I agree, Syd. Let's go."

The two detectives covered the quarter mile in record time. But within a few feet of the body, Syd stopped dead in her tracks, astonished.

The body belonged to Luke Lacount.

Chapter 58

Syd checked Luke's pulse. "He's alive!"

Marv pulled out his cell and called Clay Franklin, a medic on the cutter. "We've got an unconscious man here and we need your help." He hung up and turned to Syd. "At this point, we don't know whether Luke's our pedophile, or simply a domestic abuser."

"You're right," she said and searched for the gun she'd seen through Eli's binoculars. It wasn't on Luke's body—or in the general area. She figured his brothers had to have it. "Well, our goal was to pick up the three Lacounts for questioning. At least we've got Luke in custody, but Patrick and Frank are flying off to who knows where and…" Syd was startled when her iPhone rang. She could see it was Gina.

"What's up?" Syd answered, watching both Clay and Eli stride across the field, Lloyd at their side.

"Syd, one of the Sturgeon Bay air traffic controllers is trying to reach you. He's been contacted by the occupants of a private plane—Bonanza 499CF—who want to talk to you."

Syd's heart skipped a beat. "Have the controller call me

directly. See if he can patch me in and also record the call."

"Will do."

As Eli and Clay neared, Syd hung up and gave Eli an imploring half smile.

He shook his head wearily, as if she was more trouble than she was worth, a grin tugging at his lips.

Syd felt enormously better.

Clay squatted down to examine Luke. "So, the guy was already unconscious when you two arrived?"

"Yeah," Marv said.

"And his brothers are trying to reach me." Syd explained the surprising call from the air traffic controller.

Eli pointed at the parked cars. "Since Patrick used this airstrip, I bet one of those is his."

Syd's eyes met Eli's. "Good thinking. At the boat dock, Patrick keeps an old Ford he drives back and forth to Hemlock House. Under its front left fender is a small magnetized box where he stores the car key."

Eli's mouth tightened. "And you know this *how*?"

Not again, Syd thought and tried to change the subject. "Why don't you and Lloyd check the cars? You can call Gina to verify the license plates."

Eli looked as if he wanted to say more, but Syd was thankful when he didn't. Instead, he called out, "Lloyd," and the two headed off.

Syd and Marv refocused on Clay, who'd been monitoring Luke's vital signs. "What's the diagnosis?" she asked.

"It appears as if he was cracked on the head with a blunt object." Clay pointed out the lump.

"Should we get him to a hospital?"

"That's not necessary. They wouldn't be doing anything different than me."

"That's good." Marv handed Clay his cuffs. "Use these if he starts to come around."

Under the hooded gray sky, the scent of scorched grass continued to fill Syd's nostrils as she waited for her cell to ring. When it finally did, she motioned for Marv to follow her over to the edge of the field for some privacy. "I'll put my cell on speaker," Syd said, "so we both can listen."

"Thanks."

On the other end of the line was Pete, the Sturgeon Bay Airport traffic controller. "I'm going to patch you into a three-way-call, Detective Bernhardt, and also record it, per your instructions. Please go ahead, Bonanza-Four-Niner-Niner-Charlie-Foxtrot."

"Syd," a faraway voice said, over the drone of an airplane engine. "Have you talked to Luke yet?"

She couldn't tell if the speaker was Patrick or Frank, but that could wait. "No, he's still unconscious, however, the medic said he'll be coming around soon. Why don't you fly back, so we can all talk face-to-face?"

"'Fly back'—is that what you said? I can't do that, Syd. Luke *now* knows. I need to explain some things before he does. You'll listen to me, won't you?"

"Of course, if that's the only way. But please tell me, is this Frank or Patrick speaking?"

"I didn't catch that, Syd. Your voice is going in and out. You need to listen…"

"Okay…" She was grateful to be communicating at all. If she could keep him talking, she had to believe she could figure out the caller's i.d.

"I know you were beginning to uncover my despicable past."

Her eyes must have mirrored the excitement in

Marv's. "Why did you think that?" she prompted.

Marv gave Syd an encouraging nod.

"Well, first I discovered the research Carli was doing on the Café's computer."

"Were you the one who cleared its search history log?"

"The one that did *what*?"

Syd repeated her words, slowly and loudly.

"Oh, yes. Then, Beth called the Café and told Alice she'd given you Carli's lockbox with a research envelope inside."

Syd frowned. Beth had unintentionally tipped off their perp. "Did you steal the envelope from my cottage?"

"Yes. I was fearful of what you might find and hoped you hadn't reviewed it yet. But today, when Alice called and said you'd been asking about the travel shows, I realized you had. You've got to understand, Syd—I couldn't help myself. Mother is to blame. She sexually abused me since I was little. She's the one who fostered my craving to abduct young girls, so I could do the same to them."

Syd gave Marv a satisfied look. They were getting their confession.

But from *which brother*?

Chapter 59

The last of the shoreline flames had been snuffed out as Syd and Marv listened to the background argument going on within their perp's phone call. One brother told the other, "Shut up and let me talk. There's not much time!" His words were followed by a deathly moan.

"Is one of you injured?" Syd asked, alarmed. "I can arrange for immediate assistance if you'll land."

He sounded angry when he said, "There's nothing you can do."

She was afraid to push him further. "All right, then... Tell me about these young girls."

He sighed. "Be patient, Syd... First, I must tell you about Mother."

Rapture had filled his voice at her mention.

It made Syd's stomach turn.

"For our interludes, she'd dress up in a jumper, knee socks, and patent leather shoes, to assume the persona of a sweet little girl. Her short brown hair, the scent of ripe peaches, would be so soft and silky. Then she'd call me into her dressing room and lock the door for our 'private time.' She said she used to suck her daddy's cock, just like mine."

Syd's eyes connected with Marv's at these disturbing words. For a mother to do such a thing to her child was, in Syd's opinion, the lowest, most vile crime. She couldn't help but feel some empathy for the speaker, whether Patrick or Frank.

"I can't see your face, Syd, but I'm sure this sounds revolting. You've got to understand. Mother exerted this power. Whenever she commanded, I *had* to comply."

"Did that include the day of her death?"

"Oh, yes. Very much so…"

Syd was having a hard time hearing *him* now, and feared she might be losing the connection.

"I'll never forget how she insisted on giving me her final gift, even though her words were slurred, and her face was drooped. She asked me to dress her up in her girlish attire. Then she had me push her wheelchair into her dressing room where she performed her final act of love on me before passing peacefully away."

Syd felt as if she might vomit. Still, since the caller's voice kept fading in and out, she prayed he'd discuss Megan before she lost the connection, altogether. So Syd forced herself to play along. "I can see how much your mother must have meant to you."

"I'm so glad you understand."

A flash of lightning made Syd jump. Then came a rumble of thunder.

"I did know my relationship with Mother was wrong. And after her death…after her, I felt I might be released from her power. But instead, I sunk into a state of depression …until I came up with the perfect way to honor her memory."

As the rain started, Marv performed one of his princely acts. He removed his jacket and held it over Syd's head and phone.

She gave him a nudge of thanks, then cautiously asked, "Was Leslie Gorman your first?"

"Well Carli was actually my first encounter—but Leslie was my first keepsake."

"Why choose Carli?"

"What, Syd? I can't hear you."

Oh, no, Syd thought. "Why choose Carli?" she shouted again.

"I couldn't believe how much she resembled Mother. So I started to send Carli emails, telling her how much I liked her hair, her eyes, her smile…"

Syd hesitated. "Was this when you were a priest?"

"What, Syd? Your voice is cutting in and out. Please listen… I need to tell you about Mother's memorial service. That's when it dawned on me that Carli was close by—right at St. Anne's Camp."

Syd was frustrated not knowing which brother was speaking, but she tried not to care. Her main goal was to keep him talking before the connection dropped.

"Around dusk, I paddled a kayak over to Adventure Island. I knew Carli's cabin number, so I hiked through the woods and hid nearby for hours. I was so uncomfortable with one of Mother's silk stockings pulled over my head. But just when I was about to give up, Carli actually came out—all alone."

He sighed. "I still fantasize about our time together—the power I held over her by threatening to kill Alice. That's why I returned the next night. I waited and waited, outside Carli's cabin, so disappointed when she never came out. But just as I was about to leave, this little girl, with pretty hair like mother's, dashed out of another cabin."

Syd's eyes shifted toward Luke Lacount, who'd

finally come around. He was swearing at Clay while struggling on the ground, trying to release his cuffed hands. Syd returned her attention to the caller. "Was that Leslie Gorman?"

"Yes, that was Leslie. But unlike Carli, I was fearful she'd tell. So I gagged her and carried her back to my kayak. Then I secured her under its meshing and began to paddle back, but it was rough going. She kept thrashing around, trying to escape."

Syd closed her eyes. It was hard to listen to his matter-of-fact recounting of such a horror.

"Oh, Syd," the caller said over his brother's low moans. "You should've seen the sunrise when I arrived at the beach, close to Hemlock House. I was pumped. I now had Leslie all to myself."

Syd heard a car start up and turned to look. Eli's hand popped out of the window of an old Chevy, then he gave her a thumb's up.

She nodded, then refocused on the caller. "Where did you take Leslie?"

"Why back to my 'dressing room.'"

"Dressing room?" Syd's breath quickened as she thought back to that solitary-confinement area attached to Rose's bedroom. She knew it had been empty last Saturday. But there'd also been built-in cabinet panels and drawers...

"Oh, yes. It's where I take all my girls. Shortly after Mother's death, I dug up her casket and gently removed her body. She was the first to be placed inside my 'dressing room' for perpetuity."

Syd cringed at his words and mouthed to Marv, "We're going to Hemlock House." She pointed toward Luke and motioned for Marv to get him into the Ford.

Syd headed that way and felt the rain pelt her face.

Marv's shoes made squishing sounds in the soggy grass as he jogged toward Clay while punching in numbers on his cell.

Syd assumed Marv was calling for additional help. That would include a helicopter, in case they needed to airlift Megan out for medical attention.

If she was still alive.

"So, you took Leslie back to your dressing room?"

"What, Syd?"

Frustrated, she repeated her words.

"Oh, yes. Once inside, I enjoyed her numerous times—while Mother looked on. I knew she was pleased. I considered going back for Carli the next night, but with everyone searching for Leslie, I was afraid I'd be caught."

"What finally happened to Leslie?" Syd shouted, wiping away rivulets of rain, impeding her vision.

"Why, I suffocated her, so she could keep Mother company."

Syd closed her eyes and nearly tripped on a rut. "Did you do that to Megan Hanson, too?"

"Syd, be patient. First, I need to tell you about my other girls."

"So tell me." Syd's voice was urgent. She watched Marv yank Luke up and push him toward the Ford.

"When I went to each travel show, I abducted a little girl. Since I had my own hotel room, I could sedate her during the day and enjoy her each evening before I suffocated her. I always brought along a big supply chest, so I could squeeze the body inside. Neither the maid nor my brothers ever knew." He laughed, pleased with himself.

"You kept all the bodies?" Syd shuddered, picturing his so-called "dressing room."

"What, Syd?"

This was painful. She shouted the awful question again.

"Oh, yes—that was very important to me. So, this week, when I had the opportunity to steal Carli's body, I couldn't resist. Better late than never!"

He chuckled again. "I fooled everyone, didn't I? And it was so easy. When Zach carried in the funeral food, I discovered the hearse was unlocked. That's when I removed Carli's body and placed it under the insulated food blanket in the back of Zach's van. He then innocently transported Carli's body back to the Café's parking lot, locked the van, and headed off to school."

As Syd shook her head at her oversight, she heard the plane sputter. "Tell me," she demanded. "What's going on up there?"

"Don't worry. This will all be for the best."

The plane continued to choke, and the sobs of his brother grew louder.

"Instead of refueling, Syd, I forced my brothers to pour the gas cans along the shoreline to start the fire."

The air traffic controller broke into the call: "Bonanza-Four-Niner-Niner-Charlie-Foxtrot, are you issuing a Mayday distress signal?"

"It's too late…"

"What about Megan Hanson?" Syd shouted.

Bone-chilling shrieks, prayers, and sobs were her only answer.

Then the sound of a massive explosion rang in her ears.

Chapter 60

Accompanied by the irritating screech of old windshield wipers, Syd sped along the gravel road in Patrick's Ford. Lloyd was by her side. Marv was in the back seat with Luke, to make sure he behaved, and Eli was piloting his boat to the Chambers Island Marina. Once there, he'd drive Patrick's old Chevy over to Hemlock House.

The horrible tale kept spinning in Syd's head—but with a hole in it where the villain was supposed to be. Was it Patrick—or Frank?

She didn't know. But whichever one was the monster, he'd probably added yet another death to his head count—in addition to his own.

At the end of the call, the air traffic controller had pinpointed the plane's location, still over Lake Michigan. He'd alerted the Coast Guard to send out both a cutter and a helicopter with the hope there'd be survivors.

Everyone knew the odds were slim.

Luke now snorted from behind. "I see you got out of Al's in one piece."

In the rear view mirror, Syd's eyes found his. She knew the type—he was raring to talk—so she decided to egg him on. "I understand you did quite a job on Colette."

He huffed. "Can you believe it? I've actually been fucking a lesbo. She deserved everything I gave her and then some. But this time, she threatened to call the cops, so I knew I had to ditch this town."

"Is that when you thought of Patrick's plane?"

"Yeah, my perfect escape route. But the only way I could convince him was by using a gun."

"Too bad his plane wasn't parked on the mainland," Marv taunted. "Or you'd have made it out."

"You've got that right. But Patrick was with Frank, so I was forced to take them *both* to Chambers. Then, Alice called." Luke's eyes found Syd's again. "Frank told us you were asking about those travel shows. That's when all hell broke loose. My bro' said he needed to get something off his chest. Said he believed we'd understand."

Syd beat him to the punch. "You mean about abducting those young girls?"

Luke's shoulders deflated. "So, he already told you?"

She nodded. "He provided a detailed confession."

"I know you think I'm disgusting, but *that* one takes top honors. 'Boo, hoo, hoo,' I told him. I mean, I was abused by 'good old Mom' too, but I didn't do what he did!"

Syd wasn't going to give this bastard any comfort, yet she realized he, too, had suffered. Her lips tightened. It appeared as if Luke held the truth to which sibling was their perp.

"Which brother did you say told you?" Marv nonchalantly asked. "I just want to confirm our story."

"Well it was—Hey wait…" Luke's face slowly brightened. "You guys don't know who abducted those girls, do you?" He gave them a crafty smile, a glint in his eyes.

In the mirror, Syd watched a flush spread across

Marv's skull. They both knew he'd inadvertently handed Luke a major bargaining chip.

"But I thought you talked to my brothers." There was confusion in Luke's voice. "I was holding the gun on them both before...before *one* of them wrestled it away from me and slammed it into my head. So, what did they do after that?"

"Your brothers took off in Patrick's plane," Marv explained.

"So, the guy you're after is on the run, and you don't even know who you're chasing?" He beamed. "Sweet!"

"Maybe not." Syd decided to give Luke the bad news. "We believe Patrick's plane crashed into Lake Michigan."

His jaw dropped. "You mean...they're dead?"

"We can't be sure," Marv said. "Not until the Coast Guard arrives at the scene."

Luke's face caved in. "God damn it! If they're dead, one of 'em sure didn't deserve to die." Tears actually filled his eyes.

"Which one?" Syd tried again.

Luke looked miserable. The snot ran from his nose and joined his tears. His hands were cuffed, so he was unable to wipe away the evidence to show he honestly cared. He croaked out, "How about it? I'll tell you if you drop my charges."

Neither Syd nor Marv responded. She knew he wasn't relishing the idea of being blackmailed by Luke any more than she was.

There had to be another way.

Chapter 61

Syd reached the turnoff for Hemlock House. As the massive home emerged through the trees, she shivered—now knowing just what had gone on inside.

She handed Marv her cuffs. He secured Luke's ankles with the pair, and they left him in the car. Syd released Lloyd and thought about last Saturday—the fun he'd had on these grounds with Blinker. She would have to tell Alice to find Patrick's dog a good home...if his master was indeed dead.

At least the weather had improved. The rain had stopped, and the dark clouds were moving northward as the detectives raced toward the home. Syd located the French door that led into the solarium, and Marv used his shoulder to bust it in. The two of them then ran up the back staircase, Lloyd in the lead.

In the master bedroom suite, Syd opened the door to her right—the door into Rose's dressing room. The windowless space looked untouched.

Syd held her breath and pulled open one of the built-in drawers.

It was empty.

She and Marv yanked open seven more drawers.

The result was the same.

"Now what?" He looked distressed.

Earlier, Syd had noticed possible kick marks on the back of the entrance door. Now she saw similar ones on the back paneled section where there were no drawers. "If there's a false wall, it's got to be here. I'll go see what's on the other side."

She dashed out of the dressing room, then the master bedroom, and turned left down the hall to enter the adjacent room.

She pounded on the suspect wall—and heard Marv's muffled voice respond.

Syd was floored. She'd been certain they would find Megan in this vicinity.

Marv and Syd searched the rest of the home and met back in the solarium. Frustrated, she stood by the baby grand piano and looked over at Rose Lacount's wedding photo. Her big dark eyes taunted Syd and stimulated a thought: "There are a number of outbuildings on the estate."

"Okay." Marv headed for the door. "Let's go."

Outside, Lloyd charged down the path ahead of them. On Saturday, he'd periodically strayed from the trail, possibly picking up Megan's scent.

Syd felt sick. She might have saved Megan then.

They neared the windowless limestone garage, covered in thick vines.

"Step carefully," Syd warned, "there's poison ivy here." In addition to the two eight-foot-wide locked garage doors, she was encouraged to see a relatively new wooden access door.

Marv turned the handle, but it was locked.

Syd leaned against it and repeatedly shouted,

"Megan, honey, Megan…are you in there?"

There was no response.

Marv used his shoulder, but the door wouldn't give.

Syd added hers, and the result was the same.

"Fuck!" Marv kicked at it. "This is some damn lock!"

Through the trees, Syd heard Eli's voice call out their names.

"Over here," she yelled, and Lloyd barked.

Eli came jogging up. The two men repeatedly kicked and slammed against the access door, but it still wouldn't give.

"Hold on," Syd said. "Last Saturday, I saw a tool shed nearby."

Marv wiped the perspiration off his forehead. "Well, what are you waiting for?"

She sprinted off and located it, thankful the shed door appeared weak. Sure enough, just two kicks, and she was inside. Her eyes scanned the interior and landed on a hatchet. Syd grabbed it, ran back, and gave it to Marv. "This should help."

Marv chopped away at the access door, then reached inside to flip the deadlock. As he turned the door handle, they all held their collective breaths.

Inside, the only thing Syd could see was an old truck, up on blocks, and a pile of used tires. "Damn! This isn't it."

"Now what?" Marv fretted.

"Hey, let's not give up hope. There's one more building—a boathouse by the lake."

The two men rushed after Syd down the path. She again warned them about the poison ivy. This time, Eli stayed back with Lloyd as Syd and Marv gingerly hiked around the accessible perimeter. They noticed a door frame filled in with cement. There was no other access to the building, not even from the lake side, where a wall had been installed after the water receded.

Just as Syd and Patrick had done the previous Saturday, she and Marv now climbed the stairs to reach the rooftop. A number of rectangular cement planters were located within the railed area.

Marv shook his head. "I don't see any sort of trap door."

"Me neither." A punctured sigh of despair escaped Syd's lips. But then she noticed something. "Look, Marv. Two sets of planters are pushed together on both the north and south ends."

"You're right." Marv headed for the north set. "Come on, Syd."

She joined him and they inched them apart.

"Fuck!" Marv stood back up. "There's nothing here."

They headed for their last hope and both bent down again.

As they began to slide them apart, tears stung Syd's eyes.

There it was—a wooden trap door. It looked relatively new—and had a place for a key.

"Fuck yes!" Marv's voice said it all. He raised the hatchet and started to chop.

"Oh no…" Syd covered her nose as the most ghastly odor of rotting tissue, urine, and feces poured out.

"Fuck!" Marv chopped faster until there was enough room for them to crawl through.

He pointed his flashlight down into the depths of the tomb-like structure. The space was dimly lit by both a kerosene lantern, resting on a table, and by the transom windows along the back wall. There were also random spots where slices of light came through.

Thankfully, Syd thought, *these gaps provide a bit of fresh air.*

They descended a set of stairs into the gloom of their perp's "dressing room."

Please God, Syd silently prayed, *let Megan be here—and still alive.*

But what Syd saw made her recoil in horror. It was worse than she could have imagined.

In a distant past, this boathouse had probably been filled with fancy water crafts. Now it was bone dry. On the prior lake bed, eight chairs formed a morbid ring around a wheelchair. Within it were Rose Lacount's skeletal remains.

She was clad in the infamous jumper, knee socks, and patent leather shoes. Her photo was propped up in the pelvic area. Syd wanted to kick it. But that could wait.

She held her breath as her eyes scanned the circle of chairs. Six of them contained either a pile of bones or a small body in some form of decomposition. Each contained a Polaroid photo of the innocent missing girl…beginning with Leslie.

Carli's body was there, too, dressed in her Sunday's-best, chosen by her brother for her funeral.

But the miraculous treasure, within this dreadful structure, was seated beside Carli, gagged and tied to a chair.

Syd finally released her breath. For five days, Megan had been lost—now, she'd been found.

They surged toward her, and Syd stumbled when Megan's eyes blinked open, glazed in terror.

"My God, Marv, she's alive!"

As he untied her arms and legs, Syd removed Megan's gag.

She gulped the air and wheezed, "Is he here?" Her whole body convulsed in fear.

"No, honey, you're safe." Syd cupped Megan's face in her hands. "We're going to take you home."

"Hurry," she sobbed, "please hurry, I know he'll be back!"

Syd pulled her into her arms and let Megan cry, smoothing her grimy hair. "Don't worry, honey. I promise. He'll never touch you again."

As Marv bent down to pick Megan up, she slunk back.

Syd put her hand on his arm and her eyes found Megan's. "I promise, honey, this is a good man—a very, very good man."

Syd looked up at Marv. His eyes shined with gratitude. Syd squeezed his arm. Marv *was* a good man.

He gently gathered Megan's small, sobbing body into his arms and headed for the stairs. As he climbed, Syd followed closely behind.

It was a relief to step out into the fresh, sweet air and hear, from above, the sound of a helicopter.

Through the hemlocks, Syd watched it land on the beach. She remembered the children playing hide and seek, their excited voices carrying over Mackaysee Lake: "Olly, Olly, Oxen, Free."

Could Megan have heard them through the walls of her prison—desperately aching to escape from this hideous hiding place—back to the innocent childhood she'd once known?

Even though Megan was alive, Syd knew, like Carli, Megan would carry a lifetime of scars.

At that thought, another one dawned on Syd.

She knelt beside Megan as medics from the chopper neared. "I realize this is hard, honey, but I need to know something…"

Chapter 62

The sunshine played on the water as Eli and Syd motored back to Fish Creek. Syd buried her face against Eli's chest, her hand resting on Lloyd's silky head. Overwhelmed by the past week, she fought back tears.

They'd all cheered as Megan was airlifted out to safety, the sun breaking out from behind the clouds.

Marv had called Megan's parents to let them know the wonderful news. Their little girl was alive—and safe.

Marv had remained at Hemlock House, while Syd and Eli had driven Patrick's two cars back to the marina. The Coast Guard cutter had taken charge of Luke. A deputy was now waiting at the Fish Creek dock to transport him to the Sturgeon Bay jail. Two official boats had also arrived with staff from the department. Syd had handed them the keys to Patrick's cars and given them directions to Hemlock House. They'd be there for days to help Marv sort through the evidence.

Among it would be the heartbreaking remains of the young girls—and of the evil woman, who, in reality, had instigated their deaths.

Syd's iPhone rang, and she pulled away from Eli to take the call.

"Detective Bernhardt, this is Pete from the Sturgeon Bay Airport. I'm sorry to inform you, two bodies were recovered from Lake Michigan. The men were killed on impact when Bonanza-Four-Niner-Niner-Charlie-Foxtrot crashed into the lake."

Syd had mixed emotions: relief their perp was dead, and sorrow because an innocent man had died in the process. She had to call Alice. It was the second time Syd would have to tell her she'd lost a loved one—yet Syd still didn't know whether it was better that Frank was dead rather than alive.

Syd knew the evidence Marv was gathering could include DNA and fingerprints, which would be matched to items in the brothers' residences. That should confirm which Lacount was their perp.

But that could take weeks.

Syd phoned Alice, who was still at the hospital with Colette, and told Alice the terrible news. Once her sobs had subsided, Syd asked Alice a question to hopefully solve the puzzle.

Moments later, feeling nauseous, Syd hung up and turned to Eli. "We know Megan's abductor was mentally scarred by his mother's sexual abuse, but he had some physical scars, too."

"Okay?" Eli tilted his head.

"Alice confirmed that Frank did not have any surgical scars in his groin area... But Megan said her abductor did."

"What are you saying, Syd?" Eli's forehead creased. "I'd think there'd be only one way for you to know whether Patrick had scars in that particular area."

"Let's not assume, okay?" Syd's eyes found his. "Go ahead, Eli. Ask me if I slept with the pervert."

"Well, did you?"

She shoved him. "No, I did not! Patrick had mentioned to me, he'd had an appendectomy and a hernia repair. That's all."

Suddenly, Syd shivered and silently thanked God she *hadn't* slept with him. But the irony of it—the fact that Patrick, the man who'd been helping her reclaim her life, was responsible for each girl's tragic death—was almost too much for Syd to stomach.

Eli brushed a stray curl from her eyes. "So, Patrick's really the guy?"

Syd nodded. "I hate to admit that Marv was right. But I'm glad for both Alice and Brian—Colette, too. I know she considered Frank her mentor for so many years. And now, even if Marv can't locate evidence to connect Patrick to that sordid 'dressing room,' we won't need to accept Luke's blackmail terms. I hope he rots in jail. Maybe Colette can move on with her life…starting with her lawsuit."

"So, you figured that out?" Eli grinned. "Well then, I'll give you an update. The suing family and Colette have reached a satisfactory agreement and are settling out of court."

"That's great!" Syd beamed. She scratched Lloyd's head and earned his curved-lips smile.

"You know, Eli, it's amazing how Patrick managed to hide his secret life for so many years. I bet he never figured Carli would've been working at the Café this summer, after she'd accepted that job in Milwaukee. It was his bad luck, and hers, that she felt guilty for not fulfilling her commitment to live in Beth's condo. I'm sure if Carli hadn't died by Beth's hands, Patrick would've killed her, knowing she'd been trying to uncover his identity as her 2000 attacker."

"I agree." Eli hugged her. "But, Syd, let's stop dwelling on that awful saga and start focusing on the good things in life. And you know there are so many: our families, our friends, the water, the sun, and today's scenery. Plus, you're with your two biggest admirers—Lloyd and me."

She laughed.

"Let's just enjoy what's left of this beautiful day. How about it?" He pointed his chin toward some fishing rods and reels, secured to a rack. "Maybe today's the day to catch 'our sturgeon'… And if not today, I'm counting on lots of tomorrows."

His words warmed her like no others could. Syd felt as if she'd arrived back in her safe harbor. The anxiety and anger she'd been carrying for two years had finally dissipated.

She pulled away, her eyes glued to Eli's, and removed her jacket. "Gina says she likes my 'tats.'" Syd bit her lower lip, and, feeling unnaturally shy, she pushed up her sleeves. "Do you think you can learn to like them, too?"

"Come here." Eli pulled her to him. "I don't just like them, Sydney, I love them—as I've *always* loved you." He kissed her deeply.

It was as if Syd was back on that blacktop, right after her van crashed, waking up from her dream—the one where she *thought* she belonged to someone.

And maybe, just maybe…she did.

ABOUT THE AUTHOR

Lynda Drews, a Wisconsin native and dedicated runner, gave the commencement speech at her college Alma mater. One lesson she shared was "to journal your life." That's what Lynda did after she made the decision to retire from her global marketing career. Her first book: RUN AT DESTRUCTION (Lynda's True Crime Memoir, published in 2009, about the mysterious death of her running partner) was the outcome.

Ann Rule, the best-selling true crime author, endorsed RUN AT DESTRUCTION saying it was "Wonderfully written... a must for True Crime readers." Publisher's Weekly said: "the author and victim's shared moments, and Drews' feelings of emptiness in the decades since, are remarkable."

Lynda's second book, CIRCLE OF INNOCENCE, is a Mystery/Suspense novel that takes place in Door County: the "Cape Cod" of Wisconsin. This setting is where Lynda and her husband, Jim, spend nearly every weekend, but they still call Green Bay, Wisconsin "home." It's where they've lived since the mid-seventies while raising their two sons.

For your reading pleasure,
we invite you to visit our
web bookstore

WHISKEY CREEK PRESS

www.whiskeycreekpress.com

CPSIA information can be obtained at www.ICGtesting.com
Printed in the USA
LVOW12s0757080714

393080LV00003B/3/P